THE SECRETS OF BENES' CASTLE

The SECRETS OF BENES' CASTLE

LARRY D. STEINMAN

MainSpring Books

Printed in the United States of America
ISBN 978-1-947352-71-1 (paperback)
ISBN 978-1-947352-97-1 (hardback)
ISBN 978-1-947352-96-4 (ebook)
Library of Congress Control Number: 2020919830

Fiction / Suspense / Thrillers

MainSpring Books
5901 W. Century Blvd
Suite 750
Los Angeles, CA, US, 90045

www.mainspringbooks.com

The Secrets of Benes' Castle

This is the story of a castle that was built in 1590 in Rumania, and follows the lives of everyone who either owned or lived in the castle up to the year 2000. It tells about what these people saw and experienced during their time in the castle and how it affected their lives. One of the questions is, was the castle responsible, or was it just the people. I will leave it up to the reader to make that judgement. Please enjoy.

CHAPTER 1

Benes' castle. Built in the late 16th century, by Lord Benes', who came to Rumania from Hungary. The castle is located outside of Medias, to the east, a small village of all local people. They don't have visitors very often. The castle stayed in the Benes' family for 200 years. It was purchased by the Bernard family, in 1790. Which brings us to the present date of 1835.

The people of the village never talked about the castle very much. Most of the villagers stayed away from it. They knew Lord Bernard as a mild mannered, intelligent person. Always friendly. He had a wonderful family, who were always in good spirits. The area was a happy place for them. They knew about the tragedy's many years ago, and they were all saddened by it. But life went on, until a couple of years ago. Stories started spreading about strange things happening at the castle. Lord Bernard never left the castle anymore. It was said that people have heard screams coming from the castle. Some people have said they saw strange apparitions on the castle grounds, as they passed by at night. Some of the villagers were afraid to go out after dark. The men met in The Pub every night, to talk about the rumors flying around. When ever a stranger did come to town, they warned them not to go near the castle, especially at night. They would be better off to keep traveling. That was life in Medias.

Adam Bernard, born, 1793. Father, Lord Bernard. Mother, Regina, deceased. Regina died in 1803 giving birth to Mimi. Adam is 10 years older than Mimi. From the time Mimi is 5 years old, Adam stays with her constantly. He takes care of her and plays games with her. Then in 1811 Mimi is playing at the edge of a deep pond at the back of the castle. She falls in and drowns. Adam carries her lifeless body up to the castle. As he enters the castle, he is crying. His father comes running up to him. "It's my fault, It's my fault. I wasn't watching her. I was studying and all of a sudden I heard her scream." All the time he can't stop crying. "When I got to her it was too late. I couldn't help her. Why wasn't I watching her?" His father told him to calm down. It was an accident. He shouldn't be so hard on himself.

At the funeral, Adam breaks down. He can't control himself. He has lost his beloved sister. For several weeks, Adam rarely comes out of his room. He tells his father he wants the pond drained. He vows to never go down to the pond again. His father is taking the loss very hard, also. He starts drinking rather heavily, and never goes outside the castle. The castle now seems very dark and dreary. Empty.

In 1813, Adam is 20 years old. He leaves the castle and moves to Bucharest to attend college. He intends to study business and administration. By 1818, Adam has graduated and has been hired by a well-known firm, which helps other businesses get started. Adam works hard and long hours. He doesn't have much of a social life. Right now, that's the way he likes it, or so he thinks. In June of 1833, Adam runs into a beautiful young woman. Literally. He is walking down the street, when this young woman comes out of a shop, carrying several packages. While not paying any attention, he almost knocks her to the ground. Her name is Christine Bristow. She's originally from England.

He helps her with her packages, and begs her to have lunch with him, so he can make up for almost running over her. She accepts. It's love at first sight. Adam starts to find out maybe he would like a little more social life. Anyway, within six months, they are married. They have a beautiful apartment and are very happy.

Then, two years later, Adam receives a letter from the castle. His father has died. The castle and the fortune, now belong to Adam. There is one stipulation. Adam must live in the castle for one year to obtain the fortune. Christine is excited. She has never seen a castle before, let alone lived in one. She is ready to see the castle. "Christine, I don't know that I want to live in the castle. There are too many bad memories of that place. My little sister drowned there. The castle has never seemed the same to me." "I know, you told me about your sister. Maybe it will do you good to go back there. You might get over your feeling of guilt. We could always try it." "We will talk about it later." "It's alright, Adam, I understand. Just, think about it."

A week has passed. "Your right, Christine, we need to go to the castle. Maybe that's what I need. Besides, if I don't claim the fortune, it will simply go to the state. Better me than them. Let's get started." Adam talks to his superior about taking a year's absence. He can do his work at the castle through correspondence.

Adam and Christine take a train to Brasov, Rumania. From there, they hire a coach to take them to Medias. It's a two-day trip. They arrive late in the evening. The people remember Adam, and they greet him with friendship. Adam and Christine go to The Pub and eat before going to the castle. When Adam tells the people, he has come to claim the castle, a hush comes over the crowd. "Mr. Bernard, sir, I don't think you should go there. Especially with Miss Christine along, and not after dark." "Mr. Mayor, why do you say that?" "There have been strange things happening at the castle. Strange noises and things. It's haunted." "Certainly, you jest." "No sir, I tell you the truth." "Well, I for one, do not believe in ghosts and haunted castles. But thank you for the entertainment. I think Christine and I will go on to the castle now. Thank you all, and goodnight." "But, sir, darkness is upon us. You should wait until morning" "Nonsense. We will leave now. Thank you." "Mark my words, Adam, there is something going on up there."

As the coach reached the entrance to the castle, a light fog was settling in. The coachman unloaded the suitcases and trunks. He hurriedly turned the coach around and took off at a fast gallop. There were steps leading up a hill. The castle stood on a plateau at the top of the hill. "Adam, we can't carry all this luggage up that hill." "We won't. Azure, the grounds keeper will bring it up for us." "Let's get inside, the fog is getting thicker." They passed several large trees on the way to the door. Their bare branches almost seemed like they were reaching out for you. To trap you.

Adam was about to bang on the door, when it opened. "Why, Mr. Adam, welcome back to the castle." Adam and Christine entered the huge entrance way. "Why Marta, you haven't changed a bit. Just as young and pretty as ever." Marta, the housekeeper, was 70. She joined the Bernard family when Adam was born. She was 48 at that time. Her hair was white as the snow. She was 5' 3" with a slender build. She was still very healthy for her age. "Oh, Mr. Adam, you always did like to kid me a lot. I'm know I look my age." "Marta, this is Christine, my wife." "Welcome, Miss Christine. I hope you like it here." "Thank you, I'm sure I will." "Will you have Azure bring our luggage up to our room?" "Yes, did you need something to eat?" "No, we ate in the village before we came up here." "Very well, follow me, I'll show you to your room."

"Adam, this bedroom is beautiful, and so large." "I'm glad you like it. Tomorrow I'll show you all the other rooms and the grounds." Christine went over to the window. The fog was pretty thick, but all of a sudden, she thought she saw the shadow of someone walking among the trees. There was a knock on the door, and Christine quickly turned from the window. It was Azure with the luggage. Adam opened the door. As Azure walked in, Christine felt a chill go through her. She almost became frightened. Azure was a tall, thin man, around 60. He was slightly bent over. He had large bushy black eyebrows and a jagged scar ran down his left cheek. He set the luggage down in the room. "Azure, this is my wife, Christine." Azure spoke slowly. "Glad to meet you, ma'am." "Thank you." "That will be all, Azure, you may retire now." "Thank you, Mr. Adam."

"Adam, that man, he's strange. He made me feel uneasy." "He's alright. He's been with us a long time. He's quiet and keeps to himself, but he is a good worker. And anything you need, he will help you. You'll get used to him." "Oh, I'm sure I will. It may take a little time." Christine had forgotten about what she saw outside the window. They were both very tired from their long journey. They turned in for the night. Tomorrow will be brighter, and Christine was sure she would be happy here. It was a new adventure for her.

The next morning, the sun was shining. There was only a slight chill in the air. After breakfast, Adam showed Christine around the grounds. The castle sat on 500 acres. About half was woods and the other half was grassland. Naturally, they didn't walk the whole 500 acres, but Christine was awed by the large expanse of the property. "Adam, take me to look at the pond." "No, I can't do that. Besides, it was drained years ago. There wouldn't be anything to see." "I think you need to see it. It may help you heal." "No, I can't." "Well, I'm going to find the pond, whether you come with me or not." "Christine! Don't...... Alright! I'll go with you." As they approached the pond, Adam stopped in his tracks. "Oh, no!" The pond was full. "It was supposed to be emptied." "Probably the rain has filled it back up over the years. After all it's been over 20 years since you said they drained it." "Maybe. Maybe they never drained it. I left when I was 20 and this is the first time I've been back. Let's get away from here."

Back up close to the castle, Adam showed Christine where the flowerbeds were during the summer. It wasn't much to look at right now. Adam showed Christine around inside the castle. The first floor contained the huge entrance room. There was a great room, where guests were entertained. Christine could tell it hadn't been used for many years. A large kitchen was in the rear, with the dinning room adjoining. A library. An office where Adam could do his company work. Upstairs were 8 bedrooms, each with sitting rooms and baths. Another upstairs room that faced the front of the grounds, with a balcony. A total of 15 rooms. There was also a tower on the front two corners of the castle. There was a room below ground which contained the family burial vaults. Adam did not say anything about this to Christine.

That evening, Adam knocked on Marta's door. "Come in." "Marta, I need to talk to you about some rumors I've heard. The town's people seem to be afraid of the castle. They say they've heard and seen strange things here. What do you know about this?" "Oh, Adam. A couple of years before your father died, he started drinking a lot. He felt so alone. He had lost your mother, Mimi, and you. Oh, he wanted you to get an education. But he missed you. Even the townspeople stopped visiting him. After he had been drinking a lot, he would start yelling loudly, different things. Later on, he started going to the window at night and yelling like he was talking to someone. Several times I heard him yell, 'I can see you standing out there. Why don't you come in here where you belong? You need to sit by the fire and get warm.' I don't know who he was talking to. I couldn't see anyone." "That's probably what the people were talking about. I can understand why they seemed so afraid. Thank you, Marta."

The next several days were peaceful and quiet. Christine loved the castle. She thought it was beautiful and stylish. Adam showed Christine the family portraits hanging on the walls. He gave her a short history of each one. She was very impressed. She was very happy. It was more than she could ever have hoped for. Christine even got to know Azure better. She liked him. He was a very kind person. Everything was perfect. Or was it?

A couple of months went by, and Christine started noticing a change in Adam. He started spending more time in his office, with the door locked. He didn't treat Christine any different. When they were together, he treated her as if they had just gotten married. He was very loving to her. But she saw something in his eyes that she couldn't quite figure out. Something different. As time passed, Adam's demeanor started to change. He would become withdrawn at times and never speak to anyone.

They used to go down to the village once in a while and have dinner in The Pub. They enjoyed talking to the villagers. The people had loosened up quite a bit. Things had been quiet at the castle since Adam and Christine had moved in. The people liked having the couple come down and visit. It has been a month or so, since Adam had left the castle. He wouldn't even go outside the castle.

Adam started staying up very late and working in his office. He started staying in one the other bedrooms so he would not disturb Christine when he finally did go to bed. Christine was at a loss. She couldn't understand what was happening. What was wrong with Adam? Didn't he love her anymore? She tried to talk to him, but all he would say was that, he was alright. That he loved her, and not to worry. Everything will be ok. Christine talked to Marta about Adam. Marta said she could see a change in Adam, but she had no explanation for his behavior. She was worried also.

Then one night, as Christine was sleeping, she started getting restless. She was tossing and turning. Suddenly she opened her eyes and sat up in bed. Standing at the foot of the bed was a little girl. She didn't say anything. She just stood looking at Christine. Christine screamed and the girl disappeared. Adam heard Christine scream and ran up to the bedroom. "Christine, what is the matter. Are you alright?" Christine was crying. "Adam, I woke up and there was a little girl standing at the foot of the bed. When I screamed, she disappeared. What's going on?" "It was probably just a dream. There are no little girls here. You just thought you saw a girl." "I know what I saw, Adam. She was as real as you are. How could she be there and then just disappear?" "Marta, get Christine some hot milk. That will calm her. You drink the milk, and go back to sleep. You'll feel better in the morning. I'll be right next door." "Adam, don't leave me. Stay here with me. At least till I go to sleep." "Alright, Christine, I'll stay with you."

The next morning, as Christine was going down to breakfast, she was sure she had seen this girl. The girl didn't say anything, but she was crying. Christine knew there was no use in talking about it. Adam wouldn't believe her. He would insist it was just a dream. She could hardly eat her breakfast. She suddenly got up from the table, and went back up to her room. Marta went up to see if Christine needed anything. "Marta, what is happening to me?" "I don't know, Christine." "It is as if there is something in or about this castle that is trying to tell me something. But I don't know what it is."

A few days went by, and nothing else happened. Christine was beginning to think maybe it was just a dream. She went out to walk about the grounds. She enjoyed walking. It helped her relax. Spring was on the way; the air was becoming warmer. As she is walking in the woods, she sees something up ahead on the ground. It's a bucket, full of water, and a doll baby is in the bucket, upside down. She feels a chill go through her. She turns and runs back to the castle. She runs straight up to her bedroom. What did that mean? Who would have put that there? Why?

That night as Christine is sleeping, she starts getting restless again. She sits up and the little girl is standing there again. This time, Christine doesn't scream. She just watches. The girl is crying. Her hair looks wet, and this time she says, 'Why did he do that?' She then disappeared. This time Christine is not frightened. She is curious. That little girl is trying to tell her something. She lights a candle and gets out of bed. She is going to go down and get some milk. As she passes the foot of the bed, she stops. There on the carpet where the girl was standing, is a wet spot. Christine knows she is not dreaming this. But where will it lead?

The next morning, at breakfast, Christine tells Adam about the bucket of water, and of the girls visit. "Christine, you will stop this nonsense. There is no little girl!" "Adam, your little sister drowned. This girl that was standing at my bed last night had wet hair. She left a wet spot on the carpet where she stood. I think your sister is reaching out to me for some reason. I heard her say, 'Why did he do that?' What does she mean by that?" "That's enough! She has not come back from the grave! I don't want to talk about it anymore. Do not mention her again. Let her rest in peace." "Adam, I've never seen you like this before. What is happening to you? To us?" Adam threw down his napkin, went to his office and locked the door. Christine wanted to cry, but she wouldn't let herself. She vowed she would get to the bottom of what was happening here.

That night, Adam is pacing back and forth in his bedroom. He stops and looks out the window. There is his sister, standing in the yard down below. "No, no, Mimi, you can't be there. You are dead. You couldn't have come back. Go away, go away!" He steps back from the window, then steps forward again. She's gone. Adam runs down stairs, picks up a set of keys and goes down to the vault room. He breaks open her vault and looks in the casket. She isn't there! The casket is empty. Adam panics. Has she really come back? No. No. It can't be.

For two days, Adam stays in his room with the door locked. Several times during that period, Christine knocks on his door. He won't answer. She is worried something has happened to him. Finally, she goes up and bangs on his door. "Adam. Open this door. Answer me." "Go away. Leave me alone. I'll be down later. Go away." Well, at least he's alive. What has happened to him, that he won't come out of his room?

Christine and Marta are in the dinning room. Marta is setting the table. They hear footsteps on the stairs. Finally, Adam is coming down to eat. When Adam enters the dining room, Christine and Marta both take a step back. There hands go to their mouth. They each suck in a deep breath. "My God, Adam, what happened to you? Your hair, your face." Adam's hair had turned white. He was unshaven, and he looked as if he had aged 10 years. Adam did not speak. "Adam! You saw Mimi, didn't you?" "Yes! I saw Mimi!" Marta stood silent. She knew Mimi was back. She herself had seen her. She didn't know why, but she knew something, beyond anyone's control, was going to happen.

"Yes, Christine, I saw her. And do you know what else I saw?" "Adam, you're scaring me." "I went down to the vault underneath the castle, and opened Mimi's casket. Do you know what I saw.......? Nothing. She wasn't there! The casket was empty." He starts laughing uncontrollably. Christine became frightened. "Adam, what is this all about? You must tell me. I need to understand." Adam turned and went to his office. He fixed a glass of whiskey. He had started drinking more and more. "Marta, what is happening to us? What is it all about?" "I don't know yet. But something terrible is going to happen. It's going to be very tragic."

That night, Mimi appeared before Christine again. "Mimi, why are you here. What are you trying to tell me?" In a low monotone voice, "Yesss. I am Mimi. You must ask Adam. Ask him why he did it." Then she was gone. "Mimi, don't go. I need to talk to you." But she didn't reappear. Was Mimi wanting to know why Adam didn't watch her and try to save her? Is that what's happening to Adam? The guilt he feels for not saving her? Is she trying to punish him for some reason? So many questions. So many unanswered. What is next?

Several days later, Marta sees a coach pull up in front of the castle. A well-dressed young man, in his late 20's, gets out of the coach. Marta goes to the door and opens it. "May I help you?" "Yes, I'm Alan Bristow, Christine's brother." "Oh, please come in. Welcome. Come in and sit down. I'll get Christine for you." "Thank you, ma'am." Marta goes up to Christine's room. "Christine, there's a young man downstairs who says he is Alan, your brother." "Oh. Alan. Tell him I'll be right down." For the last few days, Christine has been in a trance like state. She hardly shows any emotion anymore. The situation has taken a toll on Christine also. Her hair has started turning grey. She looks like she has aged some also. "Hello, Alan. I didn't know you were coming. Why are you here?" "Aren't you glad to see me?" "Yes." "Father asked me to come see you. We haven't heard from you for a long time. I'm here to see if you are alright." "I'm fine, Alan."

They talk for a while. They go into the kitchen for sandwiches. Alan senses something is very wrong. "Christine, you don't act like you are glad to see me." "I am glad to see you, I'm just very tired. I haven't been sleeping very well lately." "But you look older than your age. What is wrong?" "Nothing, Alan. Some people age faster than others. I am approaching 40 you know?" "Maybe so. Where is Adam? I'd like to see him." "He's in his office working. He is very busy these days." Adam heard voices, so he steps out to see who's there. "Who are you?" "I'm Alan, Christine's brother. Don't you remember?" Alan can't believe that's really Adam standing in front of him. He's so different. "Alan. Yes, I remember. You'll have to excuse me, I'm very busy right now." With that, Adam went back to his office. "Christine, what is happening here? You are two different people from the ones I last saw. Are you in danger? Is Adam not treating you right?" "No, Alan. Adam and I are fine. It's a harder life here than we thought it would be. But it's our life now." "I think you need to get away from here. Why don't you come with me back home for a while? Father and mother would love to have you back home. Even if it's just for a while." "No, Alan. I can't do that. I am needed here right now."

"Alan, I think you should leave tomorrow morning and go back to the village. Azure can take you there. When the next coach comes through, go back home. Tell everyone that I am fine." "If you insist, Christine. But I don't like leaving you. I feel something is happening here that's beyond your control. I feel danger here." "Nonsense, Alan. Perhaps you can come back in the fall when the leaves start turning. We can have a joyous time together." "Alright. I'll leave in the morning. But you must let us know if you need help."

Adam has not done any company work for almost 2 months. His superior has sent several letters inquiring about why. He decides it is time to confront Adam. Marta hears someone knocking on the door. "Yes. May I help you?" "I'm Henry Atkins, Adam's employer. Is Adam in?" "Come in sir, I'll let Adam know you are here." "Thank you." Marta knocks on the office door. "Adam, a Mr. Atkins is here to see you." No answer. "Adam, did you hear me?" "Yes, Marta. I heard you. How could I help but hear you? Atkins…. Atkins… Oh yes from the company.

Send him away." "But he came all the way from Bucharest. It's about some work he needs from you." "Very well. Send him in."

When Mr. Atkins enters the office, he is shocked. This is not the same Adam he knew. He is so different. But Henry doesn't say anything about the way Adam looks. "Well, Henry, what is it you want? I'm very busy. I don't have much time for you." "That's why I have come here. You haven't sent us anything for almost 2 months now. Are you having problems with your reports?" "Don't question me about my work." "Your work is past due. We've had to compensate by assigning someone else to handle your cases. If you want to leave the company, you are free to do so." "I don't need your money or your work. Now get out!" "Adam. What has come over you? We were best friends. You have changed so. I don't even recognize you anymore. You look so much older. Are you ill? Should I get a doctor for you?" "Stop hounding me? There is nothing wrong with me. I don't need a doctor. Leave me alone!" Suddenly, Adam picked up a poker from the fire place, turned around and struck Henry across the side of the head. As Henry fell, he hit his head against the corner of the desk. Adam stood looking at Henry on the floor. Henry did not move. Adam knelt down. Henry was dead. Without any emotion or regret, Adam simply said, "I must get rid of this body tonight."

Around 2 AM, while everyone was asleep, Adam, started dragging Henry's body through the hall and out into the kitchen. He decided the vault would be an appropriate place for Henry. He managed to get Henry down into the vault. He opened one of the empty vaults and placed Henry in it, and closed the lid. If anyone inquired about Henry, 'Yes, he was here. But he left. I don't know where he went'. As Adam turned around to go back upstairs, Mimi appeared before him. She didn't say anything. She just pointed her finger at him, and then she was gone. Adam ran up the stairs and into his office, and locked the door. He poured himself another drink.

The next morning, as Marta is fixing breakfast, she notices marks on the floor, as if something was dragged across it. The marks led to the door to the vault room. As she looked closer, she saw some red spots along the floor. They were blood spots. What has happened now? She gets the keys and goes down the stairs. She looks around. The track of blood leads to one of the vaults. The vault lid is not all the way on. It's heavy, but she is able to move it. In horror, she sees the body of Henry. She starts shaking. "Oh, what has Adam done now?" She sees the side of Henry's face. It's terrible. "Why did Adam kill this man?" She pulls the lid back across the top of the vault, and goes back upstairs.

Marta is in a quandary. She's afraid to say anything to Adam. He might kill her also. She doesn't know if she should tell Christine. What would it do to Christine if she knew Adam had killed a man? She's on the verge of a breakdown now. For the time being, she will keep this to herself. She needs time to think. She mustn't let Adam know she is aware of what he did. Things are about to come to a head, and when it does, all hell will break loose.

Mimi appears to Christine again. "Adam has been bad again. Ask Adam what he did. You need to know. Look in the room below the kitchen. It's time Adam is stopped. It's up to you, Christine." "What is the room below the kitchen?" Mimi is gone. Christine decides it is time to find out what is happening. It's time to end this nightmare. Adam is going to talk to her one way or the other. Perhaps Marta will help her.

Marta is in the kitchen. "Marta, I want you to take me to the room below the kitchen." "Oh, no! I can't do that. Don't ask me to do that. You don't want to see it." "Yes, I do, Marta. What is that room?" "It's where the vaults are. It's where everyone is buried." "Well, what's so bad about that?" "You won't like what you see down there. Don't ask me." "I'm going to go down to that room. Now, which door is it?" "It's over there, but it's locked." "Then give me the key!" "Yes, ma'am."

Christine unlocked the door and started down the stairs. She looked around the room. There didn't seem to be anything that scary about the room, except where Adam had broken open Mimi's casket. She looked in the casket, and Adam was right. Mimi's body was not there. Christine couldn't understand why Marta was so frightened. As she walked around, she noticed a red spot next to one of the vaults. As she looked closer, she saw that it was dried blood. And there was an area where blood had run down the side of the vault. She set her candles down and proceeded to push the top open. She pushed the top about half way open and brought the candles closer. Her heart shipped several beats, and she held her breath. It was Henry Atkins, Adam's superior.

She hadn't been aware that Henry had come to the castle. It was obvious Adam had killed him. But why?

She ran up to the kitchen. She just stared at Marta. "Marta, you knew about Mr. Atkins, didn't you?" "Yes, I discovered him yesterday." "That's why you didn't want me to go down there, isn't it? Why did you not tell me?" "Oh, Miss Christine, I've been so afraid. I didn't know what to do. I was going to eventually tell you, but I just wasn't ready yet. I was afraid if Adam found out I knew, he would kill me." "Yes, your right. I need time to think. I need to figure out how to confront Adam. We'll wait a couple of days. But something has to be done about this."

A few days later, there is a knock at the door. "Ma'am, I'm Constable Arturo from the village. Is there a Mr. Henry Atkins here?" "No." "May I speak to the Master of the castle?" "Yes, come in. I'll announce you." Marta knocked on the office door. "Adam, there is a constable here to see you." "A constable? What does he want?" "I don't know, sir." "Send him in." "Yes, sir." She went back to the door. "Follow me, I'll take you to him." In Adam's office, "Yes, how can I help you constable?" "I'm inquiring about a Mr. Henry Atkins. I understand he came here to see you a few days ago." "Yes, he was here, but he left that same day." "I see. Only, no one in the village, remembers seeing him leave. And he would have had to stay in the village, because the coach didn't come through until yesterday. How do you explain that?" "I don't. I don't know what the man did after he left here." "I see. Did he have business with you here?" "Yes, he came for some reports I had for him. He is my superior." "He seems to be missing. We haven't been able to locate him." "Well, that's not my worry. He left and that's all I know." "Very well, forgive me for the intrusion, good day sir."

After the constable leaves, Marta goes up to Christine's room. "The constable was just here inquiring about Mr. Atkins." "Do you know what Adam told him?" "Well, I sort of listened through the door. All Adam would tell him, was that Mr. Atkins had been here and left. Adam told him he didn't know where the man went after that." "This evening I am going to confront Adam, and get to the bottom of all this. We can't wait any longer." "Oh, Miss Christine, be careful. You don't know what he'll do. He may try to kill you. Do you want me to be with you when you talk to him?" "No, you go on to your quarters this evening, just as always. I'll be alright."

That evening, Christine knocks on the office door. "Adam, please let me in. I have to talk to you. It's very important. Please, Adam." Silence. Then there is a click, and the door opens. "Very well, come in and talk." Christine is startled. Whatever is happening, is making an old man out of Adam. "Sit down and get on with it." "Adam, it's time we stop this nightmare, and bring what's happening out in the open. We are dying from this; whatever it is you are hiding. Help me understand, Adam." "There is nothing to understand. I'm not dying, you're not dying. I have done nothing. Now get out." "No, Adam. I won't get out until we get to the bottom of this. I know about Henry Atkins." "You know nothing about Atkins. There is nothing to know." "I know he is lying dead in a vault downstairs." "How do you know that? Did you go down there?" "Yes. I did." "Why, you had no business going down there. Who let you down there?" "I let myself down there. I just sensed that something was down there. And it turned out there was."

"Alright, you want the truth, I'll give you the truth! Yes, I killed Henry and took him down to the vault. I didn't like what he was saying to me, so I hit him. I didn't intend to kill him, it just worked out that way. Now, you want to know the rest of the story? Why I am the way I am?" "Yes, I would like to know." "Because Mimi has come back from the grave for revenge." "Revenge? Why would she want revenge?" "Because I killed her." "But it was just an accident." "It was not an accident, I intended to kill her." "Adam! Why? Why did you intend to kill her?" "I hated her. She killed my mother. She deprived me of a mother for the rest of my life." "So, how did you kill her?" "Oh, I played with her, kept her with me all the time, pretended I loved my little sister. It was all an act. When the time was right, I took her down to the pond. I picked her up, gave her a kiss on the cheek, then I threw her into the pond. It shocked her so, she panicked and drowned. I carried her back to the castle with tears running down my cheeks. My father believed me." "Adam! I can't hardy believe this. You've lived with this all these years. Didn't you even regret what you did?" "No. But Mimi has come back to make me pay for what I did. But I'm not ready to pay yet."

"Adam, I don't know you anymore. You're like a...... a...... complete stranger to me. You have killed two people, and you don't even care. You have to own up to this. You have to tell the authorities about this." "What! You want to see me hang?" "No, but if they determine you are not well, they won't hang you." "I would then spend the rest of my life imprisoned. I won't do that." "I have to tell the constable." "No, you won't tell anyone. You won't be able to." "Are you going to kill me, also?" "No, but you will never talk to anyone again." Adam got up from his chair behind the desk and walked around to Christine. As he approached her, she stood up. He hit her hard across the face. She fell, unconscious to the floor.

He carried her down to the vault room. There was a door that led to another room. In the early days of the castle, it was used as a torture room for those that broke the law. The door had not been opened since the middle of the 17th century. The hinges were very rusted. Adam pulled on the door several times before it finally broke loose. It took some strength to open the creaking door. Adam went in and lit a torch. He then carried Christine into the room, and chained her wrists to the wall. As he finished, Christine came to. She started screaming. "Adam, what are you doing? Let me loose! Why are you doing this?" "To keep you from talking." "Let me loose, I promise I won't say anything. Adam, please. I promise." "I can't trust you anymore, Christine. You'll be alright. You won't die right away. I'll even see that you get something to eat everyday until you do die." "Adam, you're crazy. You're out of your mind." "Probably so. But, you're the one chained to the wall." Adam laughed uncontrollably.

The next morning, Marta went up to Christine's room. She wanted to know what happened when Christine confronted Adam. The room was empty. Her bed hadn't been slept in. She went downstairs and searched. Christine was not anywhere to be found. She knocked on the office door. "Adam, is Christine in there with you?" "No." "I can't find her anywhere. It's as if she vanished." "Christine left last night. She won't be back. So, forget about her." Marta didn't say anything, but she wouldn't believe for a minute that Christine would leave the castle. She had to be here somewhere. Did Adam kill her also? If so, there would only be one place she could be. Marta picked up a set of candles and went down to the vault room. She checked everywhere. Even the vault that Mr. Atkins was in. No Christine. She went back upstairs.

Several days went by. Christine never showed up. Marta was worried sick. She decided to go back down and check the vaults again. Still nothing. As she passed the torture room door, she noticed something on the floor. She knew about the door, but she had never been told what was beyond that door. She knelt down. She ran her finger across the floor. It was rust. That door must have been opened recently. She put the candles down and pulled on the door. It took several tugs to start it moving. Suddenly she heard someone screaming on the other side of the door. Christine! What had he done to her? She pulled even harder. The door finally opened up. There was Christine, chained to the wall. "Christine, what has he done to you?" "Help me, Marta. Please. Get me out of here!" There was one problem. How was Marta going to get Christine's wrists loose? There was a metal bar in a corner of the room. If she could pry the chain holders from the wall, they could get Christine up to her room. Then they could get Azure to get the chains off her wrists. He would have the tools to do that.

Even though Marta was in her early seventies, her concern and fear for Christine, gave her the strength she needed. As she pried on the chains, they started to loosen. The wall was so old that the concrete had eroded enough that the chains finally broke loose. They rushed up to Christine's room. Marta went to get Azure. Christine was safe in her room. Adam knew where she was, or where she was supposed to be, so he never went into her room. Marta brought Azure back with her. After some time, he managed to free Christine's wrists. When he left, he took the chains with him and hid them where they would never be found.

Christine took a bath, and Marta brought her something to eat. They had a problem now. Adam would soon find out that Christine had gotten free, and he would know that Marta helped her. The first place he would look, would be her room. It was going on 11 PM, so, it was dark outside. But, even if they went outside, they still wouldn't be safe from Adam. The only thing to do was wait for him and face him. As a matter of fact, at this very moment, Adam was down in the vault room. He saw the open door. He saw Christine was gone, and so were the chains. "How could this happen? How could she get away? Marta!

Marta found her and got her loose. They are probably in her room right now. I'll have to get rid of both of them."

Adam banged on Christine's door. "Open this door or I'll break it in." Christine unlocked the door, then stepped back. Marta stepped back against a wall. "Come in, Adam, its unlocked." He swung the door open and stepped in. He stared at Marta. His eyes, glaring and red. "Marta, you are a bad girl, and you will pay for your treachery. He then turned to Christine, "Your time has come also. You are a liability to me." Suddenly, Mimi appeared in the room. Adam stared at her. His body stiffened. "Adam, it is time. It is time for you to pay your debt." Mimi started toward Adam. She seemed to glide across the floor. Adam took several steps backward. Mimi kept coming. Adam turned and ran down the stairs. Mimi followed him down. Christine, without any emotion, slowly started walking after them. Adam stopped in the entrance room. Mimi and Christine were still coming at him. He opened the door and started running across the grounds. Before he knew it, he was at the pond. Before he was able to stop running, he fell into the pond. He started yelling for help. Mimi and Christine stood at the edge of the pond. Just watching. As Adam splashed around, he called for help. "Christine, help me I can't move. Something is holding me down. Help me!" Mimi and Christine stood motionless. "Christine! Something is pulling me under. Please!" Both girls watched as Adam slipped beneath the water. After a couple of minutes, Adam floated to the surface, face down. He did not move. Mimi and Christine turned, and started back to the castle.

On the way to the castle, Mimi disappeared. Christine slowly went inside and straight to the vault room door. She went down the stairs and over to Mimi's casket. She opened it. Mimi had returned to her resting place. She was at peace now.

Christine returned to her room. Marta was still standing against the wall. "It's alright, Marta, it's all over. Adam is gone. Mimi is at peace. You can relax now." "But what are we going to do?" "I own the castle now. I suggest we relax, and enjoy the castle with what time we have left."

Chapter 2

Christine lived in the castle until her death, in 1877, at the age of 82. She never mentioned anything to anyone about what had happened back in 1835. All the village was ever told, was that Adam had died accidently. Never how or why. She pushed Mr. Atkins to the back of her mind, and never said a word about him. He was finally listed as missing and probably dead. For a few years after Adam's death, Christine would go to the village every so often, talk to the villagers and eat a meal at The Pub. Marta died in 1843 at the age of 80. She stayed with Christine until her death. Azure was not a well man. He died in 1838. His body just wore out. The castle remained empty until 1935, when the castle was occupied by a new family.

But, before we go there, I really should go back to the original builder of Benes' Castle. Andros Benes' was a very wealthy man. He and his family lived in Budapest, Hungary. His wealth came from his father. Andros was 5'8" and weighed 155 pounds. Not a really big man. He had never had to work, and he was rather wild at times. But he loved his family and took good care of them. His wife, Erzsi was very beautiful and she knew it. She was 5'5" and never mind her weight. Let me just say, she could sure turn heads when she walked down the street, and at parties. Then there was a 15-year-old girl, Josefa, and a 12-year-old boy, Vidor.

Before I continue, let me say, the reason I'm going back to the original owner of the castle, is because unfortunately the Benes' family had some tragedies and scandals. Knowing what the Benes' family went through during their time living in the castle, will help in understanding the future events of families occupying the castle. The history of this castle, suggests it was not always an enjoyable place to live, even as beautiful as it was. It's as though, certain people who lived in the castle, were controlled by the castle, and it always changed their lives. Usually not for the better. The question I ask, and I will probably ask it several times, is the castle responsible for the happenings, is it somehow alive, or is it just the people and the times?

Let me get back to Andros, and his family. Andros was 34 and Erzsi was 32. As I said, they were happy as a family, but Andros started becoming restless. He was getting tired of the city life, and some of the people. He yearned to go somewhere else, where it was quiet and peaceful. Erzsi was originally from Rumania, and she often said she would like to go back sometime and see the old country. Now, it just so happens, that Andros was having lunch with the mayor one afternoon. Andros mentioned that Erzsi had been wanting to go back to her home sometime. "We have talked about moving to Rumania. I guess it's very beautiful there. It would be nice to get away from the big city." "Andros, I just happen to have a flyer come through a few days ago. There is an article in it, about 500 acres for sale near Medias in Rumania. It's about 150 miles northwest of Bucharest. It's near the Transylvanian Alps. Beautiful country, I understand."

When Andros told Erzsi about the property, she became excited. "Would you really want to move there?" "You always wanted to go back to the old country, and the mayor said it is very beautiful there. I think it would be a nice change." "Oh, Andros, let's do it. I know the children would love it." "Then it's settled. The seller is in Bucharest, so we will go there and talk to him. We will stop by the area where the land is first. It's a few miles outside a village called Medias." "It sounds so quaint."

So, it ended up, they loved the land, and they purchased it. Now, what were they going to build on the land, to live in? On the way to Bucharest, they had seen several old castles. They were huge and looked so impressive. They decided that's what they wanted. A castle. They would proceed to draw up a set of plans of how they wanted it to look, then hire someone to build it for them. They hired a builder and went over the plans. Andros gave the builder a list of every detail of the castle, inside and outside. It took Andros and the builder two months to go over everything. Nothing was overlooked. Now the vault room and torture room were not part of the plans. They came in several years later. The builder estimated it would take two years to complete the castle. Therefore, Andros and Erzsi went back to their home in Hungary to eagerly await their new home.

During the building, Andros traveled to the castle about once a month, to see how things were progressing. He was well pleased with how elegant the castle was becoming. Even the villagers seemed proud of the castle. They thought it added a lot to their village. Little did they know. Anyway, the work was actually completed 3 months before the two years was up. The year was 1590. Andros and the family rented a coach, packed up their belongings, and headed for their new home.

Erzsi was ecstatic. Josefa and Vidor were in awe. It was beautiful, and exciting. After a couple of months everyone was settled in and enjoying their new life. They mingled with some of the villagers. The mayor, the constable, the higher ups in the village. They also spent time in The Pub, talking to the regulars there. The Benes' were well respected. They came to know people in the surrounding villages. They would host a party every once in a while; for the upper crust of the villages. Life was good for about 3 years, then things started to change.

It was very subtle at first. No one even seemed to notice. I mentioned earlier that Andros was a little wild at times. Especially after a few drinks. Erzsi didn't drink, except for maybe one glass of wine with dinner. This meant Andros would go to The Pub in the evening by himself. Erzsi never objected so long as he didn't drink too much. She was happy to be with the children. At least for now.

One evening, as Andros was in The Pub, talking with the old-timers, of how serene and beautiful the area was, he especially liked the view of the Transylvanian Alps. He mentioned that he and Erzsi planned to take a trip up into the mountains in a few days. "Mr. Andros, that is not a good idea. You must stay away from there. It could be dangerous. Strange things happen there." "What do you mean, strange things?" "You've heard the story of Vlad, who they say drank the blood of his victims." "Yes, I've heard of him. Don't know too much about him." "Well, he was killed, but they say he came back from the dead as a vampire. He drinks the blood of people, especially women, to stay alive. After he attacks them, they become vampires also. They become, the living dead." "Nonsense. That's just an old wives' tales. Surely you don't believe all that?" "He has a castle in those mountains, and people have seen him wandering through the woods at night. Most people don't go near there, especially at night. That's the only time he can come out."

"Well, I still intend to take a trip there. Besides it will be daytime when we go. We should have nothing to worry about. We may even look up this castle and look it over. Does anyone live there now?" "Yes, there is a man and a woman, who take care of the castle. And, of course the Master, the vampire." "Has this 'Master' ever bothered anyone here?" "Yes, The Pub owner. A few years ago, his daughter was found dead in her bed one morning." "How do you know the vampire did it.?" "She had two puncture marks on her neck, and she was drained of her blood." "Why don't you get a group together and go after him. A good shotgun should end your problem." "A gun won't kill him. The only way he can be killed is by driving a stake through his heart, and it must be done before nightfall. That's when he comes out of his casket." "What are you waiting for?" "The caretakers run off anyone who comes near the castle." "That's a very interesting story, but I must be getting back to Erzsi and the children."

A few days later, Andros and Erzsi started out for the mountains. Andros didn't bother to tell Erzsi about the story he had been told at The Pub. It was a perfect day for a trip. It was only a couple of hours to Fagaras, a village at the foot of the mountains. There, Andros stopped someone and ask if he knew the way to the castle. The man looked at him, and without speaking, turned and walked away. He asked a couple of other people, and got the same reaction. He finally went in to a tavern, and asked the barkeeper. They always know everything. "Mister, you don't want to know where that thing is." "I most certainly do want to know." "If you insist, but you would be better off going back the way you came." He was then given directions, and proceeded to go ahead.

They reached the castle around 3:00. As they drove up a narrow dirt path, they could see the castle up ahead of them. It was impressive, but at the same time, it gave off a sense of darkness and a feeling that was eerie. Suddenly the horses started acting as if they were scared of something. They tried to stop, but Andros used the whip to try and get them to move. All of a sudden, they bolted and started running at a breakneck speed. As they reached the front of the castle, they suddenly came to a stop, right in front of the door. It was as if something had called them to hurry to the front door.

An elderly man and woman, immediately came out to the carriage. "What are you doing here? We don't allow visitors. Turn around and go back." "I'm Andros and this is Erzsi, we own a castle close to Medias. We heard about this castle, thought it would be nice if we could see how magnificent it was." "You see it. Now, turn around and go. Don't come back." "I'm afraid that's impossible right now." "Why is that?" "Because the left rear wheel froze up coming up the path. One of the spindles has snapped. I'm afraid I need a new wheel." The man looked at the wheel. "Yes, you're right. It must be replaced. All right, both of you may come inside. I will ask our maintenance person to go down to the village and get you another wheel." "Thank you very much. We would like to come in and rest a while." "You must leave as soon as the wheel is replaced. You must not be here after the sun goes down."

The maintenance man was a rather slow mover. It took him 2 hours to go to the village and find a wheel. It was going on 7 o'clock before he was finished installing it. The sun had already started going down. During this time, dinner was served for Andros and Erzsi. When they were alone at the table, Erzsi ask, "Why did that man say we had to be gone before the sun went down?" "Oh, it's just that the mountains are too dangerous to travel at night. Hard to see the road and all. You know." "If you say so. But I have a strange feeling about this place." At that moment the house keeper came in to the room. "The Master says he will be with you shortly. He said you must stay the night. You can leave in the morning. The woods are dangerous at night." "Thank you. That's very kind of you." In a very low voice, she replied, "You may not think so later." "Did you say something, ma'am?" "No, I was just thinking I better get your beds ready."

As Andros and Erzsi sat at the dining room table, they noticed how attractive the room was. The table could seat around 30 people.

There were men and women's portraits along one wall. Bright red heavy curtains at each of the windows. The table was made of marble. They wondered if they would get to see the rest of the castle.

As Andros and Erzsi were talking, they felt someone enter the room. They turned and there was the Master. Tall, black hair, piercing eyes. He wore a black outfit and a cape. He approached the table. He spoke in a slow monotone voice. "Good evening. I am Count Stefan. Welcome to my home." Andros and Erzsi stood and introduced themselves. "This is a very beautiful place you have here." "Thank you. I took it over after the original owner passed away. I understand you had some trouble with your carriage." "Yes, the wheel had to be replaced." "I see. We don't get many visitors here, but you are welcome to stay the night." All the time he is talking, he is looking straight into Erzsi's eyes. She starts feeling unsteady. "Erzsi, what's the matter? Are you all right? Erzsi!" "Huh? Oh, yes. I guess I'm just tired." "Well, I will leave you two now, so you may retire. I will say goodbye now, I won't be seeing you in the morning."

The housekeeper entered the room, "I have made up two bedrooms for you. Come, I'll show you to your rooms." "Why separate rooms? We're married." "It's appropriate for everyone to have their own room, while they are here." "It's alright, Andros, I'll be ok. It's just for one night." "Well, I don't like it, but if you're ok with it for tonight, call me if you need me."

The moon was not quite full yet, but it was shining in through the balcony doors. It was 2 AM. Everything was quiet. Erzsi was sound asleep. Then she started tossing and turning. Was she dreaming? She sensed something. There was a bat flying around her balcony door. Suddenly, she opened her eyes and screamed. There, against the moonlight was the figure of someone standing there. They started coming toward Erzsi, but when she kept screaming, the figure disappeared. Andros came running into the room. "Erzsi, what's the matter? Are you alright?" He hurriedly lit some candles. Erzsi was sitting up in the bed. Andros hurried over to her. "Erzsi, what happened?" "There was the shadow of a person standing just inside those doors. He started toward me. Then he disappeared." Andros went over to the balcony doors. He opened them and went out on the balcony. There was no one there. And it was 60' straight down to the ground.

"Erzsi, are you sure you weren't dreaming? There is no way anyone could enter from that balcony." "I tell you someone was standing at those doors, then disappeared. I was not dreaming." "Alright Erzsi, calm down. I'm going over to my room and bring my things over here. I'm going to stay with you the rest of the night. Housekeeper, or no housekeeper. And we will never sleep in separate rooms again. I promise you." A couple of hours later, the bat was back at the balcony doors. But it saw Andros lying next to Erzsi, and flew away. The rest of the night was peaceful.

The next morning, they packed their belongings and prepared to leave. The housekeeper saw them off. "We thank you for your hospitality." "Do not come back again. Hospitality will not be extended to you again." The housekeeper turned and walked away. "Andros, these people are very strange. I feel there is something going on that we do not know about." "Yes, I agree. The sooner we get away from here, the better I'll feel. We won't ever have to worry about coming back here again."

When we got to the village of Fagaras, they stopped at the tavern to eat. "Well, did you find what you were looking for? By the way, where did you stay last night? I didn't see you here in the village." "Yes, we found the castle, and that's where we stayed all night." "You stayed in the castle all night? Are you people crazy?" "We had no choice. The carriage had a broken wheel. By the time it was fixed, it was too late to travel." "Nothing happened to you?" "No, other than Erzsi had a terrible dream." "Andros, it wasn't a dream, I tell you." "Tell me, did you see the Count while you were there?" "Yes, Count Stefan. He was a little strange, but pleasant." "Miss, I will tell you that maybe it wasn't a dream that you experienced, and now that the Count has seen you, I want both of you to do something for me." He pulled out two necklaces with a cross on each one. "Each of you put on one of these, and never take it off. Promise me you won't take them off." "Ok, but why?" "A vampire can't come near a cross. It will protect you." "Here we go again with these superstitions. You don't really believe this do you?" "I do, and you better also. That cross could save your life. Promise me." "Very well, we promise not to take these crosses off, and wear them at all times." "Someday soon, you both will believe how lucky you were to have survived last night, and let me warn you, it isn't over yet. The

Count saw you Miss Erzsi and he won't forget you." "Ok, I think that's enough. You're starting to scare my wife." "As you wish."

Andros and Erzsi started back home. "Andros, what was that man talking about? Why did he want us to wear this cross?" "It's just superstition. They believe dead people walk in those mountains at night. It's just legend stuff. A legend gets started and before you know it, everyone believes it. Don't worry yourself over it." "This cross is nice, but I have other jewelry I like to wear around my neck." "And a very pretty neck it is. If you don't want to wear the cross, don't. I don't intend to keep mine on." "But you promised you would." "I don't think it really protects us from anything."

When they arrived home, the children ran out to greet them. There not really children anymore. Josefa is 18, becoming a beautiful young woman. Vidor is 16, and…., well Vidor is Vidor. He would rather explore and try to figure things out, than go to school. Loves practical jokes. But he is kind hearted and loves his family. Even his sister. They all spend the evening together, talking about the trip. Andros doesn't tell everything. There's no use in scaring Josefa and Vidor. Josefa did ask about the crosses. Andros explained they were just gifts someone gave them at the village of Fagaras. They were very friendly people.

That evening there was a terrific thunder storm. Numerous lightning strikes and very hard rain. The storm ended early morning, but it rained fairly steady for the next couple of days. The family stayed inside and played games and had a wonderful time together. But Andros was anxious to get down to the village and tell them about their trip. Finally, the rain stopped, and Andros headed for the village.

"Andros, where have you been? It's been a while since we last saw you." "Just trying to keep dry." "Did you go on your trip to the mountains?" "Yes, and it was very interesting. Beautiful up in the mountains. We even went to a huge castle up there." "Which castle?" "It was called Bran Castle." "It's vacant isn't it?" "No, a Count Stefan owns it. We even had to stay overnight there." "Count Stefan! That's not good. The last I heard of him, he was staying somewhere in far eastern Romania. He's getting too close. What do you mean you stayed all night? You're lucky to be alive." "I've heard all about this Count. He seemed a little strange, but he was very hospitable." "You met him!" "Of course. We spent the night there." The man crossed himself. "Good Lord, man, you are lucky to be alive. Did anything happen while you were there?" "Not really. Although, Erzsi had a nightmare. She thought someone was standing in her bedroom during the night. But I didn't see anyone around." "You shouldn't have gone there! Now you have brought this curse to our village. We must be very careful. We must take precautions." "So, you really believe all this about vampires and curses." "Yes, and if you were smart, you would too." "Why do you say, I brought this curse to your village?" "Because he has seen your wife, and he will not rest until he controls her." "I will not sit here and listen to this." Andros abruptly got up and left for home. He had enough of this kind of talk.

Two days later, there was a knock on the castle door. Miriam, the housekeeper opened the door. "Yes, may I help you?" It was Markos, the barkeep. "I must see Mr. Andros right away. It's important." "Please come in. I'll get him for you." Andros quickly came out to the entrance room. "Markos, what can I do for you?" "Andros, you need to come with me to the village. Right away." "What's going on?" "Just come with me, please. You'll see when we get there." "All right, let's go."

When they got to the village, they went straight to the home of Alexe Rosetti. When they went in the house, Alexe was crying hysterically. "Who did this! Why! Why!" A priest was trying to calm Alexe. Andros and Markos went into his daughter's bedroom. There on the bed was Rosita. She was dead. Andros, "What happened? Why are you showing me this girl?" "Rosita was 23. So full of life." "I don't understand what this has to do with me." "Look at her throat." Andros leaned down toward the girl. There were two puncture marks on her throat. A trickle of blood was at the marks. "She was drained of blood." "You don't think I had something to do with this?" "Indirectly, yes." "You think because of our trip, I brought a vampire to this village. That's preposterous. You think it was this Count Stefan." "Yes, I'm sure it was him. Actually, it wasn't you that brought him here, it was your wife. He will not be satisfied until he has her under his spell."

Andros hurried back to the castle. "Erzsi! Erzsi! Where are you?" "I'm right here. What is wrong?" "You don't have your cross on?" "No, it's upstairs on my dresser. Why?" "Go get it and put it on." "Andros, what is wrong?" "I'll explain later. Just do it. Where is Josefa?" "Up in her room studying." Andros picked up his cross and went to Josefa's room. "Josefa, I want you to put this cross on, and never take it off." "Why? What is it for?" "Well, sweetheart, it's just a precaution. There are some rumors going around. The villagers think all the ladies should wear a cross to protect them from certain things." "You mean I'm in danger? That something might happen to me?" "No, no. Nothing is going to happen to you. Your mother is going to wear one also. It makes the villagers feel better. Besides, I'm always here to protect you. I won't let anything happen to you." "How about when I go to bed?" "Especially when you go to bed. Just don't ever take it off, then you won't ever have to worry about forgetting it. Ok?" "I'll keep it on all the time. Day and night."

Two days later, Rosita was buried. The whole village turned out for the funeral. They Mayor ask Andros to stay until everyone left. After everyone left, the Mayor and Markos, reopened the coffin. "Why are you reopening her coffin?" "We want you to see what has to be done. You won't like it, but you need to witness this. You will then know why it has to be done to these victims." Andros watched, while Markos picked up a short wooden stake and a hammer. He placed the stake over Rosita's heart and raised the hammer. "Wait! You're not really going to do that? It's obscene." Marcos, with one swift stroke, hit the stake with the hammer and drove the stake through Rosita's heart. As the stake went through her heart, Rosita's eyes opened and she screamed. A moment later her eyes closed and the screaming stopped. She suddenly looked as though she was at peace. "I don't believe you just did that. That was horrible. That girl was still alive. I saw her eyes open and heard her scream." "She was not alive as we know it. She was part of the living dead. Now she is at peace, and that stake must remain in her heart forever." "And if the stake is removed?" "She will come back as the living dead, roaming the countryside, looking for victims, because she will need blood to stay in that state."

As Andros went back to the castle, he just couldn't quite grasp what he had just seen. But he knew that the villagers had not been telling him tales. He has witnessed the truth. He realized that they really had been lucky to leave that castle alive. Then Erzsi was not dreaming that night.

She really did see the Count in her bedroom. She must be told what is happening. She will be frightened, but she must be aware of the danger.

It was getting late, so Andros decided to wait until tomorrow to tell Erzsi what was happening. He decided to go to his office library, and see if he could find any information on vampirism. He found 3 books that dealt with vampires, the occult, superstition legends. Erzsi was very tired and went on up to bed. Andros told her he would be up soon. Andros became so engrossed in the information he was reading, time passed without him realizing it.

Vampirism grew out of legend over the years. Most people view it as a legend and no more. Others believe the legend is truth. A vampire cannot survive in daylight. Sunlight causes him to decompose. He can only function during darkness. That's when he hunts his victims. Usually young women. He survives by drinking their blood. It has been said he can turn himself into a bat and back again at will. He cannot enter a room if there is garlic near his entrance. Because he is evil, a cross will make him unable to function. The most common way to end a vampire's 'life', is a stake through the heart, which must remain in his heart, or he will come back to 'life' again. The vampire must return to his coffin, each night, which contains dirt from his original burial ground. He must be destroyed during the day. That is considered the best time to end his 'life'. Also, water will cause him to dissolve. The third most common way is by fire. Burning by fire will destroy him.

Andros is amazed at what he is reading. It is getting very late. Meanwhile, Erzsi is sleeping soundly. A bat is approaching the balcony of the room that faces the front of the castle. Then a figure enters the room thru the balcony doors. He walks down the hall towards Erzsi's bedroom door. He enters. Some moonlight is shinning through the windows. The figure stands beside Erzsi, and leans down. At that moment Erzsi moves a little and the moonlight reflects off of her cross. The figure sees the cross and backs up and shields his eyes. At that moment, Erzsi wakes up, sees the figure and screams. The figure then turns and flees back the way he came.

Andros hears the scream, and hurries up to the bedroom. Erzis is hysterical. Andros hurriedly lights a candle. "Erzsi! Erzsi! What's wrong? Are you alright?" Andros gets Erzsi to calm down some. "Andros, the

Count was here in this room. I saw him in the moonlight. He was here!" "What was he doing?" "I don't know. When I woke up, and screamed, he fled down the hall." Andros ran down the hall and out on the balcony of the front room. He saw nothing. But he knew that Count Stefan had been there. Erzsi was not dreaming. Andros went back to Erzsi, "I'm going downstairs and put out those candles and I'll be right back." Andros went back to stay with Erzsi. He needed to tell her the whole story tomorrow. It's time she knows the danger.

Meanwhile at the home of Kristof Sabrisse, his daughter, Mia, age 26, is asleep in her bed. There is garlic at the windows and her door. She is also wearing a cross. Suddenly, she sits up in bed and just stares. She is in a trance. Count Stefan is standing outside her window. He does not speak, but Mia hears his thoughts. 'Mia, come to the window.' He repeats twice more. Mia gets up and walks toward the window. 'Remove that stuff from the window.' Mia removes the garlic from the window and tosses it into a corner of the room. 'Open the window.' He repeats this again. Mia opens the window. The Count comes in the window and walks toward Mia. He stops. He sees the cross she is wearing. 'Mia, take off the cross.' He repeats this 3 times. Finally, Mia takes hold of the cross and rips it from her neck and drops it on the floor. The Count approaches her.

The next morning after breakfast, which Erzsi did not eat much of, Andros told her it was time to talk about last night. "Erzsi, it's time I tell you what......." At that moment, there was a knock on the front door. Miriam came in the dinning room, Mr. Andros, the Mayor is here. He says it is important." "Thank you, Miriam, I'll be right there."

"Andros, it has happened again. Please come with me." "Yes, let us go. I have some news for you also." They went to the house of Kristof Sabrisse. His daughter, Mia was dead. Same two marks on her throat. "Well, Mayor, we had a visitor last night also. Count Stefan. I think the cross saved Erzsi's life. When she woke up and screamed, he fled." "But what can we do?" "It's time to put a stop to this Count Stefan. I've done some research, and I know how he can be stopped for good." "Really, what do we have to do?" "The Count has to be staying around the village somewhere. He has to sleep in his coffin during the day. We must find that coffin and destroy him." How do we destroy him?" "The same way you take care of these girls. Drive a stake through his heart and leave it there. That will end his reign of terror." "Alright, let's take care of Mia, then call a meeting with the men of the village to discuss what we must do."

Andros went back to the castle. He sat down with Erzsi to talk. "Erzsi, it's time you knew what has been happening and why. Count Stefan was here last night. I think your cross saved you from harm. You see, Count Stefan......." Andros told Erzsi everything about the terror they were living."........so, we are going to do what we can to stop this Count Stefan." "How horrible. I'm so scared, Andros. What about Josefa? We must protect her." "We will."

Now, Josefa is 18, your typical teenager. She is in her last year of school. She has a boyfriend, Marku. He is 19. Nothing serious, just normal boyfriend, girlfriend. Now, Marku is going off to Bucharest to attend college, and since he is leaving tomorrow, he wants to meet Josefa later tonight after their parents have gone to bed. They will meet in the woods, half way between the village and the castle. Sometime after midnight, they meet. They don't like leaving each other, but they will stay in touch. They talk for several hours. Josefa finally realizes how late it is, so they part, and Josefa heads back to the castle.

A fog has settled in. Josefa is having trouble finding her way back. She sees someone standing on the path just in front of her. She stops. "Good evening miss, are you lost?" "No, I'm going home. Who are you?" "I am, Count Stefan." The Count comes closer. She sees his glaring red eyes. She's becoming afraid. She reaches for her cross. It's not there! She left it on her dresser. She starts to back up. "Don't be afraid, miss, I'm not going to hurt you. I'm going to give you eternal life. And you will be mine forever." Josefa faints. The Count picks her up and starts carrying her through the woods.

Andros and Erzsi are on their way downstairs to breakfast. As they enter the dining room, Vidor is already at the table. "Vidor, where is your sister?" "I haven't seen her this morning." "Erzsi, why don't you go up to Josefa's room and see if she is up yet?" "Yes, I'll be right back." A couple of minutes later, Erzsi yells, "Andros, come here. Hurry." Andros runs up the stairs. "What's wrong?" "Josefa is not here. Her bed hasn't been slept in. Something has happened to her! Andros, we have to find her! She might be hurt!" "Stay calm. I'll go right down to the village and see if anyone has seen her. You stay here in case she comes back."

Andros hurries to the village. Most of the villagers are just waking up. Andros goes around to the people Josefa knows. No one has seen her. He goes to see Marku. "Josefa is missing? Oh, no. It's my fault." "What do you mean?" "I'm leaving for school today, so we met in the woods last night to say goodbye." "In the woods last night? You fool. Don't you know you cannot be out after dark? Never mind. We have to find her before it's too late, if it isn't already. Go around and get as many men together as you can, and meet me in The Pub." "Yes, sir, right away."

The Count had carried Josefa to where he was staying outside the village. By the time he got there, the sun was just starting to come up. He only had time to tie Josefa up and return to his coffin. He would finish with her that night. No one would be able to figure out where she was.

"Men, the Count has Josefa. We know he is around here somewhere. We must figure out where that is. We have to rescue Josefa, and hope we're not too late. We need to search the village. Everywhere." "Ok, we're with you. We will each take a section of town. Let's go, men." The search started. They searched barns and other buildings. They covered the whole town. They searched the grave yard. Several of the men searched the woods all the way from the village, up to the castle. Nothing. Early that evening they met again at The Pub. Everyone came up empty handed. One of the men spoke up, "Wait a minute. I just thought of something we overlooked. There are some old ruins about a mile northwest of town. Remember guys? It was built to be a school, but it was never used. It's mostly rubble now. That's probably where he is." Andros finally had some hope. "Ok, how about four or five of us hurry up and go up there. It's getting late."

They could see the ruins up ahead, so they started running. As soon as they reached the ruins, they spotted the coffin. And there was Josefa, tied up, sitting against a wall, unable to move. When she saw the men she started screaming, "Father, father, over here. Help." Andros untied her and held her in his arms. "It's ok, Josefa. I've got you. Are you alright? Did he do anything to you?" Josefa was crying. "No, when we got here, the sun was coming up and he tied me up and got in that coffin. Who is he? And what is he?" "We'll talk about that later. Right now, we have to get you home. People, the sun is going down. We have to get out of here. We know where he sleeps now. We'll come back tomorrow and finish him off."

That evening Andros got the family together. It was time to tell Josefa and Vidor what was going on. "Josefa, I know why you went to the woods last night. It was a foolish thing to do. But it's partly my fault. I should have told you the whole story about the Count when I gave you the cross. But why weren't you wearing it? I told you to never take it off." "I know. I laid it on the dresser and when I went out, I forgot about it. I'm so sorry. I promise I will never take it off again." Andros proceeded to tell Josefa and Vidor about the Count and what was at stake. (Couldn't help that.)

That night, the Count, finding Josefa gone, was furious. He knew she must live at the castle, that's where she was heading when he accosted her. So, she was part of Andros's family. He will make Andros pay dearly for this. He will pay with the loss of his wife. Every since he first saw Erzsi, he knew she was the one to be his for the rest of their lives. Tomorrow night he would act.

The next morning, Andros and 3 other men went back to the ruins to finish off the Count. When they got to the ruins, the coffin was gone. They looked all around. It was not there. "How stupid of me! I should have known, with Josefa gone, he would know he had been discovered, so he moved the coffin, because he knew we would be back today." "What do we do now?" "Search all over again. We must find that coffin before dark." "I'll go get some more men, and will start searching again." They started searching the village again. Some of the men even searched out farther than the ruins. By late afternoon, they had found nothing. It was no use.

Late that night, Erzsi becomes restless. She is asleep, but she hears someone calling her. She opens her eyes, and sits up on the edge of the bed. She puts her robe on, and starts down the stairs. She opens the door and steps outside. She is in a trance. The voice in her head keeps calling her. "Erzsi, follow the sound of my voice. Come to me. Come to me." Andros suddenly wakes up. He hears the door downstairs close.

He quickly puts on his pants and shirt, and goes downstairs. As he steps outside, he can see Erzsi slowly walking across the lawn, toward the back of the castle. She looks like she is sleepwalking. But Andros has a feeling that the Count is calling to her. Andros wants to call to Erzsi, and tell her to stop, but thinks better of it. If he follows her, she will lead him to the Count, and he may be able to confront the Count and stop his reign of terror.

Erzsi continues on down a hill behind the castle. She is heading toward a grove of trees. As Andros follows her into the woods, he realizes he has never seen this part of the castle grounds. The light of the moon is just enough to be able to see fairly well. Then he sees the Count up ahead. He also notices this area is like a little canyon. Andros sees the coffin on some level ground at the top of this canyon. The Count is standing next to it. Andros waits until Erzsi is just a few feet away, then rushes to Erzsi. He shakes her. "Erzsi, wake up. Wake up." She doesn't respond. Out of the corner of his eye, he sees the Count coming at him. They meet and struggle. The Count has enormous strength. He picks Andros up and throws him against a tree. Andros is stunned. As the Count rushes toward Andros, Andros hits the Count as hard as he can on the side of his jaw. The Count falls to the ground. Andros jumps on the Count. They roll around on the ground. Erzsi is still standing where she was, not moving, unaware of what was going on. In their struggles, Andros manages to grab a rock and hit the Count on the head. It dazes the Count for a few seconds. Andros jumps on top of him. But the Count takes his foot and pushes Andros back. He lands at the edge of the cliff, which is about 30 feet above the bottom of the canyon. Unable to stop himself, he rolls over the edge and is saved by a small tree growing out of the edge of the cliff. As he tries to hang on, the Count comes over and steps on Andros's hands, to make him let go of the tree, so he will fall to his death. But as the Count slams his foot down on Andros's hands, he loses his balance. He falls over the cliff. Down at the bottom is an old dead tree, with several branches reaching for the sky. The Count just happens to fall on one of those pointed branches. That branch pierces his back, goes through his heart and out through his chest. As Andros looks down, the Count ages to an old man, then his body starts to erode until there is nothing left but the skeleton. As this happens, Erzsi wakes up, and doesn't know where she is. Andros manages to pull himself up on level ground. He runs over to Erzsi. "What happened? Where am I?" "It's all right Erzsi, you are ok. The terror is over. The Count is destroyed."

The village is celebrating. There is singing and dancing in the streets. Up at the castle, Andros and the family are enjoying each other. They are all together and the danger is over. They are all safe. Marku has left for college. Since Josefa is graduating soon, she wants to go to a girl's school in Bucharest to continue her education. She hopes to be a teacher. So, everything is back to 'normal', whatever normal is. Unfortunately, the castle has other plans for the Benes' and the village.

Chapter 3

Twenty-five years have passed. It is 1628. Medias has grown quite a lot. It now has a library, an administration building for the mayor and a constable. And of course, The Pub. Andros is now 62, Erzsi is 60 and still a beautiful lady. Josefa and Vidor are now 43 and 40. Mayor Felix Gustav passed away two years ago at the age of 76, and Andros was elected Mayor. Erzsi has her social life. Josefa and Marku got together while they were in school in Bucharest. They married in 1608 and had a daughter Elena in 1610. She is now 18. Three years ago, Josefa and the family moved back to Medias, and Josefa became the teacher at the school after the teacher there passed away. Marku became the constable and had one deputy, Emil Toma. Vidor also went to college and became a lawyer. He lives at the castle and takes care of Andros's financial affairs. He also helps people out in the village that need advice. He has not married, although he is rather smitten with a girl from the village. Miriam is still the housekeeper. She is now 68. Markos is now 80 years old, but his health is not very good these days. He hired a woman, Brigita, 38, to take care of the customers, and take care of the books. She is slightly heavy, very pretty, and outgoing. She is perfect for the job. Markos also hired a young girl, Lucia, 24, to help Brigita. She is quiet, but polite. She has short light brown hair. Not exactly pretty, just average. Markos still does what he can once in a while, but he mostly just sits around and talks to the customers. That pretty much brings us up to date on the village and the occupants. Oh,

I almost forgot, with everyone getting older, Andros had a vault room built under the castle. The entrance would be from the kitchen. As time passed, he wanted all the family members to be interned in one area.

I need to tell you a little more about Brigita. She came to Medias several months ago from Bucharest. She never explained why she left the big city and ended up in this little village. She wasn't married, she never dated, and didn't seem interested in any of the younger men in the village. But Brigita had a goal. And after she became 'part of the village', she began working on her goal. Which will become clear fairly soon.

Now, Andros and Erzsi are still in love with each other, but sometimes, situations come up that people can't control. And most times these situations end in tragedy. I'm afraid Andros and Erzsi, are about to confront one of those situations. Will it be tragedy, or will understanding win out?

About once a month, Andros and Erzsi have a party in the great room for close friends. Tonight, is one of those parties. There are usually around 30 guests. Tonight, is no exception. Andros had met a man that morning who had just arrived in town, and had invited him to come to the party. It would be a perfect time to meet many of the townspeople. The man was 58, very well-built man, around 6' tall, dark hair with some grey starting to show through. He was not married, his wife died two years ago. Andros introduced him to several people. "Oh, there is my wife, come meet her." As they walked toward Erzsi, the man was immediately attracted to her beauty. "Erzsi, this is Dragos, he is taking over the library in the village." "Oh, how nice. I'm very happy to meet you. Did you just get into town?" "I'm very glad to meet you, also. Such a beautiful lady, and yes, I did just arrive this morning." "You must come to the castle some evening and have dinner with us, so we can get to know each other." "I would love to." "Come, Dragos, I want you to meet some more of the people."

Dragos seemed to fit right in with the villagers. He was always friendly, always had a smile. He got along with everyone. He liked his position, and felt that this was his home now. He participated in town meetings. Sometimes made suggestions, always listened to others. He was becoming very popular, especially with some of the single women, maybe even a few women that weren't single.

There was a restaurant close to the library. Erzsi eats there quite often around noon. As she was sitting at a table, ordering, Dragos entered, looked around, and spotted Erzsi. He went over to her table. "Mrs. Benes', may I join you?" "Please sit down. And my name is Erzsi." "Ok… Erzsi." After they had finished their meal, "Why don't you come over to the library with me? I will show you around. Do you read much?" "No. Even when I was younger, I didn't read very often." "We have such a selection, maybe you could find something that would interest you." "Sure, why not?"

They spent time walking up and down the aisles, looking at the different selections. Suddenly, Dragos stopped. "Erzsi, I've watched you a lot over these last few weeks, and I have fallen in love with you." "Don't Dragos, I'm married." "I know, but I can't help it." Dragos put his hands on her shoulders, drew her toward him, and kissed her. She started to pull back, then stopped. Dragos pulled back. "Erzsi, I'm sorry. I shouldn't have done that." "No, you shouldn't have, and please don't do it again." She left and went back to the castle.

That evening, when Andros came home, Erzsi seemed a little upset. "Erzsi, what's wrong? You seem nervous. Are you alright?" Erzsi was not about to tell Andros about this afternoon. "I'm ok, it's just been a busy day. I just need to relax a while." Erzsi couldn't stop thinking about what happened. She loved Andros, but when Dragos kissed her, something stirred in her. She was so confused. She could not be alone with Dragos again.

I mentioned that Brigita had an agenda. Well, she is about to put it into action. One evening, Andros and the men are at The Pub, as usual, discussing politics or whatever. Brigita is watching Andros intently. Andros is good looking, and rich. It doesn't matter that he is married. That's no obstacle. As a matter of fact, it is good that he is married. It will make things much easier. It's close to 12:00 and time for Brigita to go home. She walks over to Andros. "Mr. Benes', I was wondering if you could walk me home. I hate to go home in the dark, and also, I would like to talk to you about something. If it's not too much bother." One of the younger men, Petre spoke up, "I'll take you home, Brigita." "No, you won't. I wasn't talking to you. And I don't want to. So be quiet."

"I suppose I could, but I have to get home pretty soon." "That's ok, it won't take long."

As they reach Brigita's door, she asked Andros to come in for a few minutes. Andros hesitated, but said he would just for a minute or so. What did you want to talk to me about?" "Come, sit down with me. I just want to talk for a while. I don't know very much about you, and I'm interested in your background." "There's not really much interesting about me." They talked for a while. Then Brigita leaned over and kissed him. He drew back. "What was that for?" "I like you, and I'm lonely. I want to be with you." "That's impossible. You know that." "No, I don't." She leaned over and kissed him again. Only this time, he didn't pull away. Then, "Brigita, we can't do this. Please. I must go." He went back to the castle. Now Andros and Erzsi are both nervous and confused.

Now, Vidor is having his own problems. For the past several months, he has been going with a girl from the village, by the name of, Aurora. They seemed quite close. Vidor started thinking about marriage. He finally decided to ask Aurora to marry him, but first he had to get up the nerve, and it had to be at the right time. He even bought her an engagement ring. One evening while they were together, Vidor showed Aurora the ring and ask her to marry him. She was surprised. But she hesitated. "Vidor, I don't know. This is so sudden. I wasn't expecting this." "Aurora, I love you, and I'm sure you love me." "I need time to think." "That's alright. I'll wait. I'm sure you'll say yes."

Vidor didn't see Aurora for the next couple of days. But that was alright, she had an important decision to make. She would come around. Finally, Vidor went over to see Aurora. She wasn't home. He would come back later. But it was unlike her not to be home this time of the evening. The next evening, he went back to Aurora's house. "Aurora, I've missed you. I came over last night, but you weren't home. Is something wrong?" "No, I just had some things to do." "Why don't we go down to The Pub for a while?" "Not tonight, Vidor, I really don't feel very well." "Ok, maybe tomorrow night." This went on for a week. Vidor decided to finally get and answer from Aurora. I don't think he is going to like the answer he gets.

Vidor knocked on Aurora's door. "Vidor, what do you want?" "I want to come in and talk about us. It's time." "Not now, Vidor, I don't feel well, and I'm not ready to talk yet." Vidor pushed his way in anyway. "Felip, what are you doing here?" Felip was one of Vidor's best friends. "Vidor, I guess it's time you knew." "Knew what?" "Felip and I were married several days ago." Vidor was stunned. He looked at Felip and then at Aurora. He couldn't believe what he had just heard. At first, he couldn't speak, he couldn't even feel anything. "How could this happen? You and I were supposed to get married. I love you and I thought you loved me. How did Felip come into the picture all of a sudden?" "Vidor, Felip and I went together before I met you. But we broke up. Then several weeks ago, I ran into Felip, and it started all over again. We have never stopped loving each other. Felip ask me to marry him, and I said yes. That's why I couldn't say yes to your proposal. I was already committed to Felip. I just didn't know how to tell you." "So, you used me until you could get what you really wanted. Isn't that a laugh." Vidor started laughing loudly. "I wasn't using you, I enjoyed being with you. I liked you, I just didn't love you." "Then you should have told me as soon as Felip came back into your life." "I'm sorry, Vidor. I didn't mean to hurt you." "It's a little late to be sorry now." Now, Vidor was as angry as he had ever been. There was pure hatred in his voice when he spoke. "You will regret this, Aurora. Someday you will regret you ever knew me. That goes for you also, Felip. Someday you will regret this traitorous act. Mark my words, you both will pay for this, and I will see to it that you do."

So much dissention; is it the castle, the village, or just the way of humans? Things can only get worse. It seems the Benes' family is heading for serious trouble.

Josefa and Marku and Elena. They are still a happy family. Josefa and Marku enjoy their jobs. Josefa loves teaching and she loves all the children. Marku enjoys being constable. It allows him to interact with everyone in the village. Elena plans to go to the same school as her mother when she graduates. She sees how her mother enjoys the children and feels she would also like to teach someday.

Erzsi can't seem to get Dragos out of her mind. One day she goes into the village to do some shopping, and without thinking, she finds herself standing in front of the library. She goes inside and asks the librarian if Dragos is in. He is in his office, so, Erzsi enters the office. "Erzsi, what a surprise. I wasn't expecting to see you." "To tell the truth, I'm not sure why I came in. I just found myself standing in front of the building." "I'm glad you came in. I've thought about you quite often, lately." "That's just it, Dragos, I find myself thinking about you, also. I think I'm becoming attracted to you. I'm really confused." "I know you're married, but that doesn't stop me loving you."

Just then there is a knock on the door. Andros walks in. "Erzsi, I didn't expect to see you here." "I just stopped in for a minute. Dragos was telling me about some plans he has to expand the library." "That's why I dropped in, Dragos. I have some suggestions for some changes. They're just ideas, something for you to think about. No pressure." "Well, I'll leave you two alone, and go on with my shopping. See you at home, darling. We still want you to drop by for dinner some evening, Dragos."

Brigita has made her first move. A couple of more meetings and she will have Andros where she wants him. She feels Andros is not very strong willed. He can be easily swayed. She will approach him again tonight.

That evening as Andros sits in The Pub, talking with his friends, he can't help but looking over at Brigita quite often. He feels guilt, and that makes him drink a little more than usual. Brigita has her eyes on him, also. Finally, it's time for her to leave. Again, she asks Andros to take her home. The younger man, Petre, speaks up again. "Come on, Brigita, let me take you home. I'll take care of you." "I doubt it. I don't think you are capable of taking care of anything. And I told you before, I'm not interested. Leave me alone. Don't even talk to me." Against his better judgement, Andros agrees to take her home. The people in The Pub don't see anything wrong with Andros taking Brigita home. They know Andros. He's a dedicated family man. They don't see anything wrong.

Again, Andros goes inside with Brigita. She sees he has had a little more to drink tonight than usual. This should be easy. She gets Andros to sit down with her again. She gives him another drink. After a short while, she takes his hand and leads him to her bedroom.

The next morning, Andros wakes up and can hardly move. His head is pounding. He has a terrific hangover. Erzsi goes up to the bedroom. "Well, I see you are finally awake. How do you feel?" "Terrible. What happened? I don't even remember leaving The Pub last night." "All I know, is the doctor found you walking around like you didn't know where you were. So, he brought you home." "I feel like I've been drugged. I just don't remember anything."

Andros goes down to the mayor's office. He tries to get some work done, but he keeps trying to figure out what happened last night. As the day goes on, and his head starts to clear some, he vaguely remembers taking Brigita home again. He remembers going inside, but after that it's a blank. He thinks it is time to have a talk with Brigita. Something is going on.

Late that afternoon, Andros goes to see Brigita. "Come in Andros. I was expecting you." "You were?" "I thought maybe you were curious." "About what?" "Suppose you tell me." "For one thing, I cannot bring you home at night anymore. There's really no reason. It's not as if the village is dangerous at night. And you don't live that far from The Pub. Second, we will not have any more romantic contact. I love my wife, I do not love you. I had some weak moments, but not anymore. Am I clear?" "Well, Andros, let me make myself clear. This is not over. It's just beginning." "What do you mean?" "Don't you remember last night when you took me into my bedroom?" "No! I did no such thing." "Yes, you did, darling Andros." "Wait a minute! You drugged me with that drink. You little tramp. You set me up. For what?" "Yes, I drugged you last night. But nothing happened. It isn't you I want." "I see… so, it's really blackmail. You expect me to pay you to protect my reputation." "Blackmail is a dirty word. Let us just say, you are investing in my future." "Forget it. I'm paying you nothing." "What do you think your wife and the people around here will do when they find out you have been having an affair with me?" "But I wasn't." "When I get done sobbing and shaking, while I tell how you forced yourself on me for the last several weeks, they'll believe me. You will be an outcast. Your wife will hate you. They may even run you out of town. You may even end up in a dungeon for the rest of your life." Brigita starts laughing. "If that happens, you won't get your investment money after all." "No,

but I'll still be better off than you. There are other rich men around."
"I'm not paying you one Lei. Do what you want." With that, Andros
walked out and went back to his office. Brigita wasn't worried. With a
little time, he would pay up.

Andros went home early. He did not even go to The Pub that
evening. "Andros, you are home early. You're not going to The Pub
tonight?" "No, I'm tired, I just want to rest." "Ok, but I need to go to
the village this evening. Some of the girls and I are planning a small
party for one of the ladies. I'll only be a couple of hours. You don't
mind, do you?" "No, no. You go ahead. I have some things to sort out."
"Is something wrong?" "No, it's nothing important. You go ahead."
Andros went to his library and scanned over his books. He found what
he wanted. 'Criminal Practices'. He was looking for a solution to his
problem, if there was one. He was looking for a way to discredit her.
He needed someone to check on Brigita's past in Bucharest. If she had
something to hide, maybe he could turn the tables on her, and she
would leave him alone. Of course, there were other ways to silence her.

Erzsi went into town, but there were no ladies waiting for her. She
went straight to Dragos's house, and knocked on the door. "Erzsi, come
in. I wasn't expecting you." "I had to see you. I think about you all the
time. Dragos, I can't stand being away from you." "Erzsi, you know I
love you. But are you sure this is what you want? I don't want just an
affair, I want to marry you. But I also know it's not all that simple." "I
know, Dragos, but let us not think about that yet. I just want to be with
you." With that Dragos put his arms around Erzsi and held her tight.
They would worry about the consequences later.

Andros thought he had found one way to silence Brigita. He needed
a lawyer, but he couldn't use Vidor, he needed someone the town
didn't know. That evening, Andros, went to The Pub, still thinking
of ways to stop Brigita. A little while later, Brigita came in and started
working. As the evening progressed, Brigita kept looking at Andros and
smiling. Andros tried not to pay any attention to her. Then he made
a decision. He was going to take Brigita home tonight, and settle this
problem, once and for all. He looked at Brigita and nodded his head
and motioned toward the door. Brigita nodded yes. She understood.
She won. Or so it seemed.

Andros was a little nervous. He knew what he had to do. To get up his nerve, he had a few more drinks than he should have. But he still had his wits about him. So, when it was time, Brigita came over to Andros. Just then Petre came over and stood in front of Brigita. "Now, you're going to let me take you home tonight. I like you, and I just want us to be friends." "Friends with you? Hah! Get out of my way. You're nothing but a worm." "Brigita……" At that moment she slapped him hard across the face. He turned and walked out the door.

Andros took Brigita home and went inside with her. "So, you decided to start paying up. I knew you would. You don't really have a choice." "Yes, I do have a choice, Brigita." With that he put his hands on her shoulders and pushed her backward onto the couch. "Now, you listen to me, you little tramp, I will not be blackmailed. And if you try, I will ruin you along with me." "Andros, by noon tomorrow, I promise you everyone in this town will know about us." Brigita stood up, and as she did, Andros slapped her hard across the face and she fell back down on the couch.

The doctor in the village had delivered a baby that night. As he was walking back home, he spotted Andros standing in the middle of the street. He wasn't moving, he just stood there. The doctor went over to him. "Andros, are you alright?" "Huh?" "Andros, you look like you just saw a ghost." "Oh, yeah, maybe I did." "Let me take you home. I don't think you can make it on your own. Where is your scarf? It's cold out here. Take mine until I get you to the castle."

The next day, Andros went about his business as usual, except he was extremely nervous and jumpy. He wondered when, and if, Brigita would make her announcement. That evening he stopped at The Pub, as usual. A couple of hours went by. Markos came over to the table, "Has anyone seen Brigita today? She hasn't shown up for work. That's unlike her." Nicolae said he would go down and check on her. Andros was not about to volunteer.

About 10 minutes later, Nicolae came back in the bar, "Markos, I have to go get the constable. Brigita, she is dead." "What! Dead! What happened?" "I don't know. She was just lying on the floor, dead." "Did you check her to see if she was really dead? Maybe she just fainted." "I wasn't going near her. I'll let Marku check her." With that he headed for the constable. Several of the men, including Andros, headed for Brigita's house. As they waited outside the house for Marku, more people started gathering. Everyone wanted to know what was going on.

Finally, Marku and his deputy, Emil, arrived. "Alright everyone, move back. Give me some room. What's this about Brigita? Who found her?" "I did." "Tell me about it, Nicolae." "Markos ask me to check on her because she didn't show up for work. When I opened the door, she was lying on the floor, dead." "Did you check her?" "No, I didn't even go inside. I just closed the door and came to you." "How did you know she was dead?" "She just looked like it."

Marku went in the room. Andros figured since he was the mayor he should go in also. If Brigita is dead, that changes Andros's situation quite a bit. Brigita was lying on her back on the floor. Marku knelt down to check her. No blood. Marku did notice some bruising on her throat. Looking closer, he could definitely see heavy bruise marks on her throat and neck. By then the doctor was there. "Doctor, it looks as if she was strangled. I saw no other injuries." The doctor agreed. "By the looks of her, I would say she's been dead less than 24 hours." "That would put it sometime last night." "Yes, I would say so."

Marku, "Does anyone know when Brigita was last seen?" Markos, "She left The Pub last night. Andros walked her home." "Is that right, Andros?" "Yes, I walked her home. I said goodnight at her door and went home." "Ok, everyone, the excitement is over, go on back to what you were doing." Marku went back in the house to look around. Everything looked to be in place. It didn't look as if someone was trying to rob her. Emil went to the bedroom. He checked around the room, nothing out of place. As he stood beside the bed, he noticed something shinny underneath the edge of the bed. He picked it up and called Marku. "What is it, Emil?" "I found this under the edge of the bed." It was a pin that is worn on a jacket, and had a crest on it. Marku recognized the coat of arms symbol, and he didn't like what he saw.

Androsask Vidor to do something for him. Since Brigita was dead, Vidor would just think Andros was helping Marku with the investigation. "Vidor, I need your help." "Sure, what do you need?" "I would like you to go to Bucharest and do some research on Brigita. We know she left there in a hurry, but we don't know why. Check her background. See if she was in trouble or if someone had it in for her and tracked her here." "I can do that. I'll leave early tomorrow morning, and probably be back that evening." Andros really wanted to know if Brigita had tried her blackmail scheme back home. Maybe that's why she left in such a hurry. If she did, that would help him explain his involvement with her in case someone found out about his situation. That may get him off the hook, especially with Erzsi.

The next morning as Vidor was leaving, Marku came up the steps. "Andros, I need to speak with you. It is important." "Sure, Marku, come in." "Andros, we need to go into your office. I need to talk to you in private." "Ok, this sounds serious." "It is Andros. It is." Andros told Miriam, the housekeeper, he was not to be disturbed. "Now, Marku, what is it that's so serious?" Marku handed the pin to Andros. "Do you recognize this?" "Why, that's my pin. Where did you find it? I didn't know I had lost it. I've been so preoccupied lately, I didn't even notice it was gone." "What has kept you so preoccupied lately." "Oh, you know, just been busy lately. You haven't said where you found my pin." "Under Brigita's bed." "That's impossible." "You've never been in Brigita's house?" "No, I......" "Then how did this pin get under her bed?"

Andros was silent for a minute. He didn't know whether to tell Marku about the blackmail or not. "Well, Andros, I'm waiting." "Alright, Marku, I will tell you how it got there......" Andros proceeded to tell Marku the whole story. He didn't leave anything out. ".......and that's the whole story. Vidor is on his way to Bucharest to see if she has tried this before." "That's fine, Andros, but you lied about being in the house, and your pin was found there. It doesn't look good for you, Andros." "But I didn't kill her." "But you had reason to." "But I didn't, I swear." "I won't arrest you yet, and I will be looking into whoever else might want her dead. Let me know what Vidor finds out. I take it you won't be taking any trips soon." "No, I'll be right here."

"Andros, why was Marku here? He walked right by me and didn't speak. He didn't look very happy." "It had to do with Brigita's death. He wanted to know if I had noticed anyone who might have appeared to have something against her. He doesn't have anything to go on yet." "It's really horrible. Only a monster could do something like that. That woman never hurt anybody." "Maybe." "What do you mean?" "She must have done something to somebody." Andros walks away before he says something to make Erzsi ask more questions.

Vidor didn't get back until the next afternoon. "Vidor, what did you find out?" "We better go in your office, and you better sit down. This woman has quite a track record." "Oh?" "It seems she made her living off of older rich men. She got them to go home with her, then get them drunk, and blackmail them. Saying if they didn't take care of her, she would ruin their reputation." "Hmm, that sounds familiar." "What?" "Oh, nothing, I was just thinking." "The two men she tried this on, are in their lower seventies and they haven't traveled outside the city for a couple of years. I talked to both of them. In the end they came out alright. They didn't lose any money, and she didn't scare them, so they went to the police right away. That's why she skipped town so fast. So, neither of them killed Brigita." Andros was a little relieved. At least he could explain his involvement with some backup. It was time to tell Erzsi what has been going on. But he wasn't out of the woods yet. Marku could still arrest him for murder because of the pin. That was the only evidence he had. Did Marku believe his story?

"Erzsi, sit down, we have to talk." "Oh, you sound so serious." "It is serious. I must tell you what has been going on. You have to try to understand what happened and why." "Andros, are you in trouble?" "Yes, you might say I am. So, let me explain……" He told Erzsi everything, including Brigita's past. But he stopped short of telling about Marku and his pin. He decided to wait until talking to Marku about Brigita's past.

"…….and that's about it. I've been such a fool. I thought I was doing Brigita a favor, and I sure was." "Oh, Andros, how could you fall for that? I would have thought you would see right through her." "I never had any interest in her, so, I never thought of anything like that happening. She never came on to me." "Yes, you were a fool, Andros, but I understand. I don't blame you. Anyway, it's over. You didn't kill her, did you?!" "No, as a matter of fact I told her I wasn't going to pay her anything, if she wanted to spread her lies around to go ahead." Erzsi trusted Andros. He had never strayed from her. He was always loyal to her. But she was a little upset that he could be taken in that way. If this comes out, will the villagers believe Andros?

Erzsi has her own problems. She is in love with two men. But she can't have both of them. To try would eventually come out, and ruin several lives. She is actually in a situation where she can't win. What if Dragos won't let her go? What if Andros finds out and sets out to ruin her? I believe there is trouble ahead for all people involved. It probably won't be pretty.

Andros goes to Marku and tells him of Brigita's past. "That eliminates those two men. But there is still you and your pin and no other suspects." "You don't think I killed her, do you?" "Andros, I don't think you are capable of murder. But sometimes in the heat of the moment, things happen. When this first happened, why didn't you come to me? Those other two men didn't waste any time." "I didn't know what to do. I needed time to think. I guess I waited too long." "Alright, Andros, just stay close."

Another month went by. Marku still did not know who killed Brigita. Erzsi was still seeing Dragos several evenings a week. The villagers were still talking about Brigita. They still didn't know about Andros and Brigita, and no one was aware of Erzsi and Dragos. Although some villagers had notice them together quite often. And Andros was starting to wonder why Erzsi was spending so much time in the village. Even though the villagers didn't know about all this, they felt like there was tension in the air. Like something was about to happen.

CHAPTER 4

Marku was talking to the doctor about Brigita. "Marku, something strange happened the night Brigita was murdered." "What is that?" "As I was going home, I noticed Andros come out of Brigita's house. He stepped out into the street and just stood there, like he was lost or didn't know what was going on around him. I even mentioned he looked like he saw a ghost. He said, 'Maybe I did.' I took him on home." "That's interesting. Thank you doctor."

Marku went to the mayor's office. "Marku, what brings here?" "Andros, I am arresting you for the murder of Brigita. Come with me to the jail." "Why? I didn't kill her. I told you that." "But you didn't tell me you were in her house the night she was murdered. That the doctor found you in a daze, and had to take you home." "I don't really remember that. If I was there, it was to tell her I was not going to pay her price. Yes, I did as a matter of fact. Then I left. She was still alive then." "I'm sorry, Andros, but you're going to have to go before the Magistrate for a hearing. Until then, I have to lock you up. Let's go." "Please go tell Erzsi right away. She needs to know." "I will."

Sitting in his cell, Andros can hardly believe what's happening. He knows he didn't kill Brigita, but at the same time, what if he was so drunk, he did kill her, and just can't remember? Just then Erzsi came to see Andros. "Oh, Andros, what is happening? Why did they arrest you? You didn't kill that girl." "Erzsi, I had a lot to drink that night, and I was at her house. I told her again I wasn't going to pay her. The doctor saw me come out of her house and took me home. He said I was in a daze. What if I did kill her, and I can't remember?" "I know you, Andros, you couldn't kill anyone, no matter what." Just then, Marku came in. "Andros, you will go before the Magistrate tomorrow afternoon. There will be a hearing and then the Magistrate will decide if there is enough evidence to send you to Bucharest for trial."

That evening, Erzsi went to see Dragos. She told him about Andros. Dragos put his arms around her to comfort her. While they were sitting there, a thought came to Erzsi. 'What if Andros is convicted of murder? Then I won't have to make a decision. Dragos and I can be together.' Erzsi! That's terrible. I would never have thought that of you. I thought you were a nice lady.

Andros takes a chair and sits before the Magistrate. "Mr. Benes', you have been charged with the murder of a Miss Brigita." "Sir, I did not kill her." "The evidence presented states you were seen leaving her house the night of the killing, and a pin with your crest on it was found in her bedroom." "Miss Brigita set me up to blackmail me. I went to her house that night to tell her once and for all I would not pay her. She was alive when I left." "According to the doctor, he had to take you home because you acted very confused. If you were in a confused state, how do you know you didn't kill the young lady?" "I have never been a violent person. I don't have it in me to commit murder. The whole village knows I have never even raised my voice in anger." "Nothing else has surfaced in this case. Only the evidence pointing to you. We will meet next week at this time, and I will give you my decision on whether to turn you over for trial."

So, Andros has to spend another week locked up. It doesn't look good. Everything points to Andros. He is really starting to worry. He doesn't see any way out of this nightmare. Now, Erzsi, on the other hand, doesn't want to be alone all week. So, she starts to see Dragos more often. Some of the villagers notice this. But they are not ready to see anything too wrong with that. After all, Erzsi is very upset over Andros being charged with murder. Dragos is probably just comforting her.

Andros goes before the Magistrate again. "Mr. Benes', I see no alternative, but to turn you over for trial." "No! No! You can't. I didn't kill her." The villagers start talking among themselves. The Magistrate calls for quiet. Andros turns around to the crowd, and as he does, he sees something that startles him. He leans over and says something to Marku. Marku looks at the crowd. Marku calls out, "Petre, please stand up." "What?" "I said stand up." Petre slowly stands up. "What do you want?" "Petre, where did you get that scarf?" "Huh?" "I said, where did you get that scarf you are wearing?" "It's mine. I bought it." "Then why does it have Andros's crest in the corner of it?" "I don't know what you are talking about." Marku stepped over to where Petre was standing. He lifted up the corner of the scarf. "This is Andros's crest. Why would it be on a scarf you bought?" "I bought it used?" "Don't act stupid, Petre!" Just then the doctor spoke up. "I remember now, that night I took Andros home, he didn't have his scarf. He was shivering and I put my scarf around him."

"Well, Petre, now what do you have to say?" Petre tried to break away and run. Marku grabbed his arm and twisted it around behind him. "Alright Petre, start talking." "Ok, ok, let go of my arm." "Talk!" "Alright, I killed her." "Why would you want to kill Brigita?" "She treated me like dirt. I liked her. I wanted to be friends with her. All she did was put me down in front of everyone. Called me names. That night when she slapped me, that was it. I decided she wasn't going to make fun of me anymore." "When was it you killed her?" "I knew Andros was taking her home. I waited outside the house. They were arguing. Andros was saying something about not paying her anything. She yelled he would when she got through with him. He finally walked out. After the doctor started taking Andros home, I went in the house. Brigita was sitting on the couch, holding her face. When I walked in, she stood up and wanted to know what I was doing in her house. She told me to get out. I walked over and grabbed her by the throat. I just started squeezing as hard as I could. She fought me, but it was no use. When I let go, she fell to the floor. This scarf was lying on the floor beside the couch, and without thinking, I just picked it up." "Ok, Petre, come on, you're under arrest. I'll have to lock you up."

The Magistrate called for order. "Mr. Benes', you are a free man. I'm sorry you had to go through all this." Everyone came over to Andros to shake his hand and tell him they never did think he was guilty. Erzsi came over and pulled Andros away from the crowd. "Oh, Andros, I'm so happy. I was afraid they would send you to prison. I knew you couldn't have killed that girl. Let's go home." Erzsi is right back where she started. She still has two men to contend with. I'm sure she will find a solution. She's a smart woman.

The school year is over. Elena is preparing to go to college. Both Josepha and Marku are getting homesick for the big city. They talk it over and decide to move back to Bucharest. Josepha can get a teaching job there. Marku wants to stay in law enforcement. He knows he can become an officer in the police force there. So, they pack their belongings, say goodbye to everyone, and head for Bucharest.

The village needs another constable. Since Vidor is a lawyer, he is elected as constable. He likes that. It gives him more status in the village. He still keeps the lawyer side of his job, and continues to keep the books for Andros. But his demeanor is changing. He is becoming less patient with people. The other day he passed Aurora and Felip on the street. He didn't say anything to them, but the anger started boiling up inside him. He hadn't forgotten what they did to him. Someday, when the time was right.

The village is slowly growing. Andros is on his way to see Dragos. As he passes the front of the library, there is a window that looks into Dragos's office. Andros sees movement out of the corner of his eye. He looks in the window, and there is Dragos and Erzsi in a tight embrace, kissing. He stops short. After a few seconds, he steps back from the window. What is going on? What did he just see? He tried to rationalize what he saw. Maybe Dragos made a move on Erzsi. Only Erzsi sure wasn't fighting him. It could have been innocent, but it sure didn't seem that way. It was hard to believe Erzsi would be cheating on him. Although she had been spending a lot of time in the village lately. Maybe there is a logical explanation. Really?

At the end of the day, Andros went straight home, not even stopping at The Pub. That evening, Erzsi said she was going into the village. The girls were having a birthday party for Sofia. She said she wouldn't be more than a couple of hours. Andros was a little upset, but he said it was ok. He didn't want to bring up anything just yet.

It just so happens that the next morning while walking to his office in the village, he sees Sofia walking toward him. He stops her. "Miss Sofia, happy birthday." "What?" "I said happy birthday. I understand the girls had a birthday party for you." "It's not my birthday. I didn't have a party." "Oh, well, I must be thinking of someone else. Sorry, Miss Sofia." "Oh, that's alright, I hope I didn't miss something." "I don't think you did." "What?" "Oh, nothing. Good day."

That did it. Andros didn't know whether to be angry, hurt or what. But it was time to get to the bottom of this. Again, Andros went straight home that afternoon. "Andros, you're home early again." "Yes, I'm not feeling too well." "Oh, dear, are you coming down with something?" "I don't know." "Well, supper is ready, come and eat. Maybe you'll feel better." "Maybe."

That evening Erzsi picked up her jacket. "I'm going down to the village with the girls for a while." "Ok, dear, by the way I ran into Sofia today." Erzsi let go of her jacket. It fell to the floor. "Oh…. what did she have to say?" "For one thing, she said she doesn't feel a year older." "Oh…." "Drop the act, Erzsi. There was no birthday party, and there hasn't been any girl's meetings. You've been lying to me." "No, Andros, I haven't lied to you. We have been having meetings. I was just wrong about the birthday party." "Come clean, Erzsi. I saw you and Dragos the other day." "Where?" "In his office." "Oh, no!" "Oh, yes." "How?" "I was passing the window to his office; I saw you two with your arms wrapped around each other. You really should be more discrete. That all fits in with your trips to the village each evening." "It's not what you think." "It's not what I think, it's what I know. You really must have enjoyed my spending a week in jail. You had a free rein. When were you planning to tell me, or were you?" Erzsi stood there for a moment. Paralyzed. "Alright, Andros, it just happened. No one planed it. The longer it went, the more involved it became. I just fell in love with Dragos." "So, you don't love me anymore. Is that it?" "No, I still love you. I'm just confused. I don't know what to do."

"There is only one thing you can do." "What is that?" "You will stop seeing Dragos. You will remain married to me. It's that simple." "But what if I wanted a divorce?" "There will be no divorce. You will remain married to me. Remember, 'until death do us part'?" "I will be so miserable not being able to see Dragos, and wondering how you really feel about me." "You only have one person to blame for your situation, and that's you. You see, Erzsi, I don't understand what's happening either. All these years of marriage. You never strayed before. And I don't know of anything in all that time, that I ever did to drive you away from me." "Oh, Andros, I'm so sorry. I've messed everything up. Will you ever forgive me?" "I don't know. We will discuss this no more. You know what you must do." "You mean I must tell Dragos." "Yes, now. And you will be back here within half an hour. Understood?" "Yes, Andros." Erzsi picked up her jacket and headed for the door. How complicated life can get. How will everyone adjust to this situation? Will things ever get back to normal? A man once told me, 'There is no normal, there is only life.' Normal today may not be normal tomorrow.

"Erzsi, come in…… what's the matter?" "Dragos, Andros knows about us." "He does? How do you know?" "He told me." "How did he find out?" "He saw us in your office the other day." "We could probably explain that away." "I'm afraid not. He caught me lying about where I went last night. He figured it all out. I'm so afraid, I don't know what to do." "Ask him for a divorce. Then we can get married." "I'm afraid not. Andros made it quite clear, there would be no divorce. I am only here, because I am supposed to tell you that we cannot see each other anymore." "Well, we're bound to see each other on the street or at a party. What are we supposed to do, act like we don't know each other?" "Exactly." "How angry is Andros?" "Very. I betrayed him and his trust. He still loves me, but I feel he is going to make my life miserable." "Erzsi, what are we going to do? I just can't wipe you out of my mind." "Be patient. With time, we may yet be able to be together. Don't give up."

Erzsi was right. Andros started changing. Erzsi was not to be out of his sight at any time. He was never mean to her, but she could feel his love did not feel as strong as it used to. He was more distant. They never talked like they used to. Andros was quiet most of the time. He didn't spend much time at The Pub anymore, and when he did Erzsi had to stay at the castle. Also, when he was at work during the day. He also kept an eye on Dragos. Whenever Andros and Dragos met for whatever reason, neither one brought up Erzsi's name. They were always polite to each other, but you could feel the tension between them. Life was not easy for the three of them.

After a few months, Erzsi could not take any more of this way of living. Andros was not a husband to her anymore. The only thing she had to cling to was her memories with Dragos. She had to find a way to break away from Andros. As she was looking out a front window, she watched the grounds keeper, Boris, tending to the flowers. It was a warm sunny day, so Erzsi thought it would be nice go out and walk around the grounds. She hadn't done that for quite a while. While walking close to the woods, she spotted a plant with white flowers on it. She went up to smell it. She quickly backed away. It had a terrible smell to it. She went to get Boris, to find out if he knew what it was. "Yes, ma'am, that's Hemlock. I need to get rid of that plant right away." "Why?" "It's a deadly poison. Even to animals. You don't want it around." "Oh, my. Yes, get rid of it." Erzsi stood looking at it as Boris walked away. After he was gone, she walked over to the plant and broke off several seeds.

A couple of weeks go by, Andros starts drinking more. He never talks to Erzsi. He stays to himself when at home. He stays sober during the day and does his job as Mayor. Erzsi is at her wits end. She never sees any of her friends anymore. She never goes into town. She has tried several things to try to please Andros. Hoping that he will start opening up to her. Nothing helps. She even thought about ending her life. But she's just not that type of person. She won't give up. There must be a way.

"Miriam, why don't you take the evening off. I'll fix supper for Andros. We need some time together. I need to talk to him." "Very well, if you want." Erzsi digs in and fixes all of Andros's favorite food, including a rich desert. She sets the table and pours a glass of wine for each. Puts on her best dress to impress him. He should be coming in very soon.

Andros sits down at the table. Erzsi starts serving supper. "Where is Miriam? Why isn't she serving?" "She had something to do she will be back after a while. I thought maybe we could be alone for supper for a change." "Sure." All through supper Andros does not speak or answer any questions Erzsi asks. She tries desperately to get him to listen to her and talk to her. Even desert doesn't loosen him up. After Andros is finished, he slowly drinks his wine. "Andros, can we get past this situation? It's been several months; can't we try to start over?" "Erzsi, I wish we could, but I cannot trust you. You lied before, how do I know you won't again?" As Andros starts to get up from the table, he finds he can't move. He can hear Erzsi talking to him, but he cannot speak. He feels paralyzed. He can't move his arms. What is happening? He is looking straight at Erzsi. "Andros, did you like your soup this evening? I made it especially for you." Andros starts having trouble breathing. He feels his heart slowing down. He hears Erzsi and knows, she has poisoned him. He is dying. Another 10 minutes, and Andros falls from his chair, to the floor. He is dead. Erzsi just sits where she is, and looks at him.

Erzsi takes her time and cleans up the table, walking over Andros lying on the floor. She does the dishes and straightens things up. She goes to get Boris. She tells him to go get the doctor, something is wrong with Mr. Benes'.

She goes back in and drags Andros in to his favorite chair, and leaves him on the floor, in front of it. She sits down and waits for the doctor. After about 15 minutes the door opens and the doctor enters the room. Erzsi is crying. Tears running down her cheeks. "Erzsi, what happened?" "I don't know, he was sitting there, and all of a sudden he stood up and grabbed his chest, and said he couldn't breathe." The doctor checked him over. "I would say he had a heart attack, Erzsi. It's not uncommon at his age." Erzsi breaks down. She can't stop crying. The doctor tells Boris to go down to the village, get the undertaker to come up, and get the body. He tries to comfort Erzsi. The doctor had never noticed anything wrong with Andros's heart when ever he checked him. But sometimes, there is no warning. The heart just stops.

The whole town turned out for the funeral. Josepha and Marku came back for the funeral. Andros was buried in a vault down in the vault room. Erzsi didn't leave the castle for a couple of weeks. Visitors would come to see her, and she would be crying and feeling so alone. After all she had to play the part. She was waiting for the appropriate time when she could see Dragos again.

After a couple of more weeks, she decided she didn't care what the villagers thought, she was going to see Dragos. She figured to see him at his office the first few times, then the villagers might not think so much of it. There was no use in her becoming an outcast because of her seeing Dragos so soon. I don't know, Erzsi has never been known to be so deceitful and cunning. What will she be up to next?

She enters Dragos's office, still dressed in black. "Erzsi, come in. How are you feeling?" "Oh, I feel alright." "I'm glad to see you. I do feel bad about Andros." "Why, he doesn't stand between us anymore. You should be happy." "Why would I be happy? The poor man is dead." "Well, now we can be together again. That's what we wanted." "I didn't want it to happen that way." "What makes the difference? He's gone." "Erzsi, you seem so cold. What happened to that warm and loving person?" "I'm still here Dragos, but many things have happened lately." "Ok, Erzsi, we'll talk later."

Erzsi left to go home. She was a little upset. Dragos acted a little distant. She thought Dragos would be happy to have her back. Well, it was their first meeting in months. They had both been through a lot in those months. He will be happy to see her the next time.

In the meantime, Medias has elected a new Mayor. His name is Adrian Dumitru. He is originally from Oradea on the western border of Rumania. He came to Medias five years ago and opened a winery. He is 47 years old. His height is 5' 8", weighs 160 pounds. Dark hair, and has a scar that runs the length of his left cheek. No one knows how he got that scar. He won't talk about his past. He says, 'As long as I am a good citizen of Medias, my past is unimportant.' He is friendly, but a private person. He does not spend much time mingling with the villagers. It seems as though no one really wants to be the mayor, so, Adrian says he was mayor back in Oradea for three years, if no one wants the job, he will take. He will do the best he can. The vote is unanimous, Adrian is the new mayor.

Vidor gets along with Adrian, but he senses something sinister in him. Vidor does notice that quite often, Adrian leaves town for several days. No one knows why, because he never talks about his trips. If anyone asks, he says it was just business. Vidor doesn't bother him, but you might say he keeps one eye on him.

Three times Erzsi goes to the library to see Dragos. Each time he is not there. So, she waits until evening and goes to his house. He is not home. She is beginning to think he is avoiding her. Then one day she sees him walking down the street. She catches up with him. "Dragos, where have you been? I've looked all over for you." "I've been very busy lately, Erzsi." "I feel like you are trying to avoid me." "Erzsi, come home with me, so we can talk." "Alright, but I feel something isn't right." They get to Dragos's house. "Dragos, tell me what is going on. I thought we had big plans for us after Andros died." "It's been three, four months since we have seen each other. We haven't been able to even speak to each other." "Well, now we can. Nothing can stop us know." "I'm afraid there is something that can." "Oh, and what is that?" "Erzsi, during those months, I met someone else. We have grown very close." "What! I killed for you, and you tell me you found someone else?" "What did you say? You killed for me?" "Yes! I killed Andros so we could be together. And now you tell me I did it for nothing?" "I could never want or ask you to kill for me." "I told you I would find a way, and I did. Now you are pushing me out of your life for someone else? I don't think so." "Erzsi, I'm sorry, but things have changed. I'm in love with someone else, and that's the way it's going to be." Erzsi turned and walked out the door. She wasn't through with him yet.

The next evening, she went back to see Dragos. She had to get him to change his mind. He had to come back to her. She knocked on his door. "What is it now, Erzsi?" "Can I come in?" "Sure." "Dragos, you have to forget that other woman. Come back to me. I need you Dragos." "Erzsi, we are through. How could I love someone who murdered her husband? How long would we last before you decided to kill me for someone else? I couldn't trust you, Erzsi. That's it. Now please leave." "Dragos, if I can't have you, no one will." Erzsi picked up a small statue and hit Dragos on the side of his head as hard as she could. Dragos fell to the floor, blood pouring from his head. He didn't move.

Erzsi went to the front door, opened it, and looked around. She didn't see anyone. She slipped out the door and took a back way back to the castle. What has changed this woman. She has gone from being a quiet, loving wife and perfect citizen, to cheating on her husband and committing two murders without even hesitating. Is there something about this castle that turns certain inhabitants into evil beings? Or, is it the ground the castle sits on? Maybe it's just the people in a changing world.

Erzsi goes into the village the next morning, expecting to see everyone gossiping about Dragos. As she walks down the street, everyone is doing what they always do at that time of morning. Nobody seems excited about anything. She goes to the library. "Has Dragos come in yet?" "No. He's usually here by now. I don't know what's keeping him." Erzsi headed for Dragos's house. Is she going to be the one to 'discover' the body?

Erzsi knocks on the door several times. She tries the knob, the door opens. Of course, she already knows what's on the other side of the door. Dragos is lying there in a pool of dried blood. She calmly walks out the door, back to the main street. When she gets there, she starts screaming for help. "Help, help, someone get Vidor. Something has happened to Dragos." One of the villagers runs to get Vidor. People start gathering to find out what is going on. "Mother, what is it?" "Vidor, something has happened to Dragos. Come. Look." Erzsi and Vidor go into the house. Vidor sees all the blood and the gash on Dragos's head. "Who could have done this, and why? You found the body, mother?" "The librarian was worried because he hadn't shown up this morning. I came to see if he was alright. I was shocked. I feel like I'm going to faint......" "Take it easy, mother. Sit down here for a minute, while I look around." It was obvious the statue was used to kill Dragos. But Vidor could find nothing to indicate who might have done it. "Mother, lets go back outside." By now there is a large crowd outside in the street. "People, listen up. Dragos is dead. Someone killed him. I don't know who, yet. As far as I know, Dragos didn't have any enemies." A voice in the crowd spoke up. "Oh yes, he did." "Who said that? Please step forward." A woman in her late 30's stepped forward out of the crowd. "What is your name?" "Ursule." "Why do you say Dragos had an enemy?" "Dragos and I have been going together now for several months. Yesterday afternoon, he told me about someone he was worried about. He said they had killed once, and he worried he may be next. He told me the whole sorted story." "I see. And who is this person?" "That woman right there." She pointed right at Erzsi. "Erzsi Benes', was the person he was afraid of." Erzsi stiffened up. She didn't know what to say.

Vidor looked at his mother. For a minute he was speechless. "You're saying my mother killed Dragos?" "Yes. And I know she also killed her husband, your father." "Are you out of your mind, woman? Where did you come up with this kind of story?" "Dragos told me everything. Dragos and her were having an affair. When Andros found out he put a stop to it. She killed Andros so she could get back with Dragos. Only, he didn't want anything to do with her." "Mother, where is this coming from. Is she making this up? Why would she accuse you of all this?" Erzsi stood silent. "Mother, don't just stand there. Tell her she's lying. Tell her you don't know what she is talking about. She just made that up." Erzsi still remained silent. Tears started rolling down her cheeks. "Mother!"

"Vidor, I'm sorry." "What do you mean, you are sorry?" "Ursule is not lying. It's all true." "You don't mean that." "Yes, I do. Dragos and I had an affair for several months. When your father found out, he forbade me to ever see Dragos again. He couldn't stand to think about Dragos and me. He started treating me like dirt. I couldn't leave the castle unless he was with me. He wouldn't talk to me. I begged for forgiveness. He wouldn't listen. I wanted so much to be with Dragos. I had no life. After several months of this, I had to do something. One day I came across a plant. Boris told me it was Hemlock. A deadly poison. So, before he got rid of the plant, I took several seeds from it. I used them to poison Andros. I was afraid I was going out of my mind. I couldn't take this way of living anymore. I had to do something to break free. Then, Dragos told me he didn't want anything to do with me anymore. I couldn't take rejection from him also. I just picked up the statue and hit him. I'm so tired, I don't care anymore what happens to me. Do what you will with me."

Vidor just stood there, speechless. He couldn't believe what he just heard. Some of the people started yelling. "Lock her up!" "Hang her. She's a murderer!" Vidor took hold of his mother and started for the jail. This was the worst thing he had ever had to do, lock up his mother. The crowd milled around for a while talking. After another hour or so, they started breaking up. Vidor put Erzsi in a cell. He just looked at her. He wanted to say 'Why?', but he knew why, she had just told the whole village why.

Later that evening, Vidor went back to the castle. Emile would stay in the jail all night, in case Erzsi needed anything. He told Miriam and Boris what had happened. They couldn't believe their ears. "There must be some mistake. Mrs. Benes' wouldn't do anything like that. There must be some mistake." "There is no mistake. The whole village heard her confession." "What is going to happen to her?" "I don't know. There is sure to be a trial."

The next morning as Vidor entered the jail, "What happened here?" Emile was lying on the floor, unconscious. The cell door was open and Erzsi was gone. Vidor turned Emile over. He was a bloody mess. He had been severely beaten. Vidor poured a little whiskey into him, and put a cold wet cloth on his forehead. "Emile, what happened? Emile!" Emile's lip was so swollen he had a hard time speaking. Finally, "Sometime...... after.... midnight. A mob.... of.... villagers came in...... and beat me...... and took Erzsi from...... her cell." "Where did they take her?" "I...... don't know." "Who were the villagers who did this?" "There were some I know...... and some.... I didn't. I can...... tell you.... the ones I knew." "Never mind now, I'm going to get you up on the cot, and I want you to rest. Just stay there, don't try to get up and do anything. I'll get the doctor."

As he went outside, he grabbed the first man he came to. "Were you part of the mob last night that stormed the jail?" "I don't know what you are talking about." The man walked away. So, that's how it's going to be. No one is going to know anything. Vidor started walking toward the church. He wanted to talk to the priest. There was a huge tree off behind the church. As Vidor approached the church, he looked at the tree. His heart almost stopped. He froze in his tracks. Erzsi, his mother, was hanging from one of the branches. "How could they do this?! They had no right! They are murderers! These villagers will pay for this!" He cut his mother down, and carried her through the village, up to the castle. He placed her in one of the vaults down in the vault room. He was crying the whole time.

After a couple of days went by, Emile had recovered enough to continue his duties. He asked Vidor if he wanted the names of the people who were involved. "No, Emile, the whole village is guilty of murder as far as I am concerned. If you feel well enough, I'll leave you in charge for a few days. I need to go to Bucharest, and let Josepha and Marku know what has happened. I don't think you will have any trouble for a while. I think the village is going to be very quiet for the time being. They know what they have done." "I'll be alright, you go ahead. Take your time."

Vidor wasn't looking forward to what he had to do. He knew Josepha would be devastated. He just didn't know how to break it to her gently. After he arrived, they talked for a while. Josepha was surprised by his visit. She asked him what prompted his visit. Vidor told them both to sit down, he had some bad news. He proceeded to tell them everything that had happened. Josepha broke down and collapsed. They carried her in to her bed. Marku went for the doctor.

"Oh, Vidor, how could this all come about? Those people murdered my mother." "Yes, they did. Josepha, I promise you that the whole village will suffer for this. Someday, when the time is right and the circumstance comes up, I will get my turn. It may not happen right away, it may take years, but I swear, the day will come when I will pay them back, with interest. I will destroy that village. This I promise you!"

CHAPTER 5

Vidor is now 45. He is no longer the constable. Emile has taken over that job. Vidor spends most of his time preparing for his vengeance. Two years ago, unknown to the villagers, Vidor had a torture chamber and dungeon built underground, next to the vault room, with a common door. His mind is losing touch with reality. Miriam is still with Vidor, but she is starting to be wary of him. She says, "Sometimes, he acts like he has made a deal with the devil. He is starting to frighten me." Boris has left, he didn't like some of the things that were happening at the castle. Vidor hired Simion, 34 years old. Simion had a very obvious limp and he could not stand up fully straight. A few years ago, he was working, cutting down trees, when one fell on him and injured his back. Vidor felt Simion could be useful to him.

Vidor has married a girl from the village. Her name is Claudia. She is five years younger than Vidor. Very beautiful dark-haired woman. She is a very kind and giving person. Vidor loves Claudia very much, and Claudia adores Vidor. As time passes, a son is born. Unfortunately, the birth does not go well. The baby is fine and healthy, but Claudia never regains her health and shortly after the birth, Claudia dies. Vidor is devastated. Why does he always lose what he loves? He tries to raise the boy, but he finds it so difficult. He loves the boy, but he constantly misses his Claudia. When the boy is old enough, Vidor sends him to a private boarding school. With the loss of Claudia, Vidor's mind becomes even more warped.

Vidor feels it is time to start his vendetta against the village. He has never forgotten how Aurora and Felip led him on, and used him. Vidor thinks, 'If those two want to spend the rest of their lives together, I will help them do that. But I don't think they will appreciate the way I do it.' What does Vidor mean by that? This should be interesting.

Vidor makes one of his rare visits to the village. He sees Aurora and Felip sitting in one of the small restaurants. He goes in and approaches them. "How are you both doing?" They are a little taken aback. Vidor hasn't spoken to them in years. "We are fine, Vidor. How about you?" "I'm doing alright. May I sit down?" "Yes, please do." "I want to apologize for my behavior these last few years. I have been foolish. I can see how happy you both are. I don't want this between us anymore. I was probably angrier at myself, then you two. I would like to make it up to you. Would you both come up to the castle tomorrow evening and have supper with me?" "Why Vidor, you astound me. I never expected this. But I'm glad. I think we would enjoy coming up tomorrow evening. Say around six." "That would be splendid. I look forward to it. Well, I'll leave you two alone now. Good day." After Vidor leaves, "Well, that was a surprise. I wonder what has come over Vidor?" "Well, Felip, you know, sometimes people change as time goes on."

Vidor told Miriam that after she fixed dinner, and set the table, she could retire for the evening. Aurora and Felip arrived right on time. They talked for a while, mostly about changes that had occurred during the past several years. It was time for dinner. Miriam set all the food on the table, then went upstairs to her room. Aurora and Felip were amazed at all of the food and drink on the table. They had never seen so much food at one time, and it looked so delicious. Something that would be given as a last meal.

Everything went well. Everyone ate well. It was a pleasant get together. After everyone had finished, they went into the living area to talk some more. Vidor brought out his special wine he had been saving. He poured a glass for everyone. After a while, Aurora started yawning. She was feeling sleepy. A few minutes later Felip started shaking his head. He was feeling sleepy also. Vidor started laughing. Aurora asked Vidor what was so funny. "My dear, you look like you are about to fall asleep. So do you, Felip." "Yes, I can't seem to keep my eyes open." "It's just a little sleeping potion, I put in your drink. You will both sleep for a couple of hours, then you will wake up." "But why, Vidor? Why would you do.........?" Aurora and Felip both fell into a deep sleep.

Vidor called for Simion to help him. "We will take these two down to the torture room. You take Aurora." They carried the two bodies down through the vault room to the torture room. On one wall, close to one of the corners of the room, were two sets of wrist chains attached to the wall. Vidor and Simion fastened Aurora and Felip to those two sets of chains. At least the two of them would be close together. But that was just the beginning. Over in another corner of the room was a large pile of bricks and mortar. Vidor and Simion started building a brick partition 4' from the corner and 2 ½' out from the other wall. After that was done, they started bricking up the existing opening. They only bricked it up about 4' high. Then they waited for Aurora and Felip to wake up.

It didn't take very long till they started coming around. Naturally they were confused and couldn't figure out what was happening. Then they realized they were chained to a wall. "Vidor, what are you doing? Why are we chained to the wall?" Aurora started screaming. "Vidor, please let us loose! Somebody, help us! Vidor, why are we chained?" Both of them are trying to break loose from their chains. "Aurora, do you remember several years ago when you used me and led me on? Making me think we were going to be married, and then broke my heart?" "That was a long time ago. I didn't mean to hurt you." "But you did. And I told you someday you both would regret what you did. I said you would pay. Today is payday." "You're just trying to scare us, aren't you? You are going to let us go. Aren't you?" "No, my dear. I am not going to let you go. You both wanted to spend the rest of your life together, and you will." Felip, "How long do you think you can keep us here? People in the village will miss us. Eventually they will find us."

Vidor didn't say anything. He was quiet for a few minutes, then he told Simion to get more bricks. "No, Felip, no one will ever find you." "What are you planning on doing? Why is this brick wall in front of us?" "To give you privacy. So you won't be disturbed. We are going to brick this front wall up to the ceiling." Aurora and Felip started pulling at their chains. Desperately trying to free themselves. "You can't do this!

We will suffocate and die." "Right. That's the point. You're catching on." Simion starts bricking up the rest of the front wall. Felip is wildly trying to break free. Aurora is crying hysterically. Vidor stands back and smiles.

Vidor has to have completely lost his mind. How can he be so vicious and cruel? After a few days, the villagers are quietly asking, 'What happened to Aurora and Felip? They seem to have just disappeared.' I will wager, the villagers will never find out what happened to Aurora and Felip. Vidor is laughing hysterically inside. But he also hasn't forgotten what the villagers did to his mother.

Years have passed. Vidor is now 70 and still has contempt and I guess you could say a hatred for the villagers. He is still waiting for his chance for revenge. Some rumors have started floating around in the villages throughout the area. This may be what Vidor has been waiting for. But we will go into that later.

The village has continued to grow. There are probably around 100 new families in the village. More small businesses have come. There is a bakery, a new dress shop and another restaurant in the village. Markos died when he was 87. The Pub has a new owner and is still the place to meet. The villagers have aged, in more ways than one. In all this time, no one in the village has ever figured out what happened to Aurora and Felip. They just, disappeared. Some people still shake their head when someone brings up the subject. The villagers have a legacy to live down, and they don't like it. They remember what happened several years ago, and many villages in the area remember, and they won't let Medias forget it. And the sad thing is, the Medias villagers feel frustration and anger when the incident is brought up, but none of them feel any guilt. That arrogance could lead to trouble for the villagers. If only after a while, they would have rethought what happened, and maybe figured out that maybe they had acted a little hasty. But it's too late now. Their fate has been written on the wind.

Adrian is now 74 and still the mayor. He is and has been a good mayor. He has fit in with the villagers very well. His past is still unknown, but I feel something is about to happen that will bring his past to light.

Vidor, as I said before, is patiently waiting. It seems he has made a pact with the devil. He has two different personalities. When he is with the villagers, he is very polite, and 'caring'. He makes the villagers feel like they are good people and important people. He has them believing he is a forgiving person and that he is genuinely interested in the people and the village. If they could only read his mind.

Vidor doesn't travel any, but some of the villagers do, and he listens and hears whatever the town is talking about. It seems that a lot of Europe is going thru a period which will be a black mark for the continent, including the village of Medias, which doesn't really need that right now. Adrian hears the talk going around. He decides it's time to have a meeting and let the people know what is really happening. "People, listen to me. Quiet! Please!" As the crowd quiets down, Adrian continues. "I hear the talk going around. I think it is time to inform all of you what is spreading throughout Europe. It started several years ago before I came to this village. It was very remote and very rare. It actually died down a couple of years ago, but is starting to spread again. I never told anyone about my past, but it's time you knew."

"My job was to go to these places and put an end to their problem. I feel it won't be long until I will have to do my job here also." The crowd was becoming frightened. "What are you talking about? What is your job? Are we in danger?" "Listen! What is happening is the Devil's work. People, are being possessed by Satan. Mostly women. They become witches. They do evil work. They put spells on people that make them do strange things. Sometimes they put curses on people that causes their death. My job is to confront these witches and either drive Satan from them or destroy them, and it must be done quickly." "Are you saying these people are really witches?" "Yes, they are, and if you see one, you will know it." "How do you destroy them?" "One way is to tie them to a stake and burn them, or simply hang them, to end their reign of terror."

The crowd was gasping. They couldn't believe what they were hearing. What is he saying? There are no witches in Medias. Everyone knows everyone else. None of them are witches. Who is this man they call Mayor? Has he lost his mind? Vidor was in the crowd, and he was laughing hysterically inside. This was it. This was his avenue of revenge. He didn't care if there were witches or not. He was going to see to it that there were witches in Medias. He would invent them if he had to. He could hardly wait.

Now it so happens that a family moved into Medias about 3 months ago. They moved into a house just outside the village. There was Alex, Anamarie and Adela, their daughter. Alex had opened up a little shop with nick nacks. They blended in well with the villagers. Adela was 28, but she had the mind of a 15 or 16-year-old. The villagers had seen her a few times, but were not aware of her mindset. Actually, they were never told Adela's real age. They also didn't know that she had a problem with seizures every once in a while. The villagers were not aware of any of this because she was kept in her room most of the time. It was very rare that Anamarie would take her to town, and when she did, they didn't stay very long.

When Adela was 10, she had wandered off from the house and gotten lost. There was quite a lot of snow, and she couldn't find her way back to the house. It took a search party almost 3 hours to find her. She was unconscious, but still breathing. They got her back to the house and laid her close to the fireplace. She eventually regained consciousness, but the hours in the cold and snow, affected part of her brain. As the years went by, her learning abilities were very slow. At this stage, her mind is around 12 years behind her age. All the villagers knew was that she was not well and had to stay inside and quiet most of the time.

But back then, just as today, teenagers are teenagers. Teenagers have a mind of their own. Sometimes they want to do something, and when the parents say no, they sometimes find a way to do it anyway. Even if they have to be sneaky about it. Most of the time Adela stayed pretty quiet. She knew what she was allowed to do, and not do. But the few times she had been in the village, intrigued her. She wanted to see more. She wanted to talk to some of the villagers. She figured out a way she could get out of the house at night when her parents were asleep, so she decided she was going to do it.

About 11:00 that evening, Avram left The Pub to go home. As he is walking down the street, he sees the shadow of someone walking toward him. The person appears to have a cape and hood on. Avram calls out, "You, there, who are you?" The person stops and looks at him. Then turns and runs between two houses. Avram starts running after the person. As he reaches the back of the houses, he stops. He doesn't see anyone. They just disappeared.

Avram goes back to The Pub to tell the guys what he saw. "Avram, I think I better help you home. You're starting to see things." "I wasn't 'seeing things'. I saw what I saw. Someone was walking down the street with a hood covering their face. When I called out to them, they ran. And when I tried to follow them, they disappeared." "Ok, Avram, whatever you say. But maybe you better go home a different way. You don't want to run into them again." Everyone had a good laugh as Avram stomped out the door.

Meanwhile, Adela went back to the house. She was mad because she had run away. But the man startled her. Her idea was to meet people. The next time she wouldn't run. She quietly went back in the house and went back to bed. She knew she was going to go out at night again, and this time she wouldn't run.

It had been two months since Adela had experienced a seizure. Maybe the cause of them had cleared up. Therefore, Anamarie felt more comfortable taking Adela to town with her. They understood that Adela was a little slow. That didn't bother them. While in town, Adela wandered a short way from Anamarie. She spotted a boy, probably 16, sitting in front of a store. She went over to talk to him. His name is Luca. Now, Adela is 28, but she is not quite 5' 5", and she doesn't really look her age. Remember, she has the mind of a 16-year-old, and when she starts talking to this boy, she talks like a teenager. So, the two get along pretty well. Finally, Anamarie calls to her and tells her it is time to go home. Adela has found a new friend and she likes him.

Anamarie doesn't take Adela to town as often as Adela would like. But when she does get to town, she always finds Luca. They have become very close. Adela is still determined to go out at night and see what goes on. She sneaks out again, dressed the same as before. This time, there are two men standing along the main street talking. One of them happens to be Avram. As he is talking, he spots this figure walking toward him again. "Look, that's who I saw the other night." The other man called to the figure and said, "Come to us, so we can see who you are." So, Adela walked up to the men and took her hood off. "Adela, what are you doing out here this time of night? Was that you I saw the other night?" "I just wanted to see what it was like in town at night; that was me you saw." "Why did you run?" "You startled me when you called to me, so I ran. But I didn't run tonight. See?" "You shouldn't be out here at night alone. I bet Alex doesn't know you are out here."

Just then it happened. Adela stiffened up, started shaking and fell to the ground. She was shaking uncontrollably and fluid was coming from her mouth. Both men stepped back a step. "Avram, what's wrong with her?" "My Lord, she's possessed by the Devil." They crossed themselves and ran back to The Pub.

"Everyone, listen up, listen! Adela is lying out in the street. The Devil has taken control of her. She is shaking and foaming at the mouth." Several of the men and women followed Avram out to the street. Adela was gone. "She was here a minute ago. Avram and I both saw her lying on the ground." Adrian spoke up, "Maybe she just fell down and hurt herself. When you ran, she was able to get up and go home." "It didn't look like that to us." "Alright, but keep this to yourselves. Don't even talk about it among yourselves. Let me look into this first. I don't want a panic on our hands. It may not amount to anything, but let me find out."

Adela does not tell her parents about her attack. She definitely doesn't want them to know she went into town last night. She goes into town, the following week, with Anamarie to do some shopping. Adela looks up Luca. Luca is growing very fond of Adela, and she likes Luca very much. They decide they will be close friends for the rest of their lives. They have so much fun together, which is something Adela has had very little of the last few years. She likes this village and the people. She feels she has found a home, and she likes that. It's been several days now since her last attack, and she feels alright now.

Adela still wants to go to the village tonight and see what all goes on. She sneaks out and goes into the village. This time she goes to The Pub, and walks in the door. Everyone is a little surprised. "Adela, what are you doing here. Especially this time of night. You should be home. You don't really belong in here, child." "I just wanted to see what goes on at night. I won't bother anyone. Does Luca come in here?" "Good Lord, no, he's home in bed, where you should be." "What do you people do in here?" Everyone started laughing. "We just sit and talk and have some brew." "Oh, ok, I guess I'll go on back home now." She started for the door, but she never made it. Adela fell to the floor with another attack. Women screamed; men backed away.

Adrian went over to her. He looked at her intensely and started muttering something. The people just stared in awe. Everyone was thinking the same thing. 'She is possessed by the Devil. She is a witch'. Someone headed toward Adela's house to get her parents. After about 5 minutes, Adela started calming down. Adrian ask her if she was alright. "I'm ok, it doesn't usually last too long. I'm ok now." "You mean this happens often?" "Yes. Not as often as it used to." The people are astounded. They can't believe what they are hearing. This girl has these attacks all the time, and no one has ever been told about it. What kind of family are they? Are they all possessed by the Devil? This village doesn't want people like that around. They must be driven out of town. That girl needs to be destroyed.

Alex and Anamarie arrive at The Pub. "Adela, what are you doing here? Why did you come here? You are not supposed to leave the house at night. You know that." "I know, but I had to see what goes on in the village at night." A woman in the crowd yells out, "Your daughter is a witch. She is possessed. We must get rid of her!" "You can't do that; she is our daughter. She is not a witch. She had an accident when she was little, that's what causes this to happen." "Maybe it was not an accident. Maybe it was just a possession by he Devil." "Stop it! Stop it! Let me take her home. She'll be alright." "She needs to be burnt at the stake." Everyone starts yelling, burn her, burn her.

Vidor happens to be in the crowd. He knows what's wrong with Adela. He has seen it before. He knows she is not a witch. He must do what he can to save her. This family is new here and these people want to destroy them. They have not changed one bit since hanging his mother. As Adrian calls for quiet, Vidor steps forward. "You people have not learned one thing these past few years. All you want to do is destroy someone without discovering what is happening. Just like my mother. Oh, I haven't forgotten." Adrian ask Vidor, "What do you suggest?" "Let me take the child up to the castle for a while and observe her. I tell you, she is not a witch." Anamarie spoke up, "She is not a child either." "What do you mean?" "Mr. Benes', Adela is 28 years old." "Really?" "Yes, when she was 10, she was found frozen in the snow. There was damage to part of her brain. She has never developed mentally beyond a teenager." "I see. Let her come up to the castle with me. As a matter of fact, why don't you and Alex stay at the castle for a while, also. There's plenty of room and you won't be separated from Adela. I will do some checking; I may be able to find a way to stop these attacks. Besides, she will be safer there. You don't know what these people might do."

Well, there must be some compassion left in Vidor's heart. I can't imagine he would want to hurt these people; they weren't part of the village in those days' past. It won't take long to find out. What do you think?

The villagers were very angry and upset to know that this girl, or woman, was still in their midst. They let Adrian know that he should have taken charge. He's the Mayor. Why should Vidor take her in? His actions and attitude haven't been very friendly since you know what. Although, he has loosened up here lately. Adrian told the people to wait and see. There is no proof she is a witch. She hasn't hurt anyone or cast any spells, as far as anyone knows.

Vidor made everyone welcome. He got them settled in some rooms upstairs. Alex and Anamarie were free to come and go as they wished, but for Adela, he said she could go where ever she wanted on the castle grounds, but he asks her not to leave the castle grounds, or try to go to the village. It might not be safe. "But what about Luca, I'll miss him. I like to talk to him." "If Alex and Anamarie don't object, it's ok with me. He may come up and see you often." "Oh, thank you Mr. Benes'."

Vidor knows a little about these attacks that Adela has. Before he became a lawyer, he studied medicine for a while. He knew these attacks were not from possession, but can be caused by a brain malfunction. Knowing Adela's history, he was sure he could help her. At least he was going to try. He knew a doctor in Bucharest who worked with this type of patient. He sent a post to Dr. Marius, asking for his help.

Meanwhile, the villagers are still muttering to each other. They keep asking Adrian to do something, but he tells them to be patient and see what happens. The people are afraid Adela will put a spell on Vidor, and he will come after the villagers, and who knows what will happen. Some of the villagers want to storm the castle, take Adela, and burn her at the stake. Emil is still the constable and he warns the villagers, "You did something like that a few years ago and you haven't been able to live it down yet. Don't make the same mistake."

Dr. Marius arrived at the castle to see what he could do. "Dr., after watching Adela, do you think you can help her?" "I can try. There are several remedies available, but they don't always work." "Such as, what?" "First, there is bloodletting. I will try to remove some blood from the brain area to relieve pressure on the brain. We could also try the cathartic method, which is to cleanse and purify the body. That has to be done with laxatives. Or I could use a sternutatory. That is a pepper or anything that will make her sneeze. Only no one has ever proven that any of these things work, but none of these things will harm her." "Then we must try."

Three weeks have gone by, and Adela has had no attacks. But she has gone longer than that before. There is no forgone conclusion as yet. Vidor has been working with Adela, trying to bring her mental state to a higher level. It seems to be working some. She has come along quite well. She understands many more things. She is starting to comprehend that she is a woman, not a little girl. Vidor has sent a post to Dr. Marius, informing him of the progress Adela is making. Vidor is thinking of reintroducing Adela to the villagers, to let them see how she has improved. "Adela, how would you like to go back to the village and live? Let the villagers see how well you are doing. Your parents agree that it could be a good thing." "Yes, I miss the villagers. I like to talk to them." "Very good, then tomorrow you shall all go back to your home."

Vidor tells the villagers about Dr. Marius and what he told Vidor about Adela's condition. He tried to convince them that she cannot help herself during those attacks, if they happen again. If it does happen, the people should help her, not fear her. Most villagers seemed to understand, but there were a few who were still skeptical.

Vidor went back to his castle. Now he had a plan. The Devil was back. And he was going to start paying the villagers back for his mother. He had really become attached to Adela and her family. He would not hurt her, but she was going to play a part in Vidor's revenge.

For some time now, Adela has not had an attack. The villagers have accepted her, and even help her when she has questions. The villagers seem to be in a good place. Everything is going well. But if it stayed that way, that would be the end of my story. Fortunately, or unfortunately, however you want to look at it, good things don't always last. The village is headed for disruption, fear and scandal.

One afternoon, Vidor is in The Pub, having some lunch. He notices Adela and a couple of women walking by the window. Adela sees him, and turns to wave. Just as she does, she falls to the ground, shaking. Vidor jumps up from the table. This is what he was waiting for. This is the time.

Vidor runs out to Adela, kneels down and holds her in his arms. Even Vidor is taken back when Adela stops shaking, only doesn't move, and suddenly her eyes open and she just stares straight ahead. Not saying a word. It's like she is in a trance. Vidor starts calling her name. She doesn't respond. This is even better than Vidor had hoped for. But he was worried about Adela. She had never gone into this stage before. One of the women spoke up, "Is she alright? Is she having another attack?" "No, this is something different. She acts as if she is possessed. Someone go, get Adrian. Quick!"

Vidor carries her into The Pub and tries to make her comfortable. Adela starts moving her eyes around, looking at everyone. Still not speaking. Adrian arrives, and looks her over. He shakes his head. "Vidor, I've seen this before. Someone has cast a spell on poor Adela." Adrian plays right into Vidor's hands. "I thought so. Someone in this village is a witch." The women step back, let out a scream, and start looking at each other. Good job Vidor. Now, who will the accused be? I suspect it is going to be the wife of the leader of the mob who instigated the hanging of Vidor's mother. Does he even know who that person was, or is he just going to pick the man who seems the most obvious?

CHAPTER 6

Adrian knew what had to be done. He travels to the head of the church in their area. He explains what had happened, and what he feared. "You know I've handled cases like this many times in villages around the area." "Yes, I agree this needs to be looked into. If it is witchcraft, it must be stopped before it spreads. You go on back home. I will send someone to your village to set up a court to investigate your suspicions. He will be there within a week."

When Adrian got back to the village, he went to see Vidor. "Vidor, there will be a man here sometime this week to investigate what is going on. If he finds that there is a witch or witches among us, we must contain them until sentence is passed." "I have the perfect place. I had a torture room and dungeon built several years ago. We can keep them there. Maybe even make them admit their guilt, that is, if they are guilty." "Why would you have something like that built?" "It just seemed there might be a use for something like that. I think the time for its use, is here." "Maybe, but let's not be to hasty to start using it."

For years, Vidor had studied the men in the village. He watched their reaction to certain events, and he thought he had the man he wanted, figured out. His name was Dorin Arcos. He was 52. He was a big man, and tended to be able to influence people rather easily. Anytime there was a problem, he always wanted to deal with it, in his own way. Dorin's wife Felicia, was 48 and a very beautiful lady. Felicia was about to become Vidor's first victim. He didn't care if Felicia was beautiful, or was a fine lady. By this time, Vidor's mind was so twisted, all he could see was revenge. Vidor wanted to watch Dorin, feel the same things he felt, when he lost his mother, so quickly, and violently. He wanted to watch Dorin's face when his beloved wife was sacrificed. Felicia would be the first, but not the last.

Vidor and Adrian met Martin Lupesco when he came to town. They went directly to see Adela. After observing her, Martin just shook his head. They went back to Adrian's office. "Gentlemen, I do think you have a problem here. That girl has definitely had a spell cast upon her. Has there been any strangers in the village lately?" "No, we seldom get strangers here." "Is there anyone in the village that has done anything a little strange, or that you might suspect?" Adrian said he never noticed any difference in anyone. Vidor spoke up, "A couple of weeks ago, I saw one of the village people doing something that was a little odd." "Oh? What was that?" "I walked by one of the houses, and I glanced in the kitchen window, and the woman was mixing up something in a pot. She was pouring several little bottles of something into the pot. She seemed to be chanting something, although, she might have been singing. I couldn't tell." "Vidor, you never told me any of this." "I guess it just slipped my mind. I had other things to think about at the time." "Who was this lady?" "Felicia Arcos." "You're not serious. Felicia? That's ridiculous." "Adrian, I didn't say she was a witch, I just told you what I saw." "I can't believe that." "Gentlemen, I would say, that's a good place to start. If she can explain her actions, she will be vindicated."

The three of them went to Felicia's house. Adrian knocked on the door. "Felicia, may we come in?" "Yes, but Dorin is out in the field, working." "That's alright, we came to see you." "Oh, what about?" Vidor walked into the kitchen. Everything looked normal. "Felicia, several days ago you were fixing something in a pot. Is that right?" "I don't know. I don't remember. If I was, I was probably fixing soup for supper." "Well, someone said you were pouring different potions in the pot and chanting something. What do you have to say to that?" "I never did any such thing. What are you trying to say, Adrian?" "Felicia, come with us down to my office, please?" "Why?" "We need to talk to you, and maybe you will be more comfortable down there." "I don't want to go to your office." "Please, Felicia, it won't take very long." "Alright, but what about Dorin? He needs to know." "You'll be back home before he comes in from the field."

Everyone headed for Adrian's office, except Vidor. He stayed at the house to look around. Martin started questioning Felicia about her beliefs, and what she knew about witchcraft. "What are you talking about? My beliefs are my own, and I don't know anything about witchcraft." "Stay calm, Mrs. Arcos. We're just trying to get some things cleared up. We just want to find out if you are involved in anything that you're trying to hide." "Involved in what? You think I'm a witch? Is that what this is about?" "In a manner of speaking, yes." "You're crazy, I don't know anything about witchcraft. I'm no witch. How dare you even think such a thing?" "That's my job, to ferret out witches and get rid of them." "Well, you're looking at the wrong girl. I want my husband and I want him now. I'm not going to say another word."

Just then Vidor walked in, carrying some items. "What did you find, Vidor?" He put the items on the table. "Plenty. Herbs, root plants, and a vial of poison. All the makings of a witch's potion. Also, this piece of paper with these weird symbols on it." "Well, Mrs. Arcos, what do you have to say about these things?" "Most of the kitchens in this village have those things in them. They are used to enhance food." "What about the poison?" "That's used to keep rats away, and I never saw that piece of paper before. I don't know what those symbols mean." "Are you saying you are not a witch, Mrs. Arcos?" "I won't answer that question. It's ridiculous. I'm going back home, and I want you to leave me alone. I'm going to see my husband. He'll set you straight." "I'm afraid you are not going anywhere, just yet, Mrs. Arcos, until you answer my question." "I told you I will not answer you." "Very well. Vidor, I understand you have a place to confine Mrs. Arcos until she decides to answer my question." "Yes, I do." "Then you and Adrian take her there and confine her until she changes her mind." Felicia started yelling and screaming, "You can't do that, I haven't done anything! Let me go......"

Vidor and Adrian escorted Felicia out the back door, and around the village, to the castle dungeon. Felicia was crying all the way. They locked her in a cell, and she became hysterical. When they left, they closed the steel door and locked it.

Dorin came home from the field. He was hungry, and was glad supper would be ready. As he came in through the kitchen door, he stopped. There was no supper, and Felicia wasn't there. He went through the house calling her. She was nowhere to be found. He was starting to get a little irritated, and at the same time, a little worried. This was not like Felicia, to not be home waiting for him. He started walking down through the village, stopping to ask if anyone had seen Felicia. He stopped at The Pub. She wasn't there, and no one had seen her all day. He headed over to Adrian's office. "Hello, Dorin, come in. This is Martin Lupesco. Martin, this Is Dorin, Felicia's husband. Sit down Dorin." "No, thanks, I just stopped in to see if you had seen Felicia." "Sit down, Dorin, that's what I want to talk to you about." "Has something happened to Felicia?" "I'm afraid so, Dorin." "Is she alright? Is she hurt? Where is she?" "Felicia is alright at the present. Martin is from the church. He is a prosecutor." "Prosecutor? What's going on here?" "Mr. Arcos, some evidence has surfaced that indicates your wife very likely is a witch." "A what? Witch? You're out of your mind. Who are you anyway?" "Like Adrian said, I am part of the church system. When we get word that something is going on that is against the church's belief, I investigate, and take appropriate action." "Why Felicia?" "It was reported that your wife seemed to be involved in witchcraft. So, I am here to find out." "Where is she?" "She would not cooperate; therefore, she is being confined until she decides to talk to us." "I want to see her. Now." "I'm afraid that's impossible, for now. Perhaps in a few days." "Where is she?!" "I cannot tell you that at this time." "Who put you up to this? Who said Felicia was a witch?" "I cannot disclose that." "I'll find out. As a matter of fact, I have a pretty good idea who it was, and I will deal with him." "Don't do anything rash, Mr. Arcos. You could get into serious trouble." "You let me worry about that."

Vidor is down in the Dungeon with Felicia. "I sure am sorry about this Felicia. I know it must be very hard on you. Don't worry, I'm sure everything will be alright." "Cut the crap, Vidor. I'm sure you are the one who started all of this. You don't fool me. You know Dorin was responsible for your mother's hanging. You said you would get revenge by slowly destroying the village. So, this is your first step toward that end." "How astute of you, Felicia. But that was years ago. You couldn't prove any of what you just said. The Prosecutor is the one who is pursuing this, not me. You have to show Mr. Lupesco you are innocent, not me." "Vidor, you know I'm not a witch!" "Maybe. That's up to Mr. Lupesco to determine."

The next morning, Vidor is eating breakfast. Someone starts banging on the door. Miriam grew so frightened of Vidor; she left a couple of years ago. So, Vidor answered the door. As he opened the door, Dorin pushed his way in. "Ok, Vidor, I know you are behind this. Where is Felicia?" "I don't know what you are talking about. You won't find Felicia here." Dorin pushed Vidor aside and started going from room to room. "Dorin, you must calm down. You're getting yourself all excited." "I'm going to search every room in this castle. I know she is here." "Well, if you must. But you'll not find her." Dorin went upstairs and searched all the rooms. Vidor waited in the hall. When Dorin came back down stairs, he was puzzled. He had been all over the village. This was the only place she could have been. "I said you wouldn't find her, and you didn't."

"Ok, Vidor, who accused Felicia of being a witch?" "I assume the prosecutor did." "Who told him?" "Why don't you ask him?" "He won't tell me." "Well, then I shan't tell you either." "You'll tell me or I'll knock it out of you." Simion was standing a few feet behind Dorin. "Do you need me, sir." "Yes, Dorin may need some help finding the door." "Never mind, I'll leave. But you haven't seen, or heard, the last of me." "I'm sure."

Dorin is a mess. He doesn't know what to do. Most of the villagers avoid him. No one will talk to him. Dorin starts threatening people. Emile warns Dorin to calm down, or he will lock him up. "I just want to know where Felicia is, and if she is alright. They can't keep her from me for no reason." "It's out of my hands, Dorin, the prosecutor has full authority here. I'm sure we will get to the bottom of this soon." "But she's not a witch. You know that, Emile." "That's up to Martin to determine. That's what he does."

The village is buzzing. Everyone knows about Felicia. But what if she is not the only one. There may be others. The women start looking at each other, wondering, is she…….? Vidor watches the turmoil starting. Just as he had hoped. The village will soon be dysfunctional.

The villagers will all be so suspicious of each other, that will be the only thing on their mind.

Today, one of the women, quietly went to see Martin. One of the women has been acting strange. "The last couple of days I have watched Laura Cardia standing in front of her house like she is talking to someone, only there is no one else around her. Don't you think that's strange?" "Yes, I do. I will look into this. I hope this is not spreading." "Do you think there are others?" "Time will tell."

Martin contacts Adrian and Vidor. "Gentlemen, we may have another case on our hands." Adrian gets a worried look on his face. Vidor exhibits a slight smile. "Who is it this time?" "A Laura Cardia. It seems she talks to people that aren't there." "Aren't we going a little too far here. Maybe she was singing. A lot of the women sing hymns while they are busy." Vidor spoke up, "Adrian, we have to investigate everything. We have to find these people out. They have to be destroyed. They are not going to come to us and say 'I'm a witch'. We have to flush them out." If Vidor was younger, he would probably be jumping up and down. "Let's go talk to her."

"Oh, I guess I might sometimes. If I can say something out loud, it helps me get it clear in my head. Nothing wrong with that. Wait! What are you trying to say? I'm no witch!" "Are you sure you weren't casting spells?" "Of course not. Don't do this to me!" "Don't get excited now. That's not going to help you any. Let's go down to my office and talk this over." Meanwhile, Vidor has been looking around the house. Unseen, he pulls a sheet of paper out of his jacket pocket. "Gentlemen, look at this. Another paper with symbols on it." He shows it to Martin. Martin hands it to Laura. "What do you know about this?" "I've never seen it before. I don't even know what it is." "It appears to be symbols that are used to cast spells. Come, we'll go to my office and talk." "No! I won't go. Leave me alone. I don't know anything about that paper or witchcraft. Please!"

At the office, "Will you tell me, Mrs. Cardia, why do you have this paper with symbols on it that denote witchcraft, and what about casting spells by chanting?" "I don't know what you are talking about. I never saw that paper; I don't know what it means and I don't chant." "Mrs. Cardia, if you do not explain these things, then I will have to assume you are not telling us everything you know. Vidor, I suggest you take her to the castle and confine her. Maybe she will begin to see things our way." Vidor and Adrian take Laura to the dungeon. "Here is someone to keep you company, Felicia." "Laura, you too?" Laura is crying almost uncontrollably. As they throw Laura in with Felicia, she puts her arms around Laura and tries to calm her. "How many more, Vidor? How many more women are you going to torture to get your revenge?" "Why, Felicia, dear, I don't know what you mean." "You are the one that's possessed, Vidor. You are possessed by the Devil. I think you are the Devil himself." "Felicia, you hurt my feelings. Have you decided to admit your guilt, Felicia?" "Never! Go to......" "Ah, ah. Careful Felicia."

Another man loses his wife with no explanation, and it doesn't stop there. Three more women and a man are charged with being a witch. The man is called a warlock. There is Sonia Korzha, Angelica Miklos, Raina Tarus and Borg Tarus, Riana's husbands' brother. The men in the village don't know what to believe. The village is in turmoil. The women are beginning to believe the village is full of witches, and they are afraid they may be accused next.

Borg Tarus goes before Martin, Adrian, and Vidor. "Mr. Tarus, you are accused of being a warlock. Are you a warlock?" Silence. Borg does not open his mouth. "Mr. Tarus, are you guilty or not guilty?" Borg does not say a word. "Borg, you and Laura Tarus, were observed holding each other's hands and chanting something. Are you guilty or not guilty of being a warlock?" "I will not give you satisfaction by answering that question." "Mr. Tarus! I demand you answer my question, are you guilty or not guilty?" "I will not answer your question." "Very well, we have means of making you answer my question. Since you refuse to answer, I have no other alternative. Adrian, Vidor, you know what you must do. Proceed."

Borg was taken out to a large dirt area. There he was forced to lie down on his back. A large wooden frame was put on him, that covered his chest and stomach area. Three large rocks were put on this frame, which put much pressure on Borg's chest and stomach. Martin ask Borg if he was ready to answer the question. He replied he was not. "Very well, we will wait one hour and if you still do not want to answer, another rock will be placed on the frame, and each hour you refuse to answer, another rock will be added, until you either answer the question or die. It's up to you."

Every hour another rock was placed on the frame and Borg still refused to answer. After nine hours, the weight of the rocks finally crushed Borg's chest. He was dead. Martin's conclusion, "It was his choice to live or die. He had ample opportunity to answer. He chose not to. We would probably have had to destroy him anyway. I do not doubt that he was a warlock."

A month has passed. There are seven women confined in the castle. Most of them are growing very weak. They either sleep or stare at the walls. They can barely move. Sonia Korzha grew so weak, she died in her sleep. Felicia is a strong woman, but even she has been quiet lately. They are fed and given water, but the food is far short of what of what they need to survive. Simion watches over the women, but he doesn't seem to know what is going on, he just does as he is told.

Another three weeks have gone by. Martin believes it is time to proceed with the trials of these women. Felicia and Laura are brought before the court. "Felicia, are you, or are you not a witch?" "You know there are no witches in this village. This is a witch-hunt in which there is no proof that witches even exist. It's all in your mind." "Very well. I have no alternative but to find you guilty of being a witch and practicing witchcraft. Laura what do you have to say for yourself?" Laura stood silent, staring at Martin. "Laura, why are you staring at me like that? Are you trying to cast a spell on me?" Laura started quietly laughing, then becoming louder and louder. "Laura, stop that laughing immediately! Do you hear me?!" Laura went silent, not saying a word. "Laura Cardia, I find you guilty of being a witch and practicing witchcraft. I sentence you both to be hanged. The hanging will be at 10:00 tomorrow morning. Dismissed."

When Dorin and Lucian, Laura's husband, heard of this they were so enraged, they probably would have committed murder. Emile, with some help, had to lock Dorin and Lucian in a cell in the jail. The villagers were becoming very afraid now. Things were going too far. The people started talking among themselves. This had to be stopped. But how?

The next morning, at 9:30, Felicia and Laura were taken to the big tree behind the church. Two ropes were thrown over a branch of the tree. (The same tree, the same branch as Erzsi.) Vidor can hardly stand still. Justice will be served. Vidor's justice. The two women are placed on the bed of a horse drawn wagon. Dorin and Lucian are escorted to the tree to watch. They try to break free, but the men holding them are stronger than they. Martin reads a proclamation of the crime and the sentence. Felicia and Laura are standing motionless. They're eyes looking straight ahead. A rope is put around each woman's neck. Martin, "Do either of you have anything to say before your sentence is fulfilled?" Neither woman said anything. They just stared straight ahead. Martin took a whip and smacked the horse on the rear. The wagon moved out from under the women. As the women dropped toward the ground, the snap of the rope broke both women's neck. They were pronounced dead.

Dorin and Lucian both collapsed to their knees. Sobbing uncontrollably. After a couple of minutes, Dorin, looked Vidor straight in the eye. "Vidor, you better start looking over your shoulder from now on. I'm going to kill you for what you did. You won't know when, but it will happen. I promise you that." Vidor just smiled a little. He had nothing to fear. Afterall, you can't kill the Devil.

Two days later, Angelica Miklos was brought before Martin. The time Angelica had spent in the dungeon had affected her mind. "Mrs. Miklos, you have been charged with witchcraft. Are you guilty or not guilty?" Angelica started laughing. Then she spit on Martin. "You are a snake. You belong in Hell, along with Vidor. Do what you will, but just know, that I have put a curse on all three of you. You will burn in Hell."

Martin was taken back; he didn't quite know what to say. Then, "Angelica Miklos, you are a vile, evil person. For your behavior and actions, I sentence you to be burned at the stake. That is the only way to completely destroy you. Tonight, at midnight." Angelica started laughing again, and laughed all the way back to the castle.

As night was approaching, Adrian, Vidor and Simion, built a platform with a 6' tall stake attached to the platform. They gathered several piles of dried brush and placed them around the stake. People were milling around, wondering what was going on. They had never seen a witch burn before, and they weren't sure they wanted to. One man in the crowd decided that this town had suffered enough, it was time to end it. Since no one else seemed brave enough, he decided he would be the one. He couldn't stop what was happening tonight, but tomorrow, he would take action.

At 11:30, Angelica was escorted to the platform. As she was being tied to the stake, she was cursing and spitting on people. "Angelica, do you have anything to say before sentencing is carried out?" "Plenty. Martin, Adrian and Vidor, all three of you are murderers, and you know I place a curse on you three. You will all die a violent death, and soon. I also put a curse on this village. You people could stop this torture, but you do nothing. Many of you will die horrible deaths. Mark my words."

Adrian and Vidor stepped forward and set fire to the brush. As the fire started, Angelica started laughing. As the flames came closer to her, and she could feel the heat intensify, her laughter changed to screams. As the flames engulfed her, many people turned away. They couldn't look. Many ran back to their houses, crying. The flames continued to grow for several minutes, before Angelica's screams stopped. Finally, everyone left the scene. The fire did not die out until just before dawn.

Four days have passed. There were 3 more women in the castle, a total of 5. Then one morning, a fancy carriage entered the town. A tall man, with a black robe and a black wide brim hat on, stepped from the coach. Two other men, who appeared to be policeman, stepped out also. He asked someone where the mayor's office was. As he started walking towards the mayor's office, he walked slowly, and observed the village and the people. He felt something evil in the village. He could tell the people were nervous and afraid. He hoped he was not to late to save the village and its people.

"I am Theodore Giana. I am from the Administrative Office with the district church in Oradea. These two men are officers of the law. Which of you is the mayor?" "I am. My name is Adrian." "And who are these gentlemen?" "They are Martin Lupesco and Vidor Benes'. Martin is the prosecutor from the church, and Vidor is a citizen of the village. What can I do for you?" "A man from your village came to me a few days ago. He was very upset. He stated the village was being slowly destroyed. He said you were hanging women and burning them at the stake. He was very angry, and hoped that I could put a stop to this torture.

"Mr. Lupesco, you are a prosecutor for the church?" "Yes, I go around and free the villages from the evil of witchcraft." "Who appointed you, and where?" "Well, I guess I just decided to help the church, and do what I could, to rid the country of these horrible witches." "So, you are not actually associated with the church. Who told you to come here and do these horrible things?" "Well, no one. I heard rumors about this village, and decided to come, and see what I could do." "You took it upon yourself to torture, and murder these people, without any solid evidence that they ever did anything wrong." "I did not murder anyone, I simply punished them for their evil behavior." "Mr. Lupesco, some time ago, the church finally came to the realization, that witchcraft was nothing more than a scheme, that people were using, to get rid of people they didn't like. Some women do claim to be witches, but they are harmless. They have no power over anyone. The church does not recognize them as a menace, and therefore, does not bother them anymore."

(Women who profess to be witches, and practice witchcraft, is still prevalent today. In 2011, the Rumanian legislature passed a bill, which made witchcraft a profession, and therefore, any money they made practicing witchcraft, would be subject to an income tax.)

"Martin Lupesco, you are under arrest for torture, and murder of innocent people. Officers, take him into custody. Adrian and Vidor, you were a part of this also." "Yes sir, but we were following Martin's orders. We both had heard about witches, and we thought Martin had the authority to do what he did." "Yes, well, I'm not going to charge either of you with anything. You both will have to continue to live here, and I think you will find that is punishment enough. Do you still have any confined at this time?" "Yes, 5 women." "You will release them, take care of them, and let no more harm come to them. Is that understood?" "Yes, sir." "Yes, sir, we will do as you ask." "Very well, we will be leaving now. Good day."

After the women were released and the villagers were told what happened, Adrian and Vidor were not very popular people. The villagers were very angry, that all they went through, the torture, the killings, and their fear, was all for nothing. It should never have happened.

The following day, word got around that there had been an accident about 20 miles outside of the village. It seems the carriage that was taking Martin Lupesco back to the church, lost a wheel, and the carriage overturned. One officer had a broken leg, the other officer and the priest were not injured. Martin, was thrown out of the carriage; it landed on his chest, crushing it. He was killed instantly.

Vidor heard about the accident, but accidents happen. Too bad. Vidor was feeling pretty good. He had accomplished pretty much what he had wanted to do. He had his revenge. He showed people what It was like to lose someone they love, needlessly, in a tragic way. It would be a long time before the villagers got over what they had witnessed. It would take many years before they would forget what happened; maybe they never would.

Although Vidor was not very popular in the village, he still went in just to aggravate people. He was going to The Pub, just to see what people were talking about. Maybe he could pick up some juicy tidbit that he could use to his advantage. First, he was going to see Adrian. It had been a couple of days since he had talk to him. He tried the door, but it was locked. That was unusual. Adrian was always in his office this time of day. He knocked on the door, no answer. As he peered in the window, he saw some sort of shadow on the wall in the inner office. Something wasn't right. Vidor banged against the door and forced it open. He hurried into the inner office. He froze in his tracks. There was a rope around Adrian's neck and he was hanging from a rafter. At that moment, he heard the voice of Angelica. 'Martin, Adrian, Vidor, you are murderers. You will all die a violent death. And soon.' Now Vidor always said he feared nothing and no one. But he found himself shaking. Did she really put a curse on them? Of course not. There are no such things as curses. It's all in a person's mind. So, he pulled himself together and went to get Emile.

The word spread quickly, and a crowd gathered around. Dorin was there also, "Well, Vidor, you will be next. Remember what Angelica said. I hope it comes quickly for you." Dorin started laughing. The crowd stared at Vidor. Were they hoping the same thing? Vidor waved them off and went back to the castle. He just couldn't believe that

Angelica could be responsible for the death of Martin and now Adrian. It had to be just a coincidence.

A couple of months went by. Dorin was elected as mayor. He seemed to be better qualified and no one else wanted the job. The villagers were trying to move on. They tried to forget what happened those past few months. They actually grew closer as a village. They had learned quite a lot, and they were determined not to let anything tear the village apart again. But some things you can't control.

Vidor stayed at the castle most of the time. Only on rare occasions did he go into town. He was starting to feel his years. He was feeling very tired these days. He started using a cane. He felt more comfortable with it, because he was having trouble with his balance. He hired another housekeeper. Her name was Zelda. She was a widow woman, 64. She was fairly new to the community and decided to ignore the rumors about Vidor. She was sure no one could be that bad. She liked the idea of living at the castle, and she needed a job.

The village was growing. More people were moving in. Business was good. People were beginning to laugh and have a good time. There were village parties every once in a while. Times were good, life was good. It was 1661.

Vidor was still able to get around, although much slower. He was glad Zelda was with him. She was a big help to him. Zelda was a little puzzled, as to why there were so many bad rumors about Vidor. He treated her very well. Never yelled at her and was always polite. How could they have labeled this man as evil? The past had taken its toll on Vidor. He no longer felt anger or hatred toward the villagers. He was tired and just wanted to live the rest of his life in peace. Vidor had forgotten about the curse he supposedly had on him. And the villagers were having such a good time, they forgot about the cloud that was hanging over the village.

The villagers were going to have one of their street parties one evening, they even invited Vidor. He reluctantly agreed to go. There was music and dancing, and plenty of food to go around. Actually, Vidor found himself enjoying the music and watching the dancing. It was getting late, some of the people were heading home. But there were the die hards who kept dancing, and some still eating. Zelda was getting Vidor ready to take him back to the castle. Suddenly, one of the women dancing, collapsed. The music stopped, and someone ran to get the doctor. The doctor knelt down to look at the woman. She was half conscious, and had a very high fever.

The doctor had a couple of men carry the woman back to his office. Medias didn't have a hospital, but the doctor had a room with a half a dozen beds next to his office. The two men left the doctor with his patient, and went back to the street. The party did break up now. Everyone was headed home, and Vidor was already back at the castle.

The next morning, the doctor went in to check his patient. As he stood there, she started coughing up blood and she had several black boils on her body. The doctor shook his head. He knew what was wrong with the woman. It was happening in other parts of Europe. Just then his office door opened. When he turned around, there were two men and a woman standing there. They could hardly stand up. He could see they were sweating. He told them to come in and lay down in one of the beds. He checked each one out, and there was no doubt, the village had been hit with the Black Plague. The doctor felt overwhelmed. He was going to need a lot of help and cooperation. But he was also afraid of a panic when the news got out.

He rushed to Dorin's office. "Dorin, I need your help and I need you to stay calm. Don't panic with what I have to tell you." "Sounds serious, Doc. What's going on?" "Dorin, I have 4 patients in my office." "Ok, and?" "They have the Black Plague." Dorin stood up. "No! What are we going to do?" "First of all, stay calm. I'm going to send someone to the surrounding villages and see if the doctors there can help us. You need to call a meeting of all the villagers you can find. They will have to be told. I hope they don't panic, but step up and help us fight this. I'm going down to see Emile. He'll need some strong men to help him in case there is trouble."

The word spread fast. The villagers were scared and ask many questions. "Alright everyone, stay calm and listen. We have a lot of work to do, and we need all of you to help. This plague comes from fleas and is very contagious. These fleas are carried by rats. I need you men to start eradicating our rat population. The streets and homes need to be cleaned up so the rats have nothing to feed on. Then they must be destroyed and driven out. That's the only way to stop this outbreak. The women must help with the patients. I know it's dangerous, and you may end up getting sick also, but you may already be infected. The plague has hit almost 60% of Europe, so we are not alone. Stay brave and do what you can to help. We must all work together."

Vidor had not been to the village for several days, so he was unaware of what was happening. Zelda went to the village, and when she came back, she told Vidor about the plague. "I need to go to the village, they need help." "Vidor, you'll do no such thing. You go down there; you'll end up sick also, and probably end up dead. Just go sit down." "No. I came close to destroying that village and everyone in it. I was a foolish and evil man back then. Now I need to help those people. Maybe atone for some of my behavior. Besides, if it's in the village, it will get up here also. Nobody is safe."

Vidor went down to do what he could. None of the other villages could send help, they were overwhelmed also. The town was on its own. There were already some 150 people affected. And the list kept growing. People were dying because help couldn't get to them fast enough. Although, the only thing that could be done for them, was to try and keep them comfortable, because the Black Plague was pretty much a death sentence. It was very rare for someone to recover. This went on for two months. Those infected rose to almost 300.

After a few days, Vidor had to go back to the castle. He was wore out. After being able to rest for a few days, he was able to go back to the village to help. By then, the plague seemed to have run its course. Less and less people were coming down with the sickness. Everyone had been buried, and there were only half a dozen cases left. Those cases didn't seem to be as serious. It appeared they may even recover.

Back at the castle, Vidor was becoming tired more often. Another few days he noticed he was feeling very tired, and he wondered why it felt so warm in the castle. The next morning, he knew what was happening. He had contracted the plague. He knew at his age; he would not survive. He did not say anything to Zelda. He went upstairs to lay down. As he approached the bedroom, he stopped for a minute, then walked to the balcony that looked out the front of the castle, where he could see part of the village. He reflected on his past, and was not very proud of it. But he could do nothing about it now. He turned to go back to his bedroom. As he took a step, a very strong gust of wind blew across the balcony. It blew him backward, and he fell over the railing, and landed on the ground in front of the front door.

Zelda heard a noise out front, and opened the door. She froze as she saw Vidor lying there. Zelda told the villagers and they held a funeral. He was buried in the vault, with the rest of the family. Zelda moved on to another village. No one ever saw her again. Simion simply disappeared.

Now, was Angelica's curse really responsible for 3 men's violent death and the plague that almost destroyed the village? Or, was that just everyday life in the world at that time in history?

The castle stayed vacant until 1790, when the Bernard family bought the castle. But you already know that story. After the Bernards, the castle was vacant until 1935, when a new family purchased the castle.

Chapter 7

1935. America was in the middle of a depression. Many European countries were experiencing economic problems. Hitler, had made himself dictator of Germany. Inflation was at it's worst, and Hitler knew, he was the only one who could save Germany. Medias, Rumania, has not changed since the era of the Bernards. A few villages have electricity, Medias still does not. No one in Medias has a car. The people use horse drawn wagons for transportation, or they ride a bicycle. Farming is the number one occupation. There has been an increase in sheep herding; mainly for the wool, but sometimes the lambs are sold for food. Just about everyone has a milk cow, or two. They run freely in and around the village. Most of the villagers are very poor. There are a few who have small business, that allows them to get by.

Bucharest is quite large, with most of the amenities of the 30's. It was a large bustling city. There was still plenty of money around among the older generation of business men. Among those, was Albert Serban, 68, who decided it was time to retire. He was from the city of Brasov, and he was ready to move back there to the peace and quiet of a smaller town. His intention was to build a huge castle just outside of Brasov. Albert and Florenta, his wife, loved to entertain, and he thought people would be excited, and intrigued to have a party in a castle.

Enter, Barry Greene and family. Barry is 35, Janet is 31, and Abby is 12. They live in Cicero, just outside of downtown Chicago. Barry is an architect; Janet, enjoys interior decorating. It's just a hobby, but she has helped many of her friends decorate their homes. Due to the depression, no one is building much of anything. The company Barry worked with has closed its doors, leaving him without a job. The end of the depression is a long way off, and Barry is going to have to find another type of work to survive.

Now, besides the depression, Congress passed the prohibition amendment. All alcoholic beverages are banned. No bars, no nightclubs, no stores, no one, can sell alcohol. It is now a dry country. But, if someone wants a drink, they will find a way; if a bar or night club wants to sell alcohol, they too will find a way. For them to be able to sell it, someone has to supply it. That's where the bootleggers come in. They have a way to get the goods, and distribute it. Now, all of this, from the supplier, to the guy behind the bar, selling it, is illegal, and subject to long prison terms. There's a lot of money to be made all up the line, and all of this is because people are angry and up in arms because they have to have their drinks. It's been a way of life since the country was founded.

Barry hasn't been able to find any steady work. Some odd jobs, maybe work for two or three days, then he is let go. Barry is behind is his rent. It is difficult to keep food on the table. Barry is getting desperate.

Barry goes into a coffee shop. He has a nickel in his pocket. That's enough for a cup of coffee. As he sits down at a table, he looks up at the door. He does a double take. He can't believe his eyes. In walks his old college roommate, Skip Johnson. "Skip, over here. Come, sit down." "Well, I'll be…. Barry Greene, I haven't seen you since we left college. How are you doing?" "I'm surviving. How about you?" "I'm doing ok. Tell me what you've been up to." "Well, I'm married, and we have a 12-year-old daughter. How about you?" "I'm still single. There's a girl I'm going with, but nothing serious. I'm not ready for that yet. Are you working?" "No, I lost my job just about a year ago. Haven't been able to find anything." "Things are pretty rough, huh?"

"I'll tell you what, Barry, I can probably get you a job, and it pays pretty well." "And what would that be?" "Driving a truck." "A truck?" "Yeah, you know how to drive a truck don't you?" "Of course, I do. But what kind of truck? What will I be hauling?" "It doesn't matter what you will be hauling. All you have to do is sit in the truck while it's being loaded. Go to the address they tell you, and sit in the truck while it's unloaded. Then go home until they call you again." "Who's going to call me?" "My Boss." "And who is your boss?" "You'll meet him later. If you do your job right, you'll be making plenty of dough." "Skip, I think I know where you are going with this, and I don't think I like it. I'm not stupid. That job can get you killed." "Not if you're careful and smart." "So, your running beer and liquor for the bootleggers." "It's a job, and you know there aren't many jobs available right now." "What if the cops arrest me?" "Not to worry, the Boss will have you back out before they can turn the key on your cell." "So, if I say yes?" "Let me talk to the Boss, first. Then I'll take you to him. Don't ask a lot of questions. The less you know, the better off you'll be.

"What about Janet? She's not going to like me going against the law." "She doesn't have to know. Just tell her you got a job with the Allied Trucking Company. She won't know who that is. Tell her you transport government stuff. Can't talk about it. Hey, what she don't know won't hurt her." "If I get arrested or killed, she'll know." "Stop worrying, the boss takes care of his people. Besides, you'll be able to take care of your family, and that's what's important."

A couple of days went by, Barry hadn't said anything to Janet about his possible job. He really wasn't sure if he wanted to go that route. He had never done anything illegal in his life. Janet never complained. She just took life as it came along. She knew there were a lot of people worse off then they were. Whatever work Barry was able to get, always seemed to get them through.

Barry and Janet were counting what money they had left, when the phone rang. Barry answered, "Skip, what do you know?" Pause. "Really? When?" Another pause. "Well, I guess I'm ready. I'll try it." Long pause. "Ok, I'll meet you at the coffee shop tomorrow morning." As he hung up, he turned to Janet, "That was Skip, I told you about him the other day." "I remember." "He has a job for me. And it's not for just a few days, it's as long as I want it." "Oh, Barry, what is it?" "I'll be driving a truck, delivering goods to stores." "Driving a truck? Are you sure, you want to do that?" "Sure, it's good money. We won't have to worry about food or anything else. I would call it a lifesaver." "Ok, it will be nice to have money to spend again. When do you start?" "Skip is going to take me to his boss tomorrow morning."

The sign on the door of the office read, 'Johnny Broco' and below his name, 'Wholesale Transportation'. As Skip and Barry entered the office, a large man was sitting at a desk across from the door. He looked up as we closed the door. He was a big built man. Not fat, well-muscled. He was at least 6' 2". Probably around 185 pounds. Grey hair, wore glasses and looked to be in his early 60's. He was pleasant enough, but I sure didn't want to get on his bad side.

"You're Barry Greene?" "Yes, sir." "No sir's, just call me Boss. That's all you need to know." "That's fine with me, Boss." "Skip says you want a job driving truck." "Yes, if you'll have me." "You know what it's about?" "I think so. I think I know enough." "No qualms about what you'll be doing? No fear about the job?" "Maybe a little fear right now, but I'll try most anything once." "Don't worry, I take care of my boys." "That's what I was told."

"We make our runs at night. It's quieter then. Report tonight at 10:00 to the warehouse at this address. When your truck is ready, drive to the address the foreman gives you. Wait in the truck until it's unloaded, then go back to the warehouse. You'll get $50 for each run you make." "Ok, I'm ready." "One other thing. There may be times when I have you go make collections from our customers. Think you can handle that?" "Sure, no problem."

Barry told Janet about his job. Well, not everything. "Barry, I don't like you working at night. It's too dangerous out there. There is so much crime and people getting robbed." "I'll be alright. I'm just driving a truck from one place to another, making deliveries. I don't even have to load or unload the truck." "I don't like the idea of being alone all night, every night. I'm afraid to be alone." "I'll tell you what. Why not ask your sister, Jessie, to move in with us? We have enough room, and she lives alone. She could be company for you at night. With me making good money now, she could take what she pays for rent now, and use it for things she needs." "That would be good. I never did like her living alone. Especially where she's living. I'll talk to her."

"Ok, Barry, here are three addresses you're to deliver to. They are nightclubs. Go to the back entrance. Each one will take his share, then go to the next one. Understand?" "I got it."

Barry started toward his first destination. The Gypsy Nightclub. He knew enough not to speed. He had all night. As he was driving along, a dog ran across the road in front of him. He swerved to miss it. He missed it, but a cop saw him swerve and decided to find out why. The cop came up behind Barry and put on his lights and siren. "Oh, great. Why is that cop pulling me over? First run and I get pulled over. If he checks to see what I'm hauling, I've had it." The cop came up to the door of the truck. "Let me see your license, buddy." "Yes, sir. Did I do something wrong?" "How come you lost control back there? You haven't been drinking, have you?" "No, sir, I don't drink. A dog ran across in front of me. I tried to miss him. That's all." "Ok. What are you hauling, anyway?" "Just regular merchandise." "Let's go take a look." "But I've got a schedule to keep." "That's alright, it will only take a minute. You won't be very late."

Barry climbed down from the truck. He was shaking so bad inside, he was afraid he would wet his pants. 'As soon as that cop looks in the back of this truck, I'm dead meat.' Barry pulled the cover back at the rear of the truck. He closed his eyes as he did. He heard the cop, "Ok, you can go now." Barry opened his eyes. What he saw almost made him laugh. The very back of the truck was piled to the ceiling with wooden crates. One said Government Issue Boots. Another one said Government Issue Underwear. All the crates were stenciled with government issue merchandise. As Barry got back into the truck, he didn't know whether to laugh or cry.

When Barry got to his first destination, he was not about to sit in the truck and wait. He wanted to see how this worked. He got out of the truck and walked around toward the dock. He stayed in the shadows. As he watched, three guys pulled the government crates out and stacked them on the dock. The way they were handling them, they had to be empty. Then they started rolling out several barrels of beer and cartons of whisky. When they got their quota, they stacked the empty crates back in the truck. Pretty clever. But are they really fooling the police?

Two weeks go by. Barry's job is going well. No more police incidents. Barry is making a lot of money. Jessie moved in with Barry and Janet. They all get along and enjoy each other's company. Jessie is glad she isn't alone anymore. She helps quite a bit around the house. Earns her keep.

Tonight, when Barry checked into work, he was told the Boss wanted to see him. "Barry, sit down. We had a problem last night. Skip had an accident." "What kind of accident?" "He was making a delivery and someone ran him off the road." "Is he alright?" "No, Barry, he was killed." "No! Not Skip?" "I'm afraid so. He was thrown from the truck and it landed on him." "Skip and I went to college together. We were best friends." "I know, Barry. That's why I called you in to the office. I wanted to tell you before someone else sprung it on you." "Did they get the guy that did it?" "No, he kept on going." "You mean he did it deliberately?" "Yes. You see, Barry, Chicago is a big place. There are other people doing the same thing we do. They don't like competition, and sometimes they try to take over part of our territory so they can expand. And that's what we are up against."

"Does this happen often?" "It's been quiet for several months. I heard one of the mobs had a new leader. I guess he is hungry for new customers." "What about the police? I'm sure they saw what Skip was hauling." "They did. They came to me this morning. I had to tell them that Skip was off last night. So, if he was hauling something illegal, I didn't know anything about it. They checked the warehouse, but we keep the goods in a special room they don't know about." "So, that's it? Business goes on as usual." "That's about it, kid." "What about Skip?" "We'll take care of him. He said he didn't have any family left, except his girlfriend. We'll take care of her; see she gets along alright. She's a good kid."

Barry is hot. Someone's going to pay for Skips death. Barry has never been so angry. This puts a different light on things. Barry could be next. He could see this would probably escalate into a war. Barry decided he needed to buy a gun, he needed to be prepared for anything.

The next day, he told Janet about Skip. She had gotten to know Skip fairly well. She thoughthe was a good guy. He didn't deserve that. She hated they didn't catch the guy who ran him off the road. "I told you it was dangerous out there at night. I wish you could work a day job. I'd feel better.

A couple of nights later, Barry is on a run. He has his new gun on the seat beside him. Janet doesn't know about the gun. As he pulls around to his first stop, he slams on the brakes. There is already a truck sitting at the dock. There are three men on the dock, and they are arguing. One of the guys has a gun. Barry grabs his gun and heads toward the dock. When he gets close to the dock, he tells the man with the gun, to drop it. "You with the gun. Drop it. NOW!" The man starts to turn around to point the gun at Barry, but thinks better of it, and drops the gun. "Kick it away from you." The man kicks it away and one of the other men pick it up. "Hey, thanks, Barry. This guy was getting mean. He's trying to take over our business." "Ok, you, what's your name?" "Willie Jenkins." "Who's your boss?" "None of your business." "I'm making it my business. Now, if you don't want a neat little hole in your shirt about where your heart is, I suggest you start talking." "Alright! Take it easy. His name is Jake Wyler. We operate out of the north end." "Well, this is not north end territory. You're out of bounds, Willie. You need to go back and have Jake show you where the boundary line is." "He told me to come down here." "Well, maybe Jake needs to be shown where the boundary is. Now, get in your truck and get out of here. We'll mail your gun to you." "You haven't heard the last of this." "I'm sure I haven't."

The next day, Barry went to see the Boss. He told him what happened the night before. "When did you start carrying a gun?" "Right after Skip was murdered. I thought it might come in handy." "Well, you were lucky last night. But you did do the right thing. I don't really like the truck drivers carrying guns. If you get pulled over for any reason, and they find a gun on you, they get testy. Then I have to go and clear things up. It's an inconvenience, you see. I don't need that." "By the way, who is the big man in this area? Will I get to meet him?" "Forget it kid, let's just say the big man is on an extended vacation for a while. Don't worry about it."

"Barry, you seem to be able to take care of yourself. How would you like a different job than driving truck?" "I don't know. It depends on what it is." "How would you like the job of collecting the money from our customers?" "Sure, why not? I get kind of tired driving truck all night." "Fine. You'll start working days from now on. You'll get a list of customers, and what they owe. All you have to do is collect the money, and get the list for their next order." "Sounds easy enough." "Well, not always. But I'm sure you can handle it."

Janet was so glad Barry was going to be working days. Now, they would be able to spend more time together. Barry took his jacket off and put it on the couch. "I'm going into the bathroom and clean up." "Ok, Barry." Janet picked Barry's jacket to hang it up. It felt heavy. She felt the pockets. She reached into a pocket and pulled out Barry's gun. It scared her. Why was Barry carrying a gun around? As Barry came out of the bathroom, Janet was holding the gun in her hand. "Barry… why do you… have a gun?" "Janet, please put that gun down before it accidently goes off. I'm going to be carrying a lot of money around with me. It's for protection." Janet put the gun down on the lampstand. "Oh, Barry, what kind of business are you in? Who do you work for? Something doesn't feel right here." "It's alright, Janet. What I'm doing now is like a promotion. Everything's ok."

"I tell you what, Janet, let's go out to a nice restaurant tonight and have dinner. We haven't been out for quite a while." "Ok, Barry, maybe we can relax for a while. I need it." As they were driving to the restaurant, Barry noticed a car following them. After a few blocks, the car was still behind them. Barry made a quick right-hand turn and the car stayed right with them. "Barry, what are you doing? This is the wrong way. You're driving too fast." Barry slowed down. "Sorry, I guess I forgot where I was going." "That's not like you, Barry."

As Barry parked the car, whoever was following them, went on by. Maybe Barry was just getting too suspicious. After they ordered their dinner, they were drinking their coffee, when Barry saw a man go by out of the corner of his eye. The man went over to a table against the wall. Barry recognized him. The man never looked his way, he just kept his eyes on the singer in front of the bandstand. After the singer finished, the man gave a quick glance at Barry, then went back to watching the band.

"Janet, I'm going to the restroom, be back in a minute." As Barry started toward the restroom, the man got up from his table and started that way also. Barry was waiting for him. "Willie, you seem to be following me. Any particular reason, or do you just like my company." "I hate your guts, Barry. I don't like the way you treated me the other night. Maybe I'm here to see it doesn't happen again." Willie pulled a gun out of his pocket. "Willie, I see you got a new gun. I forgot to mail you the other one." "I'm going to see to it you don't bother me again." "Well, Willie, make your move." Just then, there was a rather loud noise out in the hallway. Willie jumped, and Barry knocked the gun out of Willie's hand. At the same time, Barry hit Willie square on the nose. Willie fell back against the wall, blood running from his nose. As Barry was coming toward him, Willie was able to straighten up and hit Barry full in the stomach. Barry went backward, falling over a trash can, and to the floor. As Willie came after him, Barry, put his foot up and caught Willie in the stomach and pushed him backward. Barry got up, and as the two came toward each other again, Willie swung a right at Barry. Barry grabbed Willie's arm and twisted it around behind Willie's back in a hammer lock. Barry guided Willie over to one of the toilets and shoved his head down in it and flushed it. Willie started screaming. As Barry started toward the door, another customer came in and saw Willie with his head in the toilet. As Barry walked out the door, "It's a shame how some people can't hold their liquor."

As Barry got to their table, he threw down some money, "Janet get your jacket, let's get out of here. Now!" Janet had seen the other man follow Barry into the restroom. As she picked up her jacket, she kept looking back at the restroom. The other man never came out. "What's going on Barry? What are you up to? What happened to that other man?" "Never mind, let's just get out of here." "Why are we in such a hurry? We never got to eat." "Be quiet and come on."

Lest you forget, let's go back to Romania for a while. Albert and Florenta Serban have rented an apartment in Brasov. Albert wants to build his castle just outside of Brasov. There are several architects in Bucharest, but Albert wants someone younger, with new ideas. The architects Albert knows can't seem to think past the 16 or 1700's. He doesn't want anything like the old Dracula type castles. They are creepy and cold. He wants something bright and warm. Something people want to come to, without looking over their shoulder all the time, wondering, when is 'you know who', going to show up. Albert decides he wants someone from America to design his new home. He puts ads in several well know papers in America.

Meanwhile, back in Chicago, Janet just knows that Barry is hiding something from her. There is something about his job that just doesn't add up. She gets her phone book and looks up 'Allied Trucking Co,'. There is no such company listed. Now, she is getting angry. Now she knows Barry has been lying to her about his job, and what he is doing. When she thought about it, Barry sure made a lot of money just driving a truck. Barry is going to have to come clean.

Barry walks in the door, "Janet, baby, I hope dinner is ready, I'm starved." Janet was sitting straight up in her chair. "Barry, sit down. There is no dinner, and there won't be, until we talk." "Baby, is something wrong? Are you ok?" "It's not about me, it's about you. Please sit down." "Ok, Janet. What is this all about?" "You. You have been lying to me since you started this job. I want the truth!" "Why do you think I'm lying to you?" "Number 1, There is no Allied Trucking Company, I checked. Number 2, in the restaurant the other night, a man followed you into the restroom, and when you came back, we had to hurry out of there. I never saw that man come out of the restroom. I don't think he was able to. Number 3, nobody makes that much money driving a truck, especially these days, and finally, now you carry a gun."

"Janet, I can explain all of that." "Yes, you will. But no more stories. I want the truth. If not, Abby and I walk out the door." "Janet, you wouldn't do that!" "I'm already packed." Barry was silent for a minute. He didn't have much choice. "Alright, Janet, I'll tell you everything." "This better be good." "I've been running booze for the bootleggers." "What! Are you crazy? You'll get arrested, or killed. Why?" "We needed the money, and this was the easiest way to get it. The cops don't bother us much. They're getting their cut. They just look the other way, most of the time." "Barry, I read the newspapers; these mob people are always shooting each other. When is your turn?"

"Janet, nothings going to happen to me. I'm just a little guy. It's the higher ups that keep getting knocked off. There is a lot of rivalry. My job now is just to collect the money." "If no one cares about what you are doing, why carry a gun? What about that guy in the restaurant? I suppose he went into the restroom with you to shake your hand and tell you what a fine job you are doing." "I had a run in with him and he followed me to pay me back. But I took care of him. He won't bother me anymore." "You didn't kill him, did you?" "No, no, I just taught him a lesson he won't forget."

"Barry, you have to get away from these people before something goes wrong. The money is no good, if you end up dead." "I don't know, Janet, the Boss may not like me leaving. I know too much. Besides, I like the job. I like the excitement and the authority I have now." "I am not going to sit here every day, wondering if you're lying dead somewhere." "Alright, Janet, alright. I'll talk to the Boss. Maybe we can work something out."

The next day Barry went around making his collections. He wasn't sure yet how to approach his Boss. He went down to the Rocket nightclub for his last collection for the day. "Well, look who's here. Willie, what are you doing here? Are you harassing the manager?" Willie stepped back several steps. "You stay away from me. Don't you come near me." "Willie, calm down. I'm not going to hurt you. Again." "Keep your distance, I'm leaving. Ok?" "Be my guest. But I better not see you around here again. You remember what happened the other night, Willie?" Willie made a hasty exit.

"Joe, what was he doing here?" "Oh, he was just fishing." "Well, I hope he didn't land anything, did he Joe?" "Hey, Barry, here is the money for the last shipment." "That's good, Joe, now where is your list for next week." "I don't have one, Barry." "What do you mean, you don't have one? You always have a list. What's going on, Joe?" "Pressure. Jake Wyler came to see me. I have to start buying from him. If I don't, he said he would burn the place down. I don't know what to do. I'm caught right in the middle. You gotta help me Barry." "Take it easy Joe, I'll get this straightened out. You know the Boss will take care of you. You've been a loyal customer."

When Barry got back to the office, he went in to talk to the Boss. He explained about Janet, and the way things were. "Barry, you should know by now that nobody quits. The only way you leave the organization, is when they put you in the ground. You know too much, Barry. We don't want you talking to the wrong people. As long as you work for me, I can keep my eye on you. You know what will happen if you make a mistake." "I understand. I'll see what I can do."

As Barry was driving home, a car pulled up along side of him. The car swerved toward Barry, forcing him to try to miss the car. He ran up over the curb and slammed on the brakes. As he got out of the car, two men from the other car came toward him. "What's the idea, you two trying to kill somebody?" "Shut up. You're coming with us." As each man grabbed one of Barry's arms, he tried to push them away. One of the men hit Barry on the head with a gun he had in his hand. As Barry slumped to the sidewalk, the two men lifted Barry up, threw him in the back seat of their car, and took off.

When Barry came to, he was sitting in a chair in an office. He couldn't figure where he was. The two men were standing behind him, and there was a man sitting at a desk in front of him. After a couple of minutes, his head cleared some. He had a good idea who the man behind the desk was. He was a thin man, about 5' 7", around 45, somewhere around 140 pounds. Dark hair combed back, and a thin mustache. His nose looked like it had run into something too many times. "I would guess you are Jake Wyler." "You would guess right. Since you are so smart, why do you think you are you here?" "That part, you'll have to tell me, since I didn't come here of my own free will." "Well, there are a couple of things I want to get through to you." "You got the floor."

"First, there is poor Willie." Barry started laughing. One of the men behind him smacked him up side the head with his fist. Barry quit laughing. "You made a mistake when you interfered with Willie last week, when he was trying to conduct some business. You even took his gun away from him. Then the other night, you accosted him in a restroom, in a restaurant. Willie doesn't like that, and I don't either. Willie is important to me." "Hey, he came after me and pulled a gun. Was I supposed to let him shoot me?" This time the other man hit Barry up side the head. "Willie only wanted to talk to you. You didn't give him a chance. So now you owe me." "Owe you what?" "Later. Second, I understand you are going to see to it that I don't infringe on your territory. If I can give a customer a better deal, that's called capitalism." "There was a line drawn between territories, and everyone is supposed to honor that line. There is no need to be greedy. Everyone's making out alright." "I think we are done talking, Barry. You two take Barry outside and collect what he owes."

Barry had no doubt things were going to get ugly. They took Barry out the back door to an alley. Each of the two guys took turns using Barry as a punching bag. He lasted about 5 minutes. He slumped to the ground, totally unconscious. Each man kicked Barry in the stomach as they left. Barry came to about 45 minutes later. He was so groggy; he just lay there for a few minutes. He tried to sit up. It was so painful. His face looked like it had gone through a meat grinder and he was sure he had at least one broken rib. He sat there for another half hour, all the time thinking what he was going to do next.

Finally, Barry was strong enough to walk. While thinking things over, Barry made two decisions. One, he was getting out no matter what the Boss said. Two, no one was going to get away with beating him this bad. He headed back inside the building, to confront Jake.

Jake had just stood up and was getting ready to leave, when Barry busted the door open. Jake froze. He watched Barry walk toward him. He quickly opened a desk drawer and pulled out a gun. "Stay back, Barry, I'll shoot you where you stand." Jake came around to the front of the desk. Barry could see that Jake's gun hand was shaking. He took two steps forward and knocked the gun out of Jake's hand. At the same time, he hit Jake with his right fist. Jake went flying back against the wall and slumped to the floor. He slowly got up and put his hand up as if to say, 'I've had enough.' But Barry wasn't finished with him just yet. "Jake, I'm going to beat you to within an inch of your life." As Barry took a step forward, Jake picked up an ashtray and threw it at him. It hit him on the forehead, and he went down.

That didn't help Barry's condition very much, but the hatred and contempt, kept him going. As he was getting up, Jake jumped on him and put his hands around Barry's throat, and started squeezing. Barry wasn't strong enough to break Jake's grip. He knew Jake's gun was on the floor close by. If he could just reach it. As he was starting to lose consciousness, he reached out for the gun. He couldn't quite reach it. He punched Jake in the head as hard as he could. It didn't knock Jake lose, but he jerked enough that Barry was able to move his body a few inches. His hand touched the handle of the gun. He took hold of the gun, stuck it in Jake's side, and pulled the trigger. Nothing happened. He tried again. This time the gun went off, and Jake fell over on the floor.

The two men who beat up Barry, were in another room and heard the gunshot. They ran into Jake's office with their guns drawn. One of the men fired at Barry, but missed. Barry fired back, and cut both of the men down. Barry went over to Jake. Jake was still alive, barely. "Barry, you are a dead man. Every cop, and every mob person in town, will be looking for you." With that, Jake breathed his last breath. Barry looked around. Barry had blown the lid off the bootlegging racket. Three dead men. No witnesses. No one would ever believe it was self-defense. Barry had to get Janet and Abby and Jessie and go into hiding.

First, he was going to see the Boss. The Boss wasn't going to like what Barry had to tell him. He knew the Boss would be home by now, so that's where he headed. He kept continuous pressure on the door bell. A woman answered the door. He pushed his way in. He yelled out, "Boss, where are you?" Boss came into the foyer. "My God man, what happened to you?" Barry walked into the front room and sat down. He was wore out. "Barry, I don't think I'm going to like your answer, but what is going on? What happened to you?" "Boss, you're not going to like this, but Jake Wyler and two of his hoods are dead." "Dead, who did it?" "Me." "You killed them?" "It was them or me." "Ok, kid, tell me what happened."

"The two hoods hijacked me and took me toJake. They beat the crap out of me." Barry went on to tell the whole story. "Jake was trying to kill me, so I had to shoot him. His two hoods came barging into the office with guns blazing, so I had to take them out also. It was either them or me. It was total self-defense." "No witnesses?" "None." "This is bad, Barry. This is going to look like I declared war on the North Side bunch. You've started a war, Barry. Your life isn't worth a plug nickel now. Everyone will be looking for you. I ought to shoot you myself, for what you have started. But I won't. I'll leave that to somebody else." "I have to get out of town. Somewhere I can hide. You need to help me." "Sorry, Barry, you're on your own. You better disappear, although you'll always have to look over your shoulder. These people have long arms. They will find you wherever you go."

Barry started for home. How can he explain all of this to Janet? This will devastate her. One thing is for certain, the Greene name must cease to exist. They must change their names, find somewhere a long way from here, and start over again. Well, there is one thing on their side. It seems that when Barry went over to the boss's house, he forgot to hand over the day's receipts. So, when the Boss figures that out, he'll be looking for Barry also. How much trouble can one person get into? And the Greene story, is not even half over.

Chapter 8

Barry rushed home to the apartment. "Janet, get Abby, Jessie and hurry up, and pack everything you can in the suite cases. We have to get out of here, on the double. Move." When Janet saw Barry's face, she let out a scream. "Oh, my God, Barry, were you in an accident?" "Something like that. We have to hurry." "What is going on? Are we in trouble?" "Yes, we have to get out here as quickly as we can." Janet rushed in to tell Abby and Jessie to start packing what they could, as quickly as they could. While she was packing, Janet ask, "Are we really in danger?" "Yes, Janet, we are. Come on, that's enough stuff, let's go." "Whose after you, the police or the mob?" "Both." As they were going down the stairs to the car, Janet started to ask another question. "Not now, Janet, I'll explain once we are away from here."

Barry headed west. After about an hour, it was getting dark, but Barry didn't notice anyone following them. He figured they were safe enough for now. Janet was really upset. She figured it was about time Barry started explaining. "Ok, Barry, you're scaring the H…. out of me. Why are we running, and leaving everything behind?" "Well, Janet, there is no easy way to put this. I killed a man tonight." "You killed a man!" "Well, actually, three men." "What! You…. you……? Abby almost wet her pants and Jessie let out a scream. "It was self-defense, Janet." "You kill three men, and you're telling me each one was self-defense? Come on, Barry." "I'm telling you it was either them or me." Barry went on laying out all of the events of the day.

"So, there you have it. The whole story." "There isn't something you're not telling me, is there?" "What? How much more could I have gone through today? Don't you think that's enough?" "So now, half of Chicago wants your head on a platter." "That's about it. The cops want me for murder, although it wasn't murder, and the mob wants me for starting a war between the territories. And when the Boss discovers what else I did; he'll be after me also." "So, there is something you left out." "Well, yes, I still have today's receipts. I forgot to give them to the Boss." "So now, you are also a thief. How much money was it?" "A…… $25,000." "And you have it on you?" "It's in my jacket pocket." "Great. You will undoubtably go down in history as the most prolific crook there ever was." "I wouldn't go that far." "Let me see, you're a bootlegger, kill three men, start a mob war, and steal $25,000. All in one day. I'd say you're on your way. The day isn't over yet." "Come on, Janet." "Remember me saying, if you don't get out of this business, something was going to happen?"

It was getting toward midnight, so Barry pulled into a motel for the night. It looked pretty run down, but it would have to do. "We have to figure out where to go from here. We have to change our names and start over. Maybe we could find a small town in New Mexico or Arizona. What do you think, Janet?" "We could go north into Canada. We could get lost up there pretty easy." "That's a good idea. I never thought of that. I never heard of any of the boys working Canada. We'll head that way tomorrow."

The next morning, they found a restaurant, so they could have breakfast. While sitting at a table, Barry looked over and saw a newspaper on the table next to him. It was a Chicago newspaper, so Barry decided to see if there was anything about yesterdays excitement. Nothing on the front page. That's good. He quickly leafed through the pages. Nothing. He laid the paper down. Janet picked up the paper and looked through it while they were waiting for their food.

"Barry!" "What's wrong?" "Nothing, look at this ad." It was Albert Serban's ad. 'Need professional architect with much experience to design a castle in Rumania. Will pay all expenses. Want an American for this project. If interested, contact Kenneth Meyer, in Trenton, New Jersey.' It went on to give a phone number and address to contact.

"Wow! That's interesting." "You can't get much further away from Chicago than that." "Janet, I think you hit it. That's an architect's dream. We could start a new life there and not have to look over our shoulder all the time. I'm going to phone this guy, and hopefully we'll be on our way to Rumania. What do you think about that, Abby?" "I'll miss school and all my friends, but it sounds exciting." "Good. Now Jessie, you don't have to take this trip, if you don't want to. You can stay here in the States. But we would like to have you go along with us. It's going to be an adventure." "I have no job now, no place to live, and it sounds exciting to me also. Let's go."

When they got to Trenton, they looked up Kenneth Meyer. He explained everything to Barry and the family. This was not a temporary job. Barry would be on the job until the castle was finished. That could be up to five years or more. If Barry was good at his job, the word would get around and he would probably be offered other jobs in the area. Barry was on top of the world. What could go wrong?

They traveled by ship across the Atlantic, through the Mediterranean Sea, to Istanbul, Turkey. It was a good trip. Everyone enjoyed themselves. It was a real vacation for them. Barry felt the past was behind him now. They could start a new life, and they wouldn't have to change their names.

When they docked, they were to go to the train station, and take a train from Istanbul to Brasov in Rumania. In case you weren't aware, Brasov is where Dracula's castle is located today. But don't worry, he's been dead a long time. But take note, in 1935, and even today, a lot of Rumanians feel that vampires still exist, and they still take precautions against them.

But back to the story. The trip from Istanbul to Brasov is scheduled to be a 15-hour trip, Including stops at certain towns along the way. Unfortunately, Rumanian trains very rarely run on time. And despite what the old movies showed; trains did not speed along the countryside. At that time, trains in Rumania, only went 25 to 35 miles and hour. The stops at towns were never exact. Trains would sometimes sit at a station for an hour or more. Nobody seemed to know why. And you may be stopped out in the countryside for hours. Again, no one knew why. It's just the way things were.

After taking a taxi to the station, Barry and the family checked in. It was 10:00 A.M., but the train was not scheduled to leave until 11:00. They went ahead to the train and settled in to their compartment. Barry and Janet were in compartment 3E, and Abby and Jessie were in 3F. They were discussing their anticipation at living in a different country, and learning their culture. It was exciting. They heard the whistle blow a couple of times, indicating the train was getting ready to move. Barry was watching out the window at the crowd milling around. He noticed a man, who looked to be in his thirties, standing by one of the columns on the boarding dock. As the train started moving, the man quickly ran to the car in front of Barry's and hopped on. Barry's window was down, and as he watched the man get on the train; he saw movement out of the corner of his eye. He turned his head and saw another man, who seemed to be about the same age, run and jump on the car behind Barry's car. Barry's thought was, 'Why do people wait until the last second, then have to run to catch the train?'

So, the train was on its way. Destination, their new city and home. Life was good. And exciting. As the train is rolling along, the conductor comes by and checks the tickets, and passports. Everyone was told the first stop would be at the border of Bulgaria. Approximately 5 hours.

A couple of hours down the tracks, Barry suggested they go to the dinning car and get something to eat. As they sat down, Barry noticed the first man he saw running to get on the train, was sitting at the next table down from them. A couple of minutes later, the other man came in to the dinning car. He stood for a minute, looking around. The first man saw him, and abruptly got up from the table and left the dinning car. The other man sat down at a table and ordered something to eat. Barry noticed that the man who left, hadn't eaten his food. The man now sitting at the table, watched the other man leave, and then looked straight at Barry. 'Don't tell me I'm being followed. No body knows I'm in Turkey. I thought everything was behind me now.'

Barry and the family went back to their compartment. Barry didn't say anything about his thoughts. Maybe what he saw had nothing to do with him. The doors in each compartment had a glass window in them. They also had blinds in case you wanted privacy. As Barry was sitting there, contemplating, the first man walked past the compartment. As he did so, he sort of glanced in their compartment. Barry had enough of this. He went out in the hall to find out what was going on. The man went around the corner and through the door to the next car. By the time Barry got to the corner, the man was coming back toward him. As he approached, he tripped and fell against Barry. It took a few seconds for the man to regain his balance. "I'm so sorry, sir, are you alright. I apologize for my clumsiness." "It's alright, I'm fine.

Barry watched the man walk on and enter a compartment at the end of the car. 'That guy had a British accent. I can't imagine anyone in England caring anything about me. My imagination must have been running wild. Oh, well.' So, Barry felt better. He relaxed and went back to be with his family. They were enjoying their train ride, but they needed to get out and stretch their legs. Only, no stops until the border.

They were running behind schedule, and it was almost dark when they reached the border of Bulgaria. The border stop was not in a town. The only thing there was a building which housed the inspectors. No one was allowed off the train. The inspectors came aboard and checked everyone's tickets and passports. When they came to Barry's compartment, they were surprised to see Americans on board. "You are a long way from home. Are you here on holiday?" "No, sir. We are on our way to Brasov, Rumania. I am starting a new job there." "Interesting. What kind of job?" "I'm an architect." "Excellent. I hope you enjoy your trip and especially your new work."

It was getting late and everyone decided to try to get some sleep. As Barry took his suit jacket off, he felt something in one of the pockets. It was a gold cigarette case. "Why Barry, when did you start smoking?" "I didn't. I don't know where this came from." When he opened it up, he saw it was full of cigarettes. He was puzzled. Then he remembered the man who bumped into him. 'He must have slipped this in my pocket when he fell. But why? It couldn't have been an accident.' "I'll be back in a minute, Janet. I think I know who this belongs to."

Barry went down to the compartment where the man had entered. He knocked on the door. No answer. He knocked a couple of more times. Still no answer. Without thinking, he took hold of the door knob and turned it. The door opened. As the door opened, he saw why no one answered. The man was lying on the floor and there was a knife sticking in his chest. Barry quickly stepped in and closed the door. He checked for a pulse, there was none. Barry checked to see if there was any ID. He found a wallet. The man's name was Jonathan Drake. There was also a card that stated he was a British Agent.

All of a sudden, Barry didn't feel so good. He didn't know what was going on, but he did know that whatever it was, now he was involved. This gold case must fit into all this. Jonathan knew someone was on to him, so he passed the gold case to me, so whoever wanted it, wouldn't get it. So, I could be next on the list. Barry left everything as it was, flipped the lock on the door so it would lock when he closed the door. Barry made sure there was no one in the hall, then hurried back to his compartment.

Back in the compartment, Barry started inspecting the gold case very closely. "Barry, what's going on? Did you see the person who owns the case?" "A…. Yes, I saw him." "What did he say?" "Actually, he didn't say anything. He's dead." "What!" "Give me a few minutes, and I'll explain." Barry saw a thin line that indicated the back of the case opened also. But he couldn't get it to open. Then, on one edge of the case he spotted a small circular indention. When Barry pushed on it, the back opened. "Well, I'll be… Janet, look at this." Inside were three strips of microfilm. He took one out and held it up to the light. It showed pieces of paper with writing on them. But Barry was unable to make out anything.

"What is that, Barry?" "It's microfilm. It seems the dead man, Jonathan, slipped this in my pocket, which I didn't know at the time, to keep someone else from getting their hands on it."

"Why would he give it to you?" "I don't know, but he was a British Agent." "Oh, no! You can't get mixed up in this." "I already am. Whoever is after this, knows Jonathan didn't have it on him. He knows someone else has it, and he'll probably figure it out before long." "You have to tell who ever is in charge about this." "I intend to. But first I want to hide this case. I don't want it found on me." Barry slipped it under one of the seat cushions. Then went to find the head man.

Barry stopped a conductor and told him he had some very important information to tell whoever was in charge on the train. He was taken to the head conductor, Milo Alexia. "What can I do for you, Mr. ……?"

"Greene, Barry Greene." "What's so important, Mr. Greene?" "There is a dead man in compartment 3A." "A dead man." "Yeah, you know, not breathing, no pulse. That kind of dead man." "You're not joking, are you?" "No, I'm not." "Take me to him. You haven't told anyone else have you?" "Just my wife, but you needn't worry. She won't tell anyone." "Let's go."

When they got to compartment 3A, "The door is locked, how do you know there is a body in there?" "Because, when I left the compartment, I locked the door so no one else would get a surprise." Milo unlocked the door, and they went in. Milo knelt down and looked at the body. "Do you know this man?" "No, I don't know him, but I know who he is." "Well, who is he" "His name is Jonathan Drake. Oh, by the way, he is a British Agent." "He what! Why didn't you tell me?" "I just did." "Do you know who killed Mr. Drake?" "No, not really." "What does that mean?" "Well, I have a suspect. But I don't want to say until we have some authorities on board." "Very well, go back to your compartment, Mr. Greene, and please stay there. I will call ahead to Burgas and notify the proper authorities."

"The conductor is calling ahead for the police to meet us in Burgas." "How long will that be?" "I was told about 2 hours. That should be about 2:00 AM." "Barry, what are you going to do about the gold case?" "Nothing, right now. I think it's better not to say anything about it yet." "Well, I'm going to try to get some sleep. You need to do the same." "Sure, Babe, I'll try."

The train rolled into Burgas at 2:20 AM. Barry was sound asleep, when he thought he heard a banging noise in his head. As he opened his eyes, he saw that someone was banging on the door. He shook his head to try and clear his brain, and opened the door. "You are Barry Greene?" "Yes." "I'm Detective Nikola Anton with Burgas police. This is Jeremy Sloan with British Intelligence. I understand you found the body of Jonathan Drake in his compartment." "Yes, I did." "Did you know Mr. Drake?" "I didn't know him, but I met him briefly." "For what reason did you go to his compartment?" "We met in the hall, and when he passed me, he tripped and started to fall. I helped him regain his balance." "And?" "Well, I knew which compartment was his, and I decided to go down and check on him. I was afraid he might be ill or something." "And then what?" "I knocked on the door several times and received no answer. I was afraid he might have passed out, so I tried the door and it was unlocked. Then, I opened the door, and saw him lying on the floor with a knife in his chest." "Go on." "I found that he was dead, so I left and locked the door behind me. Then notified the conductor."

"Let's continue on. You knew he was a British Agent." "Not until I looked for an ID to see who the person was." "So that's all you can tell me about the murder?" "Yes, that's all for now. After I notified the conductor, I came back here and tried to get some sleep. The next thing I knew you were knocking on the door." "I see. May I call you Barry?" "Yes, please." "Barry, do you have any idea who might have done this?" "Let's just say, I have a suspicion." "I see you are American. Would you tell me why you are in Bulgaria?" "My family and I are on our way to Rumania. I was offered a job there." "Doing what?" "I'm an architect. I was hired to design a castle for an Albert Serban." "Ah, yes. I know Mr. Serban. He's a good man to work for. Barry, I'm certain you had nothing to do with this murder. You were just unfortunate to be in the wrong place at the wrong time. Thank you for your help. We are going to stay on the train and do our investigation. The train will get underway in a few minutes. Thank you for your help. If you think of anything else, please call on us." "Yes, sir, glad I could help."

"Barry, why didn't you tell them about the gold case? You know that has to be important." "Yes, it's very important, and that's why I didn't bring it up." "But the murderer probably left the train when we stopped." "No, he's still on board, and he'll stay on board." "How do you know?" "Because he still doesn't have what he came after, and he won't leave until gets it." "But you have it." "Bingo! He knows it's still on the train. He knows Jonathan didn't have it on him, which means Jonathan must have given it to someone else. Pretty soon he's going to figure out who that person is, if he doesn't already know. I'm sure he witnessed all this commotion. He's going to figure out that I'm his man." "Barry, don't do this. Your setting yourself up to get killed." "I have to do this. I'm already a target. I'm in this up to my neck, I don't have a choice."

Just as Barry nods off to sleep, he hears tapping on the door window. As he starts to get up, he sees a man standing there. 'Uh-oh, that's the other man in the dinning car. I guess this is it.' Barry opens the door, "Yes." "Sir, the Detective wants to see you. Please follow me." "Sure thing." They went about 4 compartments down. The man opened the door and motioned for Barry to enter. As Barry took a step forward, the man put his hand on Barry's back, and pushed him into the compartment. The man stepped in, closed the door, and locked it. As Barry was getting up from the floor, he looked up, and stared into the barrel of a gun. "Go ahead, get up." "Do you mind pointing that cannon a different direction. It might go off." "It won't go off unless I want it to, and if you play the game right, you'll be alright." "I'm not good at playing games. Suppose you tell me what we are playing." "It's called, you have something I want, and you're going to give it to me. Simple as that."

Barry was looking the situation over, but couldn't see any move he could make without getting killed in the process. "I don't know what you mean. If you want my wallet, go ahead and take it. It's not worth getting killed over. Other than that, I don't have anything that would interest you." "Don't play dumb, Mr. Greene. You know what I'm after." "What is this, 20 questions?" "Mr. Greene, hand over the gold… cigarette… case. Got it?" "No, I don't got it. I don't smoke." "Are you really that dense?" "Sometimes my wife thinks so." "I'm losing my patients, Mr. Greene. Mr. Drake didn't have the case on him or in his compartment. He must have handed it off to someone. Then I remembered as I was following him, I saw him fall against you, and that's when he passed it you." "Oh…. That gold case? I don't have it."

Barry took a step forward. "Hold it! Don't try anything. Move back against the wall and raise your hands real high." The man took a cylinder out of his pocket, and screwed it on the barrel of the gun. "Now, Mr. Greene, since you won't cooperate, I will try another tactic. This is a silencer, that way there is no noise when I pull the trigger. Now, each time I ask for the gold case, and you refuse, I'm going to shoot a different part of your anatomy." "I don't have the case on me." "I know that. Just tell me where it is. Simple. Huh?"

As Barry stepped back against the compartment wall, and raised his hands, one of his hands touched the emergency stop cord. "Now wait a minute. Let's talk this over." As Barry spoke, he slowly wrapped his fingers around the cord. "I'm through talking, Mr. Greene." At that moment, Barry pulled the cord as hard as he could. The train lurched forward as it tried to stop. The man lost his balance, and fell against the seats. Barry jumped. He landed on top of the man and grabbed for the gun. They started wrestling for the gun. Twice, during the struggle, the gun went off. A bullet went up through the ceiling, and one out through the door glass.

Just as that bullet went through the glass door, a woman was walking past the compartment. The bullet missed her nose by about 4 inches. She screamed so loud, that the man was startled, and stopped for just a couple seconds. That was all Barry needed. He hit the man square in the face. The man dropped the gun, and Barry grabbed the gun, and stood up. "Well, Mr. whoever you are. The table has turned. Now, don't do anything except breathe once in a while. I'm sure we will have plenty of company very soon. You're not the first person I've killed, so I won't hesitate."

It didn't take long. Detective Anton and Agent Sloan were coming down the hall, being led by the woman, who was still screaming. As they looked into the compartment, "Mr. Greene you have been a busy man since you got on this train. What do we have here?" "What we have here, is the man who killed Jonathan." Detective Anton searched the man for identification. "Well, well. What do you know? This is Hans Mueller, a member of the Gestapo in Germany. What do you have to say about this, Mr. Mueller?" "I will say nothing." "I didn't think you would. Mr. Sloan will take charge of you and you will be charged as a spy, but I'm sure you are already aware of that."

"Mr. Greene, is this the man you suspected?" "Yes." "Why didn't you let us know? We could have helped. You could have gotten yourself killed; you know?" "I came close, that's for sure. But I had to do this alone. You see, I have what he was looking for." "You have it! What is it?" "In a minute. He knew I had what he wanted. So, I knew he would come to me for it." "Well, you still took a chance." "Let's just say, I've had experience at taking care of myself." Mr. Sloan spoke up, "Mr. Greene, you have the item in question?" "Yes."

The woman was still standing there, taking this all in. She couldn't believe what she was watching. "I feel like I'm watching a movie."

Detective Anton, "Ma'am, let me take you down to the dinning room to the bar. You need a nice big shot of whisky. That will help your nerves. Maybe I'll have one myself."

After Sloan secured his prisoner, Barry took Agent Sloan back to his compartment. Janet was still asleep, but she was lying on the cushion the gold case was under. "Janet, wake up. Janet." "Are we there?" "No, you have to get up for a minute." "Ok." She was still half asleep. Barry reached under the cushion and pulled out the gold case. "This is the center of attraction." "A gold cigarette case?" "Yes, there is microfilm in the back of the case." "You opened it?" "Yes, just to make sure it wasn't just a normal cigarette case. After I saw the microfilm, I closed it up and put it under that cushion for safe keeping." "I really appreciate what you have done for us. Maybe we can make you an honorary agent." "No, thanks. I just want to get back to my drawing board. It's less dangerous."

Barry told Janet all that had happened the last couple of hours. "Barry, I swear, one of these days you're going to get yourself killed. You have to quit getting mixed up in these sorts of things." "Believe me, Janet, the next time I find a dead body, I'm going to run away as fast and as far as I can get." "Oh, Barry you're crazy, but I love you."

Maybe Barry and the family will make it to Brasov without anymore excitement. They will be able to settle down to a quiet, enjoyable family life. Barry will have a good job, good income and live a long life. Really?

Chapter 9

The train pulled into Brasov station right at 8:30 AM. As Barry was getting everyone's luggage together, a man approached Barry. "Are you the Greene family?" "Yes." "I am Mr. Serban's chauffer, Andriov. I will take you to Mr. Serban's residence. I will take your baggage for you." "Well, thank you Andriov. The way these trains run; how did you figure out what time to be here?" "We are used to their schedules."

Barry and his family were met at the door by the butler. They were ushered into Mr. Serban's office. Everyone was introduced. "Barry, I'm glad you accepted my offer. It will be an adventure. And I am sure you, and the family, will love it here in Rumania." "We are looking forward to it. Will we be staying close by here?" "No, I understand architects like quiet, so they can concentrate on their work." "Well, true, but not too quiet." "Perfect. I have leased a castle in Medias. I'm sure you will like it, and I thought it might give you inspiration living in a castle. It's just outside of the village. That way you will have your privacy, and still be able to mingle with the villagers and make friends." "It sounds exciting. When will we get to move in?" "I will take you there tomorrow. It's less than 50 miles away. It's an easy ride." Abby spoke up, "You mean we are going to live in a real castle, with a moat and all?" Albert laughed a little. "No, my dear, it's a real castle, but it doesn't have a moat. But I don't think you will be disappointed when you see the castle.

They stayed at a hotel that night. Early in the morning Albert came to get them and head for their new home. First, they stopped at the site where Albert wanted to build his castle. It was about 5 miles north of Brasov. It was 200 acres of beautiful rolling land. While Albert and Barry talked, the girls walked around some. They could not believe how beautiful Rumania was. There was also a beautiful view of the Transylvania Mountains, which were about 10 miles to the west. They were sure they were going to enjoy living here.

When they finally reached the castle at Medias, they couldn't believe their eyes. It was right out of a story book. They all went in and gave a quick look around. "Barry, I'm going to send an automobile out to you tomorrow. You can use it to travel back and forth to Brasov. That way if you need to go to the property to look over something, you will have it available. If I need you for anything, I will send word." "That's great, I'm anxious to get started."

I mentioned before, there are still no automobiles in the village. Everyone uses either horse and wagon or a bicycle. The streets aren't wide enough for automobiles, but, about a mile east of the castle, there is a dirt road, wide enough for 2 vehicles to pass one another. Off of this road is a single lane dirt road that leads to the castle.

Everyone started exploring the castle. Abby and Jessie picked out the bedrooms they wanted. When they were done exploring, they went to the kitchen to see if there was anything they could eat. "Well, thank you, Mr. Serban, there is enough food here to feed an army." Just then there was a knocking on the door. Barry went to see who it was. When he opened the door, there was a man and a woman standing there. The lady spoke first. "Mr. Greene, I am Violeta and this is my husband, Deniel. I am your housekeeper." "And I am going to take care of the grounds for you." "Well, welcome. Come in please." Barry introduced his family. "I take it you live in the village." "Yes, sir." "Excellent. We were about to fix something to eat." "Let me do that for you." "Thank you, Violeta." "Mr. Greene, I will go out to the shed, and see what I have to work with." "Very well Deniel."

"Janet, this office is perfect for me to work in." "This place is beautiful. I'm really going to enjoy living here. I can't wait to see the village and meet the people." "We'll do that tomorrow morning. It's really a different world here."

As everyone turned in that evening, Barry was in the bathroom, and Janet was turning the bed clothes down. As she walked around the end of the bed, in her bare feet, she suddenly stopped. She looked down and the carpet was wet where she was standing. She started toward the bathroom. "Barry! Barry! Come here. Quick." Barry hurried to the bedroom. "What's wrong?" "The carpet at the end of the bed is wet." "Wet? How could that be?" Janet showed Barry where the wet area was. "Well, where is this wet area?" Janet looked down. It was dry. "Barry, that carpet was wet! My feet are still wet." Barry reached down and touched Janet's foot. "Yes, your foot feels as though it was wet. Maybe you spilled water on your foot and didn't realize it." "I haven't had any water." "Well, don't worry about it, I'm sure there is a logical explanation. Let's go to bed, I'm tired."

Abby was already asleep in her room. Jessie was getting ready for bed, when suddenly the door to her balcony blew open and a strong gust of cold wind swept over Jessie. She felt like someone was in the room with her. She looked around, but nobody was there. A rocking chair started rocking back and forth. Jessie was unable to move. Just as quickly as it started, the rocking chair stopped rocking and the cold wind stopped. Jessie went out on the balcony; everything was quiet. She went back in and closed the door and locked it. Jessie didn't understand what just happened, but she knew she didn't like it. She didn't know whether to tell Barry about it, or not.

The next morning Barry and the family went down to the village. Like I said, the village hadn't changed much. There was a new generation, but there were still quit a few old timers left that remembered the last tenants of the castle. The Pub was still doing business. The owner was Emilian. He was 57, but through his years in the village, he knew all the history. The mayor was Constantine. He was 68 and he was well informed also. The constable was Remus. He was 32. He heard stories, but he thought most of it was old wife's tales. But he kept an open mind.

Barry and the family went into The Pub. It was quite crowded. Everyone gathered around and greeted them. Emilian spoke first, "I understand you are an architect and are working with Albert Serban."

"Yes, that's correct." "He's a good man, he'll treat you right." One of the old timers spoke up, "How do you like living in the castle?" "We all think it's great. It's a beautiful place." "Well, you tell me what you think of it, say, 6 months from now." The man gave a laugh. "What do you mean by that?" "Oh, nothing, Mr. Greene. Just talking." "Barry, don't listen to him. He doesn't make sense half of the time. You'll enjoy you're stay here." "We look forward to it."

Later that afternoon, Albert came to the castle. Albert brought some rough drawings and he and Barry spent the afternoon in the office discussing the design of Albert's castle.

The girls went out to tour the grounds. It was a fall day. Very nice. A good day for walking. "There is so much land. It would take 2 or 3 days to see all of it." "Well, Janet, we have plenty of time to explore." Standing in front of the castle, looking west, "Mother, look, you can see part of the village from here. There is the school house." "Yes, another couple of weeks and you'll be starting school. Are you anxious?" "In a way. It will be so different. But I'm sure I'll like it."

As they walked along to the east, "Janet, look over there. It looks like there is a pond over there. Or what used to be a pond. It doesn't have much water in it now." There were several pools of water in the pond, but is was mostly just mud. Abby let out a scream. "Mother, look, over by that log in the middle of the pond. There's a skeleton behind that log. Look at the bones of the hand on top of the log." Most of the skeleton was hidden behind the log, but they could see part of the skull and some of the ribs. Jessie put her hand to her mouth, "Oh, my gosh, Janet, that's a human skeleton." "It sure is. This castle has a long history. I'm sure that skeleton has been there for hundreds of years. The other day in the village, a man made a strange statement. He said, 'Tell me how you like the castle six months from now.' I think we better talk to Mr. Serban, and see if there is something we need to know."

As the girls went back to the castle, Albert and Barry were just wrapping things up. "Mr. Serban, what do you know about this castle? I mean it's history. Things that happened." "Not a whole lot, Janet. What do you want to know?" "Did you know there is a human skeleton lying in what used to be a pond, a few hundred yards from our front door?" "No, I didn't. But this castle has been here almost 350 years. It's hard to tell what all happened in the history of the castle. Every person, every house, every castle, has a history, and most of those have tragedy in their history." "Yes, I know you are right, but after a comment I heard in the village, and what I saw in that pond, I'm beginning to think there is more to this castle than we know about." "Come now, Janet, this is 1935, what happened in the past can't hurt you now." Hmmm… famous last words.

Months have passed. It is now 1936. Barry is making good progress on his design. Janet was asked if she would like to run the library. She accepted. Abby is in school. She has made a lot of friends and is doing well with her studies. Then, there is Jessie. She is 25. She married when she was 18, but 4 years later her husband was killed in an auto accident in Chicago. It was ruled as an accident, but Jessie wasn't so sure. She tried to get someone to check the car over and see if it was tampered with. No one was interested.

Jessie helped out in The Pub part time to earn some money. While working one evening, a young man, around Jessie's age, who had recently moved to the village, came in to The Pub. Jessie went over to ask him what he wanted. There was electricity in the air. They both smiled and just stared at each other. You can see where this is going. Anyway, she brought him what he wanted, and went back to work. She couldn't help looking his way every now and then. He seemed to be watching her also. Later, she went over to see if he needed anything else. "I do need something, if you don't mind?" "Sure, what is it?" "Your name." "I'm Jessie." "Jessie. How nice. I am Paul." After the introductions, Paul said he had to go, but he would like to see her later. That was fine with Jessie.

It is now fall of 1939. Barry is now 39, Janet, 35, Abby, 17. The last four years have been good for the Greene family and Jessie. Barry has completed the design of Albert's castle and construction has been going on for a little over a year. Barry has to divide his time between the construction site and the drawing board. Janet still runs the library and likes to help with planning festivals, and other public functions. Abby will graduate next year, and has a boyfriend, Sebastian Petran. Jessie married Paul last year. No children yet. Things are going well, but there are dark clouds gathering over Europe.

Barry gets a Bucharest newspaper once a week. Barry reads what's happening and its worrying him some. Barry and the villagers talk about what is going on, but they are just not sure what it means yet. But some of the villagers and Barry feel that war is near.

Germany has annexed Austria and invaded Czechoslovakia. Hitler is looking for an excuse to invade Poland. If he does, England and France will intervene and it will mean war. England has tried to be patient with Hitler, hoping he will stop this expansion. Hitler says he will stop, but he is just playing them. England and France have a pact with Poland, in case Poland is attacked, England and France will declare war on Germany.

On September 1st 1939, Germany invaded and ran roughshod over Poland. England and France had no choice but to help defend Poland. This was the beginning of WWll, which would be catastrophic for Europe, and the rest of the world, for the next 6 years. A lot was going on in Rumania, but it was far enough away that it did not really affect the village. The villagers went on as usual. Barry kept up with the news, but it had nothing to do with him, or his family. Life went on.

Then one day, Barry was in Brasov, working with Albert. It was getting late, and Barry was tired, so he headed back home. When Barry reached the castle, it was twilight, the sun was going down. As Barry went in the front door, he called out for Janet. He called again, still no answer. She wasn't down stairs, so he headed upstairs to the bedroom. Janet was lying on the floor. She was crying and her blouse was ripped. Barry knelt down to pick her up. Her lip was bleeding, there was a bruise on her cheek, and her eye was swollen. "My God, Janet, who did this? Janet!" He helped her up and laid her on the bed. "Janet, talk to me. What happened? Who did this?" Janet sat up in bed and just stared ahead. "Janet, you have to tell me. Do you know who did this?" Janet slowly shook her head, yes. Barry got her cleaned up and helped her change her clothes. Janet never spoke, just stared ahead. "Come on Janet, I'll take you down to the doctor and then go see Remus, the constable."

As they walked to the doctor's home, it was supper time and the streets were pretty empty. As they neared the doctor's house, Janet let out a scream. "There he is! That's him! He's the one!" On the other side of the street, about ½ block away, was a man walking. He looked to be about 50, had a beard and ruffled hair. His clothes looked wrinkled as though he had been wearing them several days, or more. Barry started walking across the street to intercept him. When Barry got to him, he grabbed the man and pulled him around behind a building. Barry mumbled something and started beating the man. The man didn't try to fight back. Barry hit him one last time, and the man fell. When he fell, he hit his head on a rock. Barry stared at him, then knelt down. "Oh, no! He's dead. I've killed him." Barry got up and looked around. He didn't see anyone, so he went back to Janet.

Janet was still standing where Barry left her. Still staring. Barry was a little panicky. He figured he better take Janet back to the castle and not say anything to anyone. When the body was found, he would just say he didn't know anything about it. He and Janet had been at the castle all evening.

As they headed back to the castle, a man came out of The Pub. Janet screamed, "That's him! He's the one who did this. That's him!" It hit Barry like a ton of bricks. Janet was in such a state of shock;she thought every man she saw was the one. She had no idea who really did it. "I just killed an innocent man. What am I going to do?" Barry hurried Janet back to the castle. Barry had a lot of thinking to do. His mind was reeling. He had to have time to think.

Barry helped Janet into bed. He got her something to help her sleep. When he went back down stairs, Abby was home. "Where is mom? Did she go to bed already?" "Yes, she wasn't feeling very well. She should be ok tomorrow." "I'll go up and say goodnight to her." "No! She is asleep. Don't bother her." "What's wrong? Is she alright?" "Yes, I just didn't want you to wake her."

The next morning, after Abby left for school, Barry went up to check on Janet. She was sitting on the edge of the bed. "Janet, how do feel this morning?" "I don't know. I think I was having a nightmare last night. But it's so hazy. I can't remember." Barry sat silent for a few minutes. "You don't remember yesterday?" Barry knew he would have to tell her about yesterday. When she looked in the mirror, she would probably remember anyway. "I'm so confused. I don't know what was real and what wasn't." "Janet, you were attacked yesterday." "I was?"

Suddenly she put her hand up to her face. She walked over to her mirror. When she saw her face, she let out a scream. "Oh, no! I remember now. It wasn't a dream." "No, Janet. It wasn't. Did you see who it was?" Janet was silent for a while. She was recalling. Slowly it was coming back to her. "Oh, Barry, I feel so ashamed. I'm so sorry, everything is a blur; I don't know who did this." Barry went over and put his arms around Janet. "Janet, it's not your fault. You didn't do anything wrong. You have nothing to feel sorry for. Everything will be alright. We will get past this. It will just take time.

Barry went into the village that afternoon. He was curious whether the dead man had been found yet. He went into The Pub. "Barry, did you hear what happened last night?" "No. What happened?" "A man's body was found this morning behind the barber shop." "Really, who was it?" "Nobody knows. He is a stranger." "What happened? A heart attack?" "We don't think so. More than likely he was drunk and fell. When he fell, he hit his head on a rock. It looks like that was what killed him." "Well, things like that happen." Barry had already decided he was not going to tell Janet about killing that man last night.

Time passed, and Janet was still not her old self. She was very quiet most of the time and she wouldn't leave the castle. Barry didn't push her. He let her heal at her own pace. She was replaced at the library. The villagers were told Janet was ill, and that it would take some time for here to heal. Jessie came to visit Janet as often as she could. Barry told her about Janet's attack, but left out the part about killing a man. Barry thought it best not to tell anyone about what happened. Jessie agreed.

It is now January, 1940. Barry's project with Albert's castle is being wrapped up. Barry's work is much admired and he has two other offers to design a castle. Abby is anxious to graduate in May. Abby and Sebastian are becoming very close, but Abby wants to go to college in Bucharest before she settles down with a family. Janet has gone into the village a few times with Barry. She is doing much better and talks a little more freely now.

The villagers are starting to get a little worried about Germany. Most of them feel that Europe is heading for a full-scale war. No one seems to be able to stop Hitler. The rumor is that Hitler has his eye on France. If that happens, everyone will be involved. Rumania is having its own problems. Russia has annexed part of Rumania and taken it over. Rumania is upset and instead of remaining neutral, they are leaning toward joining Germany and the axis powers.

One day as Barry is approaching the village, he sees a crowd of people in the street, in front of one of the houses. Barry goes up to the Mayor. "Constantine, what is going on? Why all the excitement?" Constantine pulls Barry aside. "Barry, someone murdered Bela Erner last night." "No. Do you know who did it?" "No idea. Mrs. Erner said that someone knocked on the door around 2:00 this morning. Bela got up to see who it was. A couple of minutes later, she heard him scream, and when she ran to the door, Bela was lying on the floor. He had been stabbed in the chest." "How horrible. What reason would anybody have to hurt Bela? He was a friendly, popular person." It's a mystery. Remus has a job on his hands trying to find out what happened.

When Barry went back to the castle, he did not tell Janet what had happened in town. He didn't think she could handle it after what she had been through. He was going to work at home today so he could be close to Janet. Janet's condition was such that Barry didn't want her left alone. Whenever Barry had to go anywhere, he made sure that Violeta and Deniel were with her.

Three weeks went by. No clue to who killed Bela. Barry was heavily into another design project. This one was closer to Medias. Barry was thankful for that. Janet was getting closer to her old self. She could even laugh now and then. She seemed more relax. But, every once in a while, Janet would have a day where she would be withdrawn. Abby still did not know the story of what happened to her mother, or why she was the way she was. She felt Barry was keeping something from her, but when she asked him what was going on, he told her not to worry, then changed the subject.

Then it happened again. Dana Barbu was stabbed during the middle of the night. Exact same story as Bela. Mrs. Barbu gave the same story. Again, no clue. The villagers were becoming frightened. Two random killings. No connection between the two. Or was there? Was the killer and outsider, or has someone in the village become deranged. Was there a reason for the killings or was someone just picking out someone to die?

Three nights later, there was a scream. The killer had struck again. This time it was Florin Goga. The same story. Remus and Barry were discussing the third killing. "Barry, what is going on here? I feel helpless. There is nothing to go on. Just three men all in their late 50's. No other connection." "Remus, what if there is some connection. Something in their past we don't know about?" "You might have something there. I think I'll go down to the library. There is a lot of past history down in the basement. I'll see if I can find out anything."

Three days went by. Everything was quiet. Remus was still searching, but nothing yet. The villagers were all talking among themselves. 'Why hasn't Remus found the person doing this? Who will be next? It might even be me.'

Remus found what he was looking for. He knew what was going on and who might possibly be behind this. He went up to the castle. "Remus, come in." "Barry. Janet, how are you feeling? We miss not seeing you down in the village." "Thank you for asking. Most of the time I feel pretty good. But I still have days that aren't so good." "Barry, I need to talk to you about……" "Wait! Let's go into my office. Janet, will you be alright?" "Yes, I think I'll go upstairs for a while."

In Barry's office. "Remus, I stopped you because I haven't told Janet anything about what's happening. She's not well and I thought it best not to say anything." "I understand." "So, what did you find out?" "I found that four men in the village have something in common, and it isn't good." "Oh, really. Go on." "It seems that 30 years ago four men attacked and raped an 18-year-old girl, named Flora Dimir. Three of them served 5 years in prison. The fourth served 3 years. He did not participate, but he was there. Three of those men are Bela Erner, Dana Barbu and Florin Goga." "Who was the fourth man?" "I haven't been able to find his name anywhere. It just talks about a fourth man who was there. The kicker is, 6 months after the incident, Flora committed suicide. Someone has decided that it's time for revenge." "Yes, but who? Does she have any family left?" "I don't know. Right after her death, the family moved away. No one knows where."

"Remus, you know what this means." "Yes, there is still a man in the village whose life is in danger." "Only, we don't know who he is. Whoever is killing these men, could be someone in the village, or it could be an outsider. Someone we don't know." "But there have been no strangers in town lately." "Maybe he is camping somewhere outside of town and no one has spotted him." "Regardless, I'm going to have to stay awake at nights and see if I can catch this person. The bad thing is I don't know who the target is. I can't watch everybody at once." "Well, good luck Remus. Thanks for filling me in. I wish there was something I could do. But I don't know what it would be."

Barry, Janet and Abby spent the evening together. Janet wanted to be able to go out and do things again. Maybe even go back to the library. Abby talked about going to college. She talked about majoring in medical science. She was interested in research. She wanted to find new ways to help treat people. It was getting late, so everyone went upstairs to retire. It was almost midnight.

Barry was sound asleep, when suddenly, he opened his eyes and sat up in bed. He got up and lit the candles. When he turned back around, Janet was not in her bed. Was she sleep walking? Barry walked out in the hall to the head of the stairs. Just then, the front door opened, Janet walked in, and closed the door. She had something in her hand, but Barry couldn't see what it was. She started walking toward the kitchen. It was as if she was in a trance. "Janet. Janet!" She did not answer, she just kept walking toward the kitchen. Barry followed her to the kitchen and stopped in the doorway.

Janet went over to the wash basin. She had her back to Barry, but he could see she was washing her hands, and whatever she held in her hand. She then walked over to the kitchen table and sat down. She just sat and stared. Barry walked over to the wash basin. It was blood red water. He then walked over to Janet, and sat down at the table next to her. She didn't move. She had both hands on the table, and between her hands, there was a huge knife.

"Janet. Janet. Where have you been? What did you do? Janet! Answer me." Janet answered him, but it was not her voice. "It... had to....be.... done."

"What had to be done?"

"They...... had....to pay."

"Janet! Look at me! What are you talking about? Answer me."

"They......ruined......my life."

"Did you kill those men in the village?"

"I......had to."

"Why?"

"She......told me......to."

"Janet! Who told you to?"

"Flori......told me. She......had......to have......revenge. They......had......to pay......for what.... they did."

"But why you?"

"I was......the first.... person.... she has......been able......to.... contact."

Barry could hardly believe what he was hearing. How could this be? What is happening? He couldn't think straight.

He was able to get Janet up to bed. He helped her lay down. As soon as she laid her head down, she went to sleep. Barry lay down in bed, but he couldn't sleep. He had to absorb all that he had just seen and heard. Was Flori really talking through Janet? Did Janet actually kill those men? How was he going to handle this situation? What would tomorrow be like? Would Janet remember? It was almost daylight. He dreaded facing the morning.

Barry managed to get a couple of hours of sleep. He was up at 8:30. He knew he had to talk to Remus, but not to tell him what he experienced last night. As he went down stairs, Violeta was opening the front door. Remus came in. "Barry, lets go in your office." "Sure, what's up?" Barry already had an idea of what Remus was going to tell him. "The fourth man was killed last night." "Oh, who was it?" "Josif Minea." "Josif. He was always the quiet one." "Yes, I was surprised." "I thought you were going to patrol the village all night. What happened?" "I was making rounds, and around 1:00, I suddenly felt so tired and sleepy. I couldn't keep my eyes open. It was as if I was sleep walking. I had to go back to the office. I fell asleep and the next thing I knew, it was daylight. Josif wasn't married and had no family. His body wasn't discovered until this morning."

Barry was not surprised. There was no doubt that somehow, Flori had used Janet for her revenge. "By the way, Barry, I forgot to tell you about Flori's funeral service." "Oh, what about it?" "Well, the family didn't want her put in the ground, so they buried her in a vault beneath the castle here." Barry came to his feet. "What?" His mind was reeling. Now he understood. "Barry! What's wrong?" "Oh......nothing. It was just a shock to hear that she was buried here. I had no idea."

So, that's how Flori was able to reach Janet. She has been with us the whole time. After Janet's attack, she must have been weak enough that Flori was able to enter and control her mind. Now the question is, who really killed those men? Janet or Flori?

Barry went upstairs. Janet was awake. "Janet, how do you feel this morning?" "I'm so tired. I don't know what is wrong with me." "Do you remember anything about last night?" "No, should I? Well, wait a minute. I had this terrible dream last night. It was almost a nightmare. But I can't remember any of it. All I know is It was frightening." "Well, it was just a dream and it is over now. I'm sure you won't have that dream anymore."

One thing was sure, Barry vowed that no one but he, would ever know what really happened concerning the killing of four men.

CHAPTER 10

May, 1940. Germany swept over Belgium, Luxembourg, and the Netherlands. Then, invaded France. Within a few weeks, France surrendered. Hitler was on a roll. Who was next? Hitler was determined to control all of Europe and England. He had also taken over the Nordic countries. He had a treaty with Russia, but he already had in mind to invade them also, in the near future. By this time, Rumania was supplying Germany with oil, grain and minerals. But there were no military soldiers actually involved in any fighting.

Barry didn't like what was happening, but it was not his war, at least not yet. Actually, life in the village went on as usual. The war was far away. No one seemed to worry too much. Barry was still designing castles. Abby had graduated and was staying in Bucharest, ready to start college. Janet was pretty much back to her old self. She was back at the library, and that helped. Barry had talked to Jessie about her and Paul moving into the castle. He thought Janet would do better with Jessie close to her. Paul rented out his house, and he and Jessie moved into the castle.

Jessie is pregnant. The doctor says it should come due in February. Everyone is excited. Jessie was worrying that she might be getting too old to have children. She is in good health, and so far, everything looks good. A lot of planning to do. They start thinking about making the bedroom next to theirs into a nursery. It has a door that connects both bedrooms.

As October starts, the weather gets nasty. It starts out with an ice storm, then turns into a blizzard. The village ends up with about 2 ½ feet of snow. The village is at a standstill. (At least they don't have to worry about power outages.)

The sun is shining, but the snow hasn't done much melting. Paul is getting cabin fever. He's feeling restless. He goes out to the kitchen to see if Violeta would make him a nice big sandwich. As he is waiting, he sees the door next to the stove. "Violeta, where does this door lead to?" "I don't really know, sir. I've never opened it." Paul opens the door. It sticks a little, but he gets it open. He sees a flight of stairs leading down to, wherever. He gets some candles and starts down the stairs. He reaches the bottom and sees that the room is filled with burial vaults. He walks around and reads several of the names. Some of the names he has heard of. As he continues on, he notices another door. Might as well see where it leads. He tries to open the door, but it won't open. He puts the candles down and uses both hands to pull on the door. Finally, it breaks lose and slowly opens. He picks up the candles and goes in, and he can't believe what he sees. There is a dungeon and several torture tools spread around.

Paul has heard about such things, but he has never seen them. He never really believed they existed. He wondered if Barry knew about this room. Paul went back upstairs, and found Barry in his office. "Barry, do you know what is beneath this castle?" "Yes, there is a burial room where past residences are buried. Why?" "That's all you know?" "Yeah, what else would there be?" "Come with me. I have a surprise for you." "Ok."

As they went into the vault room, "This is the first time I've been down here, Paul. I knew it was here, but I had no desire to see it." "Well, you haven't seen anything yet. Follow me." Paul opened the door to the torture room and went in. Barry stopped short. "What in the world is this room, Paul?" "It is a torture room and back there is a dungeon. Right out of a horror story." "You mean they actually used this room to torture people and keep them locked up?" "I would assume that they really did. Remember, this castle was built right around 1600." "Yes, I remember Albert said the castle was about 350 years old when we moved here."

As they went back into the vault room, Barry stopped to look at some of the names. As he walked along, he suddenly stopped. There it was, 'Flori Dimir'. He looked at it for a few seconds. "Paul, lets get out of here."

Barry and Paul didn't say anything to the girls. But Barry's mind was saying, 'How many other people buried down there had a reason for vengeance?' What Barry had just seen was starting to worry him. Why was that other room down there? What kind of stories could it tell? He had heard of haunted castles, but were he, and his family living in one? The incident with Flori, the skeleton in the pond. Barry thought it might be wise to look into the history of this castle.

As so often happens, Barry had other things to think about. The history of the castle was pushed to the back of Barry's mind. He had plenty of time to pursue that later. Right now, the weather was the big problem. The sun had been out several days now, but the temperature never made it above the mid 30's. It was hard to keep the castle warm enough. The villagers pretty much agreed, this was the worst winter in about 30 years. All anyone could do was wait it out.

By the middle of November, the temperature was averaging in the upper 40's, and the snow was melting pretty quick. But with melting snow, comes mud. You just can't win. At least people were able to get out and around. Barry was slightly behind in his present project because he hadn't been able to go out to the building site. Jessie was doing fine with her pregnancy. Janet helped her a lot. Janet seemed to be in a good place now. She laughed a lot and seemed to have more energy. Things were good.

February, 1941 rolled around and Jessie was getting anxious. The time was close. The last couple of months, Jessie had been having considerable pain off and on. The doctor said everything seemed to be ok. Nothing to worry about. Jessie was bed ridden now. The doctor checked on her every day. The baby could come at any time now, therefore, the doctor had his nurse stay with Jessie 24 hours a day.

The time was here. It was 11:48 PM. Janet hurried into the village to get the doctor. Meanwhile the nurse and Violeta attended to Jessie. Janet banged on the doctor's door. She kept pounding on the door, but no one answered. Janet was ready to panic. Then the door opened.

"Doctor, it's time. Jessie is in labor." "Alright, you go on back, I'll get dressed and be right there."

Babies don't go by a clock, and sometimes they don't wait for the doctor. This baby decided he had waited long enough. The nurse and Violeta delivered the baby before the doctor made his appearance. As the baby was born, the downstairs clock chimed 12 times. Midnight. It was a boy. When the doctor got there, he checked the baby out. It was a fine-looking boy; plenty of dark hair. He was a fine healthy boy.

The doctor gave the baby back to Jessie. She held him close to her and just watched him. She was amazed. Jessie and Paul had already decided that if it was a boy, his name would be Daniel. Everyone except the nurse, decided to go down stairs and let Jessie rest. As they started to leave, suddenly as Jessie was looking at Daniel, she let out a scream. Everyone ran back to the bed. Jessie looked at the doctor, then back at the baby. Janet ask, "Jessie what's wrong? Why did you scream?" "I don't know, I thought I saw something, but it's alright now. Nothing is wrong." What made Jessie scream? As she was looking at Daniel, his eyes suddenly turned black. When she screamed, and looked back at Daniel, his eyes were normal. Jessie was sure her eyes were playing tricks on her. Paul smiled, "It's ok, Jessie, everything will be fine. You'll see."

June of 1941. Germany invades Russia. Rumania wants back what Russia took from them, so the Rumanian military join Germany in the invasion. There are German troops in Rumania now, pushing Russia back out of Rumanian. The war is now in Medias' back yard, so to speak. Barry does not worry too much about the situation. Being that, Barry and his family are Americans, he doesn't think the Germans will bother them, mainly because America is not involved in the war. But he knows deep down, it probably won't be too long before America gets involved. If so, he doesn't know how it will affect the Greene family.

It is summer time. Little Daniel is 5 months old. He appears to be very healthy. Getting bigger. Barry and Janet are enjoying their little nephew. Abby came home for a month. She starts back to school in August. Medias is expanding their library. Adding new books. It keeps Janet busy, and she likes it. Barry has two more projects pending. Everyone is happy.

It is Monday, December 7th, 1941, 8:00 PM. This means it is December 7th 1941, 8:00 AM Sunday in Pearl Harbor, Hawaii. Japan has attacked Pearl Harbor and is destroying the base and sinking our Battle ships and any other navy vessel they can find. America has been forced to enter WWII against Japan and Germany. Now, Barry is concerned because a German Battalion has gathered about 5 miles east of the castle. Will Barry and his family be rounded up, and sent to a concentration camp? Maybe they will leave them alone since they have been living here for 6 years. This is their home now.

The Germans now occupy most of Rumania. They say they are just building up the troop strength for the big push into Russia. But as time goes by, Rumania becomes more under the control of the Germans. First there is a curfew of 10:00 PM. Newspapers are censored. Group assemblies are forbidden. This is because there is an underground movement of people that would rather die than live under Nazi rule. They use sabotage and harassment to fight the Germans.

This is mainly in the populated areas. Medias and small villages are usually not subjected to this treatment. Life in Medias continues pretty much the same. Once in a while a few Germans come into the village from the battalion east of the castle. So far, they have not caused any trouble, although the villagers do not like them. They have heard stories. The soldiers have seen the castle, but they don't pay much attention to it. None of them have visited the castle.

Barry and the family don't go into the village, if they know soldiers are there. Barry wants to keep a low profile. Not get involved. It seems like more soldiers infiltrate every day. They are not easy going and cordial any more. They want to be waited on and treat the villagers like slaves. They confiscate belongings of the villagers and some even go after the girls of the village. Life is becoming harsh.

Barry is working in his office, and hears the front door open and close. He goes out to see what is going on. There is a soldier standing in the hallway. "What do you think you are doing, walking into my house without being invited?" The soldier says nothing, but walks toward the stairs. He stops and points toward the upstairs, saying in German, "What is up there?" Barry doesn't speak German, but he points toward the front door, "Out. Leave." The soldier turns and starts up the stairs.

Barry walks over and grabs the man by the arm. The soldier turns and knocks Barry down, then points his rifle at him. Barry puts his hands up as if to say 'OK, ok.' The soldier goes up the stairs. Barry gets up and follows him.

The soldier looks in the rooms. He opens a bedroom door and sees Jessie standing there with Daniel in her arms. The soldier smiles and starts toward Jessie. Jessie lets out a scream, "Stay away from me!" The soldier starts laughing and continues toward her. Barry yells, "Stop. Stay away from her." Jessie holds Daniel closer to her. She looks down at Daniel, and it happens again. Daniel's eyes turn black. At that instant, the soldier grabs his chest, gets a strange look on his face, and collapses to the floor.

Barry runs over to him. "He's dead." Jessie looks down at Daniel. His eyes are normal. She doesn't say anything, but she sure has a sense about what just happened. She holds Daniel tightly against her. As Jessie walks over and looks down at the soldier, Paul runs in. "What happened? I heard a scream." "It's alright, Paul, this soldier was about to attack Jessie, and all of a sudden, he just keeled over. He's dead." "How?" "I don't know. He acted as if he was having a heart attack. But he's too young to have a heart attack." Paul replied, "Maybe." Paul turned to Jessie, "Do not worry, Jessie, you will always be protected." Jessie didn't say anything, but she had a puzzled look on her face. What did Paul mean by that?

"Well, Paul, we have a dead German on our hands. We better figure our what to do." "If we tell the Germans we have a dead soldier here, we'll probably end up in front of a firing squad." "I Think you are right. It would be hard to explain. The safest thing to do is take him down to the vault room and put him in one of the empty vaults." "Right. If anyone comes looking for him, we'll say he was here and left, and we don't know where went." "You grab one end and I'll grab the other." Hmmm. Bodies keep piling up down in that vault room. I wonder how many more it can handle?

When Janet came home, Barry told her what happened. "I would say you did the right thing. These Germans are becoming like animals. Today, down in the village, an officer was harassing a woman. When her husband came over and grabbed the officer's arm, the officer pulled his gun and shot him, just like it was nothing." "I'm afraid things are only going to get worse. We will have to be careful of everything we do. We've been lucky so far."

In 1942, the German and Rumanian armies have pushed deep into Russian territory. They are pushing toward Stalingrad. The Germans still occupy most of Rumania. Things are only getting worse. If anyone is deemed breaking any 'German laws', they are sent to Poland to a concentration camp. Everyone is scared to death. Barry has seen instances where someone was arrested simply because their neighbor or someone didn't like them. The neighbor would make up a story of something that person did or said against Germany, and that person would simply disappear.

A German soldier was found dead behind a building in some bushes. He had been beaten to death. When the commanding officer, Major Holtz, was notified about the soldier, he decided the village would pay for this soldier's death. He did not doubt that one of the villagers was responsible. Now, Major Holtz was a short, heavy man. He wore rather thick glasses. He had no sense of humor. He was a 'by the book' officer. He was a strict officer and could be very mean, and brutal when angry.

That afternoon, the Major entered The Pub. "One of you people in the village has murdered one of my soldiers. I intend to find out who that person was. I want the word spread that I want that person. He will be punished. You have one hour for that person to step forward. If he does not come forward in that hour, the whole village will be punished. One hour!"

Everyone knew who that person was, but they were not going to talk. They would take whatever comes their way. Last night at The Pub, the soldier was drunk, and went after a man's wife. He tried to force himself on her, and she fought him. The soldier hit the woman with his fist and started tearing her blouse off of her. Just then the woman's husband came in the door. He had left for a few minutes to get something from home. As he entered The Pub, he saw what was happening. He ran over, turned the soldier around and hit him, hard enough to knock him down. As the soldier got up, he came at the man. The man grabbed the soldier's arm and twisted it behind his back and pushed him out the back door. Well, you know what the result was.

The hour went by and the people in The Pub had never even made an effort to spread the word. Exactly one hour later, the Major entered The Pub. "Well, I take it you have the man I'm looking for." No one even bothered to look at the Major. "Did you hear me? Where is the man I want?" No one said a word. "Very well." The Major left. About 10 minutes later he reentered The Pub. He had four soldiers with him. "Since you will not tell me who this person is, I will have to get nasty." He pointed to a man about 2 feet away from him. "You, stand over by that wall." He picked 10 men to stand next to the wall. "I will give you just 2 minutes, to divulge this mans name. If you do not, you 10 men will be taken outside, put before a firing squad, and shot."

There was a huge gasp. No one saw that coming. There was a lot of mumbling, but no one said anything. Now the man who did kill the soldier was among the ten. Unfortunately, Paul was also in the group. Now, the guilty man started to make a move to step forward, but the man of each side of him, stopped him from moving. The man broke lose, stepped forward, and said, "I am that man." Just as suddenly, Paul stepped forward, "No, I am the one." One after the other, all ten men stepped forward, claiming to be the man. Then the other men standing around started shouting that they were the one. The Major was so angry, he was red in the face. "Take these ten men out, and line them up. Now!"

By this time, Barry, Janet and Jessie were notified what was happening in the village. The three of them ran down to the village; they arrived as the men were being lined up. Jessie saw Paul and screamed. She started running toward Paul, two soldiers cut her off. Barry and Janet put their arms around Jessie and tried to calm her down. She looked down at Daniel and then at Paul. She was crying unconsolably. The Major ordered, "Ready." The line of soldiers cocked their weapons. "Aim." The rifles went to shoulder position. "Fire!" Every soldier pulled the trigger on his rifle. Nothing! Not a single rifle fired. There was only a loud click.

The Major yelled out, "I said, Fire!" Everyone said they pulled the trigger and nothing happened. "Alright, we'll do it again." Nothing happened again. Jessie was smiling now. Without even looking at Daniel, she knew what was happening. The Major wasn't going to give up. He personally inspected each rifle. He could find no reason for them not firing. "Reload and this time make it count." For the third time, none of the rifles fired.

Barry stepped forward. "Major, I think this has gone far enough. You are putting these men through hell every time those triggers are pulled. Stop this nonsense and free those ten men. Obviously, they are not meant to die yet." "Mr. Greene, I am in command here, not you. You do not tell me how to do my job. But, as you said, evidently these men were not meant to die yet. They will be freed."

Back at the castle, Jessie decides it's time to find out what is going on. "Paul, you and I have to talk. In private." "Sure, lets go up to our bed room." As Paul closed the door, "What is it you want to talk about?" "Paul, something has been going on for some time now, and I want to know what you might know about it." "Ok. What is going on?" "Paul, Daniel has some kind of power, and he knows just when to use it." "What are you talking about?" "Those guns misfiring was no accident." "And?" "Daniel kept those guns from firing." "Jessie, that's crazy." "No, it isn't. A 20-year-old soldier, apparently died of a heart attack, just as he was going to attack me. Twenty-year old's don't have heart attacks and die." "Jessie, those two incidents have nothing to do with Daniel." "One thing I haven't told you yet." "Oh, what?" "Each time I was holding Daniel, and his eyes turned black, just before those two incidents. Then afterword his eyes were normal." "That can't be. Jessie, are you sure your eyes weren't playing tricks on you.? You just thought his eyes changed?" "No, Paul. Remember when I first saw Daniel, I screamed?" "Yeah, I seem to remember." "That was when I first saw his eyes change." "Jessie, I think you need some rest. I'll tell you what. Let's take a few days and go up into the mountains. We'll enjoy the scenery and relax for a while. What do you say?"

Daniel is now 1 ½ years old. He is walking some now and he is talking some. One word he has learned is, 'No.' And naturally he uses it quite a bit. Jessie and Paul hire a coach, and a driver, and head for the mountains. This is Daniel's first time away from the village. Jessie is wondering how Daniel will react being away from home for a week or so.

They have been traveling for four days now, stopping in villages or inns overnight. They are enjoying the peace and quiet, and the beauty of the mountains. Daniel has been taking it all in. He seems to be enjoying this trip. They are getting quite high up in the mountains now. Jessie sees a castle way up on a hill. "Paul, look, there is a huge castle up there. It is beautiful, but at the same time, it rather frightens me." "Yes. It is the Stefan castle. I believe it has been vacant for some decades now. There is quite a legend about it." "Tell me about it." "Oh, I don't put much stock in it. The rumor is, that about 300 some odd years ago there was a Count Stefan who owned the castle, and he was said to be a vampire. He wandered around at night looking for young maidens. The legend says he actually terrorized Medias for a while. That's where he was eventually destroyed." "That sounds exciting. Can we go look at the castle?" "It's probably deserted." "That's alright, we can at least look around. I would like to see where this 'vampire' lived."

Paul gave in. They started toward the castle. While Paul was telling his story, Jessie noticed that Daniel just stared at Paul, as though he was taking it all in. Anyway, as they traveled up the lane to the castle, the horses started becoming jittery. Like something was frightening them. There was something strange about the trees and forest. The trees were bare, as if they were dead. It was very dreary, and there was only about an hour of sun left.

As the horses pulled up in front of the castle, a young man, who appeared to be in his 20's, came up to the coach. "Can I help you people?" "Forgive me. I thought the castle was vacant. My wife saw it from a distance and wanted to get a closer look at it." "I see. Well, the castle is occupied, but you may come in. It's getting dark. The Count would be happy for you to spend the night. Please come in. We have room for the coachman also." "I hate to intrude." "Nonsense, the Count will be glad to meet your wife…. And you. Oh, you have a little one. We don't see many children here."

As they entered the castle, Jessie was amazed. It was beautiful. Although, Jessie and Paul were not aware, but the interior of the castle had not changed in the 300 years. "The Count will be down soon, then we will have dinner. Please make yourself comfortable. I will return shortly." As the young man left the room, a tall slim woman, dressed in black, came in. She had long black hair that came clear down her back. Her face was rather long and shallow. She talked with a slow, distinct voice. "Welcome to our home. I am Viorica. We don't see many strangers here." "My wife, Jessie, saw the castle and wanted to come up and look at it. I'm sorry for the intrusion, I thought the castle was vacant." "Oh, it's no intrusion. We are happy to see some new b.... Ah faces. We don't get much news from the outside world. Perhaps after dinner, you can inform us as to what is happening beyond our castle." "We would be glad to. Although it is not very good news."

Just then, a man came walking down the stairs. He was tall and thin also. He had dark hair combed back, with greying on the sides. He was dressed in black, wearing a cape. He appeared to be in his mid-50's, but somehow he seemed older than that. He had a strong deep voice. "Welcome, I am Count Yorga Stefan, you have met my wife?" "Yes. We have been talking." The young man came in and announced that dinner was ready. They went into the huge dinning area. The same long table was there. The paintings were the same. Of course, Paul and Jessie did not know this.

As they were dinning, Jessie noticed that Daniel kept watching the Count. It was as though he was seeing something that Jessie or Paul didn't see. Well, Daniel was at an inquisitive age. He was probably fascinated by the way the Count was dressed. "I didn't know the castle was occupied, otherwise we would not have intruded." "Nonsense, we are happy to have you as our guest. We will have an interesting evening together. You will see."

After dinner everyone went to the living room. "So, how long have you lived here?" "Viorica and I moved here about 30 years ago. The castle has been in the family a few hundred years. I ran across the deed one day and we decided to move into the castle." "Interesting. I'm glad we came here. It's been a pleasure to meet you." "Well, thank you. Now, tell us what is going on in the outside world.

Paul and Jessie told them what was happening, and how bad it is. They talked for several hours. It was getting late. Daniel had fallen asleep, and Janet said she was very tired and was ready to turn in. "Viorica will show you to your rooms. I do my work at night, so I won't be seeing you off tomorrow. So, goodnight, and have a safe trip." Viorica took them upstairs. She put Jessie and Daniel in one room and Paul in the adjoining room, with a common door. Janet placed Daniel in the bed, then got ready herself. She decided to leave a candle burning in case Daniel woke up during the night.

During the night, Jessie suddenly felt cold air. She opened her eyes. The candle had gone out. She felt someone was in the room. She thought she saw the shadow of someone moving about. The full moon was shinning in the doors to the balcony. She looked over and Daniel was standing beside the bed, staring at the balcony. Jessie walked over to the balcony doors. One on them was open about a foot or so. She closed the door and went back to Daniel. She picked him up. He pointed toward the balcony. "What do you see, Daniel? Are you looking at the moon? It's very bright, isn't it? Daniel just pointed. Janet put him back in bed, and lay back down, wondering if she had been dreaming.

The next morning everyone had breakfast. As they were getting ready to leave, the Count walked in. "Good morning everyone. I have not gone to bed yet, so I thought I would wait to see you off. Have a safe trip to wherever you are going next." "Thank you, Count. Thank you for your hospitality." "It was a pleasure."

So, they were back on the road again. Jessie told Paul about her experience last night. Paul said it was probably just a dream. "Maybe, but I am so tired today, I can hardly move." "I think we've had a good trip. Maybe it's time to head back home." "It's been exciting, but I'm ready to head back, also."

Paul and Jessie are going back home. They are unaware of what has been happening in Medias. Things have been moving quickly and they are about to be jolted back to reality.

Chapter 11

While Paul and Jessie were away; in Medias, events were happening continually. The Major was watching the villagers very closely. He did not trust any of them. He had to be very strict with them. They had to fear him. He was afraid if given the chance, they might rebel. He decided to move his command post and staff into the village, and he knew the perfect place. The castle. So, he volunteered two soldiers and headed for the castle.

"Well, Major, what brings you to my castle?" The Major told the two soldiers to remain outside next to the door. "Mr. Greene, may I come in?" "Well, alright. What is it you want to see me about?" "About your castle." "Oh, what about it?" "Well, you know your country is at war with us." "I'm well aware of that." "Well, I could make you and your family prisoners of war, and put you in a POW camp. But you don't really cause much trouble, and you keep to yourselves and do your work. Therefore, we will not bother you. But I am going to make this my command post." "Ahhh…. Are you asking me, or telling me?" "It doesn't matter, I am making this my command post, and that's that." Barry thought for a moment. Then he put his arm around the Major's back and started walking him toward his office. "Now, Major, let's talk this over." "Nothing to talk about." As they approached the office door, Barry let his arm slowly drop down the Major's back. Then he grabbed the Luger out of the Major's holster, pointed it at him, and stepped back a couple of steps.

The Major jumped and turned toward Barry. "What's the idea? What do you think you are doing? You will be shot for this!" "I.... don't think so." "If you throw me out of here, I will destroy you and your whole family." "No, you won't." "What are you planning on doing?" "You told me that I could have been your prisoner." "Yes, and you soon will be now. I will send all of you to Warsaw." "No, because you are my prisoner, and you will spend the rest of the war in my prisoner of war camp." "You are joking. But you are not very funny. Now, give me my gun back and we will forget this incident happened. Yes?" "No. You will please come with me." Barry took the Major into the kitchen and started down the stairs to the vault room.

"What do you intend to do, bury me alive in one of your vaults?" "No, Major, we wouldn't be that cruel. See that door over on that wall? Open it." As the Major opened the door, he stopped short. "What is this room?" "It is where you are going to remain as my prisoner, until the war is over." "You can't do that." "Yes, I can. First, I have the gun. Second, since we are war with each other, your soldiers take American prisoners, and you are my German prisoner. Simple." "I will die down here." "No, I promise you will be well taken care of. You will be fed every day. As a matter of fact, you will probably have it better here, than what our American prisoners have it, in your camps." "People will be looking for me. They know I came to see you. They will find me, and that will be the end of you, and your family. You know two soldiers came with me. How are you going to explain my disappearance?" "Have no fear, I have that figured out. It will be very easy." Barry locked the Major in the dungeon.

Barry went back upstairs to find Deniel. He explained to Deniel and Violeta what was going on. Deniel and Violeta both hated the Germans because of their treatment of the villagers. They weren't too happy about being in charge of the Major, but they agreed to do it. Barry then went to the front door. The two soldiers were still standing outside the door. "The Major has agreed to stay and have lunch with us. He said you may go back to wherever it is you go." Barry hoped they understood what he was saying. The two soldiers looked at each other, shrugged their shoulders and walked away. Now, when anyone comes to question Barry about the Major, he will have the perfect response.

Barry told Janet, Jessie and Paul what transpired. They had been standing at the head of the stairs; therefore, they had heard most of it. Janet thought it was ironic, "The Major has been treating the villagers, and us, as though we were the prisoners, now, he is the prisoner." There was some mild laughter. Jessie noticed Daniel was smiling. Her thought, 'This is getting scary. I am sure that no matter what, Daniel always knows what is going on. Why won't Paul believe me?'

It didn't take long for the Major to be missed. The next afternoon, there was a loud banging on the front door. As Barry opened the door, there was and officer and two soldiers facing him. "I am Captain Karl Meyer." He then pushed his way in. "Oh, why don't you come on in?" "I did. I understand Major Holtz was here to see you yesterday morning." "Yes, he was here." "The Major has not been seen since he came in here. Do you happen to know where the Major went afterward?" "No, he decided to stay and have lunch with us. He told the soldiers who were with him to go back." "Back where?" "I don't know. Where do they usually go?" The Captain ignored that comment. "I think maybe we will search the castle for him." "Now wait a minute, you pushed your way in here, I didn't invite you, and you are not going to search my home." "Who do you think you are talking to?" "I don't know, you tell me." "I don't like your attitude, Mr. Greene." "And I don't like you barging in and making demands." Is this Captain going to end up keeping the Major company?

"Alright, Mr. Greene, I could have you arrested, but, if you say the Major left after you had lunch, I will take you at your word, for now." "Why, thank you Captain. As I said, you will not find the Major here." "Very well." The Captain and his crew, turned and left the castle. Just then Deniel came in the hallway. "I suppose you heard?" "Yes, that was a close one, Mr. Greene, and I don't think he believed you." "I don't either. I going to have to be very careful. He will probably have someone watching me all the time now. Probably all of us." Janet came in. "I hope we are not getting in too deep, Barry. These people are dangerous. One mistake and we'll be standing up against a wall." "If I stopped being rude to them, and became to cooperative, then they would be suspicious."

By August of 1942, the Battalion outside of Medias is gone. The German and Rumania troops are fighting to capture Stalingrad. The

Battalion was called up as reserve for the fight. In the next couple of months, the Germans and Rumanians will occupy Stalingrad, but at great cost.

The Germans have left Medias. Everyone is breathing easier. Things are getting back to where they should be. Now, about the Major. There are no Germans around Medias, but Germans still occupy Rumania. Barry feels that the Major must remain where he is for now. The Major is really treated very well. At this point he is given the weekly newspaper to read. Everyday, weather allowing, he is allowed to walk around the grounds outside, with Deniel watching him. Deniel carries the Major's luger, just in case the Major decides to do something foolish. They actually let him have dinner with them each evening. The Major and Barry talk quite a bit. They seem at ease with other. They are starting to understand each other. They certainly have their differences, but they listen to each other.

Barry has discovered that the Major always follows his orders, but he doesn't always agree with them. As a matter of he doesn't think Germany can win the war. Not since the Americans have entered. He thinks Hitler is crazy, and totally underestimates the American military. He thinks it won't be long before America invades the continent and when they do, Germany will never be able to stop them. There are many officers that feel the same way, but if their thoughts were known, they would be executed. "Mr. Greene, I actually feel safer here with you than up at the front. I am sure if I was with my battalion right now, a bullet would surely find me."

One morning, Deniel goes down to let the Major come upstairs. The Major is white as a sheet. "Why, Major, you look as though you saw a ghost." "No. No, but I heard them. I must see Mr. Greene." "You heard ghosts?" Deniel laughed a little. "Did you talk back to them?" "Don't be funny, get me out of here." The two of them went up stairs to find Barry. "Mr. Greene, this man says there are ghosts down there. He heard them talking." "Yes, yes. There were many of them." "Major, did you see them?" "No. I just heard them talking." "What were they saying?" "All kinds of things. I couldn't really make out much of it. But they sounded angry." Barry was getting a little worried. He knew the Major could be telling the truth. He knew from experience that the

Major could very well have heard something. "Now, Major, you may have been dreaming or you just thought you heard voices." "I know what I heard." "There are air vents down there. Maybe you just heard the wind blowing through those vents."

That evening, Paul went with Deniel to lock up the Major. The Major was begging for them not to lock him up tonight. He was shaking terribly. "Major, if it will make you feel better, I'll sit with you for a couple of hours. Deniel, you can go on upstairs." "But it was well after midnight when I heard the voices." "Alright, I'll go up and get some things, and camp out on the floor tonight. How's that?" "Yes, please."

Paul and the Major talk for a while, then Paul made a place for him to sleep. Everything was quiet for a while. Then, about 2:00 AM, a terrific storm developed. Extremely high winds and what seemed like continuous lightening and thunder. A deluge of rain. It woke Barry and Janet up. The doors to the balcony had blown open. Rain was coming in. Barry hurried over and tried to close the doors. The wind was so strong, Barry had a hard time getting them closed. Once he got them closed, he locked them. Then, just as quickly as the storm started, it stopped. Everything was calm and quiet.

The next morning, the sky was blue and the sun was shining brightly. Paul hadn't come upstairs yet, so Barry went down to wake him up. As he entered, Paul was still sound asleep. It appeared the Major was also. Barry shook Paul. Paul was having a hard time waking up. "Barry, I feel like I've been drugged. I have never slept that sound before. I can hardly keep my eyes open." "You didn't hear that storm last night?" "I don't remember hearing anything." "Well, our prisoner hasn't woken up yet either." Barry went over and unlocked the cell. As he stepped in the cell, he stopped. "Paul, come here!" The Major's face was horribly contorted. His mouth was wide open and blood had been running from his ears and his nose. "What in the world happened? He was fine last night when we went to sleep." Barry looked closely at the Major. "Well, he could have had a brain hemorrhage, but that look on his face. It's as though he was frightened to death." "Maybe he saw one of the ghosts he heard the other night." Barry didn't laugh or question Paul. He knew very well that could be the answer. But why the Major? Barry didn't say anything to Paul.

Another one for the vault room. The way bodies keep piling up, what will Barry do if they run out of vaults? He'll have to start his own cemetery.

Remember Janet telling Barry about the officer that shot a man in the village after the man tried to keep the officer from harassing his wife? Well, that officer was the Major. If you remember back a few hundred years ago, a man named Vidor. Vidor was a rather evil person. It turns out that the man the Major shot was a descendant of Vidor. Remember, Vidor is a resident in the vault room. Was Vidor responsible for the Major's death, or did the Major just die from a brain hemorrhage, which people do die from once in a while?

That afternoon, Paul went back down stairs. Something puzzled him. When he was looking around the torture room last night, he thought, something didn't fit. As he walked around the room, he suddenly saw what was different. There were four corners to the room, but one corner was different. At one corner there were two brick walls, that extended into the room. Why the extension? Was there something behind those brick walls? Paul went over to study them. He could tell the brick walls were put in long after the original walls were built. Was there something behind there? There is no use asking Barry, he didn't even know this room was here. Paul was curious enough, he thought he might come down sometime, and break some of the bricks loose, and find out what was behind them.

In the fall of '42, the German and Rumanian armies captured Stalingrad. But by January '43, the Russians had surrounded Stalingrad and recaptured the town. Germany and Rumania together lost 200,000 soldiers. Of that number 100,000 were prisoners of war. By April of '43, the Allies were bombing Rumania. Mainly the oil fields at Ploiesti, which is just a few miles north of Bucharest.

Abby was far enough away from the bombing that she was not in harms way. Next month she would be coming home for a few days, before resuming her classes. She needed a rest. The medical science classes were very intense and there was so much to remember. She and Sebastian were looking forward to spending some time in the village. She had heard the Germans had left the village. She was glad of that.

If the Germans had still been there, she considering staying on campus instead of going home.

In the summer of '43 in Medias, the war seemed far away. There were festivals, family picnics, and The Pub was doing a booming business. Abby was home again. She spent a lot of time getting to know Daniel. He seemed to like Abby a lot. Everyone was so happy, Barry forgot about the Major and Paul forgot about the brick walls down stairs.

Abby and Daniel go out for a walk. Daniel likes to walk around the grounds. Abby usually holds Daniel's hand when they walk, but today he wanted to walk on his own. They were walking on a path that lead out from the back of the castle. After a while, Abby feels they have walked far enough. She tells Daniel that its time to head back. Daniel doesn't want to. He takes Abby's hand and tries to pull her on further. "Alright Daniel, we'll go on a little way, but we have to be getting back to the castle." They go through a small wooded area. Then, the ground starts becoming rather rocky.

Abby tells Daniel to come back and hold her hand, she's afraid he might fall. But Daniel keeps walking faster. Abby almost has to run to keep up with him. Suddenly Daniel stops and looks down at something. As Abby reaches Daniel, she looks down also. She tenses up. She is not quite sure what she is looking at. They are standing at the edge of a cliff, and down below is a canyon. What Daniel is looking at, and what Abby can't quite believe, is a dead tree, with what is left of a skeleton lodged in the branches. The leg bones and the bones of one arm are on the ground.

What ever history this place has, it must have been a place of death and tragedy. As she is looking down, she see's the sun reflecting off something shinny. She tells Daniel to stay where he is, she is going down to see where the sun's reflection is coming from. She walks along the edge until she sees a path that leads down to the bottom. It's a little tricky, but she manages. As she looks around the bottom of the tree, she see's what she is looking for. She picks it up. It is a gold ring with a black stone in it. In the stone, is a coat of arms insignia. She puts the ring on. She feels chills and her body tingles for a few seconds. The ring is beautiful. She likes it.

As Abby makes her way back up to the top, she shows the ring to Daniel. He stares at the ring, touches it and smiles. "Well, Daniel, we better get back to the castle, it is getting close to dinner time." As they walk away, a strong, cool wind comes up. There is thunder in the distance, and the dead tree sways in the wind. More bones fall to the ground.

Abby shows Barry the ring. "Where, on earth, did you find that ring?" "Way back behind the castle. There is a canyon there, and a dead tree with the bones of a skeleton in it. This was lying on the ground under the tree." "A skeleton in a tree? How could that happen?" "It's at the bottom of a cliff. Evidently someone fell off the cliff and landed in the tree." "I suppose. That ring and design look familiar. Like I've seen it somewhere before. I just can't remember." "It looks like a man's ring, but I might wear it for a while. Maybe I'll give it to Sebastian."

By the fall of '43, Russia has started pushing the German and Rumanian armies back toward Rumania. Abby and Sebastian have gone back to school. When Abby left for school, she put the gold ring in her jewelry box. When she took the ring off, she felt that tingling feeling again. She had been having dreams while wearing the ring. She could see the figure of a man, only the face was blurry. She could not tell who it was, just that he was dressed in black. She was wondering if it had something to do with the ring, and now she was curious as to who it belonged to. But that would have to wait. School was the important thing right now.

In April of '44, Russia was pushing closer to Rumania. That month the Allies bombed Bucharest. Their target was industrial plants, and they did destroy several plants, but unfortunately, they didn't always hit what they were aiming for. Such was the case of one young pilot, who had not flown any missions yet. He released his bomb much too soon. It hit the dormitory where Sebastian was visiting Abby. The bomb actually landed just outside the building, but it destroyed the whole outside wall of the building. Abby and Sebastian were in a room on the opposite side of the building, but it collapsed one wall and the ceiling of the room. Abby and Sebastian were buried under the rubble.

Abby was stunned, but eventually able to get herself free from the rubble. Unfortunately, her leg was broken. The pain was terrible and the shin bone was protruding from her leg. She called for Sebastian, but he didn't answer. When she got herself free, she looked around to try and see where Sebastian was. She saw his arm sticking out from part of a wall that had fallen on him. She crawled over to where he was. She called to him, but he didn't answer. She took hold of his wrist. She couldn't feel any pulse. Just then someone came running in room, saw the situation and ran over to lift that part of the wall off Sebastian. He could only lift it so far, but Abby was able to pull Sebastian out from under it. It took all her strength and her leg pained her so, but she did it. Abby screamed. Sebastian was dead. He wasn't breathing and there was no pulse. Abby became hysterical. She lost the person she loved. If only she could bring him back to life. There should be something that could be done to put life back in him.

The man picked Abby up and carried her to the hospital on campus. That dormitory was the only area damaged. Two men and a woman were killed. Twelve people were injured, four of them critical. There weren't any classes that day, most of the people from the dormitory had gone into town. The doctor checked Abby over. Some scrapes and bruises. The main injury was Abby's leg. The bone had to be set back where it belonged, and the wound sewn up. Abby had to be put out because of the pain involved. When Abby came to, the doctor came in to talk to her. "Abby, everything went well. You'll be in a cast for at least six weeks. You will have a scar on your leg. But, Abby, when that bone broke, it splintered some and you lost a few hundredths of a millimeter of bone. This means when the bone fuses together and heals, that leg will be a fraction shorter than your other one. You will have a slight limp for the rest of your life. But it should not interfere with anything you want or need to do. You can live a normal life." Abby heard what the doctor was saying, but the only thing she could think about was Sebastian. She could worry about her leg later. What was she going to do without Sebastian?

Abby was able to keep up with her classes. Even though she was in a wheel chair for a while, her classmates helped her as much as they could. Now Abby focused totally on her studies. She even went to the library and took out other books on medical science. She had a purpose now, and that was the most important thing in her life.

June 6th, 1944. United States and her allies have successively pulled off the largest invasion in modern history. The D-Day invasion of France; and now they are starting to drive the Germans back toward Germany. August '44, Russia has pushed the German and Rumanian army deep into Rumania. It's obvious the Axis is losing this particular battle. Rumania doesn't like being on the losing side, so they sign an armistice with the Allies and are placed under Russian occupation as a puppet state. Rumania then declares war on Germany.

Since the Germans invaded Rumania, they have occupied Brasov as a headquarters, and have terrorized the town. They have taken thousands of men, women, and children from Brasov, and put them in concentration camps, so that the officers and soldiers could take over their houses. Since Albert's castle is a few miles outside of town, he hasn't been bothered too often. But he is very disturbed about what is happening to his Brasov. He is waiting for the day the Germans are run out of town. When that time comes, he vows to go in, and help drive them out.

He doesn't have to wait long. In September, working with the Allies, the Rumanian army attacks Brasov to drive the Germans out. Albert hears about the attack and decides to help. He goes in and puts his old uniform on, although, it used to fit better than it does now. He attaches a sword to his hip, and grabs his old rifle. Just then Florenta walks in the room. "Albert! What in the world do you think you are going to do?" "I'm going down and help take back Brasov. They will need my help." "You old fool, your 76 years old. You can't even make it out the door without sitting down to rest. By the time you make it to town, it will all be over. Our boys will do alright without your help." Albert stood there, for a moment, shaking his head. "Oh, I know, Florenta, your right. I just wanted to do my part." "Dear Albert, sit down and I will fix you some tea."

The Rumanian army along side the Russians continued to push the Germans westward out of Rumania. The Rumanian army continued to fight along with the Russians in Hungary, Yugoslavia and Czechoslovakia until the war ended in May of 1945.

Back in Medias, and other small villages, the end of the war was welcomed, but nothing changed. Everything continued as usual. Barry is 45 now. Janet 41. Abby is 23 and has one more year of college. She spends the majority of her time studying. She has a goal now. She studies everything she can find, about the body. What the purpose of each body part is, how it functions and how the body regenerates. What does it take to keep the body functioning, and if it is possible to restart the body after it stops functioning? At this point in time, many strides have been made in medical science, but there is still so much unknown.

Daniel is just over 4 years old. He is rather quiet. He actually seems a little more advanced for his age. He still gets into trouble once in a while. Nothing serious. He is a very curious person. He seems to study everyone and everything. It's like he is trying to figure out what makes people tick.

Jessie and Daniel go into town to get something from the bakery. As they walk along, a man driving a horse and wagon, pass them. Just as the horse approaches Jessie and Daniel, it suddenly starts rising up on its hind legs, and snorting. The horse goes wild and starts running as fast as it can. The horse breaks loose from the wagon and it tips over throwing the man out of it. The man is not hurt too seriously. He manages to get up and looks at his wagon. There's not too much damage that it cannot be fixed. But he is going to have to find his horse. He looks at Jessie and Daniel and tries to figure out what just happened. Neither Jessie or Daniel even looked at the horse. Jessie ask the man if he was alright. He said he was, so Jessie and Daniel walked on into the village.

As Jessie is looking around the bakery, Daniel stays right with her. A woman and her son, who is about the same age as Daniel, come into the bakery. As the woman looks around, the boy starts wondering around. He starts running around the store. As he makes a turn, he runs into Daniel and knocks him down. Daniel gets up and steps toward the boy and just stares at him. The boy sees Daniel's eyes turn black. The boy screams and runs clear out of the store and heads home, leaving his mother standing there. "What just happened? Why did my son scream and run out? What did you do to him?" "Daniel didn't do anything to your son. Your son was running and knocked Daniel down. Daniel just got up and stood there. He didn't do anything." "Something had to scare him. But I'm sorry about what happened. I will give my son a good talking to when I get home." "Don't be too hard on him. He was just being a little boy."

When Jessie got back, she called to Paul. "Paul, come upstairs with me and Daniel. We have something to discuss." "I'll be up in a few minutes." "You will come up now! This is important." "Ok, ok." When they got upstairs Jessie was shaking. "Ok, Jessie, what's so important? Why are you shaking? Is something wrong?" "Yes, there is something terribly wrong, and I want answers." "Slow down, Jessie. Stay calm and we will sit down and talk this out. What ever it is that has you so upset."

Jessie told Paul about the two incidents that morning. "Why is that so upsetting? Strange things happen every day. Why is this so special?" "Paul, you don't get it. A 20-year-old dies of a supposed heart attack. Six rifles don't fire after three tries, and now this morning." "And?" "And! Don't you get it? Paul, I think you know more than what you are telling me." "Jessie, I don't know what you are talking about." "There is something special about Daniel. I don't know, whether it is good or bad. But I am going to take him to a doctor, or someone, who can explain what is happening to, or with my son." "That's ridiculous, Jessie, there is nothing special about Daniel." "Then, what did you mean, when you told me, I would always be protected? By whom, Daniel?" "It was just a statement, nothing uncanny about that." "Yes, there is. You keep giving excuses, but you know what is going on, and I am going to find out, one way or another."

"Alright, Jessie, I'll explain everything. Hear me out, and try to understand." "Alright, but this better be good." "Just be patient with me. It started many years before I met you. I started worrying about becoming old. I couldn't stand the thought of being old, ugly and alone. I became obsessed with the thought. I became desperate. I would do anything to stop that from happening. Then something happened. You haven't noticed in the years we have been married; I haven't aged any. I look the same as I did ten years ago. No one in the village has even noticed." "Paul. What are you telling me?"

"Jessie........., I made a deal with the devil." "You what?" "The devil came to me......" "The devil came to you! What do you mean....? 'The devil came to you'?" "I didn't see him. He didn't come to me in person. I could hear him in my mind." "I see. And?" "He said I could keep my youth, if I did something for him." "And, what would that be?" "He wanted a child. So, if I gave him a child, I would never grow old." "Oh, my God...... Your telling me, I gave birth to a son of the Devil? That he is part of Satan? That he is Evil incarnate? Oh, Paul, how could you?" Daniel is watching, and smiling. "Jessie, listen to me. He is your son; he will protect you and me." "Paul, you are as evil as the Devil himself. I will not raise the son of Satan. To know that I gave birth to him, makes me sick to my stomach. He must be destroyed. And you...... Stay away from me and don't ever touch me again." Daniel is not smiling anymore.

Jessie turns, and leaves the room, to go down stairs and tell Barry what is happening. As she reaches the head of the stairs, she suddenly loses her balance, and falls down the flight of stairs. Barry was standing in the hall when Jessie fell. He had heard them yelling, but couldn't make out what they were talking about. Barry ran over to Jessie. He lifted her up in his arms. She was still alive. She started whispering something. Barry leaned closer to her, so he could hear what she was saying. "Daniel...... must be......destroyed. He......is the son......of Satan. Paul made....... a deal......with the Devil. Daniel's...... eyes." Jessie breathed her last breath. Barry sat with Jessie in his arms. Janet rushed into the room just then. "Barry, what happened? Jessie......" "Janet, Jessie fell down the stairs. She's gone." "Oh, Barry, no......" She knelt down next to Barry. Then Paul came out of the room upstairs. "What happened?" "It's Jessie, she fell down the stairs." Paul ran down the stairs to Jessie. "Is she alright?" "No, Paul, she's dead." "I told her to be careful going down the stairs." Barry looked at Paul. Why would Paul warn her this time? She goes up and down those stairs several times a day. Jessie was a careful person. Why was Paul so calm? What did Jessie's last words mean?

Chapter 12

After the funeral, Jessie was placed in a vault in the vault room. Janet was very disturbed. She just couldn't believe Jessie could be that careless. After Jessie's fall down the stairs, Barry carefully checked out the stairs and the head of the stairs. The stairs and landing were all wood. No carpeting. Everything was smooth, no cracks. There was nothing slippery on the steps or the head of the stairs.

Barry didn't tell Janet what Jessie's last words were. He was still trying to figure out what she meant. It didn't make sense. Did Jessie know what she was saying? Knowing what he had observed in the past, he decided to keep and eye on Paul, and Daniel. He also thought, now was the time to check out the history of this castle.

Paul decided it was time to move back to the village since Jessie was gone. He had no tie to the castle now. Barry tried to talk Paul into staying at the castle; he had good living conditions, and he was still part of the family. "I wish you would reconsider and stay with us here. We get along fine, and we will be able to watch Daniel grow. He's going to be a fine boy and we want to be close to him." "I don't know, Barry, I don't want to be in the way. You and Janet need your privacy. Daniel will still be part of your life." "Nonsense. We have our privacy. We can watch Daniel when ever you have to go somewhere. Besides, you and I have seen some strange things in this castle, and you never know when I might need you again." "Alright, Barry, we'll stay, at least for a while." Barry felt relieved. He needed them close, so he could watch them. He wasn't totally convinced that anything was wrong, but something in the back of his brain told him, stay alert.

Barry went down to the library. He told Janet he wanted to go down in the basement, and see if he could find any history of the castle. "What brought this on?" "Oh, I'm just curious. I've been thinking about it for a while. I'm sure some interesting things have happened at the castle in the past. We've seen a few ourselves." "Ok. I've never been down in the basement, but you can go down and look around. Let me know if you find anything interesting."

Barry got a set of candles and headed for the basement. It was pretty messy. Cobwebs all over everything. It looked as if it had been 100 years or more since anyone had been down here. With the exception of Remus when he was checking on the story of Flori. He slowly walked around the basement to get the layout. He didn't really know where to start, but there were plenty of papers, maps and books to look through. Barry picked a random spot and started looking through all the paperwork.

After a couple of hours, Barry ran across a stack of papers bound together. He started reading the top page. There were a few sentences, that told Barry he had found something of interest. The package contained 30 pages of print. After he read the pages, he took a few minutes to digest what he had just read. It was the report on the witch hunt. That didn't surprise him too much. He knew about the witch stories back in the medieval days. What did grab his attention, was the fact that the suspected witches were held in the dungeon below the castle. Searching further, Barry came across a packet that had a name on the front sheet. Count Stefan. Barry recognized that name right away. He was astounded at what he read. The terror he brought on Medias and his destruction. So, the Count met his demise right here on the castle grounds. Then Barry remembered, 'Wait a minute. Abby was talking about bones near a tree. I didn't really think too much about it. After all, there are someone's skeleton in a pond somewhere here. But from what I am reading, Abby must have found the Count's skeleton. Then that ring she has must be the Count's.' Barry searched through some more of the papers. On one of the pages was a drawing of a coat of arms. It was the same as what was on the ring. He must notify Abby that the ring could be dangerous.

Barry found a box that was sealed. Inside were rolled up papers, like scrolls. They were very yellowed and fragile. Some of the writing had almost faded away. He carefully unrolled the papers. Some of them were so old, he couldn't open them without them crumbling. He could tell they were like a diary the mayor kept of happenings in the village. One page caught his eye. The writing was pretty faded, but when he held it close to the candles, he could make out some of it. What he could read, disturbed him. All he could make out, was that a little girl, that lived in the castle, had drowned in the pond, and many years later, her brother disappeared, with no explanation. Barry could not make out a date that this occurred, but that was enough for him. He didn't need any more history of the castle. With what he had found, and what Janet and he had witnessed in the past months, there seemed to be something evil about the castle.

That evening, as Barry and Janet were relaxing, Barry felt that Janet should know what he found out that morning. "Janet, you know I was searching the history of the castle this morning?" "Oh, yes. Did you find anything interesting?" "That's putting it mildly. I think you should know what I found this morning, and it's not going to be pretty." "Really? Go on." Barry proceeded to tell Janet what he found out about the castle. "So that, plus what we have experienced since we have been here, doesn't make for a very happy home." "Oh, Barry, I feel chills going through me. That is a horrible history. Is this castle haunted?" "Haunted or evil. Either choice isn't good." "Maybe we should have stayed in Chicago." "I don't know. Back in Chicago, I would either have a tombstone at my head or serving a life prison term. I think I can cope with this."

"Barry...... Maybe we should move away from here. Maybe to Brasov or even Bucharest. We may not be safe here." "I don't want to move to a big city. I like it here at the village. Since we know strange things happen here, we must just be aware of what goes on around us. Besides, there's never a dull moment." "Yes, well, I should have known from your past in Chicago, that you do like adventure. Alright, I'm with you." "Good. I knew you would be." One reason Barry wanted to stay where they were, is to keep an eye on Paul and Daniel. But he did not tell Janet that reason. Jessie's words kept going through Barry's mind. What she said was hard to believe, but he couldn't dismiss it.

The next couple of years were pretty calm. In Medias the war was pretty much forgotten. Albert passed away at the age of 78. His body just gave out. Barry and Janet were doing well. Barry noticed nothing too outstanding about Paul or Daniel. But times were good and Daniel was still pretty young. Abby was 25 now, and had a good job in Bucharest's largest hospital. The hospital had a huge lab for research, and that's where Abby worked. She was very happy there.

Then in the fall of 1949, things started to change. Daniel was approaching 9. He was slightly bigger that the other kids his age. He was quiet. He usually had a group of friends around him. He never seemed to get into trouble, but he wasn't a very good student. He had absolutely no interest in the school or school work. He was close to failing. Paul didn't seem concerned, he just shrugged it off. Barry tried to talk to Daniel about his school work, but Daniel always sidestepped the subject. He didn't want to talk about it. He had other things to do.

The principle called Daniel into his office. "Daniel, you know you are failing, and I know you have been missing from class several times. This must stop. You must participate in school and bring your grades up to a passing level." "I don't like school. It's a waste of my time." "Well, Daniel, that's no excuse. If you don't want to do the work, and help yourself, I will have to talk to your father about putting you in a special school for children like you. Do you understand?" "Yes, may I go now?" "Very well. Go on."

The next morning, as the principle unlocked the door, and went into his office, he was shocked. Papers were thrown all over the floor, everything on his desk was on the floor. Chairs overturned, there were pictures drawn all over the walls, done with crayons. He went to check the classrooms. Some of them were a mess also. He was livid. He had a good idea who did this, and they were going to pay for this vandalism.

There was a knock at the castle door. Violeta answered the door. "Is Paul here? I need to talk to him." "Yes. Come in." Paul came to the hallway and Barry was just coming out of his office. They both greeted the principle. "There will be no school today." Paul, "Oh, what happened?" "Someone broke into the school last night, and made a mess of my office, and some of the classrooms. May I see Daniel, please?" "Why do......? You think Daniel had something to do with this?" Barry spoke up, "Wait a minute. Daniel didn't have anything to do with what happened at the school. He was here all evening." "And how do you know that?" "Because, he told me about your talk with him yesterday. He wanted me to help him with his books so he could start improving his grades. We spent the evening working on his books, until he went to bed." "He didn't get up during the night and leave?" "No, I was up most of the night working. He never left the castle." "I'm sorry. I apologize. I know Daniel is not one who gets into trouble very often. Because of our conversation yesterday......" "I understand. It's alright, don't let it worry you. Did you report it to Remus?" "Yes, he's down at the school now. I think I'll go check with him."

A few nights later, Remus is sleeping in the jail, when he is awakened by a loud noise. He runs to the door and steps outside, but doesn't see anyone around. Doesn't hear anyone running. As he scans the area, he notices the bakery window has been broken. He goes over to investigate, and sees a good size rock inside on the floor. The baker lives in the back of the bakery. He comes out of the back the same time Remus approaches the window. "What is going on Remus?" "I wish I knew. I don't understand. In all the time I've been here, we have never had a vandalism problem. Now there has been two instances in just a few days."

It didn't take long for the word to spread. No one could understand why. This was a peaceful village. Everyone got along. Especially since the war had ended. Remus did not have a clue. He did not know where to start. He would talk to the school kids again, but he didn't think that would get anywhere. The school kids all said they didn't know anything about what was going on. Even Daniel had a solid alibi. Barry said Daniel never left the castle after he came home from school that afternoon.

A few days later, a strange thing happened. There was no school that day, and Paul was working, so Barry took Daniel down to the library to find some books that would help Daniel with his studies. As they are walking toward the library, two men across the street are talking.

Omor and Uta were good friends, and they were just talking small talk, about the weather and so forth. Daniel suddenly stopped and turned toward the men. Suddenly the two men started arguing. Next thing, they were fighting. Then Uta pulled a knife and stabbed Omor in the stomach. Barry looked down at Daniel, and for a moment he thought he saw something in Daniel's eyes. It was so quick; Barry couldn't be sure, but Jessie's words came back to Barry, 'Daniel's eyes.' Barry didn't say anything, but wheels were turning.

Someone had already run to get Remus. By the time Remus got there, it was all over. Uta was holding a knife in one hand, and Omor was lying on the street dead. "Uta, what happened?" "I don't know. We were just talking, and then, all at once, we were arguing and began fighting. I don't remember pulling my knife. Why would I do such a thing? We were good friends. We never once had an argument. What is happening?" Uta started to break down. "Take it easy, Uta, I don't understand this either, but it happened. Can a couple of you guys take Omor over to the doctor's office? Uta, I have to place you under arrest. Please come with me."

Back at the castle, Barry went into his office. He started to write down strange events that occurred since Daniel was born. Then he went back to see if there was anything to link Daniel with those occurrences. Daniel was present at the firing squad incident. He was also present when the young German collapsed. He was sure Daniel had nothing to do with the Major. But what about the school, and the baker's window? He couldn't have had anything to do with that, because he was here when those things happened. Why would any of the school kids suddenly become vandals; they never did anything like that before. Unless. Had Daniel taken over the will of some of the children? Was he controlling them? There wasn't enough to go on yet. It's too early to confront Daniel. Barry needed to confide in Janet what Jessie told him, and what Barry had observed. She needed to watch Daniel also.

That evening, up in their bedroom, where they would be alone, "Janet, sit down, I have some things to tell you. This is not going to be easy, and you must keep an open mind." "Ok, you sound so serious." "I am. First about Jessie." "What about her?" "Janet...... I don't think her falling was an accident." "What! What do you mean?" "Jessie told me some things before she died." "Why didn't you tell me?" "Because what she told me, was so bizarre, I had to have time to sort it out. Well, what Jessie told me, and what I have observed, leads me to believe what she said. It concerns Paul and Daniel." "Ok, so…. What?" "Janet, Jessie said that Paul made a deal with the Devil, and Daniel is a son of Satan." "Are you serious? You're out of your mind. My sister gives birth to a son of the Devil? I don't believe that for one minute. Where did you come up with this?" "Those were Jessie's last words. I have gone over some things that have happened in the past, since Daniel was born, and I observed something this morning that convinces me Jessie was right."

"Remember the firing squad, when the rifles wouldn't fire, and Paul was one of those against the wall? Remember the young German soldier that collapsed and died when he tried to attack Jessie?" "Yes, but that doesn't prove anything. Daniel was only a baby. I'm sure there is a logical explanation for those things." "This morning, I took Daniel into the village, to go to the library. On the way, he suddenly stopped, and stared at two men who were talking. Suddenly they started arguing, and one of the men pulled a knife, and stabbed the other one." "So?" "The last words from Jessie were, 'Watch Daniel's eyes.' Janet, I looked down at Daniel just then. Just for a fraction of a second, his eyes were black. The next second they were normal." "Barry, it's hard to believe what you are telling me, but you are scaring me."

"Janet, I also believe Daniel is responsible for the vandalism that's going on." "He couldn't have done those things. He never leaves the castle at night." "He doesn't have to. I think he is controlling some of the kids at school. He has them under a spell, and they do what ever Daniel tells them." "Barry, do you know how ridiculous this story sounds. This sounds like something right out of a horror movie." "That may be, but I believe this is real. Janet, I need your help." "How?" "Just watch Daniel. Don't make it obvious, just see if you notice anything out of the ordinary." "Alright, but I still think you need to see a head doctor."

Barry went to see Remus. "Remus, there are three students I would like you to bring to your office this afternoon." "Oh? Who are these students, and why?" "They are Alexandru, Darius and Gabriel. I think they are responsible for the vandalism, and I think I have a way to make them confess." "It's against the law to beat up kids, you know." "You know I wouldn't do that." "I know. But how do you expect to get them to confess?" "You bring them here, then watch." "What excuse do I use to get them here?" "That's up to you. I'm sure you can handle it."

With everyone gathered together, Barry looks at each of the three boys. Darius speaks up, "Are we in trouble?" "Not really. I just need some information from you." This time Gabriel speaks up, "About what?" "You three are close friends of Daniels, is that correct?" "Yes." "Does he ever boss you, or tell you to do things you didn't want to do?" Alexandru, "No. He's nice to us. We're good friends." "Boys, think back, now. Did Daniel ever talk about something, and then later, you felt like you were being pulled to do something. Say, late at night." The boys all looked at each other. Darius spoke up, "Are we going to be in trouble?" "No. Anything you say here is just between us. It will never leave this room." The boys all looked at each other again. Then Gabriel whispered something to the other two, and they shook their head up and down. Then Gabriel spoke, "Mr. Greene, we do have something to tell you. But don't get mad." "No, no, Gabriel, Remus and I won't get mad at you. We just want to try to understand what is happening."

"Alright, the three of us all had the same experience. We talked about it, but we don't understand what it means. One day, when the four of us were together, Daniel said something about, 'Wouldn't it be something if someone went in one night and messed up the school? You know, threw things all over the floor, wrote on the walls, knocked desks over.' That night the school was broken into, I had a terrible dream, and so did Darius and Alexandru. At least it seemed like a dream. The dream was that we trashed the school. Only none of us remember being there, and when I woke up, I still had my clothes on. I know I took them off when I went to bed earlier. Darius and Alexandru said the same thing." "I see. You don't remember being at the school, but you saw yourselves at the school." "Yeah, that's it." "Is there anything else?" "Yes." "Go ahead Gabriel." "A few days later, Daniel said to me, 'It sure would make a mess if someone threw a rock through the bakers window.'" "That night I had another dream." "Oh, and what was it?" "I had a dream about the bakery window being broken. But I don't remember doing it. Did we really do those things?" "Well, maybe, but I want you to put those dreams out of your mind. Forget them. Don't talk to anyone about this meeting. Not even your parents or any of your other friends. Understand?" "Yes, sir."

"Remus, I'm sure you don't understand any of this, but I think I know what is going on. I'm not going to try to explain it to you yet, but let me handle this. Forget everything you heard here today. Trust me on this. Boys, don't worry. No one will know of this except us. Not even your parents will know. You're not in any trouble, and try to forget about it, and move on. I do suggest you stay away from Daniel for a while."

Barry didn't say anything to anyone that evening. He needed time to figure out how to handle this. He wasn't really afraid of Daniel, but he also did not know the limits of what Daniel could do at this point. If Daniel really is what Jessie said he was, maybe there is a chance he could be saved from his destiny? Could Daniel be reasoned with?

That night, Barry woke up. He thought he heard footsteps in the hall. He put his robe on and went out to check. As he looked down the hall, he could see the outline of Daniel out on the front balcony. As he walked out onto the balcony, he called out, "Daniel?" Daniel jumped and turned around to face Barry. "What?" "What are you doing out on the balcony this time of night?" "Just looking down at the village."

While Daniel was looking down at the village, at Gabriel's home, Gabriel started coughing and chocking. His mother was trying to helping him, but she didn't know what to do. At the same time, Darius's mother was tending to Darius. He said his chest felt like it was on fire. He couldn't breathe, and Alexandru, he was having his own problems. His head hurt so much that he couldn't hear anything and he couldn't focus his eyes. This lasted about 3 or 4 minutes, then everyone's pain subsided. The boys were alright.

Back on the balcony, Barry ask Daniel, "Why were you staring at the village? Were you trying to communicate with someone?" Daniel stiffened up. "Daniel, I know about your friends." As Daniel took a step forward, suddenly Barry felt such pain in his chest that he bent over. Just as suddenly the pain stopped. "Well, Daniel, I guess what your mother told me is true." "My mother didn't understand, she wanted to destroy me. I couldn't let that happen." "So, you killed your mother." "I couldn't let her destroy me." "Are you going to kill everyone that defies you?" "Probably not."

"Were you planning on having your friends do some more of your dirty work?" "No, I was punishing them. I know they talked to you and Remus." "You didn't kill them?" "No, they are alright. But I don't think they will talk to you again." "Daniel, can I talk you out of doing these things? Can you try to get rid of your evilness? Become a decent human being?" "Don't worry, I have just been testing my powers, and now that I know what I can do, nothing more will happen for a few years. Can I change from evil to good? Only time will tell, but don't count on it."

"You said nothing will happen for a few years. What is your objective? What is your purpose?" "What it has always been. To control the world and its people. To see that the people of the world enjoy all the pleasures in life, they seek to have. To show the world that my father is stronger than your God, and to turn to him." "Daniel, I think you are being deceived. Your father wins once in a great while, but God always comes out on top. Satan does not have enough power to overcome God." "Maybe he and I together can change that."

"The majority of the people believe God is the only answer. What about those that defy you and won't come over to your side?" "We will destroy them." "Daniel, you are delusional. Satan has tried to do this since time began. He hasn't succeeded yet, and he won't. Daniel, all you will end up doing, is destroying yourself. Mark my words." "We shall see, won't we?"

"Daniel, I'm going to work on you, very hard, to make you see the truth." "Very well, I like a challenge. I will learn your ways, and for everything you try to teach me, I will point out to you how naïve you are." "Daniel, come with Janet and me to church this Sunday." "No! You know I can't enter a church." "So, you admit that God would show you his power, and that power would overshadow yours." "I didn't say that. I'm not ready for a confrontation yet." "Because you will not have the power until you are older. Is that what you are telling me?" "Maybe."

The next morning, Barry went to Paul. "Paul, Daniel and I had a long talk last night. I know who he is, and what his purpose is. I also know your part in this." "I'm glad you know. I made a terrible mistake. I was so selfish. Daniel is my doing, and no one else's. I was so stupid to think I could stay young the rest of my life." "That's in the past. The thing now is to help Daniel." "The is no help for Daniel. I know he is responsible for Jessie's death. He will kill anyone who gets in his way." "I also know he caused Jessie's death, but we had an intense discussion last night. I think there is a chance for Daniel." "A chance for what?" "A chance to save him. To drive the evil out of him and bring forth the good in him." "Barry, that will never happen. I know this Satan; he will never allow it." "Daniel has agreed to allow me to work with him, and try to show him the truth." "Very well, if you think there is a chance, I will help in any way I can. But don't turn your back on him. Always be aware."

That evening, Barry told Janet about his talk with Daniel and Paul. "The three of us have a big job ahead of us. We must do what we can to get rid of the evil in Daniel. Work with him. He'll let you. He's agreed not to do anymore harm." "Alright, I'll do whatever I can. But what if it doesn't work?" "If he does not change, there will come a point when he cannot be allowed to continue his purpose." "How will you know when that time is?" "That's the big question. But I think we will know when we reach that point."

It is summer, 1952, and Abby is unaware of what is happening back home. She is absorbed in her research work. She works so much; it is wearing her down. She has a co-worker, Artur. He is the same age as Abby. He tells her she needs to get away from her work for a while. Go with him and have dinner. Relax a little. She finally agrees. While having dinner, Artur gets Abby to open up a little. They talk for a long time. Abby starts to enjoy herself. They get along very well together. During their conversation, Abby begins to really see Artur for the first time. She likes what she sees. She still has this obsession about Sebastian, but she is starting to realize there are other people around her. She needs to start living again.

CHAPTER 13

bby is still bound to her research, but she realizes she is still young and has a life to live. She and Artur spend a lot of time together now. Up to this point it has just been friendship. But Artur feels he is starting feel more than just friendship with Abby. He knows about her past with Sebastian, and he has the feeling that Abby has not let go of Sebastian yet. Artur hopes he can make Abby forget about Sebastian and start thinking more about him.

Artur is 5' 8" tall, muscular build, dark hair, has a close-cut beard that hides a scar he received when he was a teenager. He was born and raised in Bucharest, during the world wide depression. In grade school, he was bullied quite a bit. At that time, he was a little shorter than most of the kids. After a couple of years, he had enough, and decided to do something about it. He started working out, and by the time he was in high school, everyone who saw him knew they sure didn't want to mess with him. As a matter of fact, he became a sort of leader to them. Everyone knows what they say about power, and Artur was no exception.

He began to think he could own the world. He could do what he wanted, and nobody could do anything about it. It was pretty bad in those days. Nobody had much money. They had to get by the best way they could. Artur figured out a way to help his parents keep food on the table. He got two of his closest friends together and told them of

"

his plan. The friends went for it. It was a way to get money and have an adventure at the same time.

The plan was to go to other parts of the city where they weren't known, and rob the small grocery stores. They would wear some kind of mask so they couldn't be identified. But they needed something to force the owner to come across with the money. One of the boys remembered his dad had a gun he kept in a closet. He said his dad had probably forgotten it was there, so he would sneak it out. He said he wouldn't load it though; he didn't want anyone to get hurt. They would split the money and give it to their dads. They would say they got a job after school to help out.

The day was finally here. The boys headed out. They found a grocery store that looked easy. So, they put their masks on and went in. When they approached the counter, the man behind the counter let out a chuckle. "Boys, what's this, it isn't Halloween." "We want your money." "You what? Are you trying to rob me?" Just then, a voice behind them, "What are you up to boys?" The boys turned around quickly, and looked straight at a policeman standing in the doorway. The boys wanted to run, but there was no where to run. "Ok, boys, take off those masks, and step forward." The policeman blew on a whistle, and within no time, there were two more police at the door. Artur suddenly panicked. If they find that gun, we are really in trouble. They searched the boys and found nothing, then called for a wagon to take the boys to the nearest station.

While waiting at the station for their parents to arrive, Artur was wondering about something. While no police were around, "What did you do with that gun you had?" "I didn't have it." "What?" "Yeah, I never had a chance to get to it." "Well, I'm glad you didn't get it. We would be in a lot more trouble if you would have had it. This way its just robbery, not armed robbery. They probable won't be too hard on us."

But sometimes things don't go the way you want them to. Artur figured they would just get probation since there was no weapon, and they didn't actually get to rob the store. But they went before a hard judge, and he sentenced each of the boys to reform school until their 18th birthday. Which meant just under two years. The boys were led away for a different kind of adventure. Would they learn anything, or would they come out with hardened minds?

It didn't take long for Artur to decide he didn't like what he was seeing. Artur's impression was that some of these kids were the boss, and if you didn't like it, you might end up with a knife in your back. I know, no weapons were allowed in here, but you didn't have to be too smart to know how to fashion a spoon into a sharp point. They could be lethal. Artur stayed away from them as much as he could. He hung around mostly with his two friends.

Artur figured out that, if he didn't want a life in this kind of world, he needed to finish school and get a diploma. He talked to the warden of the reform school, and ask about continuing his education while he served his time. The warden informed him that everyone was required to continue their schooling, and that if he did well, he would have a diploma when he was released. That suited Artur just fine.

Artur concentrated on his schooling. That was the most important thing to him right now. Then Artur made a mistake. One evening in the barracks two kids started fighting. They started out arguing, then it turned into a fist fight. The one kid was quite a bit bigger than the other. When that started, Artur went over and grabbed the bigger kid on the shoulder. In the blink of an eye, the bigger kid swung around and slashed Artur cheek with a knife. In a second, two guards were there. One grabbed Artur and moved him back a few steps. The other guard had hold of the big kid. The guard holding Artur, "Artur, you're bleeding pretty bad. Let's get you to the doctor. I'll help you. Take that other kid to isolation."

The doctor cleaned the wound and stitched it up. "This will heal alright, but it will leave you with a scar." The guard spoke up, "Artur, I saw what happened, and you should have let us handle the situation. We were moving in when you stepped in." "I was afraid he was going to kill that little guy." "I know, but that's why we are here." Artur made a decision right then. He would get his diploma, and when he was released, he would find some way to go to college and make something of himself. This criminal life was definitely not for him.

So, Artur fulfilled his goal, became a respected medical researcher, and now has met a girl he likes, and hopes to spend a lot of time with.

But Abby is aware that Artur never speaks about his past. She has asked him, but Artur always says that was a different world, and doesn't want to talk about it. So, Abby knows nothing about him other than when she met him at work.

1955. Electric utilities are expanding quite a bit. There is an electric line that runs down the road east of the castle. Barry arranged to have an electric line built to the castle. It makes life so much easier. A few of the village businesses asked to have electric installed. But the majority of the villagers still don't want it. It cost money every month, and they say they can't afford it. They've lived without it all these years and they don't miss it.

Daniel is 14 now. He is still quiet. He is an observer. He mentally analyzes everything. He thinks how rich and happy these people could be if they would just listen to him. They could have everything, and never have to work again. It's about time he starts showing some of the people what they are missing.

Barry spends a lot of time with Daniel, but Paul has become withdrawn. He stays in his room a lot, and he has started drinking quite a bit. Daniel has told Paul what he intends to do in the near future. "Daniel, you can't go on with this. I don't think Barry will be able to change you. I don't think you can change. You are your father's son, and nothing will change that. Barry is wasting histime." "Yes, you are right, I won't change, and no one, or nothing will stop me." "Then why do you lead Barry on? He thinks he is making progress with you." "It keeps him happy. He thinks he is doing something good." "I want no part of it. I must find a way to stop you." Daniel laughs. "You are a part of this, and if I were destroyed, you would be destroyed right along with me. But that will never happen."

Janet was up in the bedroom looking for her hair brush. It was no where to be found. She thought maybe she had left it in Abby's room. As she is looking through Abby's things, she opens a drawer, and sees the gold ring Abby had found. Out of curiosity she puts the ring on. A strange feeling goes through her body. It's as though she is mesmerized by the ring. She starts to take off the ring, but something is keeping her from removing the ring. She pulls on the ring, but it won't come off. She suddenly feels that she must keep the ring on, but she isn't sure why.

That evening at dinner, Barry noticed the ring on Janet's finger. "Where did you get that ring?" "It was in Abby's room in one her drawers. I tried it on, now I can't get it off. So, I thought I would go ahead and wear it for a while. Unless Abby wants it back." "Do you know where that ring came from?" "No, where?" "Abby found that ring on the castle grounds in a small canyon. She said there were skeleton bones in the tree and on the ground. In my research the other day, I found that the ring belonged to a Count." "A Count? He must have been important." "Oh, he was. He was Count Stefan, supposedly a vampire. He was destroyed at that tree." Janet took in a deep breath. "This ring belonged to a vampire?" "That's the story." "How interesting. Oh, well, since he has been dead 200, or 300 years, I don't think it can do any harm now." "I suppose not."

Since Janet was running the library, and she was in town quite a lot, the villagers started noticing Janet's ring. But when they looked at the ring closer, they would back away. Usually the response was, "You shouldn't be wearing that ring. Do you know who it originally belonged to?" "Yes, but the person has been long dead." "Longer than you think, but mark my words, if you wear that ring, nothing good will come of it." "I don't understand." "That ring will only cause you pain and danger, and maybe to us also." "You can't be serious?" "You heard what I said."

Abby and Artur are spending a lot of time together. They seem so at ease with each other. They both like pretty much the same thing, and both always seem to think the same way. Abby is starting to think more and more about marriage, but so far, Artur has not even come close to hinting about getting married. Abby was getting a little tired of waiting for Artur to make his feelings known. One evening, while they were together, "Artur, do you ever think about getting married?" "No, any woman could do much better than me." "Why do you say that?" "You know I never talk about my past." "Yes, but, what does the past have to do with anything? That's over with, this is the present." "Yes, but my past is not pretty." "What were you, a serial killer or a gang boss?" "No, no, nothing like that." "Then tell me what you were, it can't be that bad." Reluctantly, Artur told Abby about the attempted robbery, reform school and how he got the scar. "Artur, that is your 'terrible past'? You shouldn't be ashamed of what you did, you should be talking about what that incident did for you. Look where you are today. You changed and for the better. You have a good life." "I was always so ashamed, I never looked at it that way. I suppose you are right. But I'm still not proud of what I did." "Here I was thinking the worst of you. Don't you know many teens go through bad times, and get into trouble, but when they turn around like you did, that's something to be proud of."

Abby and Artur married. They had the wedding on the castle grounds. There was a huge turnout for the wedding. Abby was so glad to be back home for a while. Barry and Janet welcomed Artur into the family. They liked Artur as soon as they met him. They were sure Abby made the right choice. Abby said they would stay at the castle a few days, then take a trip through the mountains for a few days, then head back to work.

Janet showed Abby the ring. "I forgot all about that ring. You go ahead and wear it if you want, I don't really care about the ring." "Tell me, Abby, exactly where did you find this ring?" "Well, if you take a straight-line north, from the back of the castle, you will come to a small canyon. It's about a 20-minute walk. The ring was on the ground at the bottom of the canyon next to some old bones." "I see, do you know who the owner of the ring was?" "No, do you?" "It's unimportant. Don't worry about it."

Artur met Daniel. After talking to him for a while, he thought Daniel to be much older than his age. He seemed so informed about things. He talked about how the village would change after he graduated. He would bring the village to life. He would make it a place of pleasure and profit. The villagers would not want for anything. "Tell me Daniel, how do you intend to do all of that? Do you have some magic wand?" "Let's just say, I have my ways of doing things." Artur was a little perplexed. Who was this teenage kid, who talked like he could control people's lives?" Artur walked over to Barry. "Barry, who is this Daniel? He talks like he is going to change the world, and everyone's lives. Who is his father?" "His father is Paul. He isn't here today. You know how teenagers talk. They think they know everything." "This boy talks like he really does."

The next couple of days were happy days. It was so nice to have Abby home for a while. They didn't get to see her very often. Artur watched Daniel at times. He still couldn't figure Daniel out, but he felt there was much more to Daniel than what could be seen. Daniel didn't talk to Abby very much. He spent most of his time away from everyone, or he would go into the village. Abby thought about how much Daniel had changed since those days she used to walk him around the grounds. Abby also noticed that her mother sometimes would sit, and just stare, as if she was in a trance.

"Mother. Mother!" "Huh? Oh, what is it Abby?" "You looked like you were in a trance." "Oh, no. I was just thinking about something." "What could you be thinking of so deeply?" "Oh, nothing. Abby, take me to that canyon where you found the ring." "What's so important about that canyon?" "I don't know. It's like something is pulling me toward that place. I want to see what it looks like." "Ok, I'll take you there. But you are starting to worry me."

On the way to the canyon, dark clouds started gathering in the west. The wind picked up a little. Janet observed everything around her as they walked. When they reached the canyon, they could see lightening in the storm clouds. A strong gust of wind came through, that gave Abby and Janet chills. The storm looked as if it was coming their way. They stopped at the edge of the canyon and looked down. "Down at the bottom of that tree is where I found the ring." Janet looked at the skeletal bones on the ground below the tree, and at the few rib bones still in the branches.

"Why are you so interested in this ring and that skeleton down there? Is there something you want to tell me? Do you know who that person was?" "Yes, I know who it was. I was just curious to see for myself." "Well, don't keep me in suspense, who was he?" Janet told Abby who the 'person' was and 'what' he was. "Do you really believe he was a vampire? You know those things weren't real. They are just legends from old wife's tales. They didn't really exist."

The storm is getting closer, and Abby tells Janet they better get back before they get caught in the rain. Just as they turn and take a few steps, lightening strikes the dead tree. The tree splits and falls to the ground. Janet stops and turns around. All of the skeleton bones are on the ground now. It's as if the bones have all come back together. Abby looks at the bones and Janet. Janet just stands staring. "Mother! Mother!

Let's get out here, you are scaring me. Mother, come on." Janet looks at Abby, "Yes… Let us…go." They quicken their pace as they head back to the castle. It is just starting to rain lightly.

"Janet, where have your two been? We've been looking for you." "We just took a walk around the grounds." "Abby, is something wrong, you're white as a ghost." "It's nothing, dad, we had to hurry to get back before the storm hit." "Did you and Janet have a mother, daughter talk?" "You might call it that."

Abby and Artur left, and headed back to Bucharest, and to their work. Abby talks to Artur about her mother. "It seems like something or someone is trying to control her, and she can't do anything about it." Abby told Artur about their experience at the canyon. "You don't believe in the undead, do you?" "Abby, that is probably the biggest legend in Rumania. People claim they have seen them. There have been bodies of girls and women found, that had the blood drained from them. A lot of people still believe they exist, even today." "I don't know, it just seems a little hard to believe." "Well, I'll tell you something that does bother me. I know he is part of your family, but there is something strange about Daniel. He makes me nervous." "I know what you mean. He is so withdrawn. He seems to sit back and study everyone. Like he is analyzing them." "Well, let's talk about something else and enjoy our journey."

Abby and Artur decide to stop in Brasov, and rent a horse and buggy, to go up into the mountains. Most of the roads in the mountains aren't fit for a car anyway. It's a beautiful sunny day, not too hot. In their traveling, they come to a village called Cimpina. It's in the foothills of the Transylvania Mountains. They decide to rest and get something to eat. It's a clean, neat little village and the people are very friendly. As they go back to the buggy, a woman approaches Abby. She says her name is Camilia. She appears to be in her early twenties. "I understand you are going up into the mountains." "Yes, why?" "I hate to impose on you, but do you think I could go with you?" "Why do you want to go up in the mountains?" "My husband is up there, and I want to join him. It won't be out of your way, and I won't be a pest. I promise." Abby and Artur talk it over and decide it might be nice to have some company. Besides, it's too far for the woman to walk. "We would be glad to have you with us. Is there anything you have to take with you?" "No, everything is already up there."

Late in the afternoon, they pass a beautiful lake down in a valley. The water is deep blue. They pull over and rest for a while and enjoy the lake. Artur noticed it was getting late. Artur is a smart man and all, but he doesn't always look ahead very far. He hadn't thought about where they would be able to stay the night. He hoped there was a village not too far down the road. All they could do is start out and see where they ended up.

As they traveled, Abby talked to Camilia. "Are you from the village of Cimpina?" "Yes, I was born there." "What made you decide to live in the mountains?" "We like it there." As Abby and Camilia talked, the sun was starting to go down. Artur was about half asleep, and the horse just more less went the way it wanted to go. Suddenly Abby said, "Oh, look." and pointed up ahead. That made Artur wake up. Up ahead was a castle. The Stefan castle. Artur hoped someone was living there, and maybe they would be able to spend the night.

As they stopped in front of the castle, a man in his 50's came out to greet them. "Welcome. May I help you?" "We're sorry to intrude, but it's getting dark and we have no place to stay the night." "Oh, that's no problem. We would like you to stay overnight. We don't get many visitors, but when we do, we like to have them stay awhile." "Very good, we would be honored." "Come then, I will get your luggage brought in."

As they entered the castle, they were amazed at the interior. (It had not changed since Jessie and Paul had been there several years before.) They were invited to sit down; they were asked if they wanted any refreshments. "Count Stefan will be down later and dinner will be served. Please make yourselves comfortable, and if you need anything, just pull that cord there, and I will be at your service." As the man left, Viorica entered the room. She was still beautiful and still had very long black hair. She introduced herself, and sat down. They talked for about an hour. It was dark outside now. Viorica asked about what was going on in the outside world.

There were footsteps on the stairs. "Welcome to our home. My name is Count Yorga Stefan. I hope you are comfortable. The Count seated himself and they continued to talk for another hour, then dinner was served. It was a wonderful meal, served with red wine. Abby spoke up, "Several years ago, my aunt Jessie and her husband, Paul, stayed overnight here. It was back during the war." The Count thought for a minute. "Of course, I remember. They had a small boy with them." "Yes, Daniel." "He must be a teenager by now. How is he doing?" "He's doing alright. Sometimes he seems older than what he is." "Yes, I could tell he was going to be someone someday." "Oh?" "It's just something you sense."

"Count, in all these years, you don't seem to have changed any. Neither has your wife. You both look the same as when Paul described you both, those many years ago." "As for Viorica, she does not age very fast. She takes good care of herself. I figure she will be just as beautiful many years hence. As for me? Paul was probably describing my older brother." Hmmm…. I don't remember an older brother. "We were not exactly twins, but we looked very much alike. So, I probably look now, as he looked then." "Oh. Is your brother here?" "No, unfortunately he passed away a couple of years ago." "Oh, I'm sorry."

It was getting late, so everyone thought it was time to turn in. The Count excused himself, he said he had work to do. Abby and Artur were shown to their bedroom. They watched Camilia go into her room two doors down. Abby opened the doors to the balcony. There was a light, cool breeze that was just right for sleeping. The night was quiet. Everyone would sleep well.

Before they went to sleep, the wheels in Abby's head were spinning pretty fast. "Artur, the Count doesn't make much sense. Paul specifically described Count Yorga and his wife. This man says he is Count Yorga, and Viorica is his wife. I thought the older man was Count Yorga and Viorica was his wife. Did this man marry Viorica after his brother died? Was there really ever a brother? Do these people never age, and the 'brother' just a cover up to explain their looks." Artur let out a small laugh. "I hear what you are saying, but it boggles my mind. I think we better get some sleep."

About a half an hour after the sun came up, Artur woke up. He felt refreshed. He woke Abby and they got ready to go down to breakfast. Viorica was already at the table. "I've had my breakfast; you go ahead and sit down; I'll have something brought in for you." Abby looked around. "There are only two places set." "Yes?" "What about Camilia?" "Who?" "The woman that was with us last night." "There was no one with you last night." Artur spoke up, "But there was a woman with us. She came with us from Cimpina." "I'm sorry, but I tell you there were only you two here last night." Abby, "But we saw her go into her room last night. It was two rooms down from us." "Come, I will show you that room. You will see no one slept in that room last night." Viorica took them to the room they described. She opened the door and stepped in. What furniture that was in the room, was covered with sheets. There was no bed in the room. There were plenty of cobwebs all over.

"As you can see, this room hasn't been used in years." "Artur, what is happening here?" "I don't know, Abby, it's so strange." As they started back down stairs, they ran into the man who helped them last night. "Giani, remember these people coming in last night?" "Yes, ma'am." "Did you see the woman with them?" "No, ma'am, there was just the two of them." "Very well, you may carry on." Viorica took them to another room upstairs. The room was very dark, only one candle burning. The Count was sitting at a desk. "Count, Miss Abby says there was a woman with them last night when they come in. Did you see anyone with them?" "Why, no. They were alone when I came down the stairs last night. I'm sorry, people, but there was no one with you."

Abby and Artur look at each other. Were they losing their mind? Something was wrong. But what? They went back down stairs. They went through the motion of eating their breakfast, but their heads were swimming. What was happening? The woman was with them all day, and evening. Where did she disappear to? There had to be an explanation. Obviously, they weren't going to get the answer here.

As they start down the lane from the castle, Abby remembers something. "Artur, I've been thinking back to last night." "And?" "Did you notice, that the Count and his wife, never once looked at, or talked, to Camilia, the whole evening?" "Now that you mention it, I did notice, but I didn't think anything about it." "Do suppose they ignored her for a reason?" "I don't know. Unless they knew her, and had some specific plan for her. Then, told us she was never there to confuse us." Just then Abby screamed, and pointed her finger, yelling, "Look! Artur, Look! Over there." Artur couldn't believe his eyes. A woman in a flowing white dress, was coming through the woods toward them. As she got closer, they could see that it was Camilia. It was as if she were floating. Abby and Artur were speechless. Camilia spoke slowly, "I……can't find….my husband. Have…. you seen…. him?" At that she turned, and started going back into the woods. Artur jumped off the buggy, and ran to catch up with her. "Camilia!" She went behind a tree, and when Artur got to the tree, she had disappeared. She was nowhere to be seen.

Artur slowly walked back to the buggy. He just stood there for a minute. "She went behind a tree, and just disappeared. Vanished." "Artur get back in the buggy, and let's get out of here. This is scaring me to no end." Artur got back into the buggy, and started on down the lane. He didn't know what to say. "Artur, I want to go back to that village." "Why?" "I want to know if anyone there knows Camilia. She said she was born there." "Yes, maybe we can get a logical explanation for this, whatever it is.

Back at the village, Abby and Artur decide to go to the local pub. That's where most news comes from. They sat at a table, ordered some coffee, and ask the bartender if they could talk to him about something. The bartender sat down, "What is it you want to talk about?" "Do you know a woman named Camilia?" "No……I've never heard that name before. Hey, Sergiu did you ever hear of a woman named Camilia?" "No, I never did." There was an old timer sitting at a table nearby. "I've heard the name." "You have? Please, come join us." The bartender was curious, so he stayed at the table also. The old man spoke, "Why do you want to know about Camilia?" "Well, yesterday as we were getting ready to leave for the mountains……… Artur and Abby told their story. ………This morning as we left the castle, we saw her walking in the woods, and as I went after her, she just disappeared." The man stared at Abby and Artur for a moment. "I'm sorry folks, but what you just told me, is impossible." "Why do you say that? We saw her." "Camilia was born here and she married a local boy. One day her husband went up into the woods to hunt some game. After a week, he hadn't come back. Camilia became so upset, she decided to go look for him. She never came back either." "Well, then she is up there, still looking for her husband." "I'm afraid not. You see that all happened over 200 years ago." "You're joking." "No, sir. It's part of the history of this village.

Neither of them was ever seen again." "Then her ghost is still up there looking for her husband." "Well, I won't say you didn't see something, but that's the story of Camilia."

Sitting in the buggy, "Artur, let's go back to Brasov and get our car and go straight home. I've had enough of this trip, to last a life time." "Me too."

CHAPTER 14

So, Abby and Artur had an adventure they probably wouldn't tell their children. They did decide not to tell anyone about their experience; no one would believe them anyway. Would you?

So many things have been happening, I need to go back several months, and talk about Daniel. Although no one seemed to notice, Daniel had a plan and decided it was time to put the plan into action. Daniel knew that when he turned 18, and started to put the 'big' plan in motion, he would need help. So, now was a good time to recruit that help. He would have plenty of time to indoctrinate the help to his purpose.

He approached his best friend one afternoon, "Grigore, let's go somewhere we can talk." "Sure, what's up?" Daniel knew of an old abandon house at the south edge of the village. "Grigore, I need someone I can trust. Someone who will not question me, and will stand by me, no matter what I say, or what happens." "I can do that." "Grigore, I don't think you understand. You are going to see things you have never seen before, and you will do things you have never done before. They won't be pretty." "That's getting pretty deep. Go on." "If you are to be my assistant, you must think as I think. One slight hesitation, and it could destroy you." "You have my full attention."

"Grigore, I was born with a purpose. You can become part of that purpose and reap the benefits with me. In a few years we will start changing the world, with this village being the first assignment."

"Daniel, I've watched you for some time. I know you seem to have a certain power over people. Who are you?" "I am my father's son." "You mean Paul is behind all of this?" "Don't be stupid. Of course, he isn't. He was just the instrument to give me life." Then Daniel looked straight at Grigore, and his eyes turned black. Grigore backed away. "You…… You…… You are the Devil!" "No, Grigore, I am his son." Grigore stood silent for a full minute.

"What do you mean, you are going to change the world?" "We will take the world away from their God, and we will give people everything they long for. Riches, happiness, and the freedom to do what ever they wish." "And what do you get in return?" "Their souls." "And what about my soul?" "I think I already have it, Grigore. Think of the life you will have. To live life as you never thought you could. Do you like adventure?" "Yes…." "Then join me. Own the world!" "Ok, Daniel, I'm with you. What ever it takes." "There is no backing out. Once you are in, the only way out is death."

"We will use this old house for our meetings. We must recruit more followers. We will pick 5 of the most vulnerable students. There must be two girls included in our choice. They must be indoctrinated to my will; I will take care of that part." "Well, I know at least 3 students who can be easily swayed." "That's good, I know the two girls I want in our group."

After a few days, the newcomers were accepted. Whether they actually understood what they were getting into, was anyone guess. Their main thought was the adventure they were about to start on. Daniel had taken care of everything. In the living room of the old house, he had drawn a circle on the floor. Inside the circle was drawn a pentagram. There was a candle at each corner of the pentagram. He had black robes and hoods for everyone. There was also a long marble slab table against one wall. Above the table, there was a large dagger hung on the wall. On another wall, there was an alter type structure, that had a candle on each side of it, and a thick book on the alter that was entitled, 'The Secrets of Hell', and the picture of a goat's head with horns, on the wall.

The night of indoctrination arrived. Everyone gathered at the old house. As each person entered, Daniel handed them a robe and hood. When everything was ready, Daniel stood at the edge of the circle, and told the rest to stand at a point of the pentagram, but stay outside of the circle on the floor. One by one, he had a student stand in the center of the pentagram. Daniel then uttered incantations and had each member swear allegiance to him. When this was done, Daniel talked to them about their jobs, and their purposes. These people were completely under his control. The meeting was adjourned, and the schedule was to meet once a month.

At the time this was going on, it is also when Janet put on the gold ring and felt this attraction to something she could not identify. It was also when Paul, knowing what Daniel was doing, became more withdrawn and started drinking heavily. Barry could feel the tension in the air. He was worried about Janet. He wanted to help Paul, but Paul told him to mind his own business. But Barry still thought he could change Daniel.

At the second meeting, Daniel got down to serious business. He had everyone line up around the circle. He then sacrificed an animal and let the blood drip into a brass goblet. He then passed the goblet around, and had each person drink from it. He then read from 'the book', and talked about all the pleasures they, and the world, would experience.

At the third meeting, Daniel tells the group that his father wants a sacrifice. That it must be a young virgin. Earlier that evening, Daniel had abducted a 21-year-old girl who was not married. He was keeping her locked in another room, and at the proper time, he led her out to the marble table. She had on a long, white gown. She seemed to be in a trance. She stood very still and stared straight ahead. She was obviously under Daniel's spell. Two students picked her up and placed her horizontally on the table. Daniel then read from different portions of 'the book'. Then Daniel took the dagger off the wall and stood over her. He held the dagger high above her. Daniel told her to wake up. She blinked her eyes a couple of times, then saw the dagger above her. As she screamed, Daniel brought the dagger down and stabbed her in the heart. The screaming stopped. Her eyes closed and she lay still. The students did not move. They did not blink. They were completely under Daniel's control.

So, back to the present. Daniel and his cult keep a low profile. They only meet once in a while. It's been three years now since the cult was started. Daniel is waiting until his 18th birthday. That is when Daniel comes to full power. Lately, Janet seems to have conquered her feeling of being pulled against her will. She is back to being herself now. For some strange reason, Paul has quit drinking. He goes out more often, and he writes a lot. But he is still a quiet person. He seems to be working towards some sort of goal. But he will not talk about it, even when asked what he is working on. Barry is accepting the fact that he just is not getting through to Daniel.

It is 1959. About a month ago, Janet started having this feeling again that something was calling to her. That she was being called to do something. Several times she walked back to the canyon. Nothing had changed. Everything looked exactly the same. Sometimes she was sure she heard a voice calling her. One night, Janet was awakened by a voice in her head. It said, 'Come to me, come to me now. It is time.' Janet quietly got out of bed, put her robe on, and started down the stairs. She went out the front door and started walking. The voice kept calling her, but then, the voice suddenly stopped. Janet looked around her; she was standing in the middle of the village. Her thought was 'What am I doing here in the middle of the night? How did I get here?' Janet looked around, saw she was all alone, so she turned and hurried back to the castle.

The next morning, Janet debated whether to tell Barry about what happened. As the morning wore on, she decided she did need to tell Barry what has happening to her. "Maybe you were just sleep walking." "I have never walked in my sleep, and what about the voice?" "Well, you were dreaming about someone calling you." "Barry, I think I better tell you something." "Ok, shoot." "Remember way back, when I put this gold ring on?" "Yes." "Then you told me the history of the ring." "Go on." "Sometime after I put the ring on, I started feeling as if something or someone, were pulling me somewhere. It was just a feeling, and I did not understand what was happening, or what it meant."

"When Abby and Artur were here, I had Abby take me back to where she found the ring. It was a frightening experience for both of us." "What frightened you both so much?" "That was when the storm came up so quickly." "I remember that." "As we were standing there, lightening struck the tree and split it in half. The rest of the bones fell to the ground, and what really frightened us, was when the bones hit the ground, it looked as if the skeleton was whole again. At that point, we ran back to the castle as hurriedly as we could."

"Are you saying, you think the Count is calling you for some reason?" "I don't know what to think. If it is the Count, why did I end up in the middle of the village last night?" "And then again, maybe it is just a reoccurring dream." "What ever the answer, I want this ring taken off. There must be a way to get it off of my finger." "I'll get ahold of Deniel. I'm sure he has a tool to cut the ring off."

"Yes, I can get the ring off. It's too tight on the finger to cut it off. That gold is soft enough, I should be able to take a very small file, and file a break in it. Then pull it apart." "Just so you can take it off without taking my finger off with it." Deniel gave out a small chuckle. "I'll do my best ma'am." After a few minutes of careful filing, the ring came off. Janet felt relieved. Later, she took the ring and walked back to the canyon. Looking down at the skeleton, she let the ring drop. She walked back to the castle hoping her nightmare was over.

Daniel's birthday is just a couple of weeks off. Daniel informs his followers, that next week will be a special meeting. There will be another sacrifice to celebrate his coming to power. This will be a special offering.

Since Janet had the ring removed from her finger, she has felt much better. There have been no voices, although there have been periods in the past, where she never heard the voice. Then one night, Barry is having trouble sleeping. He will doze off, then suddenly wake up. On one of those instances, he feels the bed moving. He looks over, and sees Janet get out of bed, and put her robe on. She then heads toward the stairs. Barry starts to call her, but hesitates. He wants to see where she is going. Is she hearing that voice again? He decides to follow her from a distance.

Barry put his pants and shirt on, and starts down the stairs behind her. He follows her out the front door, and she heads towards the village again. Janet walks to the middle of town, then turns left and follows a path that leads to an old house. As Barry waits at the corner, before following Janet, suddenly he feels a hand on his shoulder. He jumps and turns. "Paul, you scared daylights out of me. What are you doing here?" Paul put a finger to his lips. Then whispered to Barry, "You are going to need some help." "Oh?" Paul motioned Barry to start walking toward the old house.

Janet reaches the house. She goes up on the porch, and stops at the door. There is dim light coming from inside. She opens the door and enters. As she steps inside, a voice says, "Welcome, Janet. Please come forward to me." Janet approaches Daniel. She is in a trance. Daniel stands in front of Janet, "Janet, you have the honor of being a special sacrifice tonight, to celebrate the beginning of my full powers. Two of the followers lift Janet up, and place her on the marble table.

Barry and Paul step up on the porch, and quietly open the front door. As they enter the room, Daniel is standing at the marble table. He has the dagger in his hand, and he is holding it high above Janet's still body. Paul yells, "Daniel! Stop!" Daniel backs up a couple of steps, the dagger still in the air. Paul runs toward Daniel, and stops in front of him. Meanwhile, Barry has run to Janet, and lifts her up from the table, and carriers her back across the room. "What is the meaning of this, Paul? What are you trying to do?" "I am going to stop you, once and for all." "You cannot stop me, Paul, and you know that." "But you are wrong, I can destroy you." "You realize that by destroying me, you will also destroy yourself?"

Without saying a word, Paul pulled his hand from behind his back. In his hand was a 6" silver cross. Without hesitation, Paul pushed the cross against Daniel's forehead. Daniel's forehead burst into flames. Within seconds, Daniel's whole body was in flames. That quickly, Daniel was nothing more than a pile of ashes on the floor. As this took place, Janet came out of her trance, asking what happened. At the same time, the student followers all collapsed to the floor. Paul stepped back and grabbed his chest. He instantly started aging. As Paul became his true age, he collapsed to the floor. His body could not take the sudden age transition; he lay on the floor dead.

A few minutes went by as everyone tried to digest what had happened. The students finally stood up, took their hoods off and looked around. Barry was the first to speak. "Are you kids alright?" "I think so, but what just happened, and where are we? Why are we here?" "You don't know what just happened? Don't you know what you have been involved in these past months?" "No, we remember listening to

Daniel speak to us. Then things would go blank for periods of time. We went to school as always, everything seemed normal to us. Except for periods we can't account for." "Well, you were all under the spell of Daniel. He had you brainwashed into doing things you definitely would not have done otherwise. Daniel was an evil person. He was using you to help spread his evil. Since you were not aware of what was going on, and this situation would be very hard to explain rationally, and no one would probably believe it, I suggest you say nothing to anyone. Try to push this scene out of you mind, and go back to your normal lives. Take those robes off and go home."

"Barry, what was going on? Why did I come here?" "Janet, the voices you heard, and the feelings you felt, had nothing to do with the ring. It was Daniel. He was preparing you for tonight." "Preparing me for what?" "He was preparing you to be a sacrifice for Satan." "A sacrifice? You mean......?" "Yes, my dear, he came within seconds of plunging a dagger through your heart." Janet started shaking. "It's alright, Janet, Paul and I were following you to see just what was going on. Paul stopped Daniel just in time." "Where is Paul?" "He is over there on the floor. He is dead." Janet let out a scream. "But that's an old man." "Yes, when Daniel was destroyed, Paul's spell was broken also. He became the age he actually was. His body couldn't take the change. Come, let's go home. The nightmare is over."

Daniel's rein was ended. It can be said that, Paul, through desperation and persuasion, brought Daniel into the world, but in the end, gave his life, to destroy Daniel, so that humanity would be saved from another attempt of world domination by evil.

Chapter 15

A couple of months have passed. Barry still has requests to design a home for someone, but mostly commercial buildings. In this day and age there aren't many requests for castles anymore. Last month, Barry and Janet went to Bucharest to spend a few days with Abby and Artur. They told Abby the whole story about Daniel. "Why did you not tell me, about Daniel, when you found out who he was?" Janet responded, "You were better off not knowing. It could have put you in danger." "Yes, and your mother, and I, and Paul were the only people that knew about Daniel." "What about the followers he had?" "They never really knew what was going on. I just told them Daniel was an evil person, and try to forget the incident and move on." Abby shook her head. "I always thought there was something different about Daniel, but I never expected that." Artur spoke up, "I could tell there was something strange about Daniel. Remember, I talked to you about that." "Yes, but I dared not say anything. You understand now?" "Yes, I do."

Abby and Artur are doing very well. They are dedicated to their work. But they still have a social life. There is a night club they like to go to, called, Night Life. It has a nice atmosphere, and it usually has a singer for entertainment. They know the owner, Joey Duncan. He is an American also. He was from Cleveland, Ohio, but left about 5 years ago. He said things were getting too hot. It was time to become scarce. Joey was mostly on the level, but once in a while some of his transactions were a little shady, you might say.

One night, Abby and Artur are at the club, they are discussing their work. Abby is getting a little frustrated. She wants to expand her research in a different direction. She wants the research center to bring in some chimpanzees. Because they have a higher degree of intelligence than most animals, she thinks they would be a great help in her research for working toward her goal of human restoration of internal organs. She is thinking about quitting, and going out on her own. She wants to have her own laboratory, where she wouldn't have anyone telling her what she can and cannot do. Artur tells her not to do anything hasty, give it some more time.

Joey walks up to their table, and asks if he can talk to Artur for a minute. "Sure, Joey, sit down. What do you need?" "Forgive me, for interrupting, but I need to ask for a favor. It's very important." "Sounds serious, Joey, what's up?" "It is serious." Joey pulled a large envelope from his jacket. "This envelope has important documents in it. I can't keep it here in my office. Certain people would like to get their hands on it. Can you keep this envelope for me, and put it in a secure hiding place?" "Sure, I could do that, but why don't you put it in your safety deposit box at your bank? It would be safe there." "Because, if something happens to me, no one would know it was there. These documents have to eventually get to the Rumanian Intelligence Bureau." "Are you in danger?" "No, not at the present. There is really nothing going on right now, but probably in the near future, those documents will become very valuable."

When Abby and Artur get back home, Artur tries to think of a safe place to hide the envelope. It had to be somewhere no one would think of looking. Everywhere he looks is so obvious. Drawers, under cushions, behind a picture, wait, Artur thinks he found the perfect place. He pulls the bottom drawer out of the desk, and tapes the envelope to the outside back of the drawer, and replaces the drawer back into the desk. Unless someone pulls the drawer clear out of the desk, it should be safe.

Back in the village, Barry and Janet are enjoying lunch at The Pub, and talking with the villagers that are there. Everything is peaceful now. Barry and Janet start back to the castle, stopping to talk to people on the way. When they get back, Barry decides to do some work in his office. As he is working, he sees something on his drawing that could be a problem. He goes over to the library in his office, to check his books, to see if he can find a solution to his problem. As he pulls out a book, he notices what looks like paper rolled up behind the books. He pulls the roll of paper out, and takes it over to his desk, and unrolls it. It appears to be a set of plans. The plans are faded some, but with a magnifying glass, he is able to make out the writing. As he looks over the plans, he sees it is a drawing of the vault room and the dungeon. As he looks at the drawing more closely, something doesn't look right.

The vault room looks alright, but something is missing in the other room. At first Barry can't figure out what's different. After looking with the magnifying glass, he spots the difference. The southeast corner. The drawing shows nothing but the two walls meeting at the corner. Barry remembers that Paul told him once about one of the corners that had two brick walls extending out into the room. But they don't show up on the original drawing. Something has been added afterward. Barry heads for the kitchen to go down and check out the torture room.

As Barry enters the room, he sees the walls Paul was referring to, and that don't show up on the original print. Barry ponders, 'Why would someone brick up that corner, unless their hiding something?' He inspects it closely, but finds no opening of any kind. Not even a small hole. He decides to try to remove a few of the bricks and find out what is in that small space. He sees a box of tools against one of the walls, and finds a hammer and a chisel. Just as he picks up the tools, he hears Janet calling him.

Barry starts back toward the stairs. "Barry, come quick, Isac is here. There's been an accident." Barry hurries up the stairs. "What happened, Isac?" "It's Virgil, he was up on the roof doing some repair work, and he fell. The doctor says he needs to go the hospital, because he doesn't have the facilities to treat him. Could you drive Virgil to the hospital in Brasov?" "Sure thing. Bring him up to the car." So, the wall is forgotten for now.

It's late when Barry gets back home. He goes to his office and cleans up his desk, quickly, and puts the rolled-up prints in a bottom drawer in his desk. He's very tired, so he goes up to the bedroom. Janet is in bed reading. "How did it go with Virgil? Is he going to be ok?" "I think so. Their going to keep him in the hospital for a few days. He has a broken leg and some internal bleeding. The doctors think he'll be ok. Virgil's wife asked if I would take her to the hospital tomorrow morning, she is going to stay with him until he is released."

A couple of months have passed. Abby and Artur are at the club, having dinner. Abby talked to her superior about what she wanted to do. They rejected the idea. She is supposed to be working on antibodies for certain diseases', not on her private projects. As Abby is talking, Artur sees a man across the room at a table, with a woman. He looks familiar, but Artur can't quite place him. The woman is talking, but the man seems more interested in the hallway, down which, Joey's office is. The man says something to the woman, and gets up and heads toward Joey's office. At the same time, the woman gets up and leaves the club.

Artur feels something is wrong. He gets up and goes down the hall. As he approaches the office door, he hears what sounds like a gunshot. He stands still for a moment, startled. Then opens the door and steps in. Just as he opens the door, he sees a door to the outside closing. He couldn't see who went out. On the floor, was Joey. Artur bent down, there was blood all over Joey's shirt. Artur saw a gun lying on the floor, a couple of feet away. He reached over and picked it up.

Unfortunately, there was an off-duty police detective in the club also. He didn't see the man go down the hall, but he did see Artur go down that hall, although he didn't really think anything about it. But when he heard the shot, he quickly went down the hall, and when he got to the office door, there was Artur, bending over Joey's body, with a gun in his hand. The detective pulled his gun. "Drop the gun, now!" Artur turned toward the voice, and saw the gun pointed at him. "I said drop the gun!" Artur put the gun down and slowly stood up. "I am Detective Sorin, move over to your right." Artur moved slowly over, "It's not what you think. I didn't shoot him." "Sure, you just happened to be coming this way, and there he was, laying there dead." "Look, I'm telling you, I didn't shoot Joey. I heard the shot, and when I came in the office, someone went out that exit door." "Did you see who it was?" "No, I just saw the door close." "Naturally. Look, I saw you come down the hall, and then heard the shot, and there you were with the gun in your hand. But you didn't shoot him." "I swear I didn't shoot him. I picked the gun up without thinking. I didn't shoot him, I tell you. Joey and I were good friends."

Abby watched Artur go down the hall, then she heard the shot also. Then the detective runs down the hall. Abby becomes frightened, and hurries down the hall to the office. "Artur, what's going on?" Then she sees Joey lying on the floor, and the blood. She lets out a scream. "Someone shot Joey, and this detective thinks I did it." "Who are you lady?" "I'm Abby, Artur's wife. Artur wouldn't shoot anyone." "Well, he was holding the gun when I walked in. It looks pretty bad to me." Detective Sorin picked up a phone and called headquarters.

Back at headquarters, Artur was locked in a room with a table and a chair, and a single light bulb hanging from the ceiling. No windows. Abby was in the detective's office, hoping to get to see Artur. The detective came in, "I'm sorry, Miss Abby, but you cannot see your husband. He is to be interrogated later this evening, and then locked in a cell." "Why can't I see him just for a few minutes?" "He is charged with a capital crime. Until we line up all the evidence, and get his story, no one can visit him." "When will I be able to see him?" "It could be a few days. The lab will check the gun your husband used. That could take 2 or 3 days. Then he will be arraigned, and charged. I'll let you know when." "So, you have already found him guilty." "No, ma'am, I'm just telling you the procedure. Now, please go on home, I'll be in touch."

Barry and Janet traveled to Bucharest to stay with Abby. They couldn't believe Artur would ever hurt anyone, let alone kill them. He just wasn't that type of person. Five days went by, no word from the detective. Abby was at her wits end.

All this time, Artur has been locked in a cell by himself. The only time he sees anyone is when the guard brings him food. They had questioned Artur for 4 hours the night he was arrested. They even tried a little strong-arm tactic for a while. The story was the same over, and over. The detective wouldn't buy it. He finally gave up and had Artur locked in a cell. Maybe Artur would change his story when the lab report came back on the gun.

After a week went by, the lab called the detective, "What did you find out about the gun? I'm anxious to send this guy up the river." "I'm afraid that's not going to be easy." "Why?" "Well, the guys prints are on the gun, like you said they would be, but, that gun was never fired, and it isn't even the same caliber as the bullet we took out of the victim." "What! You must have made a mistake." "No mistake, it's just like I told you." "Great. Well, I'll have to figure some way out of this."

Detective Sorin called down to the cell block, and told the guard to bring Artur up to his office. Then he called Abby, and told her to come down to his office. When Artur entered the office, Sorin told him to sit down. Artur was a mess. He still had the same clothes on as when he was arrested. His hair needed combed. He still had a slight bruise on his left cheek, some dried blood on his chin. "Now what do you want? I told you a thousand times, I didn't kill anybody." His speech was a little slurred. "I know, I know, that's why I called you up here." "What? What did you just say?" "I said, I now know you didn't kill Joey. The gun evidence showed it hadn't been fired and was a different caliber, than the bullet that killed Joey. You didn't have any other gun on you, and there was no gun found anywhere in the office." "You put me through hell, and now you tell me it was all a mistake?" "Now, calm down, Artur."

Just then, Abby, Barry, and Janet entered the office. "Artur! What did they do to you?" "After all I went through, and now he decides, I didn't do it. Doesn't that make you want to laugh?" "Well, Mr. detective, what is this all about?" "Miss Abby, the evidence confirmed that Artur was innocent. We just made a mistake. It happens." "Some mistake. It looks like you tried to beat it out of him. Is that standard procedure?" "Sometimes it's necessary." Artur spoke up, "It took you a full week to check a gun?" "The lab is very busy."

It felt good to be back home. The first thing Artur did was shower and change his clothes. He then joined the family in the living room. "I'm glad that's over with. I think I was starting to go crazy in that cell." "What happened that night?" "Well, Abby, I saw a man in the club that looked familiar. Then, when I saw him go back toward the office, I thought I better go check on Joey. When I reached the office door, I heard a shot. When I went in the office, Joey was lying on the floor. When I knelt down to check Joey, I saw the gun, and picked it up. Which I know now, was a stupid thing to do. When Sorin walked in, there I was holding the gun." Barry asked, "You didn't see anyone else in the office?" "No, but someone went out the exit door, only I couldn't see who it was. I'm sure it was the same guy I followed into the office. I wish I could remember where I've seen him." Abby, "Let's not talk about it anymore tonight; you need to rest."

Barry and Janet went back to Medias, Abby and Artur tried to get back into the routine of things. Artur was having a hard time getting over his experience. That was even worse than reform school. There was no recourse against the Bucharest police department. No one there even said 'Sorry'. But as time went by, Artur was able to push it further back in his mind. He thought it was time to get back to living again. That part of his life was over now. Or was it?

Abby and Artur are spending a quiet evening at home together. There is a knock at the door. Artur goes over and opens the door. It's the man from the club that looked familiar to Artur. "Yes, what is it you want?" "Artur, don't you recognize me? It's been a lot of years, buddy." "Sergiu, I'll be...... Come in. What do you know? Abby, this is Sergiu, we went to school together." "Yeah, buddy, even reform school." Sergiu let out a laugh. "Yeah, well, that's true also." "Oh yes, Artur has told me about the three of you." "By the way, Sergiu, what ever happened to Valentin? Have you seen him lately?" "Well, Valentin bought it about 4 years ago. Reform school turned him mean. He got mixed up with some bad people. He got into a shootout with the police, and he took a bullet in the chest. I tried to talk to him, but he just wouldn't listen." "I'm sorry to hear that. What have you been up to lately?" "Oh, I just sort a help people out. Someone needs help with something, I see if I can help them out. All kinds of different things. They talked about old times for a while. "Hey, I gotta be going. I got a busy day tomorrow. It was good to see you again. Nice to meet you Abby." "How did you ever find where I was?" "Oh, I just did some asking around. Well, good night."

"Well, that was a surprise. Showing up like that after all this time." "It's no surprise, Abby." "What do you mean?" "He was here for a purpose." "What purpose?" "That was the man at the club that night Joey was shot. Sergiu is who I saw go into Joey's office. I just didn't recognize him at that time. I have a feeling he shot Joey." "Oh, no, why would he shoot Joey, and why did he show up here tonight?" "I think he saw us at the club that night. I think he recognized me, and looked me up to see if I knew anything. He was looking for me to slip up and say something." "Now what?" "I don't know, the next move is up to him. I'm sure he'll be back." "What are we going to do?" "Just wait."

Back at the castle, Barry and Janet are thinking about going down to The Pub for a while. Then, there is a knock at the door. Barry opens the door, takes a step backwards. "Boss?" Barry just stands there. "Well, Barry, are you going ask me in, or should I just stand here. Barry didn't know whether to ask him in, or slam the door shut, and run. "Oh, yes, come in. I was just shocked to see you after all these years." "I was just as surprised to find you were over here also. I figured you were buried in a field somewhere outside Chicago. How did you ever manage to end up in Rumania of all places?" "I'm an architect remember? I figured the family and I had better disappear after that incident. I really had no idea where to go, then we saw an ad in a paper, which offered a job over here, to design a castle for a guy. So here we are. I had so much work coming in, we decided to make this our home." "You designed this castle?" "No, it is over near Brasov. So, what is your story?" "After your little episode, total war broke out. No one had ever bumped off a head man before. You made it look so easy, everyone went after everyone else. As I walked out of the office one night, a bullet missed me by about six inches. That was enough for me, plus the police started really cracking down on our racket."

"What brought you to Rumania?" "Well, like I said, things were really heating up, and prohibition had been lifted, so, bootlegging wasn't profitable anymore. Actually, some of the gangs even went straight and started selling legally. I had too many enemies, so I had to disappear also." "But why Rumania?" "My parents were originally from here. I was born after they moved to the states. I have a sister here, who moved back here when she was in her 20's. This was the perfect place to disappear to." "Amazing. So, what are you doing these days?" "Actually, I'm straight these days. I work with an investment firm in Bucharest. No more crooked dealings."

"By the way, Barry, you owe me something. You know?" "Ah…. Yes, I know. Twenty-Five thousand dollars." "You know, it took me several days, before I realized you hadn't given me that money." "It helped us get a good start over here. I'll see that you get it back." "Oh, that was a long, long, time ago, Barry. Besides, it belonged to the big guy, I was just an intermediary." "I thought you were the big guy." "No, but you were supposed to think I was. That way, you wouldn't get nosey, and try to find out things you weren't supposed know." "Well, I'll tell you, I don't want to know who he was. It's safer that way. But, at least take half that money, you always treated me right." "Well, alright, if that's what you want."

"By the way, you haven't said how you knew I was here." "You were in Bucharest a couple of weeks ago. I just happened to see you one day. You were with another man and woman. But I didn't get a chance to get your attention. After some checking, I found out you were here in this castle." "That was our daughter, Abby, and her husband, Artur." The three of them talked for a while, the 'boss' had dinner with them. "Hey, I have to be going now. If you get back to Bucharest, look me up. I'll buy you and Janet dinner." "Sounds good to me."

Abby can't relax. She is worried that Sergiu will come back and cause more trouble. There has been so much upheaval lately, she just wants to get away, and leave it all behind, but she also knows that's not possible. It's been a week since Sergiu came to see them. She wishes Sergiu would go a head and do something, if he's going to. The waiting is the worst part.

Abby didn't have to wait long. There was a knock at the door. "Well, Sergiu, back so soon. Come in." "This isn't a social call, Artur, it's business." "What business could we have together?" "I want the envelope." "What did you say about an envelope?" "Don't play stupid, Artur. I know you have it, and I want it." "How do you know I have this 'envelope' you are talking about?" "I knew Joey had it, that's why I was there that night. I didn't get a chance to look for it because you interrupted me." "Yeah, sorry for the inconvenience." "I went back later, and looked for the envelope, but it wasn't there. Joey's partner, not knowing what was going, told me Joey had given you the envelope a couple of weeks before, so, here I am." "Yes, so you are. Well, I don't have the envelope, I passed it on to someone else." "Who?" "Sorry, I can't tell you at this time." "Maybe I can help you tell me." "Never mind, Sergiu, you can beat on me, I won't tell you, and if you kill me, you never will know." "Maybe, but I'm sure Abby would talk without too much persuasion." "You touch Abby, and I'll take that gun away from you, and shove it down your throat." "Ok, Artur, ok. We'll leave it at that. But I will find where that envelope is." Sergiu left.

Artur started breathing again. Abby started crying. "It's alright, Abby, it's over." "No, it is not over. It won't be over until someone else gets killed." "Calm down, Abby, we'll get through this. As a matter of fact, I had forgotten about the envelope, until Sergiu brought it up. I think it's time we find out what is so important about that envelope." Artur walked over to the desk and pulled out the bottom drawer and took the envelope from the back of the drawer. "You're not going to open that, are you? It's not addressed to you." "We seem to be in this pretty deep, and I want to know what we are putting our life on the line for. I think we have that right." Artur opened the envelope and pulled out two pieces of paper. "Artur, what does it say?" "It's a list of names, and a list of addresses, in various parts of Bucharest and Brasov."

"What does it mean? Who are these people?" "I don't know. Most of these names look as if they are Russian names." "Is Sergiu on the list?" "No, he is probably their gun for hire and messenger boy. He's too low on the totem pole for anyone to worry about yet. The names on the list are probably all of the people who must be involved in something big. We have to get this to the Rumanian Intelligence. We'll do that first thing tomorrow. In the meantime, I think I need a drink. Let's go down to the club for a while." Artur taped the envelope back on to the drawer and put it back in the desk.

As Abby and Artur entered the club, Artur spotted Sergiu over at his regular table by the wall. Artur's thought was, 'Is he going to follow us everywhere?' They sat at their regular table; Sergiu never once looked their way. Artur decided not to start anything. The lights dimmed down, and a woman came out, and sang a couple of songs. After she finished, the lights came back up. Artur noticed that Sergiu had left. Maybe he just came in for the music.

It was getting late, so Abby and Artur started home. Artur kept watching to see if they were being followed. There didn't seem to be, so Artur relaxed some. As Artur unlocked the door to the apartment and turned the light on, he stopped so quickly, Abby walked into the back of him. "What's wrong, Artur?" Artur walked on in to the apartment. When Abby stepped in, she inhaled a deep breath. "What.......?" The apartment was a mess. The desk drawers were opened and the contents thrown all over the floor. Couch cushions on the floor. Every piece of furniture with a drawer in it was open with everything thrown on the floor. Even the bedroom was a mess. "It looks as if Sergiu paid us a visit while we were gone." "Oh, Artur, how are we ever going to get this mess cleaned up?" Then it hit Artur, he better check that bottom desk drawer. He pulled the drawer all the way out. The envelope was still taped to the back of the drawer. That was luck.

"Well, the envelope is still here. We're lucky he didn't pull the drawers all the way out." "Artur, we're getting in too deep. Someone's going to get killed, and it will probably be us." "Abby, we'll be alright. Tomorrow we'll get this to the right people. We just have to play it smart; keep our eyes and ears open. We'll get through this."

Early the next morning, Artur is rudely awakened by someone banging on the door. He slowly gets up and stumbles to the door. He's not fully awake yet, but that's about to change, really quick. He is about to unlock the door, but before he can, whoever is on the other side of the door, breaks it open and barges in, knocking Artur backward on the floor. It is Sergiu. "I said I would be back." "Well, you could have waited 10 more seconds. You didn't need to break the door down." "You took so long, I thought you might be planning something stupid." "The only stupid around here is you Sergiu. I could kill you right now, and get away with it. It's called self-defense."

By now, Abby is out in the room with her robe on. "Artur, are you all right?" "Yes, physically." "You big ape, why don't you leave us alone?" "When I get what I want, I will. In the meantime, we are all going on a little trip together." "We're not even dressed. Besides, I don't feel like taking a trip." "You're dressed enough. Now let's go!" "If I ever get my hands on you......" "Forget it, you're not big enough. Move."

There was a driver in the car. Abby sat up front with him. Artur got in the back with Sergiu. Artur was sitting behind Abby. They drove west, through town, and out to a rural area. All the time, Sergiu held a gun pointed toward Artur. They drove for about an hour. "How far are we going, Sergiu?" "Shut up!" "Ahhh…… Touchy." Without warning, Artur swung his right fist around, and hit Sergiu square in the face, at the same time he grabbed Sergiu's gun. The gun went off and hit the driver in the back of the head. He collapsed on the wheel, the car started swerving, heading for a tree. It glanced off the tree, and rolled over a couple of times, landing upright.

No one moved for several minutes. Everyone was rather dazed. When Artur opened his eyes, Sergiu was still sitting there with his gun pointed at Artur. "Are you alright, Abby?" "Yeah, just a little bruised in a couple of places." "Well, Artur, it looks like the only thing you accomplished was wrecking the car and killing the driver." "Well, that's something." "Yeah, but not enough. We still have someone to go see. We'll just have to continue on foot. It isn't too much farther."

After about half and hour of walking, they came to a gravel drive. "Up the end of this drive is where we are going." "Sergiu, why don't you go on up, and bring a car back to get us. We'll wait." "You go ahead and make your jokes, but before long you won't be laughing at anything."

The lane was around a quarter of a mile long. Then, they came to an old two story farm house, which had seen better days. They went up on the porch. "Artur, you open the door and step in. Abby, you follow Artur, and I'll be right behind you. Don't make any quick moves." They entered a large living room, with not much furniture, but lots of spider webs. Sergiu pointed them toward a door off to the left.

The room they entered, was probably a bedroom at one time. Now, it had a table in the center of the room, with four chairs. There was a couch against one wall. Two stuffed chairs against another wall. There was a refrigerator and a cooking stove. There were three men at the table, and one man on the couch. The man on the couch opened one eye when they walked in, then closed it again. Two of the men looked to be Rumanian, but the other two looked to be Russian. The man on the couch was told to get up, and Artur and Abby, were told to sit on the couch. The man went over and sat at the table.

Artur was getting a little worried, but, "What will we talk about while we're waiting for, whoever it is we're waiting on?" "Quiet! We will talk when the General gets here. Until then, don't talk." "Who's the General?" "I said shut up!" Artur was trying to figure out what was going on. Whatever it was, it was big. Artur was forming an idea, but he didn't want to get too far ahead of himself. He needed more information. If Artur was right, it could mean the life or death of Rumania.

A door opened, and a man walked in dressed in a Generals military uniform. Definitely Russian. "Who are these people and why are they here?" Sergiu spoke up, "Sir, this is Artur and Abby. Artur has the envelope, or knows where it is." "You idiot, why did you bring them here? You were told not to ever bring anyone here." "They wouldn't cooperate. He refuses to hand over the envelope. I didn't know what else to do." "They will have to be disposed of after we are through with them. Well, Mr. Artur, what do you have to say for yourself?" "Nothing, Sergiu said it all." "We will soon rid you of that smugness, Mr. Artur."

"Look, General, I don't have any envelope with your name on it." "I know you don't, but the one you do have is the one I want." "It's against the law to read other people's mail." "Mr. Artur, are you really that stupid?" "Only when I want to be." One of the men at the table got up and walked over to the couch beside Artur. After Artur made that last remark, the man hit Artur on the jaw with his fist. Artur fell over on Abby's lap. He shook his head, and tried to sit up. Abby screamed. "Mr. Artur, let me put it this way. If you give me what I want, you live. If you don't, you die." "If I die, I won't be able to tell you anything." "If you die, I'll just find another way to get what I want." Abby spoke up, "Then go find that other way, and let us go." "Forget it, General, one of the first things you said when you came in, was that you would have to dispose of us. Why help you when we are going to die anyway?"

"Alright, suppose I tell you I will let you live, if you promise to never divulge what happened here." "General, that's as old as the hills, but it never works out that way, you know that." "Mr. Artur, you are straining my patience. There is only one solution left for me. Miss Abby, that is your name, I understand, please stand up." "Whoa, General, what do think you are going to do?" "Shut up! Take Miss Abby and place her on one of the chairs at the table. Tie her hands behind her." "Wait, don't you touch her." The man who tied her up, stood in front of her. The man suddenly slapped Abby across the face so hard, she almost passed out. Artur started to get up. The man beside him pushed him back down. The man facing Abby raised his hand again. "Wait! Stop! I'll give you the envelope, I'll give you the envelope. Don't hurt Abby anymore."

As Artur yelled out, he stood up. As the General turned toward Abby, Artur quickly turned and hit the man beside him so hard in the stomach, he fell to the floor. As the General turned back around, his nose ran into Artur's clenched fist. He went flying backward, landing on the floor. Before Artur could move again, Sergiu had his arms around Artur, and squeezed so tight, Artur almost passed out. Within seconds, the rest of the men were in front of Artur. One of them hit him hard on the side of the head.

As the General started to get up, a voice from outside, "This is the police. The house is surrounded. Come out one at a time with your hands up." Inside, everyone stood still and looked at each other. "You have 30 seconds to come out, or we start shooting." "What are we going to do, General?" "Let me think a minute." "You have 20 seconds left." The General yelled out, "We're coming out don't shoot." "General, you mean you are going to give up?" "No. We have an advantage." As he spoke, he looked at Artur and Abby. "These two will be our ticket out of here. They won't take the chance of hitting them." One of the men untied Abby and brought her to where Artur was. The General, "You two will be right in front of me when we walk out. Don't try anything. My gun will be right against Abby's head. The rest of you fall in behind." "You have 10 seconds left." "Ok, ok, we're coming."

The General had Abby slowly open the front door. He put a hand on Artur's shoulder, and the gun against Abby' head. They walked to the edge of the front porch and stopped. "You gentlemen will move away, let is walk to our car, and leave. If you do not, this woman will die." No one moved, the minutes went by. The General didn't know it, but the police actually had the advantage. Behind a tree, several yards from the General, was a man standing with a sniper's rifle. The cross hairs were lined up with the General's forehead. He waited for the right time. His finger resting on the trigger.

Abby was unable to stop crying and screaming. The man in charge of the police just happened to be Detective Sorin. "Artur, you should be more careful how you dress, especially those shoes." Artur dropped his head down to look. At that instant, the sniper pulled the trigger. The bullet hit the General in the middle of the forehead. He never knew what hit him. He flew backwards from the impact of the bullet. Abby fainted and fell to the ground. The rest of the men threw their hands up. "Don't shoot, don't shoot." Except Sergiu, he pulled out his gun and one of the policemen shot him in the chest. He fell to the ground, dead. Artur straightened up. "Sorin, I don't have any shoes on." "I know, but it got the job done." Artur leaned over and helped Abby up. "Is it over, am I alive?" "Yes Abby, everything is over, and you are very much alive. Thanks to our 'friend' detective Sorin."

Sorin walked up to Abby and Artur, "That little maneuver worked really well." "What do you mean, 'That little maneuver'?" "I knew when I mentioned your shoes, you would look down. That's all it took for our sharp shooter to do his job." "And what if your man missed or was off a little? Abby and I would probably have a hole in our head now." "Our man didn't miss, and you are both ok. Why don't you two go get in my car, and I'll drive you back to your apartment. You have something that man over there wants."

A man with grey hair, probably around 50, in a dark blue suit, came over to Artur. "I am Cezar Balan, with the National Intelligence Department. I believe you have something I want." "You bet I do, and the sooner it's in your hands, the better Abby and I will feel. It's getting too dangerous around here. A guy could get killed." Mr. Balan let out a laugh. "I see what you mean. Come, we will talk on the way to your apartment." Abby sat up with Sorin, while Artur and Cezar sat in the back.

"By the way, Sorin, what prompted you and your people to come out to that house?" "You did." "What? I didn't even know that house existed, until we arrived there. I didn't even know what we were in there for. Of course, I knew it wasn't going to be anything fun. So how did I lead you there?" "I've had a tail on you and Abby for the last couple of weeks." "Why, you still think I killed Joey?" "No, I knew you didn't kill him. I got an anonymous phone call that Joey had given you an envelope a few weeks before, and that Joey was killed by someone who wanted that envelope pretty bad." Cezar spoke up, "You see, Joey was one of our agents. He was holding on to this envelope until we were organized to move on this group. Evidently, he knew his life was in danger, and since you were good friends, he figured you would know what to do when the time came."

"Did he tell you I had the envelope?" "No, after Joey was killed, we had no idea where it got to. We assumed the people we were after had it. That worried us. Then Mr. Sorin called us and told us about the phone call. We think it was Joey's partner who placed the call. He didn't want to get involved, so he didn't give his name. So, anyway, we felt relieved you had it instead of the group." "So, Mr. Detective, since I had the envelope, you were just going to sit back and wait for someone to come to me for it." "I guess you could put it that way." "Why didn't you move in when Sergiu came up to kidnap us?" "Sergiu was just a messenger. We knew the head man was called 'The General', but we didn't know where he was at. So, we let you lead us to him."

"So, you were using Abby and I as bait, and it never occurred to you, to let is in on what was going on?" "We couldn't take the chance. You would either have backed out, or you would have been so nervous, you would have blown the whole thing." "Well, Detective Sorin, I think you owe Abby and I something." "You're absolutely right. I'm going to treat you and Abby to the best meal the club has to offer, including Champaign, the whole works." "Well, thank you. We will accept that."

At the apartment, Artur took the bottom desk drawer out and took the envelope off the back of it. "Here you are, Mr. Balan. I am glad to be rid of it." "I assume you know what is in here." "Yes, sir, Abby and I looked at the contents. Since we were in so deep, we decided to see what we were protecting. To us, it's just a list of names and locations. Other than that, we don't know what it means." "Because of what you have been through, I feel you deserve to know just what is going on. The 'General', a Russian, although Russia is not involved, was planning to oust the present government, and install his own. He wanted to be Rumania's dictator. The list of names and locations are his groups that would act when he gave the word. They would take over different utility's, radio stations and local government offices, all at the same time. Without a leader, they are harmless, but we will round them all up."

"Well, I'm glad that's over with." "Think of the adventure we had, Abby. You don't get that every day." "Thank Goodness. That was enough to last me a life time. I just want to get back to my research. It's less dangerous." "How right you are."

CHAPTER 16

It is 1965 now. Barry is 65, Janet is 61, Abby and Artur are 43. Barry has slowed down a little, he doesn't seem to have much energy anymore. Janet is still at the library. She is feeling her age a little, but her health is still pretty good. Violeta and Deniel passed away a few years ago. Clare is the housekeeper, she is 51. Bela is the grounds keeper, he is 52. They are good people, and very helpful to Barry and Janet. Barry and Janet like them very much.

Abby and Artur have had a quiet, peaceful life, since their adventure. Only, Abby is still a little unhappy with the administrative department. She thinks they keep too tight a rein on her. She is starting to form an idea in her mind. She won't tell Artur, until she does some investigation.

One afternoon, there was a knock on the door. Clara opened the door, "Yes. Can I help you?" "My name is Bert Allen, Is Mr. Barry Greene here?" "Yes, step in and I will get him for you." Barry was upstairs resting. Clara knocked on the door and told Barry someone was here to see him. "Who is it Clara?" "His name is Bert Allen; he appears to be American." "Very well, I'll be down in a minute."

"Hi, I'm Barry Greene, you are an American?" "Yes, I'm Bert Allen." "So, why are you here?" "I am with Enterprise Studio's in California. I am a movie director." "Interesting. How would that have anything to do with me?" "We are shooting a movie, and I would like to talk to you about doing some filming outside and inside your castle." "Really? Why this castle?" "Barry, if I may, we have been looking for an interesting place to film, and in our research, we found there is quite a history behind your castle." "Oh? What kind of movie is this?" "Naturally, it's a horror movie, with some humor in it. We would like to incorporate some of the history into our film. It will give you some publicity."

"Well, Mr. Allen, I don't want any publicity. I don't want anyone hanging around the grounds or knocking on the door, because they think there is something to see here." "That's alright, we will keep your name and the location of the castle out of the credits. That's no problem. Let me explain what's involved. We will shoot several scenes out on the grounds, and several scenes inside. We will not destroy anything, and any messes we make, we will clean up, and you will be handsomely paid for the use of your castle." "Well, as long as my name and location are not released, I think it might be interesting to see how you film a movie." "If you or your wife would like to be in a scene, we can do that. We will need some of the people from the village to be extras." "That might be interesting, we'll see." "Very good. It will take a few days to get all of our equipment up here. I'll keep you posted."

Barry was starting to get a little excited. This was a new experience for them. Maybe they would have a good experience for a change. He decided to go down to the library and tell Janet, instead of waiting until she got home.

"Janet, how would you like to be in a movie?" "Be in a movie? What are you talking about? You haven't been drinking, have you?" "No, but I have some news for you. A movie studio wants to shoot a movie at the castle." "What? Really? Why?" "They heard about the history of the castle, and they want to use some of that history, and the castle." "They are going to come up here and shoot a movie, and we will be in it?" "He said he could arrange to have us in one of the scenes. He's going to use some of the villagers, also." "Who is this guy?" "His name is Bert Allen, with Enterprise Studio's." "It sounds fun. We could use some good entertainment for a change." "There is one thing, though, I don't want Mr. Allen to know about or use anything about Daniel." "Definitely not."

After about a week, everything was set up, and ready to go. There were three lead actors and the lead actress. The actress was Helen Duval, age 32. The three actors were, Jonathan Howell, age 42, Jason Taylor, age 35 and Arthur Tate, 52. Two co-stars were, Judith Day, and Amy Burke. They each had their own trailer to sleep in, as did the director. Everyone else stayed in the inn in the village. There were just enough rooms, if they doubled up. They were used to that. So, after some confusion in the beginning, everything was finally organized. It was too late in the day to start shooting any scenes without any preparations; everyone was too tired anyway. Some of the crew and the director went down to the village to meet the villagers.

The next morning, everyone started rehearsing a scene, going over their lines and positions. Bert was finally satisfied and called for a shoot. The cameras were set up and the scene started. They shot three scenes that afternoon. Two of them required several retakes. Twice, Helen got her tongue twisted, and messed up her lines, and everyone started laughing. But they had enough scenes to call it a day, although, they intended to shoot a night scene later.

Around 10:00 that evening, they were ready to shoot the night scene. Helen and Jason were to meet secretly outside the castle. After several minutes Arthur (her husband) was to come on the scene and confront Helen and Jason. The scene was going along fine. Suddenly, Helen let out a scream, and started shaking. "Cut! Helen, what's the matter? What happened?" Jason put his arm around Helen. "Helen what is it? You're shaking." Bert ran over to Helen. "Helen, calm down. Tell me what's wrong." Finally, Helen was able to talk. "Bert, there was someone standing over there." She pointed with her finger. "He was horrible looking. The left side of his face was a bloody mess. He was looking right at me." "Harry, go around the side of the castle and see if you see anyone. Helen, are you sure it wasn't Arthur getting ready to come on the set?" "No! It wasn't Arthur. I don't know who it was, but I saw him, as sure as I see you." Harry came back, "I didn't see anyone."

The next morning, the film was developed, and the editor went through the scenes to see if everything looked as it should. As he looked through the night scene, he stiffened up. He ran the film back to make sure of what he saw. He stopped, ran out of the trailer, and found Bert. "Burt, you better come look at yesterday's shoot. I think we have a problem." Bert headed for the trailer to look at the film. "Scroll through the night scene." As Bert went through the night scene, he saw what the editor was talking about. There was small white place on the film, they couldn't make out. "Put that frame in the projector and blow it up on the screen. Maybe we can make out what it is." They took a close look at the frame. "It almost looks like someone standing there. Do you think one of the crew got in the way?" "I don't know Bert, its very blurry." "It looks to be transparent. Was the moon out last night?" "Yeah, it was about ¾ full." "This is probably just the reflection of the moon on the lens. It happens sometimes. It doesn't matter, we never finished the scene. We'll try it again tonight."

They plan on shooting some scenes inside this afternoon. They are going to use the great hall for some scenes. They have invited some of the villagers up to participate in the scene. It's going to be a celebration of Helen, returning to the castle after several years away. Barry and Janet will be in the scene. Barry will make a toast to Helen, and Janet will tell her how happy she is that Helen is back. They rehearse the scene a few times. Then, they are ready to shoot. Barry gives the toast, and as everyone starts to drink to the toast, the bulbs on the lighting fixtures all explode. At the same instant, Barry starts to choke. He drops his glass and grabs his throat.

Janet yells, "Barry!" Barry collapsed on the floor. A couple of the crew tried to help Barry, but there wasn't much they could do. Barry's face turned blue as he tried desperately to breathe. Just as suddenly as it started, it stopped. Barry lay there gasping for air. After a few minutes, he came around and was alright. "Barry, what happened? What made you start choking?" "I don't know, Janet. It just started and I couldn't do anything. I've never done that before." Bert called for a break. They would try later. One of the lighting crew was checking the light standards. Bert, "What caused those lights to explode?" "I don't know. I never experienced all the bulbs going at once. There must have been an awfully high electrical surge. That's all I can think of." "See what you can do. We'll try the scene again in an hour."

They tried the scene again. Everything went well this time. Barry did his toast, and Janet said her line. The complete scene lasted about 10 minutes. They only had to reshoot one part twice, which isn't too bad. Sometimes it takes more than twice. But when Bert said 'That's a wrap', a strong, chilling, breeze swept through the room. Everyone felt it. Barry and Janet, looked at each other, but didn't say anything.

That night they set up to shoot the night scene. They used a different place, and a different position, so the moon wouldn't interfere. "Ok, Helen, you're a little uncomfortable, because you don't want Arthur to catch you and Jason together. Got it?" "Yes, I have it." The scene went well. They didn't even have to reshoot any of it. Bert called it a night. Some of the crew and actors went down to The Pub to relax a while.

Barry and Janet went up to their room. Now, they don't know about the problem with the film from that first night scene. "Janet, I'm sure you felt that chilling breeze this afternoon." "Yes. It sort of frightened me. And that choking you went through. It scared me to death. Are you thinking, what I'm thinking?" "Yes, dear, knowing the history of this place, and what it is capable of, I have a feeling someone, or something, doesn't want this movie filmed here."

"That's my feeling also." "We'll see how it goes, but we may have to have them stop filming their movie here."

The next morning, as the editor goes over yesterdays filming, everything looks good. Then he gets to the night scene again. Guess what? He goes and gets Bert again. "Now, what?" "Bert, this is something different. You better come and look." As Bert scrolls through the night scene, he sees what looks like a man's shadow near the edge of the frames. The shadow appears to be a man standing against the castle wall. "From now on, I'm going to make sure all the crew members are back behind the camera. We're wasting a lot of time on reshoots." "Ah…. Bert, I don't know of any of our crew members that are that big. Whoever that shadow belongs to must be at least 6 ½ feet tall. And weigh 200 pounds or more." "Yeah……, you're right. That is an awfully big shadow."

"What do you want to do with it?" "I tell you what, we'll leave it in the film. This is a horror movie, and people watching the movie, will be wondering what it has to do with the plot. Therefore, they will continue to watch, to see what part it plays." "But it doesn't have anything to do with the plot." "But those who notice it, will be talking about it. Word of mouth could make a lot of people want to watch the film."

That night they are going to shoot the rest of the night scene. Helen and Jason were holding each other and talking, when Arthur came on the scene. There was an argument. Helen tried to tell Arthur nothing was going on. Arthur started yelling at Helen, and she turned and ran away. Jason and Arthur argued for a couple of minutes. "Alright people, this is where Jason and Arthur are arguing. Now we're going to finish the scene where Jason and Arthur start fighting. You two have rehearsed this, so you understand what moves to make. This will take a while because we have to choregraph these fight moves. Alright, lets get started."

Jason tells Arthur to calm down. At which point Arthur hits Jason and knocks him to the ground. Jason tells Arthur he doesn't want to fight him. Arthur lunges toward Jason, but Jason is too quick. He sidesteps Arthur and hits Arthur in the stomach. Arthur falls to the ground. As Arthur lays on the ground, trying to get up, Jason, to Arthur, "Your too old to be fighting me, let's stop it, right here." Jason grabs Arthur's hand to help him up. As Arthur rises, he hits Jason and knocks him backward. Then Arthur grabs Jason around the neck and starts choking him. (That's not in the script.) Jason tries to get free of Arthur, but Arthur won't let go. He squeezes harder. Jason can't breathe and starts losing conscience. Bert runs toward Arthur. "Arthur what are you doing? Let go of Jason. Arthur!" Bert and two of the crew are trying to pull Arthur off of Jason. He won't let go. One of the crew hits Arthur across the side of the face. Arthur let's go and falls to the ground. Jason collapses to the ground, trying to catch his breathe. Finally, Jason is able to sit up. Arthur sits up, "What's going on? What happened? I thought we were going to shoot this scene." "You don't know what just happened?" "No, my jaw hurts, did Jason slip and hit me?"

"Ok, everyone, that's it for tonight. Arthur, you and I and Jason are going to my trailer. We're going to talk about what happened here." The three went to Bert's trailer. Bert poured everyone some coffee. "Ok, Arthur, tell me what happened." "I don't know what happened. I told you, I was saying my lines to Jason, the next thing I knew, I was lying on he ground with a sore jaw." "You don't remember grabbing Jason around the neck, and choking him till he almost passed out?" "I what! I never did that." "Look at Jason's neck. It still has the imprint of your fingers and bruising." "I don't remember any of that. Jason, if I did that, I'm sorry. I would never knowingly do that to you. We have always been friends. You know that." "I know, Arthur, it's alright, I'm ok now. This is all such a mystery." "I hate to get behind schedule, but we need a day off. I think I need to have a talk with Barry, tomorrow."

The next morning, Bert went to talk to Barry. Barry and Janet were sitting in Barry's office. "Come on in, Bert, sit down and have a cup of coffee." "Yeah, I think I need some coffee." "Well, Bert, what's on the agenda for today?" "There is no agenda for today. We're taking today off. Everyone needs it." "Ok, what can I do for you?" "I need to have a talk with you and Janet." "Sure, you sound serious." "It is. Believe me." "Ok, shoot." "There have been some strange things going on around here." "Ah…… Suchas what?" "Well, first of all……." Bert went on to tell Barry and Janet about everything that has happened. "…… so, you see I think there's a curse on this movie, and I think what happened to you the other day, is part of that."

"A curse, huh? Janet and I came to that same conclusion the other day." "You did. But why?" "You know this castle has quite a history. Right?" "Yes, that's why we chose it for filming." "Do you know what the history is?" "No, just that there has been a lot of violence here in the last couple hundred years." "Exactly. Bert, I want you to come with me. I want to show you something. This may change your mind about filming your movie here."

Barry took Bert down to the vault room. "Bert, you see all these vaults, some with names and some without?" "Yes, so, what about them?" "There are very few empty vaults here. But in all those that contain a body, just about every one of those people died a violent, and horrible death." "So, you think the ghosts of these people don't want me to film a movie here at the castle." "Well, that's one answer." "You don't really believe that?" "Well, I've seen a few strange things here, and I have read some of the history. Do you have another explanation?" "I have to think about that."

As Barry and Bert are about to leave the vault room, Bert spots the door to the torture room. "Barry, where does that door lead?" Barry hesitated. "It's a……. torture room and a dungeon." "You're kidding." "No, I'm not kidding." "Fantastic! I need to see it." Barry tried to think of some excuse, but Bert would probably sneak down here and go in it anyway. "Ok, Bert, I'll even let you open the door." Bert opened the door and stepped in. "This is great. We can shoot our scenes here, instead of back home on a set." "I don't know, Bert, you may be getting in over your head." "Take it easy, Barry, we'll be ok."

Bert got all the crew and actors together. "Listen up people. I found the perfect place to film the torture scenes. There is actually a torture room and dungeon below the castle here. It would be perfect and authentic." "You want us to set up our equipment down there now?" "Yes, I'll show you where it is, and then you can set up the scene. Come on." Barry went down to watch them set up. There were still several sets of chains attached to the walls. There was also a device that a person lay down on, and with the aid of a crank, would tend to make you taller, or longer, which ever way you want to look at it, but either way, it caused a lot of pain.

"Now, Judith and Amy, you will be shackled to the chains on the wall. Your brother, Simon, is unconscious on the floor. Arthur, you have become demented, and twisted, the past few years, since Helen ran off with Jason. You hate all women. Arthur, you drag Simon into the dungeon and place him on the cot. Then you threaten to disfigure the girls. Places everybody. This is a shoot."

It was about a 10-minute scene. It all went smooth. The girls screaming and trying to get loose, begging to be let go. Some blood on their blouses, and arms. "Cut. Good job. We will take a break before going on. Simon, come on out and get ready for your part in this scene. Take a break for lunch." Everybody headed back upstairs. Bert looked around, "Where is Simon? We need to go over his scene." Everyone looked around, he wasn't there. Bert headed back down the stairs to see what the hold up was. Simon was still laying on the cot. "Simon, wake up. I want to go over your next scene." Simon didn't move. Bert went over to Simon to wake him up. As Bert went to shake Simon, he stopped, and stepped back a few steps. He just stared at Simon. Simon wasn't moving. His mouth was wide open, as is he were trying to scream, and his eyes were wide open, looking straight up at the ceiling.

Bert turned and ran back upstairs. He was panicky. "Where's Barry!" Someone said he was in his office. Bert ran to the office. "Barry, come with me, something has happened. You have to see this." "Ok, Bert, calm down." Barry followed Bert down to the dungeon. "Look at Simon. He's dead. Look at his face." Barry looked Simon over. There were no marks on Simon, just the twisted face. "Bert, Simon looks like he was scared to death by something, or someone. None of you saw anything, or heard Simon yell out?" "No, in the next scene, Arthur was supposed to drag Simon out of the dungeon and chain him to the wall also. Simon never made a sound while he was laying there. I thought he was just asleep."

"Leave everything as it is. Have one of the crew go to the village and get Remus. Have him bring the doctor with him. I warned you, strange things happen here." "Yeah, but I never expected anything like this. Now I'm not sure what to do. Simon was a good friend. I don't understand what's happening." "I told you, you just didn't believe me."

Remus and the doctor came down to the dungeon. The cast and crew are wondering what is going on. Where's Simon? Why is the constable and doctor here? The doctor checked Simon over pretty close. "Bert, did Simon have a bad heart or any other ailments?" "No, doc, as far as I know, he was very healthy. He was only 35." "I'll have to get him to Brasov and do an autopsy to find out what the cause was. But off hand, he looks like he was scared to death. Barry, can you take me and Simon to Brasov in your vehicle? Bert, can you get a couple of your crew to take Simon upstairs." "Sure thing." Remus, "Well, I don't need to hang around, it looks like no crime was committed. But, doc, you'll need to notify the authorities in Brasov." "Yeah, I will."

Bert got everyone together and told them what had happened. Everybody was in shock. This was the first time anyone had experienced a death on the set. Needless to say, there would be no more scene shooting the rest of today. Everyone split up and went to their trailers and such, to digest what had happened. No one felt like talking.

The next couple of days were a little chaotic. No one really wanted to go back to work yet. Bert had to figure out what to do about Simon's character. Bert went into the village to The Pub, then walked around the village. Maybe he could find a villager that looked enough like Simon, with enough make-up, that the audience wouldn't notice. If the villager could at least finish the dungeon scene, maybe the writers could have the character disappear later.

A man came out of a shop and almost ran over Bert. When Bert looked at the guy, he had his man. The features were similar, but the hair was the wrong color, and the eyes were a different color, but if the man wanted the job, they could dye his hair, and put the correct color contacts in his eyes. "Oh, Mr. Bert, I'm sorry, I guess we both tried to occupy the same space there." "That's alright, no harm done. What is your name?" "Augustin Anton, sir." "You heard about the death of one of out actors?" "Yes, sir. I did." "I need someone to replace him for a scene. Would you consider trying out for that character?" "I never did any acting before. I've never even seen very many movies." "That's alright, would you be willing to try?" "I guess so. Sure."

In the meantime, the doctor came back to the village. He went to see Barry and Bert. "I performed the autopsy on Simon." "What did you find?" "I could find nothing wrong. All of his organs were healthy. There is no explanation. His heart just stopped. I think he was scared to death." "But, doc, we were all down there with him the whole time. No one heard, or saw anything that would cause that." "No, but, evidently Simon did."

Everything was starting to get back to normal, so Bert decided to try the next part of the dungeon scene. When they got done with Augustin, he was a pretty good double for Simon. But, could he act the part. They did a couple of rehearsals, and Augustin was pretty good. This time Barry was in the room for the shooting, in case something should happen again.

In this scene, Arthur forces Augustin out of the cell, and chains him to the wall next to the girls, who are rather quiet now. They have worn themselves out screaming, and trying to break free. Judith, "Why are you holding us here? We haven't done anything to you." "You were trespassing." Amy, "We were lost. We were just asking for help." "Yes, then you would have run off with this man, just as my wife ran off with my friend." Augustin, "You're crazy! We didn't have anything to do with your wife." Judith, "What do you mean, we would have run off with Jerry? He's my brother. We are over here on vacation. We don't live here. We are Americans. And what about Jerry, he's not a woman, let him go."

"It's just his misfortune that he was with you. I can't let him go; he has seen too much. You are all alike, and you must pay the penalty." "What penalty?" "Slow death."

Now, Arthur will take the chains off of Amy, and place her on the stretching table. As she lays on the table, Arthur will pull her arms above her head, and tie her hands to one end of the table. Then he will take her feet, tie them together, and tie them to the other end of the table. Then, the turn of a crank at one end of the table, will start stretching her body. The crank was tested earlier, and it was so corroded and rusted that it would not turn. Which was good, because then they would not have to disassemble it to keep it from operating. They didn't want any more accidents.

So, after Arthur makes sure Amy is secure, he turns to Judith and Augustin. "Now watch closely, and see how you will die. I may do you next Jerry, so watch closely." Suddenly, there is a clicking noise. Everyone stops and listens. Arthur turns around, "The crank is moving!" Then Amy feels the tension building on her body. She starts screaming. Arthur grabs the crank to try to stop it. It won't stop. Arthur keeps trying. Amy is screaming and trying to get loose. But Arthur can't stop the crank. Barry reaches into the tool box and pulls out a knife. He runs over to the table and cuts the rope attached to the Amy's feet. Then steps over and cuts the rope tied to her hands. The crank stops.

Arthur helps Amy off the table, and back upstairs. She is still shaking, and crying. Arthur pours Amy a drink. "Amy, drink this. Are you ok?" "I think so, but I sure thought I was going to die." Everyone was back up in the kitchen now. No, wait. Someone's missing. It's Barry and Judith. Bert runs back down to the room. "Barry, what's going on?" "I got Augustin loose ok, but I can't get the chains off of Judith. The screws won't turn. It's as if they were rusted." Both men worked on the arm bracelets. Judith was becoming frightened, and started to cry. They tried oil on the screws, they tried a wrench, they wouldn't budge. "The only thing left is to try sawing the chains." Barry went over to the tool box. Just as he picked up a saw, the bracelets let loose on their own. "Bert, we need to go have a talk. Come, Judith, let's go upstairs."

Bert and Barry went into Barry's office, and closed the door. "Bert, I would say that this castle does not want the publicity. I will even go further, and say, the people down in that vault room, don't want this movie made here. Maybe not anywhere." "I hear what you are saying, but......" "But, what?" "I don't believe in ghosts and haunted castles. At least I didn't. But I don't have any logical explanation for what is happening." "I don't either, but then I don't have any explanation for a lot of other things that have happened in the castle."

"Why do you and Janet stay here? I would move somewhere else and leave all this behind. Is it worth it to go through these strange things?" "This has been our home for 30 years. I can't imagine living anywhere else, and except for a couple of times, the castle has really been good for us. It doesn't usually involve us too much. I guess we're just used to it." "Why don't you go back to America?" "Well, let's just say, we had to leave the states in a hurry. Even though it's been 30 years, I don't know if it's safe to go back. Let's just leave it at that." "Ok."

"Barry, I would like to do a couple of shots at the front of the castle with Helen, Jason and Arthur. Then I will think seriously about whether to continue, or pack it up and go home." "That's alright with me." "I'll get the cast and crew together. We'll try it now, while there is still enough light left."

Bert set the scene up. Helen and Arthur would be talking by the front door. Then Jason would enter. Helen and Arthur would talk about a gala they were going to host. Just as Jason was entering the scene, the ground started shaking. Suddenly a concrete block from the balcony above broke loose and started falling to the ground. When Arthur felt the shaking, for some reason he looked up. He saw the block falling, he grabbed Helen by the shoulders and pulled her to him. The block landed where she had been standing.

Helen put her arms around Arthur and held him tight. She was shaking terribly. Arthur took Helen over and sat her on a small bench. "Helen, that was close. Are you alright?" "Arthur, is someone trying to kill us all?" Everyone gathered around. "Barry, that's it. We're through here. I'm not supposed to make this picture here. We'll go back to the states and try and finish this movie. If anything happens over there, I'll burn every foot of film we have already."

Barry and Janet are alone again. "I'm glad that ordeal is over with. I'm glad Bert decided to quit when he did. Janet, I think this castle is alive, and the people down in that vault room aren't quite as dead as we think they are. I think their spirits are still roaming around. Do you think we should move away from here?" "I don't really think we should. What ever this is, has never really harmed you, or me, or Abby. It's as if we are supposed to be here." Janet laughed a little, "Maybe this castle wouldn't let us leave." "You may be right."

Chapter 17

It's now 1972. Barry is 72, his health is not very good. He has to use a cane when he walks. He has quit working; his hands aren't very steady anymore. Janet is 68, she is doing fairly well, health wise. She has retired from the library. She planted a good size flower garden; she spends a lot of time in the garden. Abby and Artur are both 50 now. Remus is 69. He retired. There is a new constable now, his name is Cornel Abbot. He is 47. Bela and Clara are still with the Greene's.

Abby and Artur are still working at the hospital, but Abby is totally fed up. Her agenda of what she wants to do, is now an obsession with her. "Artur, I am really unhappy working here." "I know. I can tell." "Am I that obvious?" "No, no, I can just tell that you are not happy here any longer." "I have been thinking about something for some time now. I have done some investigating, and I think it will work." "I'm almost afraid to ask." "Artur, let's quit our job here, and move back to the castle." "What? What on earth why? We can't do any research there." "Yes, we can." "How?" "We can build our own lab down in the torture room." "The torture room? Oh no! That place has a history, and I don't want anything to do with it. I intend to grow old."

"Oh, Artur, be sensible. Nothing has happened there in several years. Besides, I think there is probably a logical explanation for the things that happened there. You don't really believe in ghostly spirits, do you?" "In a word. Yes! Too many weird things have happened at the castle and that room." Abby chuckled a little. "Artur, what am I going to do with you?" "Keep me away from the castle, for one." "Artur, stop clowning around. You know where clowns belong." "Yes, I know, in a circus. Go on. I'm listening. But really, I am a little leary about that castle."

"I have priced what we would need for a lab, and we have the money. No one could tell us what to do, and no one would be looking over our shoulders. I want to do my own research. It would be perfect." "I know what you want to do, but is it ethical?" "Of course, it is. I'm not going to kill anyone." "What will I work on?" "I have a couple of projects related to what I'm doing that you can process." "Alright, but we can't quit the hospital until we are completely set up in the castle." "I'll go along with that. Oh, Artur, thank you. I love you."

Janet got a letter from Abby, telling them what they planed on doing. She hoped it would be alright with her and dad. Janet was excited. Abby was coming home. She hurried upstairs to tell Barry. She went into the bedroom; Barry was on the bed taking a nap. "Barry, I just got a letter from Abby. They are coming back to live here with us. Isn't that exciting? I can hardly wait." Barry didn't say anything. "Barry, did you hear what I said?" She shook Barry to wake him up. Barry didn't move. He was gone.

Dr. Vasile, from the clinic, checked Barry. "You know his health was bad, Janet. His body just quit working. His heart probably couldn't take it anymore." "I know he's been sleeping an awful lot these last couple of days. I just wasn't ready for it yet." "Go over to one of the other bedrooms and get some rest. I'll give you something to relax you some. I'll take care of all the arrangements. You just rest. I'll notify Abby."

Abby's supervisor brought her a telegram. After Abby read it, she went over and sat down. "Abby, what's wrong?" "Oh, Artur, dad passed away this morning. We have to hurry to the castle." "What happened, Abby?" "It was his health. His body just gave out." "Let's go home and pack some things."

The whole village turned out for the funeral. He was always an important figure in the village. Everyone thought a lot of Barry. Barry was interred in the vault room. One of the very few down there, who had died of natural causes.

Abby and Artur moved back to the castle, and set up their equipment in a room that is now called the 'Lab'. Everything was perfect. They had exactly what they needed to start work on Abby's project. There were electrical panels for electrical experiments. All kinds of glass vessels for mixing chemicals. There was also a concrete vat that contained a powerful acid. When working with animals, it was easier to dispose of them in the acid, than to take them out and bury them. They had everything they needed, except a subject.

Janet was missing Barry. She was glad Abby and Artur were back home. She would have felt very lonely without them there. Janet thought back about their life and marriage. They had gone through a lot of things during their long marriage. But they always stuck together and supported each other. Now, Janet would have to start a new life, without Barry. Who knows what the future holds in store for Janet?

Abby and Artur were ready to start Abby's project. Artur went to work on some chemical compounds that Abby needed for her work. Abby needed some organ tissue to test her chemicals on. But she didn't have any. She needed some donations of animals that had just died. She thought about talking to the villagers, about letting her know, whenever one of their animals died. Then she got a telegram from the hospital. A zoo near Bucharest was experiencing several smaller animals dying for some unknown reason. The hospital suggested the zoo contact Abby. She could do autopsies to help find out the cause.

That is just what Abby was looking for. Her project was to determine a cause of death in animals, and then find a way to correct the cause. Possibly rejuvenate the organ that caused the animal to die. Abby was excited, to say the least. A van arrived with several animals that had died that morning. Included was a spider monkey, a fox and a lion cub.

Abby got down to work. She started with the spider monkey. Artur assisted her. After a complete investigation, she could find no apparent cause of death. This puzzled her. She had Artur get the fox. Again, she could find nothing wrong. What was she missing? "I don't see why these animals died. Everything about them looks healthy. Let's look at the lion cub." The same story. No cause visible. "Artur, this is frustrating. Something caused these poor animals to die. Do you see anything I'm overlooking?" Artur took a closer look. Then he spotted something. "Abby, look closely at the lungs." Abby looked closer, took an instrument, and moved the lungs around. She saw it then. "Artur, there is a light greenish tint inside the lungs. Get the other two animals and we will check them." After checking closer, she could see the same green in their lungs.

She removed one of the lungs, took a small sample, and put it under a microscope. She ran a couple of tests of the sample. "I have it, Artur. It's some kind of cleaning agent. After breathing in this agent for a while, these animals suffocate. I need to call the zoo right away."

Abby came back to the lab. "What did you find out?" "It's what they use to clean the concrete flooring in these animals' habitat. It has a certain chemical in it that when inhaled, coats the lungs of the animals." "Why didn't it affect the larger animals?" "Because of their height. Their breathing system is far enough above the floor, they are not affected. It's just the poor little guys that breathe this chemical."

Abby was a little disappointed. She needed an animal that she could use to test her formulas. She was sure that if an organ quit performing, there had to be a combination of chemicals that could make that organ healthy again. If she could do that, she could save lives by making an organ healthy again, before the person died. She was obsessed with this theory, and it would make her famous throughout the world. Obsessions often have a way of getting side tracked to a different direction. Abby has not told Artur of what her final goal entails. He will slowly start learning as time goes by. Actually, Abby herself isn't really aware of where this is going to lead her.

Janet was very happy when Abby and Artur came to stay with her. But Abby and Artur spend so much time in the lab, she doesn't get to see them as much as she would like. Janet is curious about what they are doing all that time in the lab, but when they do spend time with her, they won't talk about what they are doing. Janet does notice that Abby appears very tired lately. It's making Abby look older than her 50 years. Artur looks a little peaked also, but he seems to more concerned about Abby. He wants her to slow down some, but she won't let herself slow down.

One of the villagers brought Abby her dog that had died. So, Abby went to work on the animal. The dog was 9 years old, so it wasn't really considered old yet. Abby went to work, and found that part of the heart muscle looked dead. "Artur, bring me the vile marked C. I used it on a muscle and it brought color back into the sample. Maybe this will work on the heart." She injected the serum into the dead muscle. Minutes went by, nothing happened. Then slowly the dead muscle began to show color. But the heart never obtained full color. Abby injected a little more serum. Nothing happened. Abby started to massage the heart, hoping the muscle was improved enough to start the heart beating. After a few minutes, Abby gave up.

"Well, Artur, we came close. Maybe the serum needs something else. We must find the right formula. I know it will work. We need to find the right combination. We can do it, Artur, we can do it. I'm so excited." "Yes, I know. We need to stop now for a while. Actually, we need to take a day and go some where and rest for a while. Then we will be fresh, when we start again." "Artur, we can't stop now. We are making progress. We have to keep going." "Abby, you're tired, I'm tired. We need some rest. If you want to keep going, ok. I'm dead tired, and I'm going to take a day, and go somewhere, and rest. So, are you coming with me, or are you going to stay here in the lab and work?" "Alright, Artur, we'll take a day and rest. I suppose you're right." "I know I am. Come, let's relax for a while and enjoy ourselves."

Abby and Artur went to the village and looked through some of the shops. They stopped at The Pub to have dinner, and talk to some of the villagers. They spent the evening with Janet. All this time, Abby's mind kept drifting back to the lab. A few times, Artur had to bring Abby back to reality.

Some time went by, and Abby was not making much progress. She had some success, but she never reached the level she was looking for. She was becoming impatient, and started yelling at Artur more often. He was trying to control himself, but he was starting to get very irritated at Abby's fits of temper. It got to the point where Artur would simply leave the lab and go into the village. That upset Abby even more.

Then Abby got a break. One of the villagers brought Abby a lamb that had just died. It was actually a pet of his daughters. The two were inseparable. The daughter, who was 10, was very upset. Abby told the girl, she would do what she could for the lamb, but she also said she couldn't make any promises. The girl said that it was ok, she would understand.

Abby put the animal on the table and started to work. She discovered there was a growth on the heart. If she could work quickly enough, she may be able to resuscitate the lamb. She extracted the growth and sewed the hole left in the heart. She injected serum A into the heart, and started massaging the heart. Her hope was that the brain would survive. Within a few minutes, the heart started pumping blood through the arteries. She was able to get the lungs working. Within minutes, the lamb opened its eyes, and started trying to move. She quickly sewed up the incision, and wrapped a bandage around the lamb to protect the incision. She gave the lamb a sedative, to keep it from moving around for a while.

Abby went into the village to find the little girl. "Your friend is alive and doing well, so far. I will have to keep her with me a few days, until she gets stronger. I don't know if what I did will keep the lamb alive for very long. But, if she survives for four or five days, I would say she will be alright." "Oh, thank you, Miss Abby, I knew you could help her."

Later that afternoon, Artur came down to the lab. Abby told him what had transpired. "I'm amazed and very happy for you. This is what you have been striving for." "Yes, but the only reason I succeeded, was the lamb was still warm when they brought it to me. If they had waited a couple of hours, it would have been too late. Don't you see, Artur, if we can perfect this serum, and it will work on humans, think how many lives we could save." "That's fine, but what human is going to let you experiment on him. I don't know if that is even ethical. You can't play God." "I'm not. I'm trying to advance medicine to save lives. Everything that has been accomplished in medicine, has had to be tested on a human also, to see if it works." "You're not a medical doctor, or a surgeon, you are a medical researcher. You are not qualified to experiment on humans." "No one is going to stop me, Artur, not you, or anyone one else. If you don't want to help me, maybe you better go back to the hospital and work."

Artur thought about the situation for a while. He thought about Abby's advice of going back to the hospital. He decided that he needed to stay with Abby. She needed someone to rein her in. Maybe he could keep her from going too far. All he could do was try. He was afraid this obsession would cloud her mind. How far would she go?

Bela, the grounds keeper, was trimming some bushes, when he started feeling pressure in his chest, and finding it hard to breathe. He turned, and started walking back to the castle. Abby was coming out the front door just then, and saw Bela having a hard time walking, and holding his chest. Abby opened the door and called Clara. She then went to Bela and helped him sit down on a bench. She knew he was having a heart attack. Clara came running out, and Abby told her to hurry and get the doctor.

Dr. Vasile, checked Bela. By then the pressure had eased some, and Bela was breathing easier. He was helped down to the clinic, where some tests were done. There was nothing they could really do. Bela was told to stay in bed a couple of days, and given some medication to take. Bela would have to slow down, not overwork himself, and stay on his medication, and he should be alright. Artur told the doctor, he would keep a watch on Bela, and help him with his work when he needed it.

Janet feels so lonely without Barry by her side. She hardly ever sees Abby; she spends almost all of her time in the lab. Janet has a hard time walking; she's afraid she will be confined to a wheel chair before long. Because of her legs, she stays in her bedroom most of the time. Clara brings her meals up to her.

Abby is becoming impatient; she is not making much progress. She has experimented on a few animals now and then. She has had some organs rejuvenate, but they don't live very long. The animals had been dead too long.

Abby misses her dad. They really were a close-knit family, and now she worries about her mother's health. She doesn't want to lose her, also. If she was only able to get around. Abby would take her to the village so she could interact with villagers. Abby knows Janet is lonely. "If only there was something, she could do........." Then it hit her. "What if mother would let me inject her with one of my serums? I'm sure she would be able to walk again. It would make her legs healthy again. I must go talk to her."

"Mother, it's hard on you, not being able to walk." "Yes, it is. But that's the way it is. I just have to accept it." "No, you don't have to accept it. I think I can help you walk again. I know I can help." "Oh, you have a magic wand to wave over me?" "No, something better. I have a serum that will heal your legs." "You're not serious?" "Yes, I am. I have seen it work on several animals." "I am a human being, not an animal. What makes you think it would work on me?" "It heals tissue and muscle. It will let you walk again." "I don't know Abby, what if something goes wrong?" "It won't. I won't let anything happen." "Alright, but I hope you know what you are doing." "Everything will be fine. You'll see."

Abby went to the lab to get everything ready. Abby was happy, her mother would walk again. Abby fixed more of the serum, picked up a clean hypo and headed upstairs. She was glad Artur was in the village. She was sure he would object, and try to stop her. This was Abby's first real chance to prove the serum would work on humans. Maybe after Artur saw the results, he would be proud of her, and help her continue her work.

"Alright, mother, lift your skirt up, so I can work on your legs, and make them well. I am going to put two shots of serum in each leg. It won't hurt. It shouldn't take very long before we see the results." "I'm still a little worried about this, but I can't walk anyway, so I suppose it's worth a try." Abby went to work. She injected both legs. All that was left, was to wait, and see what happens. Several minutes went by. Her legs started getting some color in them, and they swelled, just ever so slightly. Janet could feel a tingle in her legs, almost as if her legs were coming alive. "There is a warm feeling in my legs." "It's working, it's working. Don't try to get up yet. Give it some time to work." They both started laughing. They were both very happy.

Abby told her mother she was going to go back to the lab for a few minutes; not to try to stand until she came back. While she was in the lab, Artur came back. "Artur, I have done it!" "Done what" "My mother is able to walk again." "You want to run that by me again?" "I injected mother's legs with the A serum, and it's working. Come upstairs with me. You can see for yourself." "Abby, you're going too far. You could end up killing your mother." "Nonsense, come on." "You know, if I had been here, I never would have allowed you to do this." "I know, that's why I waited until you weren't here." Abby started laughing.

Artur followed Abby up the stairs, shaking his head. He was afraid Abby was losing reality; this obsession was warping her mind. As they entered Janet's bedroom, "How do your legs feel?" "They feel good, they feel alive again." "They look good also. They have regained their color. I think it's time for you to try to walk. What do you think?" "I'm ready." Artur just stands there. Has Abby really succeeded in healing Janet's legs? Will she be able to walk?

Abby helps Janet stand up. Janet waits until she has her balance, then takes a step. She waits, then takes another step. She then slowly starts walking. "I'm walking, and there is no pain. I'm still a little shaky." "That's because it's been so long since you have walked. It's like learning how to walk all over again. As your strength returns, you'll become steady again. That's enough for now. You don't want to do too much at one time until you are stronger."

Back down stairs, "Well, Artur, what do you think now?" "I'm not sure what I think. I am amazed at what I saw. If it continues to work, I applaud you. But what if it doesn't last? What if it does more harm than good? You are playing with your mother's life. I'm not sure you are qualified to do that. You are not a medical doctor, and if something goes wrong, how is that going to impact you? Are you going to be sorry, or are you just going to move on, and try it on someone else?" "I'll cross that bridge when I get to it."

Several days have passed. Janet is getting along very well. She has even walked down to the village and back, no problems. Oh, just a side note, the lamb Abby worked on, lived for 3 weeks, then passed away. Abby did not work on the lamb again. Anyway, when the villagers learned about what Abby had done for Janet, people started going to Abby and asking if she could cure their arthritis and different aches and pains. But Abby told them she couldn't really help them. They should rely on the doctor to help them. It's not that she didn't want to, it was because she was told by Dr. Vasile, 'do not practice on these people, you are not a doctor'. Naturally, the doctor found out what Abby did for Janet. He was not very happy. He told Abby that research is fine. But do not experiment without the approval of a doctor, and the doctor must be the one to administer any new serums. He was not going to report what Abby had done, but he was concerned about Janet. She was not to continue with her experiment, and the doctor said he would keep a close eye on Janet and Abby.

Artur was glad Dr. Vasile had gotten involved. She didn't have to listen to Artur, but she better listen to the doctor. She could have her research license revoked, and possibly get jail time for practicing as a doctor. Abby was angry at the doctor, but she knew the rules. But in her mind, she decided she would continue helping her mother with whatever she needed.

Two more weeks went by. Janet's plan for the day was to go down to the village, and visit the library. She hadn't been there for a while. She woke up that morning feeling great. The sun was shining; it would be a good day. She threw back the covers and started to get out of bed. She couldn't move her legs. She pulled up her nightgown, and started screaming.

Abby was in the kitchen eating breakfast when she heard her mother scream. She ran up the stairs as quickly as she could. "Mother, what is……?" She stopped short. Janet's legs were swollen, and the skin was very black. Artur came into the room and saw Janet's legs. "Abby, what……?" "I don't know! I don't know! I'll be back in a minute."

Abby went down to the lab, measured out some of the serum, and ran back upstairs. "Abby, what are you doing now?" "I'm going to try more serum. It will bring her legs back." "Abby, the doctor told you not to continue this. I'll go get the doctor." "Don't you dare! I'll handle this, and if you say anything to the doctor, I promise you, you will regret it. Do you understand me?" "Abby……" "Don't say a word." Janet is crying hysterically, "Abby, am I going to lose my legs?" "Quiet, mother, you'll be alright in a minute." Abby injected the serum into Janet's legs. After a few minutes, Janet's legs started reversing back to a healthy state.

"Well, Abby, how many times are you going to continue reinjecting you mother's legs?" "As many times as it takes. I told you before, she can't walk anyway, so why not continue?" "Well, then, since she can't walk anyway, why don't you just cut her legs off? It would be more human than what you are going to be putting her through every 3 or 4 weeks." "Artur, I think you should leave the room, and let me finish what I'm doing." "Good idea."

Artur left and went down to The Pub. He needed a drink, maybe two. As he was going to The Pub, Dr. Vasile approached him. "Artur, how are Janet's legs?" "When I left a few minutes ago, they were fine." "So, Abby has given up on this dangerous experimentation?" "You would have to ask Abby that question. It's hard to tell what goes on in her mind. If you will excuse me, I'll be moving on." "Oh, yes. Good day Artur."

Artur sat down and ordered a drink. A double at that. He started talking to several of the people around him. The sun had gone down, and Artur had a couple more than he should have. He was in pretty good spirits now. He saw a woman across the room at a table by herself. She looked to be in her 40's. Attractive lady. Artur had never seen her before. He got up and went over to her table and ask if he could join her. "Sure, sit down. My name is Sonja." "I'm Artur. I don't remember seeing you here before. Are you new in the village?" "I moved here about 6 months ago. My husband died, and I just couldn't stay in that village any longer." "I'm sorry to hear that. But welcome to Medias."

They talked for a couple of hours, then Sonja said she had to be getting home. "I'll walk you home, if you don't mind." "Yes, I would like that." Artur walked her home, and they sat on a bench in front of her house for a while. Suddenly, Artur leaned over and kissed Sonja. He quickly backed away. "Forgive me. I shouldn't have done that." "It's alright, it was just a kiss. No harm done. If I would have objected, you would probably have a very red cheek right now." They both laughed. "Yes, but I am married." "It was just an innocent kiss. Do not let it worry you. It will stay between you and me."

It was late when Artur got home. Abby was in bed, but she was awake. "Artur, where have you been?" "The Pub." "Ah, yes, I can see that now. Do you feel any better?" "I ran into the doctor this afternoon." "Oh.......?" "He ask some questions, but I didn't lie, I just kind of went around them. He seemed satisfied, but I don't know." "I meant what I said, Artur, don't tell him anything." "I hear you." "Come to bed." "I think I better sleep in one of the other bedrooms." "Suit yourself."

Abby and Artur don't talk to each other much anymore. Artur has taken over a separate bedroom. He very seldom goes down to the lab anymore. He spends most evenings in the village. Abby has become angry, and frustrated; she is tired of working with animals. She wants to move on, if you know what I mean. Abby sometimes feels she actually hates Artur. He won't help her, and he spends every evening down in the village.

Artur goes down to The Pub every evening, but doesn't drink too much anymore. He has a new interest. Sonja. He is becoming very attracted to her, and he thinks she feels the same about him. "Sonja, I'm falling in love with you." "I feel the same way about you. But there is one complication, you're married." "It's not a marriage anymore, just on paper." "Would she give you a divorce?" "I don't know, but I think it is time to find out. We don't have a life together anymore." "Don't do anything until you are ready. I'll wait for you." "If I can get a divorce, you will marry me?" "Yes. I will."

Abby feels that Artur's attitude has changed recently. Not towards her, but as if he has another interest, and he is enjoying it. Abby thinks maybe she better find out what's going on with Artur. She hears Artur leave for the village. Well after dark, Abby heads for the village. She figures he is in The Pub, so that's where she heads. As she walks past a small lane that leads back to some houses, she hears voices. She stops. As she looks down the lane, she sees Artur and a woman. She steps into the shadows to watch and listen. She can't make out what they are saying, but while she is watching, they embrace and kiss. "So, that's it. He's been cheating on me. If he thinks he can toss me aside for someone else, he better think again." Abby quietly turned and went back to the castle. A plan was already forming in Abby's mind.

Chapter 18

Janet was feeling good. She was down at The Pub having lunch. Dr. Vasile came in The Pub and saw Janet, so he walked over to her table and sat down. "Janet, how are you doing these days? I see your legs are still working." "Yes, but I had a setback a couple of weeks ago." "Oh, what do you mean?" "The serum wore off, and Abby had to reinject my legs again." "I told Abby, under no circumstances, was she to use that serum again." "She had to do something; my legs were turning black." "Oh, Janet, obviously there is something wrong with that serum. Tomorrow, I want to take you to Bucharest, to the hospital, and have them try to determine what is going on with your legs. You hear me?" "Alright doctor, if you think it is best." "Please do not say anything to Abby." "Alright, if you insist." "I do."

Janet left The Pub, and started back to the castle. As she approached the edge of the village, she started losing her balance, everything seemed to be going around in circles. She collapsed, unconscious. A couple of the villagers ran over to her. One of the villagers saw the doctor come out of The Pub, and yelled as loud as he could for the doctor. He immediately ran over to Janet. She was face down, so the doctor turned her over. Her skin color was becoming dark, even her face. The doctor checked her heart. No pulse. She was dead.

The doctor had her carried over to the clinic. He then headed for the castle. "Clara, may I come in? I need to talk to Abby. It's extremely important." "Of course, doctor, I'll get her, she's in the lab." "I think I better go down there and talk to her. I want to see what she has been doing down there." "Very well, follow me." Abby has been keeping the lab door locked at all times. She won't allow Artur or anyone else in the lab anymore. The doctor banged on the door. Abby opened it a couple of inches. "What do you want?" "The doctor is here to see you. He said it is important." "Tell him to go away, I don't want to talk to him." The doctor spoke up, "It's about your mother, Abby." "What about her?" "Abby, let me come in, we have some talking to do." "No. Go away." "Abby if you don't let me in, I will have to get Cornel to force you."

"Alright, come in." The doctor entered the lab. He looked around the lab, trying to quickly see what Abby might be into. "Abby, your mother is dead." Abby felt like she was going to collapse. "No. No. It can't be. She was doing so well. Why are you telling me this? It's a lie. Isn't it?" "No, Abby, it is not a lie. She is at the clinic. She collapsed on the street." "What happened?" "You happened, Abby. Your serum killed your mother." "That's not true! It was healing her." "You gave her more injections, didn't you?" "Who told you that?" "Your mother, before she died." "Yes, but I had to." "I would have thought that after the first shot failed, you would come to me." "But I didn't have time. She needed it right away." "Abby, whatever that serum is, the second shot was enough to affect her whole body, and when it failed, it failed the rest of her body also. That's what killed her."

"Oh, doctor, I feel like I want to die. I wanted to help her, and I ended up killing her." "Well, that's not all of it, Abby." "What do you mean?" "I have to report this to the medical board in Bucharest." "What will they do?" "They will do an investigation. You will be called in to testify." "It was an accident." "I doubt that the board will see it that way. Naturally you will lose your research license. But worse than that, you will probably be charged with involuntary manslaughter." "They can't do that. I thought I was helping her. I wasn't trying to kill her." "They'll know that, but you are still responsible for your mother's death. You will also be charged with practicing beyond your qualifications. Whether you go to prison, or not, you will never be allowed in the medical field again" "Doctor, what have I done? I have messed everyone's life up, including mine. How soon will they arrest me?" "There will be a meeting of the board first. It will probably be in a couple of weeks.

Then, you will be called in to testify at that time. Abby, do not try to run from this. They will eventually find you, and it will go a lot harder on you." "I know. I won't run." "Just stay calm. No one's made any decisions about anything yet. It may not be as bad as you think."

Abby went up to her bedroom to rest. She had a lot to digest. Her life, and her future, were up in the air. Artur was walking down the street, heading back for the castle. He heard people taking about Janet, so he ask what they talking about. When he heard, he ran to the clinic. He saw Janet's body, then ran back to the castle. He ran to the lab. He knocked on the door, but no one answered, so he ran up the stairs to Abby's bedroom. "Abby, I just heard about your mother, what happened?" "I killed her Artur. It's as simple as that." "What do mean, you killed her?" "Just what I said, the serum was too much, it affected her whole body, and that's it." "Abby, I'm so sorry. I begged you not to use that serum. Why didn't you listen?" "Because I thought I was doing the right thing. Now, I could end up in prison." "Abby, if you would only have listened to the doctor and me." "Well, I didn't. Now, go away, and leave me alone."

Artur felt bad for Abby, but she had been warned time and time, again. She just wouldn't listen. This was no time to talk about a divorce, so Artur went to see Sonja, and tell her what was going on. He knocked on her door. "Artur, your back so soon." "Yes, I have to talk to you." "Ok, come in." "Did something happen?" "Yes, a lot happened." "You haven't been gone that long." "It didn't take long. First, Abby's mother is dead. Second, Abby could end up in prison." Artur went on to tell Sonja what happened. "So, you see, it is not a good time to talk about a divorce." "I understand. We have time, and we have each other. We'll just have to be patient, and see how things play out."

A few days later, Dr. Vasile came to see Abby. "Abby, the medical board is ready to talk to you. You are supposed to meet with them tomorrow afternoon in Bucharest. I will be going with you." "Why, to make sure they convict me?" "No, Abby. I have to go also, because I'm the one who notified them about you. Abby, I am not your enemy. I wish I could help you find a way to solve this dilemma, but you have to realize the severity of what you have done." "I know, doctor, I'm sorry. I'll be ready."

The next afternoon, Abby and Dr. Vasile, sat in the waiting room. Finally, a man came up to them and said the board was ready. They were ushered into a room with a table and two chairs. Behind the table sat 5 doctors. "Miss Abby, we have looked over the complaint that was filed against you. We called you here, to hear your side. What you did, and why you did it." "Gentlemen, I am a medical researcher........." Abby went on to tell her side of the story. Although she did leave a few details out. She placed a lot of emphases on why she did what she did. ".........you see, I was desperate to help my mother. I didn't want to lose her, also. It was hard enough to lose my father; I could not lose my mother." "Thank you for your testimony, Miss Abby. We will evaluate all of this, and call you back in a few days. Thank you."

After Abby was back home, she was tired, so she went upstairs to rest for a while. She hoped the board would understand, and be lenient with her. But, if she didn't get away, with what she was planning, it wouldn't make any difference what the board did.

Abby went down stairs. Artur was not around. That didn't surprise her. She figured he was with his new lover. She knew that it was over between her and Artur. There was no marriage anymore. But one thing she knew for certain, no one else was going to have him either. She would see to that. She knew exactly what she was going to do, and how to do it. But she had to be careful. She didn't know if Dr. Vasile was watching her, or not. But she would find a way to achieve her revenge.

A week later, Dr. Vasile, and Abby were back in Bucharest, appearing before the board. "Miss Abby, we have gone over everything, looking for a solution to this charge. We could just revoke you license, and let it go at that. But the result of what you did, cost a person their life. Your own mother. If you were that concerned about your mother's health, why didn't you call Dr. Vasile, and get an assessment from him? You could have told him, of what you had been working on, and he would have advised you on whether to try your serum. I'm not saying he would have approved. You are not a doctor, and had no right to experiment on your mother. So, you in essence, you caused your mother's death, we have no alternative, but to turn this over to the grand Jury. Abby sat motionless. She showed no reaction.

"Is there anything you want to say, Abby?" Abby shook her head no. "Very well, the grand jury meets two weeks from today. They may take no action, or they may recommend you be turned over to the authorities for trial. Either way, you will be notified. That is all." Abby and Dr. Vasile left and headed home.

"Abby, I hope you realize just how serious this is." "Not much I can do about it, is there? I've done all I can do. It's up to them." "Do you have a lawyer?" "No, I've never needed one." "Well, I suggest you find a good lawyer, just in case." Abby was thinking, 'I don't need a lawyer, because as soon as I complete my little surprise for Artur and his lover, I will simply disappear. No one will ever know what happened to me.'

Before Abby executed her revenge scheme, she had to try an experiment first, to see if what she was planning would work; but she needed help. She thought she knew someone who would help, whether they wanted to, or not. What she had planned, was not exactly legal. But she didn't care anymore. How much more trouble could she get into; her life was ruined anyway. The only thing on her mind now, was Artur and his 'lover', and how to punish them. Especially, Artur.

Some time ago, Abby noticed Bela was acting a little strange. His attitude seemed to change. Maybe it was his heart problem that changed him. Abby did notice that Bela would go down to the village every evening. When he came back, he would go straight up to bed. Clara didn't seem to notice anything strange, so Abby quit worrying about Bela. Then one evening, when Bela came home, Abby was opening the door to go out. They ran right into each other. Then Abby noticed something. Bela had the smell of perfume on him. Abby didn't say anything, she just let him pass by.

Abby started thinking, 'Is Bela having an affair, also? What is this, a common pastime?' She thought it might be worth finding out what Bela is up to. The next evening when Bela left, Abby followed him, staying in the shadows. Bela went into The Pub. Abby stayed outside, but carefully looked in through the window. Bela went over to a table where a woman was sitting, and sat down opposite her. They reached across the table and held hands. Abby waited. After about 10 minutes, they both got up from the table, and started for the door. Abby went deeper into the shadows, so she wouldn't be seen. She watched them walk down the street to a house, the woman opened the door, and they both went in. Abby knew there was no proof that anything she saw, or thought, was as it seemed.

Abby waited a couple of days, then approached Bela. "Bela, I need you to help me with something." "Ok, I'll do what I can." "It's something I have to do in the lab, and I need your help getting me something." "What do you need?" "A body." "A body? I don't understand." "Bela, what we are going to do, is not exactly legal, and it could be messy." "Oh no, Miss Abby, I don't go against the law." "Well, Bela, if you refuse, I will be obligated to talk to Clara." "About what?" "About your nightly forays to The Pub, and the lady at the table you visit." "How do you know about that?" "You made a mistake one night when you let your girlfriend get perfume on your jacket." "You followed me?" "Yes, and I know where she lives."

"That's blackmail! You wouldn't do that. You wouldn't tell Clara?" "I don't like the word 'blackmail'. Let us just say, you keep my secret, I'll keep your secret, and yes, I would tell Clara. Now, are you ready to co-operate." "I guess. I don't have much choice." "Excellent, I'll let you know when I'm ready for you."

A couple of nights later, two young men, who were good friends, were in The Pub, and drinking pretty heavy, started arguing over a girl. Next thing, they stood up, and started swinging at each other. Two older men, pulled the two apart, and told them to go home and sleep it off. So, the two young guys left. But they didn't go far. As soon as they were out on the street, they started up again. Only this time, one of them picked up a good size rock, and hit the other one on the side of the head pretty hard. The man fell to the ground and didn't move. The other man knelt down to check his friend. He shook him, but he didn't move. The man realized that his friend was dead. He panicked. He didn't intend to kill his friend. It was an accident. He was getting ready to run, but two men came out of The Pub, and saw him leaning over the body. There was no use in running, the men knew who he was. So, one of the men went to get Cornel, the constable.

The next day there was a funeral, and the young man was buried in the cemetery. That was Abby's que. It's was time for Bela to go to work. "Bela, tonight we have work to do." "Yes, Miss Abby. What is it?" "Tonight, we are going out to the cemetery, and retrieve the body of the man that was buried today." "Oh no. You can't do that!" "I'm not going to, you are. I'll help." "Please don't ask me to do that. I don't go to the cemetery in the daytime, let alone at night, and I don't like to mess with dead bodies." "I'm not asking you Bela, I'm telling you." "Ok, Miss Abby, but it will be a quick job. I don't intend to spend much time there." Abby laughed at Bela. "Alright, Bela, we'll make it quick, just for you."

Abby waited until about 3:00 in the morning. Then she called Bela, and they took a wagon to the cemetery. "Ok, Bela, start digging." "What about my heart?" "Don't worry about your heart. That dirt is still loose, you'll be alright." Bela looked all around. "Are you looking for ghosts or what? Start digging." "Alright, alright." Bela started digging. It didn't take long to reach the coffin. Bela pried the lid up, and started shaking. "I don't like this at all. Who's going to take the body out of there?" "You are." "Oh no, I'm not going to touch that man." "I'll help you, now let's get him in the wagon." They got him in the wagon, closed up the grave, and headed back to the castle. Bela was trying to hurry; he was scared to death someone would see them. "This sure is a bumpy path." "That's alright, Bela, our passenger back there, doesn't mind."

When they got back to the castle, Bela, still shaking, helped Abby carry the body down to the lab. "I glad that's over, please don't ask me to go through that again." "You won't have to. I will need your help in a few days, but it won't have anything to do with dead bodies. Now, go on back upstairs."

After Bela left, Abby locked the door, and began working. What Abby was about to do had to work, her next project depended on it. Abby set up what she needed. A large glass container, some chemicals, two low power electrodes and whatever. She went over to the body, made an incision, and removed the heart. She quickly put the heart in the glass container containing the chemicals. She took the two electrodes and attached each one to the heart. The goal was to make the heart start beating, and continue beating; pumping the chemical through the heart, in place of blood. If this worked, it would be a medical breakthrough. She could be famous. But that was not her intention.

This was only a prelude to her final project. Only one person would ever know about this.

Artur was in bed asleep, but earlier in the evening he had been with Sonja. "It's been several days now since Abby's mother died. I think it's time to approach her about a divorce. That is if I can ever catch up with her." "Do you have any idea how she will respond?" "We haven't even seen each other since her mother's funeral. I have a feeling she is so wrapped up in her work in the lab, she probably hasn't even thought about me." "Why don't you give it a couple of more days. By then, it may have been long enough, she won't fight you." "Yeah, you may be right."

Back in the lab, Abby is getting ready to test her experiment. She turns on the power panel, goes over to another panel, and sets the pulse time. Then she goes over to another switch, and turns it on to connect the power to the electrodes. She goes over to the glass container and watches. Several minutes; nothing happens. She goes over to the body, and drags it over to the vat of acid, lifts the body up, and dumps it into the acid. When they were at the cemetery, they covered the grave up again, so no one would ever know there was no body in the casket. Abby then walks back over to the glass container. Then, she sees some slight movement of the heart, but the beating does not increase. She goes over to the power panel, and increases the power level. As she watches, the heart beat grows stronger, and levels out at 60 beats per minute.

That's fine, but how long will the heart keep beating? That is the key. It must keep going until Abby decides to turn the power off. She must keep the heart beating, until the final act of her project. At least two days, maybe three.

After three full days, the heart is still beating strong. That is enough time, so Abby goes over to the power panel, and turns it off. The heart continues to beat for about ten seconds, then stops. It has served its purpose, so Abby disconnects the heart, and disposes of it in the acid. Within seconds, it is no more. Now, Abby can proceed with the final step of her little game.

The next day, Abby tells Bela to come with her into the village. As they are walking in the village, "Bela, see that house there with the red shutters?" "Yes. What do I have to do? Kill somebody?" "Bela, knock it off. You don't have to kill anyone. Let's go back to the castle....... Wait! See that woman coming out of the house?" "I see her. So?" "Remember what she looks like." "I...... don't think...... I'm going to like....... this." "Quit worrying, you're not going to hurt anyone." "Then what am I going to do?" "Let's go back to the castle, and I'll explain everything."

"Come down to the lab tonight after midnight. Then I will tell you what I want you do. Before we proceed, Artur must be up in his room asleep." "Miss Abby, I don't know which I fear the worst, having Clara know about my friend, or going to prison." "Bela, calm down, you're not going to prison. No one will ever know of your involvement in what I'm doing. Now, go on about your business, and make sure you are on time tonight."

Bela knocked on the lab door; Abby unlocked the door for him. "Ok, Miss Abby, let me have it. I know I'm not going to like it." "Bela, after you do this one last thing for me, I will never ask you to do anything again. That's a promise." "Well, you say that now, but I'm not going to hold my breath. What is it you want me to do?" "I want you to go down to that woman's house we looked at today, and bring that woman to me, here in the lab. Do it very quietly. Don't wake up the whole village. Got it?" "How am I going to get her here, if she doesn't want to come?" "Use your brain, you'll think of something." "Ohhhh...... I'll probably get shot on the way back." "Well, if you do, make sure you get that woman here before you die." "I'll do my best. Ohhhh."

It's 1:00 in the morning. Bela knocks on Sonja's door. No one answers, so Bela knocks again. Finally, a voice on the other side of the door, "Who are you? What do you want?" "I'm Bela, from the castle. Miss Abby needs you to come up to the castle, right away." Sonja opens the door a couple of inches. "Why would she want to see me, especially at this time of night?" "I don't know, she just said it was an emergency. That you need to come right up." "Is this some kind of joke?" "No, ma'am. Miss Abby sent me to get you." Sonja wondered if something was wrong with Artur. Maybe he had an accident. "Just a minute while I get dressed." "I'll wait."

When they got to the castle, Bela told Sonja that Abby was in the lab. He would show her the way. As they went down the stairs, they entered the vault room. Sonja stopped. "Wait a minute, what is this place? It sure doesn't look like a lab." "No, this is the vault room. This is where all the past residents of the castle are buried. The lab is in the next room." "I sure don't like this." Bela knocked on the door.

Abby opened the door. "Come in Sonja. Welcome." What is the big emergency?" "Just a minute, I'll get to that." "Miss Abby, can I go now?" "Yes, Bela, you may go. I want you to know, I will never need your services again. You are free to do what you want. I will not bother you again. I promise." Bela smiled. "Thank you, Miss Abby. I hope you mean that." "You have my word."

Abby locked the door. "Now, Abby, what is so important, to drag me up here?" "I'll show you. Come with me" Abby guided Sonja toward the dungeon. She opened the cell door, and pointed toward one of the corners. As Sonja leaned forward to look, Abby pushed her into the cell, and quickly locked the cell door. "What are you doing? Let me out of here!" "In due time Sonja, when I am ready." Why are you doing this? What are you going to do? Abby, let me out!" Sonja was starting to really panic. "Calm down, Sonja, we are going to play a game. You, Artur and I." "So that's what this is about. Artur." "Well, what do you know, you may pass Go and collect $200." "What do you want me to do, give Artur up, so you can have him back?" "No, it's went too far for that. I know Artur and I have not really had a marriage for some time."

"Then why not give him a divorce?" "No, then I would be admitting defeat. Artur and I are married until death do us part. So that's what we will concentrate on." "So, you are going to kill Artur, and make me watch." "Heavens no, that's too easy. I told you, we are playing a game." "Abby, if you don't let me out of here, I'm going to start screaming my head off." "Save it. No one outside this room would ever hear you." "Ok, what's my role in this game?" "You're going to be the star of the game." "Abby, please stop this nonsense, and let me go home."

"Sonja, how about a cup of coffee? We'll each have a cup of coffee, and discuss the latest fashions." "I don't want any coffee. I want out of here." "Sonja, you are not being very sociable. Please, have some coffee with me." Abby went over and poured two cups of coffee. When Abby handed the cup to Sonja, she threw the cup at Abby. "Sonja, that was not a very friendly gesture. Please take mine, I'll go pour me another cup." "Ok, I give up." Abby poured another cup of coffee. As they drank their coffee, "Abby, will you stop this stupid game and let me out?" "In few minutes, just be patient. Drink your coffee." As Sonja drank the coffee, she started feeling drowsy. "I can't stay awake. What did you do?" I just put something in it to make you sleep." "But that was your cup of coffee I drank." "Yes, I was way ahead of you." "But why……?" "You wanted to give your heart to Artur, and so you will." At that point, Sonja fell to the floor, sound asleep.

Abby proceeded to get everything ready for Sonja, after which she opened the cell door, and proceeded to lift Sonja up on the operating table. She opened Sonja's blouse, and made an incision down Sonja's chest. She carefully removed Sonja's heart, and placed it in the glass container containing the chemicals. She connected the two terminals, went over to the power panel, and switched it on. Set the heart rate and turned on the switch. After several seconds, the heart started beating; 60 beats per minute. She then took Sonja's body over to the acid vat, and slowly rolled the body into the acid. Thus, ended the first step in Abby's plan. Right now, Abby was very tired. She would go up to bed and get some sleep. She would wait three days before implementing step two.

Artur headed down to the village. He went into The Pub, looking for Sonja. She wasn't there, so he headed for her house. He knocked on the door, no answer. He knocked a couple of more times, still no answer. Oh well, he would catch up with her later. His plan was to travel to Bucharest this morning. He intended to stop at the hospital, to see if his old job was available. He also intended to look up a couple of friends he hadn't seen in a long time.

He stopped at the hospital and talked to his supervisor. "I was wondering if my old job was still available. I'm thinking about moving back here, and I need a job." "You and Abby are moving back to Bucharest?" "No, just me. Abby and I are estranged, we don't even see each other anymore." "Oh, I'm sorry to hear that. But I thought you were doing your own research now." "No, it's all Abby's. I don't even go into the lab anymore. I think Abby is going places she shouldn't be going." "Well, see me after you get settled, and we will see what we can work out."

Artur visited a couple of friends, then headed back to the castle. It was evening, so he went on down to the village. He went into The Pub and looked around. He didn't see Sonja anywhere. He asked the bartender, "Have you seen Sonja at all today?" "No, she hasn't been in here today." Artur headed for her house again. He knocked, no answer. After knocking several times, he gave up and went back up to the castle. Artur couldn't understand where she could have gone.

The next two days were no different. Artur couldn't find Sonja. He asked so many people about Sonja, he figured he had talked to everyone in the village. She had not been seen in The Pub for the last three days. Now, he was becoming fearful that something had happened to her. If she was going somewhere for a period of time, she would at least leave him a note. He went to her house. He knocked on the door several times. No answer. He tried the door knob. The door was not locked. That's strange. He opened the door and entered. He looked through all the rooms. In the bedroom, the bed was not made. Her nightgown was on the floor. Now, he was sure something was wrong. He went to see Cornel. "Cornel, Sonja is missing. No one has seen her for three days." "Maybe she went to see a family member back home." "No, from what I know, she would never go back to the village she came from." "Maybe there was emergency." "She would have left me a note, or something? I just left her house; the door was unlocked and her bed was not made. It's as though she left in a hurry, or was forced to leave." "Now, don't get excited. I'll go down and check the house, and ask around." "I talked to everyone in the village, no one has seen her the last three days either."

Artur went back to the castle. Abby was waiting for him. "What's the matter, Artur, you look like you lost your best friend." "Nothing is wrong, leave me alone." "Don't get testy. Come with me, I want to show you something." "Not now I'm tired, and I have things to do." "Oh no, this you'll want to see. Trust me. Come to the lab with me." "Alright, let's get this over with."

Abby unlocked the door and let Artur enter. "Ok, what do you want me...... What in the world is that? What......" "It's a heart. It's been beating for three days now, and still going. Isn't that something?" "Why? Whose heart is it, or was it?" "That will be of great interest to you." "Abby, what you are doing is against all medical practice. For what purpose is this?....... What do you mean 'of interest to me'?" "Artur, I know we don't have a real marriage anymore, but we are still legally married." "I know that." "Yet, you went ahead and were having an affair with Sonja, weren't you?" "I figured you knew about it, but you never said anything."

"Well, I'm saying something now. I have decided that if I can't have you, then nobody else will either. But I don't want you to be all alone, so I have arranged for you, and Sonja, to be close to each other. She wanted to give you her heart, so there it is." At first, Artur didn't catch what Abby was saying, then he looked at the heart in the container. He almost passed out. At first, he couldn't talk. "That......is......Sonja's heart? Abby! Why? You are insane! You are a monster! I should kill you!" "But you won't." "You killed Sonja!" "No, I just took her heart out while she was drugged. She didn't feel a thing." Abby started laughing uncontrollably. "Abby, you will be executed for this monstrous thing you have done." "I'm already on my way to prison for my mother's death, but they won't get me, I'm going to disappear where no one will find me." "Not if I can help it." Artur quickly started toward Abby. Abby picked up a knife off the table, and in Artur's haste, he ran into the knife. The knife went all the way in. Artur fell to the floor. Within a couple of minutes, he was dead.

Abby looked at Artur on the floor, and shook her head. Then she calmly pulled Artur over to the acid vat. She lifted him up, and rolled him into the acid. As she did so, she suddenly started hearing a sound. At first, she couldn't figure out what it was. As she turned around, she looked at the heart. It was beating very fast. The sound was getting louder. She was hearing the heartbeat. 'Thump, thump, thump, THUMP, THUMP, THUMP'. Abby couldn't stand it. She turned the switch off. She still heard the sound. She turned the heart beat rate to zero. Nothing happened. She went to the power panel. As she reached to turn the power off, she received a shock. The power panel arced and caught fire. The sound was unbearable. She went over to the table; if she could destroy the container, maybe the sound would stop. Something would not let her touch the container. The sound was deafening. She quickly started backing away from the table. Suddenly, she backed against the acid vat, fell backwards into the acid....... The thumping stopped. The heart was stilled.

Four days later, Cornel was notified that the grand jury had recommended Abby be charged with involuntary manslaughter. Cornel was instructed to arrest Abby, and transport her to Bucharest for trial. Cornel went to the castle, and knocked on the door. Clara answered the door. "Miss Clara, is Abby here?" "I don't rightly know. I haven't seen her for days now." "How about Artur?" "I haven't seen him either. Now, Abby might be down in the lab. I'll show you where it is."

Clara was going to knock on the door, but she noticed it was slightly open. She pulled the door open, and Cornel and she went in. "There's no one here. Is there another room off of this?" "No, this is it." Cornel noticed the blackened power panel. Then the glass container caught his eye. The heart was lying in the bottom of the container, not beating. "What in the world was this woman doing down here? Isn't that a heart in there?" "I don't know, I don't want to look. I just want to get out of here." Cornel went over to the acid vat. "This looks like a tub of water." Cornel was just about to put his hand in the 'water', and Clara yelled, "Can we get out of here?" Cornel stopped and turned toward Clara, "Alright, Clara, we'll go back upstairs. It looks like Abby has just disappeared."

Abby, true to her word, disappeared, and no one would ever know where she went. What went wrong with Abby? Until her and Artur moved back to the castle, she was a fairly level headed, average woman. What made her go off the deep end? Was it Artur, her mother's death, her obsession? Or is there something in that castle, that drives certain people mad?

The villagers all wondered what happened to Abby, Artur and Sonja. To them, it's still a mystery. Clara and Bela moved back to the village. Bela decided he was better off with Clara, and he never strayed again. The castle was empty until 1980, when a new victim, I mean, resident, moved in.

Chapter 19

If you remember, Bert Allen, the movie director, tried to shoot a movie at the castle. Things did not go well, so Bert went back to the states to finish his movie. The rest of the filming went without incident. The film was released and did very well, probably because the word got around about things that happened during shooting at a real castle in Rumania.

Bert could not get the experience at the castle out of his mind. He had seen things, that if he would have just been told about, he wouldn't believe. But the fact is he witnessed those things. He couldn't deny what he had seen. The more this weighed on his mind, the more he wanted to know. He had a friend, Larry Hart, who had written a couple of books on medieval castles in Germany. They were just matter of fact histories. Nothing unusual. Bert decided to go see Larry.

"Larry, I have a proposition for you that I think you might be interested in." "Oh, what's that?" "I know you have written history books about castles. I have a castle you might be interested in." "Ok, what castle is that?" "It's a castle in Medias, Rumania." "I heard about that, but I thought it was just publicity for your movie. Why would I be interested in that particular castle?" "Because that castle has a history, and I think it would interest you very much." "You trying to say it's haunted?" "Larry, I saw things happen there, that are beyond explanation. Things I would never believe if I hadn't witnessed them." Larry let out a small laugh. "Well, you have my interest, now convince me."

"First of all, there is a vault room underneath the castle. It contains the bodies of just about everyone who owned, or lived in the castle, since it was built. Probably 90% of those people died a violent and horrible death." "Ok, so?" "While we were there shooting the movie, a lot of strange things happened, which shouldn't have. It was as if someone, or something, didn't want that picture made there. It was trying to drive us away. I tell you, it succeeded. I had to come back here to finish the movie." "So, what did this castle do to drive you away?" "There were things that showed up on the frames of the film that shouldn't have been there. No one saw these images while we were shooting. Except, one time, Helen thought she saw something while we were shooting, but at the time, we thought she was just imagining things. Now I think she really did see something."

"That's not very much to go on. The film could be due to reflections. You know that. When it's dark, a lot of people think they see something that isn't really there." "Yes, but what Helen described, showed up on the print, although it wasn't very clear." So, tell me more." "One of the cast died for no reason the doctor could identify. The man looked like he had been scared to death. There is a dungeon below the castle. While shooting down there, one of the girls almost had her body pulled apart by a torture machine, that we inspected, and determined that is was so rusted it could not work. Which is what we wanted. But during shooting, the machine started to operate, and nearly killed the girl." "How did you stop it?" "We couldn't. We had to hurry and cut the ropes holding the girl." "What else?" "Helen was almost killed when a piece of concrete fell from a balcony, and landed right where she was standing. The only thing that saved her, was Arthur pulling Helen out of the way just in time."

"Well, Bert, I am interested now. What do you want me to do?" "I will contact Barry Greene, and ask him if you could go over and stay with them for a while. Delve as deep as you can into the history of that castle, from the time it was built. This could be a best seller for you." "Bert, I think you have something there. This could become an adventure." "I guarantee that." "You make the arrangements and I'll talk to Kristy, and get things in order. I'm sure Kristy will be excited about a trip to Rumania." "Ok, Larry, I'll be in touch."

Bert sent a telegram to Barry, hoping he would go along with Larry poking into the history of the castle. Bert just had to know what all has happened in that castle; it might make a good movie. In the reply to his telegram, Bert was notified that Barry and Janet Greene, had both passed away. The castle was vacant at this time, so Bert put in a call to the land office in Bucharest, to inquire about the status of the castle. It was property of the state. Bert made arrangements to lease the castle for a year. He felt that would be plenty of time for Larry to do the research and to write his book. If not, he was told there probably wouldn't be a problem to extend the lease. Everything was ready. He hoped Larry was ready.

The village of Medias has not changed a bit since Abby has disappeared. There is a new pub owner. Cornel is still the constable; he is 55 now. The older generations of people still dress as they did hundreds of years ago. The younger villagers, most of them try to keep up with a more modern dress. Most of the villagers still travel as they always have. Bicycles or horse and wagon. That's because most people, very seldom leave the village. A new mayor was elected 4 years ago. His name is Stanislav Randa. He is 54 years old.

Larry is 28, and Kristy is 27. They met in college and married after they both graduated. That was four years ago. They are not ready for a family yet. Larry does a lot of traveling, doing research for the books he writes. Kristy travels with him. She helps with the research and tries to keep things in order.

They are met at the castle by Mayor Randa. "Welcome to Medias. We've been expecting you. The villagers are looking forward to meeting you. They know you have come here to write a book, but they are a little apprehensive about what kind of book." "Thank you for the welcome. We are here to write a history of this beautiful castle. We understand it has a very interesting background." "Well, I've lived here for 5 years. I only know bits and pieces about the castle. Many villagers won't talk about it. The villagers, through the centuries, have endured a lot since this castle was built. If the villagers had their way, they would have destroyed the castle after the last inhabitants disappeared. But they are afraid to go even close to the castle. So, I don't know if you'll get much cooperation from them. I understand there is quite a bit of history of the castle down in the archives of the library." "I'll check that out."

So, it's been several years since anyone lived here?" "Yes, I understand there was some strange things happening here, and after the disappearance of the couple who lived here, plus one of the village women, that door has been locked since Cornel, the constable, locked it that day." "When was that?" "That was in 1973. So, I have no idea what it looks like inside."

"Well, Mr. Mayor, suppose you unlock the door, and we will see how bad it is." The Mayor unlocked the door, and everyone entered. Larry and Kristy couldn't believe their eyes. Kristy spoke first. "This is amazing, it's beautiful. I love it." "Well, I must say I'm surprised. This is the first time I've been in the castle, but it looks as if someone has been living here all the time. Everything is sparkling." "Mr. Mayor, I think we are going to like it here. Kristy sure approves." "Well, here are the keys, I'll leave you now, and let you get settled in."

Larry and Kristy started exploring. Larry was glad there was an office, where they could work. They went up stairs and checked out all the bedrooms. Kristy was happy about the master bedroom. It was large and the décor was perfect. They looked in the great room, then to the kitchen. "Bert said, that down below the castle, there was a vault room, and a torture room. He said the entrance was in the kitchen." Larry spotted a door next to the refrigerator. "That must be it. Let's go down and look."

They went down the stairs into the vault room. "Look at all these vaults. I'll have to make a list of the names. Bert said, most of these people met a violent death." "That doesn't sound very encouraging. Larry, are you sure you want to live in this place? It's beginning to get spooky." "We'll be alright, we're just going to write a book." "Yeah, but what if somebody doesn't want this book to be written? You heard what the Mayor said about the villagers." "They are just superstitious, and they are so afraid of this place, they won't come near it." "I suppose you're right."

Larry went over to the door to the torture room. As they entered, Larry was a little surprised. "This was supposed to be a torture room. It looks a lab to me." They started looking around. "There's the dungeon, it's still here." They inspected the dungeon. Then Larry spotted the acid vat. It was still about half full. Larry started to lean over the vat, when he noticed a slight smell coming from the liquid. Just then, Kristy let out a slight scream. "Larry, what is that?" Larry turned around to see what Kristy was concerned about. On the table, was the glass container, still full of liquid, and something lying in the bottom of the container. Larry walked over to the table. "Good grief, Kristy, that looks like what was once a heart." The heart was still in the container of liquid, but it had shrunk quite a bit, and was fairly wrinkled. Larry looked at it for a moment, then turned around and looked at the vat. There was a rubber glove on the table, so Larry put it on and reached in and picked up the heart. He took it over to the vat and dropped it in. Within a minute, the heart was dissolved. "Just as I thought, Kristy, this vat is full of acid. I'm going to get someone to dispose of this stuff, it's too dangerous to have around." "Larry, I've seen enough. Let's go back upstairs."

That afternoon, Larry and Kristy's luggage and trunks were delivered from the airport. The new housekeeper and groundskeeper introduced themselves. Christian and Ana Moldovan, ages 52 and 48. The day was spent unpacking and arranging their belongings. Larry went down to the office to look around. Later, Larry and Kristy, walked around the grounds. They discovered the pond. There had been quite a lot of rain the last year or so, and the water in the pond was fairly deep. They spotted the path that led back behind the castle. They decided to explore it.

They reached the canyon. The grass had grown about a foot or so tall. Larry and Kristy walked to the edge of the canyon. Kristy grabbed Larry's arm. "Larry, look down there, those are bones. Do you think they are human?" "Could be, let's go down and look." They made their way to the bottom of the canyon. "It certainly is human" "Larry, look, there is something shining between the rib bones." Larry reached down and picked up the gold ring. "It's a gold ring, but it looks as if it's been cut or sawn through. The stone has some sort of crest on it. I would like to know who the ring belonged to, and who's skeleton that is." "Put it back down, Larry. I don't like the looks of this." "No, I think I'll hang on to it. Probably when we start searching records, we will find out what this is about."

They went back up to the top of the canyon. As Larry was walking through some tall grass, his foot hit something. He pulled the grass back away. "Kristy, there is some type of wooden box here. It must be hundreds of years old. Whatever it was has fallen apart, and the wood very dry and aged." Kristy came over to look. "Who knows what it was.......? Wait...... Look at that one board there, it looks like a drawing or something on it." Larry knelt down to get a better look. He brushed some dirt off of the board. As he looked closer, he could make out the outline of a crest. "Kristy, the crest on this board is the same as that on the ring. I can barley make out the word Count and an St, but that's all. This was a coffin, which evidently belonged to that skeleton at the bottom of the canyon." "Why would someone dump his body into the bottom of the canyon?" "That is a good question. I'll be looking closely for information on this incident."

The sun was going down when they arrived back at the castle. It had been a long day, and Larry and Kristy were both wore out. So, the plan was to sit back and relax for a while, go to bed early, and start work tomorrow. They would go down to the village sometime after noon, to The Pub, and introduce themselves and talk to some of the villagers.

After breakfast the next morning, Larry went into the office to clean out the desk, so he could put in his own things, and arrange it to fit his own purpose. He started going through the drawers first. Most of what he found, was of no use to him. There was quite a lot of drafting equipment, which, he didn't want to throw away, so he stored it in an empty cabinet. One drawer he opened had a journal in it. That interested Larry. He felt like he hit the jackpot. It was a journal that Barry kept, and it appeared to contain information on just about everything that Barry and his family had experienced while living in the castle. He put the journal back in the drawer.

Larry was elated. While doing the history of the two castles in Germany, he found that the mayors, the constables, and the doctors, in the villages had kept logs, or journals, which went back hundreds of years. Even some of the villagers had kept diaries or records of things they experienced. If Larry was lucky, the same would hold for this village. The only difference would be, the villagers in Germany were eager to work with Larry. The people in Medias, either hated or feared the castle. He probably wouldn't get much cooperation.

In a bottom drawer, Larry found the rolled-up floor plan of the torture room. He unrolled the plans and look them over. It wasn't very complicated. It showed the dungeon, a few torture machines, chains attached to one wall. He rolled the plan back up and placed it back in the bottom drawer. Through out the morning, Larry had the office pretty much like he wanted it. Since he and Kristy would both be working in the office, she would have her put in her own little touches.

That afternoon, Larry and Kristy went down to The Pub. Since it was lunch time, there were quite a few people in The Pub. As they entered, all eyes were trained on them. As they found a table, Larry turned to the group. "Hello, everyone. I am Larry and this is my wife, Kristy. We have moved into the castle. I am a writer and Kristy is my assistant. We hope to get to know all of you while we are here." "My name is Anatolie Stoica, why are you here?" "I have been hired to write a history of your castle." "It's not our castle; it is evil, and you would do better to forget it, and go back to where you came from." "Mr. Stoica, I'm sorry you feel that way, but we have been hired for a job, and we intend to complete that job." "Do what you need to, but you both heed my words, you'll find out. Don't expect any information from me." "No sir, Mr. Stoica, I won't. But thank you for your input."

A young girl stood up. "My name is Sabina Hagi. I'm nineteen, and I was born here. I've heard stories, and I've seen some things, and I don't mind telling you about them, but you probably won't believe me." "Well, Miss Hagi, I would like to hear what you have to say, and I promise I will keep an open mind. Let me assure everyone, I am not here to make a spectacle of the village, or to put you people, or your village, in a bad light. Many people in the world feel they have had strange experiences that no one believed. I think they would like to know they are not alone. The history I write about this castle, I hope, will let people see their experiences were through no fault of theirs. Just like what ever has happened in this castle, is no fault of you people, or the village."

"Larry." "Yes, Mr. Stoica." "Since you put it that way, maybe I've been a little hard on you. I think I understand why you are doing this, but I'm still afraid you're going to have trouble with that castle." "Thank you, Mr. Stoica, we will keep our guard up."

An older woman stood up, "My name is Soreana Bogdan. I've lived here all my life. My husband kept a diary, up until he passed away. I would be willing to make it available to you." "Well, thank you, Mrs. Bogdan, I may ask for your help later."

Later, they went to talk to Cornel. "Yes, the mayor told me all about you and your wife. So, you came here to write a history of the village." "No, we are going to write a history of the Benes' Castle. Of course, being so close to Medias, the village will be part of that history. As I told a group of the citizens, this is not an expose for the tabloids. This will be as factual as I can make it, but portions of the book will be left to the reader to determine whether they believe certain aspects." "Well, that's neither here nor there, for me. The law has no interest in what you write in your book." "I do need your help." "In what way?" "You keep a log or register of what goes on each day, right?" "Yes." "Would I have access to those records?" "Yes, they are public records. That's no problem." "How about past constables records?" "Those you will find in the basement of the library." "Very well, Kirsty and I thank you."

The next stop was to the mayor. "Sure, I'll help in any way I can, as long as it's possible and not against the law." "I understand. I presume any information from years past, back to when the castle was built, I will find in the basement of the library." "Yes. I'll leave word with the library to give you access to what ever you need." "Thank you, I appreciate that."

"We will stop in and see the doctor, although I don't look for him to be of much help." They entered the doctor's office. "Is the doctor available for a few minutes?" "I'll find out." The receptionist switched on the intercom. "Larry and Kristy are here. They would like to talk to you for a few minutes." "Send them in." "Please, go on in."

"What can I do for you?" "I was wondering, in our research, if we would be able to look at your past records?" "No, I'm afraid that is not possible. Those records are privileged, and are not available to the public." "I understand that, but at some later date, would you be willing to share with me, what you can, about things you have seen or experienced, while you have been the doctor here?" "I suppose there are some things we could discuss." "Thank you, doctor, I would appreciate that."

Back at the castle, Larry sat at his desk to work out his plan of action. He had to decide whether to start back at the beginning when the castle was built, or start with the recent past, which would still be remembered readily by the villagers. He started to make a list of people he wanted to talk to, but he figured most of the information would come from the archives at the library. He made a note of what he, and Kristy, had seen back at the canyon. He hoped he would find what that was all about.

As Larry sat at his desk, he started thinking about the lab. Something bothered him. He seemed to think there was something down there that didn't fit. He went back down to the lab to look around. The first thing he noticed, were the chains on one wall. He noticed there seemed to be a set missing. There were holes in the wall where they had been. He made a note of that. He went over to the power panel. It was obvious it had been on fire at one time. He looked over the lab table. It looked like a normal lab setup. Nothing unusual, or out of the ordinary. He walked over to the dungeon, opened the cell door, and went in. Nothing really to see in there, except a cot over in one corner.

Suddenly, there was a clanking sound. Larry turned around; the cell door had banged closed. There wasn't anything to see in there anyway, so Larry took hold of the cell door, only when he pushed on the door, it didn't move. He tried again. The cell door would not open. He started jiggling the door. It would not open. Larry thought about calling out to Kristy, but if she was upstairs, she probably wouldn't hear him. He took a couple of steps back, wondering what to do next. As Larry stood there, he heard a click, and the cell door slowly swung open. He didn't waist any time leaving the cell, but he didn't understand what just happened. He decided he had enough of the lab for a while. Then he stopped. That's what was different. The corner with two brick walls.

He hurried back up stairs to look at the torture room plans again. He laid them out on his desk, and unrolled them. Sure enough, the plans did not show the brick walls. They were not part of the original plans, which means they were built sometime later. Why would someone enclose a corner of the room? There was no opening in either wall. Had they been built to hide something? Larry was going back down to the lab, and find out what was behind those walls, if anything.

Larry went down, and looked the brick walls over, very carefully. Not even a little hole in the bricks. Larry looked around, and saw the tool box against one wall. He found a chisel and a hammer. He commenced chipping away the mortar between the bricks. The mortar must have been pretty old, it crumbled fairly easy. He pulled the first brick out, but he couldn't see anything. There wasn't enough light in the lab to show through one brick opening. He removed 4 bricks. As he looked in the opening, he still couldn't see too much. But what he did see, made him jump back. His eyes must be playing tricks on him. He was sure he didn't really see what he thought he did. With 4 bricks out, he was able to pull more bricks out with his hands.

Well, he did see what he thought he saw. Two skeletons, hanging from chains on the wall. He stepped back. He was excited, and scared to death, at the same time. He removed a few more bricks. The clothes were pretty much intact, so he could tell that one had been a woman and the other a man. Larry was sure of one thing; this castle definitely had a history. It may not be supernatural, but Larry was sure it was going to be an interesting history. The disappearance of Abby, the canyon, the cell door and now this. It was time to have a long talk with Kristy.

"Kristy, this project gets more interesting all the time. We haven't even really started yet, but things are progressing pretty fast." "What do you mean?" "You know about Abby's disappearance, and the canyon. Well, something else has popped up. I think we need to be prepared for whatever we find out about this castle." "Well, don't keep me in suspense. What did you find?" "Come with me down to the lab, words wouldn't do this discovery justice. It has to be seen." "I'm right behind you."

As they entered the lab, Kristy saw bricks scattered on the floor, where the brick walls were. "Looks as if you have been busy. What do I need to look at?" Larry walked over to the brick wall. "Come, look in the opening here." As Kristy looked into the opening, her mouth dropped open, she stepped back away. "Larry, how did you know what was in there?" "I didn't know." "What made you start taking bricks out of the wall?" "These two walls did not show up on the original prints of the torture room. They had to be built later. I couldn't figure any reason for the walls to be there, so I decided to see if they were hiding something. I started tearing bricks out, and that's what I found." "How horrible. I would bet money they were alive when those walls went up." "I'm sure they were. There is probably not much chance this will show up anywhere in the archives. I'm sure who ever did this, never told anybody about it." "There is one chance. In our searching we may find where a man and a woman went missing in the past." "That's a good possibility. I'll have to start writing this stuff down, so I can remember to keep an eye open for it while we are searching.

After they went back upstairs, "Kristy, I forgot to tell something that happened while I was in the lab." "Don't tell me you have something else to show me?" "No, but while I was in the lab, I walked into the dungeon, and while I was standing inside the dungeon, the cell door slammed shut. When I tried to open it, it wouldn't open. No matter how hard I tried, it wouldn't open. Then just like that. There was a click and the door slowly opened by itself." "That's a little weird." "Bert told me that when they tried to shoot his movie here, strange things happened, and he decided the castle didn't want him to shoot his movie here. Maybe this castle doesn't want us to write a history about it either." "Oh, Larry, you don't believe that, do you?" "Well, I don't want to, but maybe there is something to what Mr. Stoica said. Let me just say, I don't think we should be surprised about anything we find out about this castle."

The first thing Larry and Kristy did, was go to Bucharest to the land office. Larry wanted to obtain a list of everyone who had owned, or lived, in the castle. It was not an easy job. The current records only went back about 100 years. Anything older than that was stored in the basement. (Everything always goes to the basement.) A clerk said she would show them where the older records were kept. Larry knew that the castle was built somewhere around 1590, so the clerk brought them all the books from 1500 up.

Larry opened the book to 1590 and started down the list. Not too far down the list was Lord Benes', who had built the castle. This was going to take some time. Larry had no idea how long each person had owned the castle. After about 3 hours, Larry and Kristy had the complete list of Benes' Castle owners. Kristy compiled the list in order, with all the information they were able to find.

Andros and Erzsi Benes', built the castle, and moved into the castle in 1590. Andros died in 1625. The property was transferred to Vidor Benes' that year. It would have gone to Erzsi, but she was accused of poisoning Andros, and killing her lover, Dragos. She was hung by the villagers, so the property went to Vidor, because Josepha wanted nothing to do with the castle. Vidor died in 1661.

The castle was vacant until 1790. Lord Bernard and Regina purchased the castle. They had a son Adam. Regina died giving birth to a girl, Mimi. Mimi died when she was 8 years old. Lord Bernard died in 1835 at which time Adam inherited the castle. Adam was married to Christine until he died in 1837. The castle went to Christine until her death in1877.

The castle remained empty until 1935. Albert Serban bought the castle, for Barry and Janet Greene to live in, while Barry designed a castle for Albert. Barry and Janet had a daughter, Abby. Albert died in 1944. Barry and Janet continued to live in the castle, until their death in 1973. Abby and her husband Artur both disappeared that year also. After that, the state took over the castle and property. The state leased the castle to Bert, so that Larry and Kristy could live in it, while writing the history of the castle.

"Kristy, we have everything we need here. I think our next step, is to go to the library and see what they have. Looking at this list, I think we should start right with when the castle was built and work our way up to the present." "I think that's best. I feel we are going to run into a lot of surprises, and I think we need to take them as they come, and not skip around, or try to work backwards.

Larry and Kristy took a day to rest, and go down to the village. They went to The Pub to get something to eat. They talked with the people in The Pub. The villagers were becoming more friendly with Larry and Kristy. Soreana Bogdon brought her husbands diary. Some of the older villagers offered to help, if Larry or Kristy had any questions as they proceeded. A few of the villagers were still worried that this book might put too much light on the village, and they would be flooded with tourists wanting to see the castle. They still lived by the old ways, and they didn't want the village to change.

The day came to start digging into the castle's past. The librarian escorted Larry and Kristy down to where all the information was stored. "Kristy, I'll start on this end, and you start at the other end. I doubt if there is any order to this mess." There wasn't. The first thing Larry found out, was who Count S, was. "Kristy, that coffin at the canyon. I found a packet here that says 'Count Stefan' on it. I would say that's our man." "That should be interesting. I'm really curious as to who this guy was. Larry, I found a folder here that says 'Plague' on the front." "We may find more information than I thought we would." "Larry, here is another folder 'Witch Trials'." "I was just thinking, what do these things have to do with the castle, if anything?" "I see what you mean. These things may be interesting, but may have nothing to do with the castle." "Exactly."

Larry and Kristy gathered up everything that might have a story with it, and boxed it up to take back to the castle. Most of what they found was simply village business, village get togethers, new businesses coming in, and elections. Nothing to help with the history of a castle. What they did have, they took back to the castle, and spread everything out on a table in the office.

As they went through the information, they would determine if it was of any value, then place all documents that were of interest, on another table, in chronological order. Larry read the account of Count Stefan. It did mention the castle, so Larry put in on the 'keep' pile. After he read the account of the Witch Trials, he put it on the 'keep' pile. One of the owners of the castle, Vidor Benes', was mentioned several times. So, it went. Larry and Kristy spent a couple of days sorting, and classifying, all the paperwork they were interested in keeping.

What they didn't need, they took back to the library. Larry and Kristy started with the earliest dated papers. The first paper told of the building of the Benes' Castle in 1590. Owners Andros and Erzsi Benes'. It seems the village was excited about having a castle built close to them. They welcomed the family with open arms. There was mention of a Count Stefan, in 1590, that terrorized the village for a short time. He reportedly was a vampire. Andros informed the village that he had succeeded in destroying Count Stephan, but he never said how or where. The next thing they come across is about a young lady that was murdered, in 1628. Andros was accused of the murder, but the real murderer was finally exposed. A few years later, Erzsi poisons Andros, and ends up killing her lover. Erzsi is hanged by some of the villagers.

Then in 1646, the Witch Trials started. Several women were held captive in the dungeon below the castle. A few of them were hanged, one was burnt at the stake. An administrator from the main church came to the village, and put a stop to the witch hunting. That was a black period for the village.

In 1661, The Black Plague hit the village hard. After several weeks, the plague eased up. It wiped out almost half the people in the village. That was another dark period for Medias. Soon after the plague, Vidor fell from the castle balcony, and died.

"Kristy, so far, none of what we have discovered, seems to be tied to the castle, at least not directly." "The only time the castle is mentioned, is when the women were held in the dungeon. There is nothing supernatural about that." "The weirdest information was about Count Stefan. A vampire. Really? Even that story doesn't mention the castle." "Larry, let's read Mr. Bogdan's diary." "That would be during the period when Barry and Janet lived here. Let's read through the second owner first. Then, when we get to Barry and Janet, we will tie the diary in with that era."

After a break, Larry and Kristy started with the Lord Bernard era. The Bernards took over the castle in 1790. "The only thing here, is a story about the daughter, Mimi, 8 years old, accidently drowned in the pond on the castle grounds. Then in 1835, after Lord Bernard dies, Adam and Christine move into the castle. It seems Adam eventually lost his mind and went crazy. All the villagers ever knew, was that Adam died after some kind of accident. "Kristy, we are not getting much book material here. Every village has its stories and tragedies, and none of this information, on the surface anyway, has anything to do with an 'evil or haunted castle'. Let's take a break tomorrow, and spend the day in the village. We need some time off."

Chapter 20

After a day off, Larry and Kristy, were ready to dig in, and see what they could come up with. So far, they didn't have much. "Well, Kristy, let's start with where Barry and Janet moved into the castle....... Wait a minute. I just remembered; Barry kept a journal after they moved in. It's in this desk drawer." Larry pulled the journal out of the drawer. This is Barry's first hand account of living in the castle. I think there will be a lot more of what we are looking for here, than in the village information. Let's put that aside, and go through the journal. I'll go through what Barry has to say, while you take notes. Ok?" "Ok. You are going to read it out loud, right?" "Oh, yes. You won't miss anything."

"The first thing Barry and Janet found, was a human skeleton, in the bottom of the empty pond. Barry never did find out who it was, or what happened. There is nothing until September of 1939, when Germany invaded Poland. Oh, here is something. In September, Janet was assaulted, but didn't know who the attacker was. It seems that Barry took Janet into the village late that night. She saw a man, and told Barry he was the man. Barry confronted the man and accidently killed him. While going back to the castle, Janet pointed to another man and said that he was the one. Barry realized, that Janet was in shock, and didn't know who attacked her. Barry had just killed an innocent man, for nothing." "Did they find out Barry had killed that man?" "Evidently not."

"This sounds interesting. In 1940, four men in the village were stabbed to death over a period of two or three weeks. One night, Barry was awakened in the middle of the night. Janet was not in the bed. Barry thought he heard the front door open and close. When he went down stairs, he saw Janet walking toward the kitchen with a knife in her hand. When he got to her, he noticed the knife had blood on it. When he asked Janet what she was doing, Janet spoke, but it was not her voice. The voice claimed to be, Flori, a young girl, who had been assaulted by these four men, when they were in there 20's, where as she committed suicide. After all these years, she was able to use Janet for her revenge. He did find out that Flori had been buried down in one of the vaults below the castle. That's how she was able to take over Janet's body. Janet never had any memory of killing four men, or of possession by Flori. Barry never told anyone about Janet's involvement, after all, he surmised, who killed those men, Janet or Flori."

"You talk about supernatural, that's it." "I don't know, Kristy, do you really think the dead can take over a person's body, and make them kill someone? That's pretty far out." "But Janet didn't know the story about Flori and the men. Why would she kill four men she knew nothing about? Barry had a good question, who really killed those men?" "I know, we have to keep an open mind. Let's continue on and see what lies ahead."

Janet had a sister, Jessie, who came over with Barry and Janet, when they moved into the castle. Jessie married a man from the village, Paul. In February of 1941, a boy, Daniel, was born to Jessie and Paul. In 1941, Germany occupies Rumania, and there are a lot of Germans in and around Medias. "Listen to this, Kristy. A German soldier forces his way into the castle. He goes upstairs and sees Jessie. Jessie is holding Daniel in her arms, and as the soldier starts toward Jessie to attack her, he suddenly stops, grabs his chest and falls to the floor, dead. He looks like he had a heart attack. But he's only 20 years old. It was as if something stopped him from reaching Jessie." "You think the castle, somehow, saved Jessie and Daniel?" "I don't know, there have been young people, as young as 20, that have had heart attacks." "Yes, but this one sure happened at the right time." "Listen to this, they carried the soldier down to the vault room, and put him into one of the empty vaults. No one ever figured out what happened to the soldier."

"Kristy, here is one you might try to explain. A German Major decides to execute 10 men, from the village, by firing squad. Paul happened to be one of them. Jessie and the baby were pleading with the Major, not to kill these men. Naturally, he ignored her. He ordered the squad to fire, but the guns didn't fire. He ordered it again, and again, the rifles didn't fire. He tried a third time, same result. The Major got a little nervous, and called off the execution." "It looks as if something is protecting Jessie and her family. I wonder what would have happened if Paul hadn't been in that group?"

Larry continued to read. "It seems that later on, the Major tried to take over the castle as his headquarters, Barry objected, and a scuffle ensued, where as Barry got a hold of the Major's gun, and escorted him down to the dungeon. After a few days, the Major was found dead on the cot in the cell. The doctor said it looked like he had been scared to death. That's the same thing Bert told me, about one of the actors, while they were filming here. He said the actor was lying on that cot, while they were filming another scene. When they went to tell the man, they were ready for his part, he was dead. Bert said the man's face was contorted, as if he had been scared to death." "Larry, this is really getting weird. It's as if some force is protecting some people in the castle, and destroying anyone who threatens them." "Let's look at Mr. Bogdan's journal, and see what he observed during this period."

Larry and Kristy read through the journal. There didn't seem to be much about the castle in any of his entries. When he talks about the war period, he talks about the firing squad incident, but it's more just in passing. He doesn't try to explain what his thoughts were. Mr. Bogdan tells about the Germans searching all the houses, it seems a young soldier was missing. Later on, he talks about the Major also being missing. No body knows what happened to him, but no one really cares. "Kristy, it appears that none of the villagers ever connected these 'happenings', with the castle. Yet the villagers feel that the castle is haunted or evil. I think the answer to that lies in the history much further back in time." "Larry, I'm dead tired. Let's turn in for the night. Why don't we go down to the village tomorrow morning, and talk to some of the people? Maybe we can find some extra information that was never written about." "Good idea. I'm with you."

The next day around noon, Larry and Kristy, went down to The Pub for some lunch. They hoped to talk to some of the older villagers who could remember back a little further in the past. They spotted Mr. Stoica sitting at a table by himself. Larry and Kristy ask if they could join him. "Sure, sit down. I have a feeling you are here for a reason." "Well, yes sir, we have a reason." "I see, you want me to enlighten you on some of the villages past." "Yes, if you don't mind." "No, I'll help if I can. A lot of history has been passed down through the generations. What do you have in mind?" "Kristy and I have been going over the war years here in the village." "Yes, that was a pretty rough time. People were always fearful of the Germans. They had a habit of making people disappear." "That's exactly what I want to talk about. I read that a young soldier disappeared. Then later, the Major in charge, also disappeared. Did you ever wonder what happened to them?" "We didn't care what happened to them. We never did find out." "Did anyone blame it on the castle?" "No, not that I know of." "So many of the villagers are afraid of the castle. They think it's haunted, or evil. What do you think? What started this fear?" "I think the castle generates an aura of tragedy, pain, and heartbreak."

"Do you think the castle still generates these things." "Maybe not at the moment, but I feel it could, and probably will." "Like I ask before, what started this fear, and when?" "People's fear of the castle started way back, within a few years after it was built. Each generation has its own reason for fearing the castle. A lot of things have happened there. Things that can't be explained. Now, if you excuse me, I have to be going. You go on with your research, if you have questions, I'll help if I can. I still think you should not stay in that castle."

"Well, Kristy, he wasn't much help. He gave us nothing explicit." "The only thing we learned, was that things started happening not long after the castle was built, and continue to happen even today. But the only real information we are finding, comes from Barry's journal." "Yes, and that gets me to thinking, are there other journals hidden in that castle? If there is, that's where our real information will come from. We'll finish with Barry's journal, then I think we need to do some searching." "This is getting exciting. Maybe we will find hidden panels, and passages. Just like in the old movies." Larry looked at Kristy and gave a little laugh.

Larry starts reading the next portion of Barry's journal. "Barry is talking about Daniel, Paul and Jessie's son. He says that as Daniel approached his teen years, Jessie started seeing some strange things happen when they went to the village. Daniel was a quiet child, but Jessie and Barry started noticing something different, as if there was another side of Daniel that nobody else noticed." Barry's journal went on to say that in his teen years, Daniel started showing a cruel side. It was very subtle, but it was there. Janet never seemed to think there was anything wrong, and Barry decided not to talk to Janet about it, just yet. Jessie started putting two and two together, and realized she had to talk to Paul about her suspicions.

"Oh my……… Kristy, listen to this. You won't believe what Barry is talking about." "Try me." "Jessie went to Paul, and told him she thought there was evil in Daniel. Whereas, Paul told Jessie, that he knew Daniel was evil. Kristy, listen carefully. Paul told Jessie that Daniel was a son of Satan." "I don't believe it." "I said you wouldn't, but that's only half of it. When Paul was younger, he made a deal with the devil, that if the devil could let him stay young and never age, he would give the devil a son." "Larry, this is more like something out of a horror movie." "I know, but Barry wouldn't write this kind of thing in a journal, unless he at least thought it was true." "Read on. What's next."

Larry continued reading. "Where was I? Oh, it says when Jessie realized what Paul said, she looked at Daniel, then back at Paul. She told Paul that Daniel must be destroyed. He cannot be allowed to complete his mission, what ever it is. As she started to go down the stairs, she tripped and fell. Barry ran to Jessie, and before she died, she was able to tell him about Paul and Daniel. Barry was sure Daniel had caused Jessie to fall. When Barry confronted Daniel, he confirmed to Barry who he was." "Well, Larry, I'll say one thing, after hearing this, what ever we find as we go on, will not surprise me. I understand why the villagers want this castle destroyed. After having this castle next to this village for several hundred years, I'm surprised the village survived, and the villagers still have their sanity."

"Barry goes on to say, that he hoped he could change Daniel, but soon found it was useless. Daniel started a cult, with some teenagers, who were under his spell, and even used a girl for a blood sacrifice. Paul and Barry decided something had to be done. They followed Daniel to where he held his rituals, where Paul was able to destroy Daniel, with a cross. After Daniel was destroyed, Paul assumed his real age, and died. It sounds like Barry could have written a book of his own." "How true, but you will be writing it for him."

"The next thing Barry talks about, is when Bert tried to shoot his movie here at the castle, but we both know all about that." "Yes, and at this point, I would say that Bert is probably right about his suspicions." "After our book is published, Bert can rerelease his movie, and probably make a mint." "How true."

"The last journal entry is in 1972. I wonder why he stopped writing?" "Maybe because he died?" "That's probably it. I think we need to go down and talk to Mr. Stoica. Let's take a break, and see what we can find out."

Larry and Kristy found Mr. Stoica at his regular table. "So, you ran into another brick wall." "I guess you could say that. Barry's journal stops in 1972. Can you tell us anything about that period?" "1972. Yes, that's the year Barry died." "Tell me it wasn't a violent death." "No, Barry died in his sleep. He was 72. Abby and her husband moved back to the castle a few days after her dad died." "What can you tell us about Abby? I don't think we will find much information about her."

"Abby was a good girl. She became a medical researcher, and married Artur. They lived in Bucharest, and as far as I know, they lead a fairly normal life. After she and Artur moved back to the castle, she changed completely. A full 180 degrees." "What do you mean?" "She rarely came to the village. She was not very friendly. She seemed to be obsessed about something. Then an odd thing happened. Villagers started taking their animals up to the castle. They said she was trying to save their lives, or bring them back to life. Eventually, Abby and Artur split up. He still slept at the castle, but he spent most of his time with a girl named Sonja. Then one day, all three of them disappeared. To this day, no one knows where they went, or why." "There is a lab in the castle, but you don't know what kind of experimenting she was doing?" "You know Bela and

Clara?" "Yes." "Talk to Bela. He was the grounds keeper at that time. I have a feeling he might know what was going on. A while before Abby disappeared, Bela started acting very strange. Any time anyone ask him if something was wrong, he would say, he didn't want to talk about it. Try talking to him. Maybe he'll talk to both of you." "Thanks, Mr. Stoica. Kristy, let's go look up Bela."

Larry and Kristy knocked on Bela's door. Clara opened the door. "Is Bela at home?" "Yes." "Can we talk to him for a minute?" "I suppose so. Come in. Sorry the place looks a mess." "Oh, don't let it bother you." "Follow me, Bela's in the kitchen." "Hello, Bela, remember Kristy and me?" "Yes, I remember, Mr. Hart. What is it you want?" "We would like to know about when you were the grounds keeper, when Abby and Artur lived in the castle." "There's nothing to tell." "Can we ask you some questions?" "No, I don't want to talk about it." "Bela, we know something happened up there, and I think you know what it was. We would really like to know what Abby was up to, in that lab." "Why, so you can print it in your book, and get me into trouble?" "Yes, we want it for the book, but your name will never be mentioned. Whatever you tell us, we will attribute to an anonymous source." "No, can't do it." "Bela, you have had this locked up in you for several years now. Don't you think it might help to get this off your mind?"

Bela thought for a few minutes. "Clara, I'd like to talk to Larry and Kristy alone. Do you mind?" "Yes, I do mind. If you were mixed up in something, I have a right to know about it. I deserve an explanation of why you have been acting the way you have these past years." "Yes....... Your right Clara, you have the right to know." "Larry, I could be sent to prison for what I know, and did. I want you to understand that." "Like I said Bela, your name will never be mentioned."

"Several months, after Abby and Artur moved into the castle, they were having problems, and Artur moved out." "I know, but why?" "Abby was doing things in that lab, that Artur didn't agree with. She got tired of his attitude, and told him, if he didn't like it, move out." "He didn't approve of what she was doing in the lab." "Right. Anyway, Abby came to me one night, and told me she wanted me to help her with something, something she couldn't do by herself. When she told me what it was, I refused. There was no way I could do what she wanted me to do." "What did she want you to do?" "I'll get to that in a minute. Anyway, she knew something about me, and she threatened to expose it, if I didn't help her. After arguing for a while, I agreed to help her." "What did she have on you?"

"Well, Larry, I was having an affair with a woman in the village. Oh, don't worry, I told Clara about it right after Abby disappeared. Clara and I are alright now." "I see, but what did Abby want you to do." "A young man had died and was buried that morning. Abby wanted me to go with her, and dig up that body." "Why?" "Hold on. So, we went to the cemetery, dug up the body, and took it back to the lab." "Bela, how could you do that?!" "Calm down Clara, remember, Abby had my back to the wall. I had no choice." "So, what happened then?" "When we got back to the lab, she made me leave." "Then you don't know what she did with the body?" "Well, yes, I found out a couple of nights later."

"Abby called me to come to the lab one evening. When I entered the lab, I couldn't believe my eyes. There on the table, was a glass container, with liquid in it, and a heart suspended in the liquid." "It was the heart of the man from the grave?" "Yes, it had to be. That thing was beating, just like it was alive." "Well, actually it was. Abby was keeping it beating by electrical impulses. But you didn't see the body." "No, I didn't see it anywhere." "Go on with your story. What happened next?"

"Abby had shown me a woman named Sonja, and where she lived. She wanted me to go to her house, and bring her back to the castle. This is 1:00 in the morning, mind you. Anyway, I said, 'What if she won't come?', and Abby says, 'You'll think of something'. I told her I didn't want anything to do with that. She as much as said if you don't, you'll end up living alone, or worse, you could go to jail. She reminded me about the body. So, I did what she said." "How did that go? Did Sonja go to the castle with you, or did you have to force her?" "She refused at first, but I told her there was an emergency at the castle. She thought maybe something happened to Artur, so she came with me."

"So, what happened when you got to the lab?" "What happened was a little strange. Abby told me I could go on upstairs. As I started to leave, she came over to me, and said the strangest thing. She knew I hated what I had been doing. Abby told me she would not be needing me anymore. I said, 'Not until the next time, I suppose'. Then Abby said, 'No, I will not ask you to do anything for me again, I guarantee you, you are free'. When I left the lab, that was the last time I saw Abby, Artur, or Sonja. I have no idea what went on after I left. They all just disappeared."

"So, Bela, you never told a single person about your experience?" "Not even Clara." "Oh, Bela, why didn't you ever tell me what you went through. I would have understood, I could have helped you." "Clara, I was just scared to death." "Well, Bela, you can relax now. No one will ever know from me what you told me. Since this happened several years ago, and Abby and the other two, have never been found, I doubt that you would ever go to prison anyway. But I do think, you and Clara, should still keep this to yourselves. It's hard to know how the villagers would react. I would say in this case, what they don't know, won't hurt them." "Well, Larry, I do feel better getting this off my chest. I thank you and Kristy for understanding. Especially you, Clara."

On the way back to the castle, "Kristy, that was very revealing. I'm beginning to believe that Benes' Castle, is evil. Something is causing some of these people to go off the deep end." "I agree with you, these strange occurrences just keep multiplying. I really would like to know what happened to Abby, Artur, and Sonja." "I think I know, Kristy." "What?" "I don't know what happened that night in the lab, but for some reason, all three of them ended up in that vat of acid. Don't ask me how, but I think that's why there has never been any trace of them."

"Kristy, let's go see the doctor, maybe he will cooperate and tell us something about Abby." "Let's make this our last stop, I'm getting tired." Larry and Kristy entered the doctor's office. Things were quiet, so the doctor said he would tell them what could. "I'll tell you everything I know, but if anyone asks where you got the information, you didn't get it from me." "Fair enough, go ahead." "After Abby and Artur moved back to the castle, Abby became a different person." "I know, we've been told that." "Anyway, I don't really know what went on in the castle, but, Janet, Abby's mother, was in poor health. She couldn't walk very well. One day I was called to the castle. It was an emergency, and when I got there, Janet's legs were black. It turns out, Abby had developed a serum, and she thought it would help Janet to walk. It did the opposite. I told Abby not to give her any more shots of that serum. Janet needed to go to the hospital. Abby was frustrated, she didn't want to lose her mother, but she gave her another shot of the serum." "You didn't know she did that?" "Not until it was too late. The second shot spread through her body and she died." "How did Abby take it after she realized her mother had died from the serum?"

"She was devastated. Not only did she lose her mother, she was the cause of it." "I think I see a problem here." "You bet. Abby was only a medical researcher, not a doctor. Her license could be revoked, and she could be charged for her mother's death." "You informed her of this aspect." "She knew what she had done. She was very disturbed over, not just of the charges she could face, but her mother was gone because of her actions." "So, what was the result?" "She went before the medical board in Bucharest, where they questioned her pretty intensely. A couple of weeks later she went back before the board, and she was informed her license had been revoked, and that her case would go before the grand jury, and she may be charged with involuntary manslaughter." "So, what was the result?" "Abby was charged and ordered arrested. But when Cornel went to arrest her, he couldn't find her. He searched the whole castle, and no sign of her. She had just disappeared. For some reason, Artur and a woman named Sonja disappeared at the same time."

"Well, doctor, you have been very helpful, and between you and me, I don't think any of those three will ever be found." "Do you know something I don't know?" "No, doctor, just a hunch."

As Larry and Kristy entered the office, they stopped in their tracks. The office was a mess. Books and papers were scattered all over the floor. Kristy picked Barry's journal up off the floor. Several pages had been ripped out, and torn into little pieces. "Larry, this is scaring me." "Yes, we know none of the villagers would do this. They won't come near the place." "Larry, I really think something doesn't want you digging into the past. It doesn't want your book written, just like it didn't want Bert to shoot his movie here. I feel as if this castle is alive and watching us." I know what you mean, but I'm not going to stop now. This makes me want to work even harder to find out it's secrets." As Kristy went over to the desk, "Larry, there is a key on the desk. Did you put it there?" Larry went over to the desk to see what Kristy was talking about. "I didn't put it there. I've never seen it before." "I haven't either, and I know it wasn't here when we left this afternoon."

"Kristy, this makes no sense. First, it appears that we aren't supposed to be digging into the past, but then we find a key on the desk. That key is telling us to look for something we need to see. I think there are two forces working here. One doesn't want the history known, the other one does for some reason." "We seem to be in the middle of a battle, Larry. What does that mean for us?" "Since we are in the middle, I would say, everything depends on which force is the strongest. With our persistence in moving ahead, and with the help of, shall we say the 'good' force, maybe we can defeat the 'bad' force." "I have one question." "What's that, Kristy?" "How do we know which force is the 'good' one, and which is the 'bad' one? Maybe we are not supposed to divulge all this information. Maybe it is supposed to stay hidden. If so, that switches who you think is the 'good' one, and the 'bad' one." "Hmmm. Kristy, you make a good argument there. All I can say is, we keep going until we either succeed, or fail. Let the forces fight it out." "Alright, Larry, just so one of them doesn't permanently knock us out of the competition. I don't want to be know as one of those violent deaths, like those people down in the vault room."

"Kristy, we need to find out what this key opens. It may be in this office, or it could be anywhere in this castle. We'll start here in the office. We'll check everything that uses a key to open." Larry and Kristy proceeded to check out everything in the office. They checked the desk drawers, to see if there was a box or container that had a lock. They checked all the cabinets, inside, and out. They checked behind pictures for wall safes, or little doors that might hold papers or such. They even rolled back a rug on the floor, to see if there was something under the floor boards. Nothing. They checked the great room, the dinning room, even the kitchen.

"Kristy, this is getting us nowhere. Let's go back to the office, sit down, and think about this." "What good will that do?" "We will take some time, and think about, if you wanted to hide something, where would you hide it? We might come up with something that will help us." "I don't know, but if you want to try it, we will."

As they went into the office to sit down, "Larry, did you leave those books lying on the floor, over by the library wall?" "No, I didn't." "I'll go pick them up." Kristy picked up the books, ready to place them back on the shelf. As she placed the first book on the shelf, she stopped. She took a closer look. "Larry, come here. Look at this." Larry walked over to Kristy. "Look at the wall behind where these books belong. There is some kind of crack in the paneling, and it sure is a straight, clean crack." Larry took a closer look, then started pulling books off the shelf. "Well, I'll be...... Kristy, this is what we have been looking for. Give me the key." The paneling behind the shelves, had a small door, with a lock. Larry inserted the key, turned it, and the door opened. Larry reached in and pulled out a thick booklet of papers. On the front sheet, was the name, Vidor Benes'. Larry was excited, "Kristy, we hit it big. This looks like a journal or diary written by Vidor Benes', the son of the family that built the castle." "Ooooh, I'll bet this will be interesting."

Larry started reading the diary. "Vidor didn't start writing until 1628, unless there is a separate set of papers, for before that time. Kristy, check through the information from the library, and see if you can find out how old he was at that time." Kristy searched through the information, after some time, Kristy found when Vidor was born, and did some quick math. "According to this summary of birth dates, Vidor would have been 40 in 1628. Strange he didn't start writing when he was younger." "Maybe life was boring before he reached 40, or he just wasn't interested in keeping track of events."

Larry went back to the diary. "Well, he starts out with a bang. It says he was going with a girl named, Aurora. He thought they were going to get married. Then without telling Vidor, she married some guy named, Felip. When Vidor found out, he was vivid with rage. He even confronted both of them, and informed them, they both would pay for what Aurora had done to him. He says he told them he would pick the time and place for his revenge." "That's a heck of a way to start out a diary." "I guess we'll have to wait to find out. He goes on to another subject."

"It seems that Andros became involved with a woman at The Pub, named Brigita. It turns out Brigita wanted to set Andros up, so that she could blackmail him. So, Brigita turns up dead, and Andros is charged

with her murder. As they were about to come to trial, the real murderer
was exposed. Erzsi, his wife, didn't blame him, she understood what
happened."

"Some months later, a man moves to the village, named Dragos."
Larry reads on for a couple of minutes. "I'll say one thing, Vidor sure
picked a good time to start writing his diary. Like I said before, maybe
nothing really happened until this period of time." "Well, Larry, I
remember one of the other papers said the villagers were excited about
the castle at first. It was several years later when they said strange things
started happening." "I remember reading that. So, this must be when
everything started. From what I just read; everything starts to snowball."
"Well, don't leave me hanging. What happened?"

"Within a few weeks after Dragos moved to the village, it turns out
Erzsi and Dragos are having an affair. Andros finds out about it, but
does nothing, other than barring her from seeing Dragos. He makes
her a prisoner in the castle. She is only aloud to leave when Andros is
with her. Of course, this sets her off. She almost goes out of her mind,
because she can't see Dragos. But then, she gets her break. One evening
as they finish dinner, and having a glass of wine, Andros, suddenly grabs
his chest, and falls to the floor, dead. The doctor said Andros had a heart
attack." "How convenient for Erzsi. I suppose she runs back to Dragos."

"How right you are, only Erzsi gets a rude awakening." "How so?"
"It seems that in that interval, Dragos moved on. He had another love,
Erzsi was out." "Love denied. I'm sure she didn't take that news very
well." "She sure didn't. When she found out, she took a small statue and
bashed his head in. So much for Dragos." "Wow, when she hits, she hits
hard." "Then she tries to cover it up by talking to some of the villagers,
that she hasn't seen Dragos for a while, maybe someone should go, and
check on him. They discover his body, and Erzsi almost gets away with
it, except one of the village women, seemed to know more than anyone
else. Her name was Ursule. She points to Erzsi, and tells the constable,
Emile, 'There is your murder.' The constable asks Ursule how she knows
Erzsi did it." Larry reads down a few lines. "Kristy, you won't believe
this, get ready for a bombshell." "What! What!" "Ursule is who Dragos
was going with after he dropped Erzsi."

"Good Lord........ Andros didn't die from a heart attack, Erzsi poisoned him!" "You're kidding, how did Ursula know that?" "Erzsi had told Dragos what she had done, so she could be with him. Dragos had then told Ursula about it. Since Erzsi had nothing left, she confessed to everything. Vidor just couldn't believe what his mother was saying. Erzsi said there was no use in denying it, it was all true. So, Emile locked Erzsi in a cell in the jail. The next morning, Vidor goes down to the jail to see his mother. As he enters the jail, Emile is lying on the floor, unconscious, the cell door is open, and Erzsi is gone. Vidor is informed that during the night some villagers, stormed the jail, knocked Emile out, and took Erzsi from her cell."

Vidor is beside himself. Vidor takes off and starts looking for Erzsi. Oh, Kristy, this is not good." "Did he find her?" "Yes, but too late. He started for the church, and as he approached, he saw Erzsi was hanging from a tree behind the church. The villagers had lynched Erzsi." "That sounds like something from the old West, not the 1600's." "Evidently that was the tipping point for Vidor. Of course, Vidor would like to know which villagers were involved in this horrible event, but no one is talking, and they probably never will. Kristy, I think I can see where Vidor is headed." "What do you mean?" "In his diary, Vidor decides the whole village is to blame for what happened, and he vows to make the whole village pay. He vows to destroy the village and everyone in it." "Oh, Larry, Vidor almost sounds like a mad man, he must be losing his mind. But I can't help sympathize with him, after all he has gone through."

Larry turned the page, and his eyes lit up. "Kristy, I think we are about to find out who our guests down in the lab are. Vidor writes that it is time to take revenge on his lost love, Aurora and Felip. It's been a few years now and Vidor knows exactly what he is going to do. He invites them to come up to the castle and have dinner with him. He's sorry how he treated them, and he wants to make it up to them." "I suppose they fall for it." "You got it. After dinner he drugs them, then, he and the grounds keeper, Simion, take them down to the torture room, and chain them to the wall. They brick up the two walls, but only half way. Oh, Kristy, you talk about cruel. You can spell it V-i-d-o-r." "He's going to torture them." "Not physically, but worse. He waits until the drugs wear off, when they can understand what's happening, and tells them since they want to be together forever, he's going to help them do that. He and Simion brick the walls on up to the ceiling. Kristy, he basically, buried them alive!" "There goes my sympathy for Vidor. The man is now totally insane. Larry, I'm beginning to have doubts about what we are doing here. If this is what happens to people who live in this castle, I don't know if I want to stay here, or continue with this book." "I know we have found a lot of things that have happened here, but is it the castle?" "I'm really beginning to think so. Look at what has happened to us since we moved in here. Those have just been minor things, what's in store for us next?"

"What do you say, we go down to the village and relax for a while. It will do us good to leave this behind us for a few hours." As Larry and Kristy were ordering something to eat, Anatolie Stoica came over to their table. "May I sit and join you?" "Of course, Mr. Stoica, you are always welcome to sit with us. Can I order you something?" "No, thanks, I'll just drink my coffee. How is your work progressing?" "Very well, actually." "Do you still contend there are no influences in the castle? You haven't heard or seen any strange goings on?" "Mr. Stoica, I would be lying if I said nothing strange has happened up there. There are a few things that have happened, that neither of us have an explanation for." "Would you care to tell me about them?" "Mr. Stoica, you seem to be a pretty level headed person. You have lived here a long time." "Ok, but that doesn't mean I don't still have my doubts about that place." "I know, and Kristy and I are starting to feel the same way. Let me ask you a question." "Go ahead." "Would you be willing to accompany Kristy, and me, when we go back to the castle?" Now Mr. Stoica had to think about that for a few minutes. He had never been to the castle, and he wasn't sure he wanted to go now.

"Listen, Mr. Stoica, I want to show you something at the castle, that no one who has lived in this village, since that castle was built, has ever known about. I discovered it, and I think it's time that this piece of history is made public. It is not a pretty sight." "You really sound serious. Since you put it that way, I'll go with you." "What do think, Kristy?" "I agree someone needs to know about this, but if it gets out, the villagers will be even more angry, and fearful of the castle. I'm afraid they might be just frightened enough; they will storm the castle and try to destroy it." "Miss Kristy, if it's that bad, I'll put off making it public until you and Larry decide that it is ok to do so." "Well, then, shall we head that way?"

When they arrived at the castle, everyone went into the office. Larry explained about things that had happened in the office, including the key, and the hidden diary. "I'll admit, those things are hard to explain. It just confirms my suspicion, that there is something about this place, that is not natural. So, what is it you want to show me?" "Come with us." They went down through the vault room. "Now, this is quite a burial ground here. Everybody who ever lived here must be entombed here." "Just about everybody, and this room has quite a history of its own." They entered the lab. Larry and Kristy stood in the doorway. "Go over to those brick walls and tell what you see." Mr. Stoica walked over to the walls. "What do you want me to see, other than a brick wall?" "Brick......... What do you mean brick wall, don't you see them?" "The bricks, yes, anything else, no." Larry and Kristy ran over to the brick walls.

"Larry, what is going on?" "I don't know, Kristy, but I sure am glad Mr. Stoica is with us to witness this." As the three looked at the wall, every brick was in place, just where it was supposed to be. There were no bricks on the floor. There was no opening in the bricks. "I don't get it!" "I don't either Larry, what's so secret about a brick wall?" "It isn't the wall that's the secret, it's what's behind it." Larry looked closely at the bricks. "Look they are still loose. There is no mortar between them." Larry started pulling the bricks out again. Finally, when the opening was big enough, what was behind the wall was visible. When Mr. Stoica saw the skeletons, he was speechless. His mouth dropped open. Finally, "Larry, what went on here?" "You can credit Mr. Vidor Benes', the son of the builder of this castle."

"I've heard his name mentioned, but no one seems to know anything about him. You say he imprisoned these two people in here?" Larry proceeded to tell Mr. Stoica the story of the skeletons and the walls. "These people were alive when Vidor did this; can you imagine the terror these two went through?" "Yes, but what bothers me, is if you took those bricks out of the wall, and you didn't put them back in, how did they get there." "Mr. Stoica, I swear, I did not put those bricks back into the wall." "Larry, I think you, and Kristy, are dealing with something stronger than both of you, and it could destroy one, or both, of you. If you don't mind, I think I will go back to the village. I don't intend to come back here again; I think this should be kept secret for the near future.......and I still think you should get out of this castle." As Mr. Stoica left, Larry put all the bricks back into the opening.

Chapter 21

Larry and Kristy went back to reading Vidor's diary. "There isn't much interesting here, until 1648. That's when the witch hunts began. Looks like Vidor had a big part in that. He said it was the perfect opportunity to get his revenge with the villagers for lynching his mother. Kristy, this shows just how demented Vidor was at this time. He would pick certain women, whose husbands, he was sure had a part in his mother's death, accuse the women of being a witch, and provide false evidence to help convict them. They hung several women, and burned one at the stake, before an administrator from the church intervened and put a stop to the witch hunt." "Innocent women killed, because of one man's urge for revenge, and years after the event. Talk about a son of the devil. This guy qualifies."

"Now, here's something interesting. According to Vidor, the woman burned at the stake, put a curse on the three men responsible, and said they would die a violent death. Vidor says, two of the three men, did in fact die violently. He says, 'I am the third, but I will not succumb to this curse'." "But he did. Remember the information from the library stated he fell from the second-floor balcony. After reading about this witch hunt, I have a feeling, his death was not an accident." "I agree with you. I don't think he was able to side step the curse. You know I would never have said anything like that a couple of years ago. This place is starting to convince me otherwise."

"There is only one entry left. It's dated 1661. That makes Vidor 83 years old. Well, it looks like old age has mellowed Vidor. He no longer has hatred for the villagers, and he even makes a heroic gesture. The Plague hit Medias in that year, and at his age, risking his life, he went to the village and helped everyone he could, for several days. That's the last entry, so he must have died shortly after that." "What a story. I would say we have enough information here for this book to be a best seller." "We're not finished yet." "Oh, what did I forget?" "One more family. The Bernards. Somehow we have to find their story."

Several days go by. They look around for any information about the Bernard family. While Kristy continues to look for something they can use, she looks at every book in the office library, hoping there is a diary among the books. Meanwhile, Larry starts working on the book itself. He goes through his notes, makes a sort of outline on where he wants to start, and how to progress the story line. "Larry, I don't think we are going to find anything about the Bernards, other than the information we found at the library in the village. I think I'll go upstairs for a while." "Huh. Ok, go ahead."

Kristy is sitting at her vanity table, combing her hair, then gets up and goes over to her night stand. There are a couple of books on the stand, that were taking up too much space. She picks them up and takes them over to her vanity. She opens the bottom drawer, and puts the books in to get them out of the way. At least for now. When she closes the drawer, it won't go all the way closed. She pushes on it a couple of times, but it won't close all the way. She knells down on the floor and pulls the drawer out. As she looks into the opening, she sees a small, thin book. Kristy pulls the book out, and looks at the front of it. It says, 'Christine Bernard'. She opens it up, and there it is. Christine's diary. Kristy looks through a few pages, and she knows this is what they have been looking for. She gets up and hurries down to show Larry.

"Kristy, you doll. Where did you find this?" "Underneath one of the drawers in my vanity. Quite by accident, I might add." "This is the final piece of the history. Up to this point, anyway." "How do you want handle this, Larry?" "I think we will go through Christine's diary first. That will fill up the empty space, then we will have the complete story. After that, we will go about organizing how we want to unfold the story.

I'm a little anxious to start writing the actual book." "Alright. I will say, this is probably going to be the most interesting book we have written."

Just as they get started, suddenly the ground and the castle start shaking. Everything starts moving around. Kristy slides out of her chair. Larry holds onto the desk tightly. It lasts for about 45 seconds, although it feels like longer than that. "Larry, what's happening? Is it an earthquake?" "I don't know, but I'm sure glad it stopped. Let's go down to the village, and see if it did any damage down there."

As they entered the village, no one seemed to be shaken up. Everyone was acting like they always do. There didn't seem to be any damage to any of the buildings. They went into The Pub. "Are you people alright?" Mr. Stoica answered, "Yeah, why?" "There's no damage?" "Damage from what?" "Didn't you feel the shaking?" "What shaking?" "The earthquake?" "Earthquake! We don't have earthquakes. What are you taking about? You haven't been drinking, have you?" Everyone laughed. "A...... No, no, I haven't been drinking." "Then what's this all about?" "I...... A....... I thought I heard a loud noise. Kristy, let's get out of here." Larry took Kristy by the arm, and hurried out the door.

As Larry is pulling Kristy back toward the castle, "Larry, what's going on? Why are you pulling me? Let go of my arm." "I'm sorry, Kristy. Don't you get it?" "Get what?" "There was no earthquake. The village never felt a thing." "Meaning?" "Kristy, the only thing that was shaking, was the castle." "The castle? Oh, no, another warning." "Exactly." "The whole thing could have collapsed and killed us." "I don't think so, Kristy. That castle has no intention of destroying itself, but it is going to, and does control everyone in it." "You really believe that now, don't you?" "It has convinced me."

"Kristy, get Christine's diary, and you read it and I'll take notes." "You are going to continue with this book, even though you feel as you do about the castle?" "Kristy, I'm going to finish this book, unless the castle kills me first." "I see. Do you want me to continue the book after your dead?" "Kristy!" "I think I'll move down to the village until you finish the book. Just in case the castle gets too angry." "Kristy, knock it off." "Larry, you're starting to act like some of the villagers. You're starting to let all of this get to you. That's not like you." "I guess you're right. Here we are arguing. We don't do that." "It seems like a trait of this place. We just have to rise above it, and be stronger than ever." "Kristy, did I ever tell you, I love you?" "Once, let's get to work."

Larry and Kristy started on Christine's diary. "Her diary starts in 1835. That's when Lord Bernard died, and Adam and Christine moved into the castle. Adam was very hesitant about moving back to the castle, because of the bad memories of when he was a child. There was a little sister, who was 10 years younger than Adam. Adam and Mimi were always together. When Adam was 16, little Mimi drowned in the castle pond. Adam was devastated. He felt guilty; that it was his fault. But he agreed to move back. Do you think that's her skeleton in the pond?" "No. That was an adult skeleton."

"Things were great for quite a while, then Christine started seeing a change in Adam, mentally, and physically. Larry, I was hoping this family might fare better than the others, but it looks they won't. One night, Christine, is abruptly wakened. She sat up in bed and there was a little girl standing at the foot of the bed. As Christine looked at her, the little girl disappeared. Christine didn't mention it to Adam; at this point in time, they were sleeping in separate bedrooms. Adam looked like he was aging more every day, and it was hard to talk to him."

"Kristy, it looks like the castle is going to work on this family, like all the others." "Anyway, the little girl, Mimi, keeps appearing to Christine, and now she talks to Christine, something about, ask Adam why he did it?" As Kristy reads on, "Listen to this, Adam's boss came to see him; they got into an argument and Adam killed him. Takes the body down and throws it into one of the vaults." "One of the violent deaths, I guess. It looks like Adam is going to take after Vidor."

"In more ways than one. Listen, Christine finds out and confronts Adam. He admits it." Kristy reads on in silence for a minute. "Larry, this....... It's......." "It's what, Kristy?" "It's horrible. It turns out, now get this, Adam killed Mimi." "What?" "He threw her into the pond on purpose to drown her." "Why on earth would he do that?" "Oh...... I see. Well, Adam hated Mimi because his mother died giving birth to her. So, therefore, Mimi deprived him of a mother." "So, Adam's condition now is because of his past."

While Kristy reads on, "Because of what Christine knows now, Adam hits Christine and knocks her down. He then takes her to the torture room, and chains her to the wall." "Where have I heard that one before. Since she is writing this, I assume she somehow got free." "Yes, Marta, the house keeper, eventually found her, and was able to set her free." "I'll bet Adam wasn't happy about that." "No, as a matter of fact, right after Christine was set free, she and Marta, went up to Christine's bed room. Before long, Adam was busting the door down, to get to Christine and Marta. Larry, remember that I read earlier, Christine mentioned that Mimi had appeared to her several times." "I remember."

"Well, it looks like justice won out again." "What do you mean?" "As Adam is going after Christine, Mimi appears in front of all of them. She tells Adam it's time for him to pay for what he did. At this point, Adam starts running down the stairs, with Mimi and Christine behind him. As Adam ran, for some reason, he ended up at the pond. He was running so fast he couldn't stop, and fell into the pond and drowned." "So, that's who the skeleton in the pond belongs to. What happened to Christine and Mimi?" "Mimi disappeared and never showed herself again. Christine continued to live in the castle, peacefully until she passed away." "Yes, I remember she passed away in 1877, at the age of 72." "That is all there is, Larry." "That covers everyone and everything."

"Now all we have to do, is put it all together, and start writing." "Do you know how you are gong to start out." "Well, I think I am going to start with this story, and then go back to when the castle was built, and go forward from there."

"Kristy, let's go down to the village for a while. Maybe they have forgotten about my little episode the other day." "I could use a break. If anyone brings that up, just tell them you don't remember. That'll confuse them."

At, The Pub, Larry and Kristy saw Mr. Stoica sitting at his regular table. They went over to join him. "Well, Larry, Kristy, sit down. Is there anything new, that I don't want to know about?" That got a laugh. "Not really, but we did find out whose bones are in the pond." "That would be, Adam Bernard. I know that story." "Well, anyway, we have finished our research, and are read to start putting it all together." "Anymore interruptions, or strange things happening? By the way, what was this, about an earthquake the other day?" "Oh, I don't know. I was probably dreaming. Nothing to worry about." "I wasn't worrying. So, your ready to write your book. You think you know the whole history of that pile of rocks." "I think we pretty well have it covered." "How much of it do you believe?" "I believe that castle is a living entity. I think it controls the majority of people that live, or have lived there." "How about you, Kristy?" "I feel the castle does have an influence over the people who live there. But it seems there are certain residents that the castle does not influence. I have no idea why it is that way." Mr. Stoica, "I think the castle should be locked up and remain empty, better yet, it should be destroyed."

Three months have gone by, and Larry and Kristy are making progress on their book. "Larry, it's late. I'm going to go on up to bed." "Ok, I'll be up in a little while." Larry continued working. When he looked at his watch, it was after midnight. It was time to stop for the night. As Larry headed for the stairs, he looked down toward the kitchen. He did a double take. Someone was standing in the doorway to the kitchen. "Who are you? What are you doing here?" The figure didn't say anything, just started laughing. "I said, who are you? What do you want?" The figure just kept laughing. Larry started toward the kitchen. As he got closer, the figure disappeared. Larry rubbed his eyes. Did he really see what he thought he saw, or was his mind playing tricks on him? Maybe he has been working too long.

The next morning, Larry decided not to tell Kristy. He still couldn't comprehend what happened. "Kristy, I think we should take the day off, and not work on the book. It's a nice day, let's spend it down in the village." "Well, ok, but what brought that on?" "I just don't think we should work ourselves to death on this book. We have plenty of time." "Are you sure there isn't something wrong? Did something happen?" "Kristy, everything is alright, ok?" "Alright, but I don't want to stay in this castle any longer than we have to. I'm starting to really worry." "We'll be ok, just bear with me."

A couple of weeks went by. One afternoon, while Larry and Kristy were working, they started hearing strange noises. It sounded like a scraping sound. They couldn't really figure where the sound was coming from, so they went out into the hall. It sounded like it came from the kitchen. It couldn't be the house keeper or the grounds keeper, they had let them go several weeks ago. The sound was coming from down below in the vault room. As Larry and Kristy started down the steps, the noise stopped. As they entered the room, no one was there.

Then Kristy let out a scream and grabbed Larry's arm. "Larry, look!" Kristy pointed to several of the vaults. The tops of the vaults had been slid open part way. Larry went over and looked in each vault. They were empty. But there were names on them. "What is it Larry?" "The vaults are empty." "Larry, let's get out of here. I'm scared."

"Kristy, I think it's time we leave here. The books almost finished. We have enough information;let's take the notes we have, and the diaries, and head back home." "I think you are right. This place is giving me the creeps." We'll go to Brasov, book a flight, and make arrangements to have our luggage picked up. We should be on a flight home by tomorrow afternoon."

Larry and Kristy got into their car, to head for the airport. "Bert will not believe how right he was about that castle." I'll tell you, Larry, if we hadn't witnessed it ourselves, I wouldn't believe it either." As they are talking, Larry is trying to start the car. "What's the matter, Larry?" "The car won't start. It's turning over all right, but it won't catch." "Is the battery alright?" "Yes, dear, the battery is alright, but it won't be, if this thing doesn't start." Larry didn't know much about cars, but he got out and lifted the hood. He was wasting his time, and he knew it. He slammed the hood down. "Kristy, let's go back inside. I'll try it again after a while."

They went out in the kitchen and fixed a sandwich and coffee. After about a half an hour, Larry decided to go try the car again. "You wait here, I'll see if I can get the car to start." Larry headed for the door. He was thinking how nice it would be to be back home again. As he turned the door handle, and pulled, nothing happened. The door wouldn't open. He tried again, nothing. He was pulling as hard as he could. "Kristy, come here." Kristy hurried in to Larry. "What's wrong?" "This door won't open. I even tried the key." "There is a door in the kitchen area. Let's try it."

"This one won't open either. I don't get it." "I do, Larry." "What?" "The castle doesn't want us to leave. It's not going to let us leave." "Maybe it doesn't want us to leave, but it's not going to stop us. I'll break one of these doors down." "Larry, those are thick, solid doors. They were built so they couldn't be broken down." "I'll bust out a window." Larry picked up a chair, went to one of the windows, and swung the chair as hard as he could at the window. As the chair hit the window, the backward thrust, threw the chair backward, and knocked Larry to the floor. "Kristy, we're trapped." They went back to the front door. They both pulled on the door as hard as the could.

Then somebody started laughing. Then the laughing grew louder. It sounded like multiple people laughing. Larry and Kristy turned around. There were figures standing in the kitchen. There were about a dozen figures standing there. They were almost transparent. Larry started toward them. "What do you want with us? Why are you doing this?" Then there was a large noise. Larry turned back towards the door. The huge glass chandelier in the hallway had broken loose. It was falling right where Kristy was standing. Before anyone could move, it hit the floor, crushing Kristy. Larry ran to Kristy. It was too late. Larry looked at the figures standing in the kitchen. His mind was reeling. His face was twisted in anger. He started toward the figures, then stopped. He looked up, as if he was yelling at the castle. "You have killed your last person. You will no longer make people go mad. I'm am going to destroy you once and for all. You have come to your end."

Then Larry turned and went into the living room. He walked over, and set the curtains on fire. He then, calmly went to the dining room, and did the same. He went all through the castle, calmly setting everything on fire. The laughter stopped; the figures disappeared. Now Larry was laughing. The flames grew higher. Larry was laughing uncontrollably. It was becoming an inferno. Larry walked back to the front door, and watched the flames encompass the whole interior. Larry turned around and tried the door; this time it opened. He continued to stand in the doorway, just watching.

Down in the village, people out in the street saw flames shooting out the windows of the castle. The whole village came out to watch. Cornel came out of his office to see what was going on. When he saw the flames, he started running toward the castle. None of the villagers even attempted to follow him.

When Cornel approached the castle, Larry was still standing in the doorway. Cornel ran up to Larry, "Larry, what happened? Where is Kristy?" Larry spoke in a low monotone voice, and pointed to the hallway, "The castle killed her." Cornel ran in to where Kristy was lying. He could tell she was dead, but he went ahead and tried to pull the chandelier off of her so he could pull her body outside. It was useless, he couldn't budge it. The flames were getting close now, so he ran back outside. Cornel pulled Larry away from the doorway. They stepped back several feet. The heat was so intense, the outside concrete walls started cracking. A few more minutes, and the walls started collapsing. After about 15 minutes, the castle was nothing but a pile of rubble, piled up on the ground.

Larry looked up, "Did you see that?" "What, Larry, see what?" "All of the spirits have left the castle. They are free now. The village is free now. They don't have to fear anything anymore. The castle is gone." "Larry, you're not making any sense. Come down to the office with me, we can talk about what's going on, and what happened. Ok?"

As they walked through the village toward Cornel's office, everyone stood still, no body said anything, they just watched Larry and Cornel pass by. The villagers didn't know what was going on, but everyone knew one thing; the castle was gone, destroyed, finally. The village could live without fear for the first time.

When they went into the office, Cornel had Larry sit down, and poured him a cup of coffee. "Larry, we need to talk about this, do you think you are up to that? We have to sort all of this out." Larry continued, almost as if in a trance. "Yeah, I think so. So much has happened in these last couple of hours." "I know, Larry, but you have to try. First of all, what happened to Kristy?" "It was the castle. It caused the chandelier to fall on her. Cornel, she is dead." "I know, Larry, I know the chandelier fell on Kristy, but why do you say the castle did it? You make it sound as if the castle intentionally caused the chandelier to fall." "It did." "Why?" "Because Kristy and I were going to leave the castle, and go back home to finish the book. We had enough of the strange things that were gong on in the castle."

"Strange things? We'll talk about that later. You're saying the castle tried to stop you from leaving?" "Yes, when we tried to leave, the castle locked the door so we couldn't get out." "So, what did you do?" "We kept pulling on the door, trying to open it. Suddenly, all this laughter started, and when we turned around, the spirits from the bodies in the vault room, were standing in the kitchen, laughing at us. When I started running toward them, the chandelier fell. Don't you see, the castle was going to destroy Kristy and me, just like it did everyone who ever lived in the castle."

"Larry, you really believe that, don't you?" "Of course, I do. I witnessed it. I saw it with my own eyes." "Larry, are you sure that all of that 'history', you went through, didn't cloud your mind, and make you think the castle was evil? I'm sure there is a logical explanation for anything that happened in that castle over the years." "No, there isn't. I know the castle was evil, but no one will ever know why."

"How did the fire start, Larry?" "I started it." "So, you started it. Why?" "After Kristy was killed, I couldn't let another person ever die in that place. It had to be destroyed. Look how many people it has destroyed since it was built. Someone had to end it, so, I did." "If you say so, but tell me Larry, why didn't it destroy you also? When I got to the castle, the door was open, and you were standing in the doorway. Why would it let you go?" "I don't know. I was watching everything burn, and without thinking, I turned around, and the door opened. Maybe I was stronger than the castle." "I see."

"Larry, you realize you are in a little trouble here. You destroyed property that did not belong to you, and if conditions had been different, the fire could have spread to the woods, and to the village. On top of that, you are not making much sense about any of this." "Don't you see, I have broken a curse. I have saved the lives of future people, and families. It had to be that way." "I'm going to have to lock you up for now, Larry. Tomorrow, I will have to transport you to Bucharest. This whole thing has to be presented to the authorities there." "It doesn't matter. I have nothing left anyway. No matter what happens to me, means nothing. I know what I did was right." "Ok, Larry, come on, I'm going to put you in a cell, and I want you to lay down on the cot and rest. Think about what you are saying."

Cornel went outside; just about the whole village was gathered outside, waiting to find out what was happening. After Cornel got the crowd to settle down, "People, listen to me. As you can see the castle has been destroyed." There was clapping and cheering, and jumping up and down. "Listen, people, listen. Kristy is still in the castle. She was killed when a chandelier fell on her." There many, Ohhhhh's. "When Kristy was killed, Larry went out of his mind, and he set fire to the castle. Larry is resting right now. Tomorrow, I will have to take him to Bucharest, to face charges for burning the castle down, maybe more." The villagers yelled, "Noooo! Noooo! He did us a favor. He was able to do what we wanted to do, and couldn't. Noooo! Noooo!" Cornel tried to calm the crowd down. "Quiet! Please! Quiet!" Finally, the crowd settled down. "That castle belonged to the state, Larry had no right to destroy it. I'm glad the castle is gone also, but the law is the law."

"What will happen to Larry? He won't go to prison, will he?" "That I don't know, but there is another issue here, that I cannot discuss. What happens to Larry, will be up to the authorities to determine." "He didn't kill Kristy, did he?" "No, that was strictly an accident. But it was the trigger that set Larry off." Mr. Stoica spoke up, "We are all behind Larry, we will do what ever it takes to help him."

The next morning, Cornel, takes Larry out of the cell. "Larry, turn around, and put your hands behind your back." "Why?" "I have to put handcuffs on you." "I'm not going to do anything. I told you, I don't have anything left, so why would I try to get away?" "It's procedure, Larry. The law requires it. Come on."

As they are on their way, Larry starts getting restless. He starts talking to himself, but does not make much sense. Larry is sitting in the back seat. He turns around and tries to open the rear car door. "Larry, stop it, calm down. What are you trying to do?" "I have to go back. I have to go back." "Why?" "My book, I have to get my book." "That was probably burnt up in the fire." "No, it was in a fire proof box. We have to go get it!" "We'll get it later, Larry, just sit still." Cornel was sure glad Larry had those handcuffs on. Suddenly, Larry leaned forward, turned around, and hit Cornel in the back of the head with his cuffed hands. Cornel was stunned. He lost control of the car for a few seconds, but managed to slow down, pull off the road, and stop the car.

Cornel shook his head, and tried to gain his senses. Before he could turn around, somehow, Larry had managed to get the rear door open. He bailed out on the ground, and hurriedly got up and started to run. Cornel saw what was happening, and got out of the car at the same time.

Cornel was a little older than Larry, but he was in good shape. When Larry stumbled a little, that was enough for Cornel to catch up with him. Cornel tackled Larry, and they both went down. Larry hit his head, and that took the fight out of him. He had a slight headache, but he was alright. Cornel got Larry to his feet, and they walked back to the car.

"Larry, that was stupid. You can't get away." Larry looked pretty rejected. "I know……. But I have to get my book. It confirms everything I said." "Alright, Larry, I'll get the book, but after I get back to Medias. Right now, we are going on to Bucharest. Get back in the car, I guess I better put a seat restraint on you. Don't try anything else." "I won't. I'm ok now." "I heard that one before."

Cornel went to the main police precinct, and to the district attorney's office. Cornel introduced himself, and Larry. "What can I do for you, Mr. Abbot?" "I have a situation here, that needs your attention." Cornel relayed the whole story to the DA, Lucian Lupul. The DA turned to Larry. "Mr. Hart what do you have to say about all this?" "Shouldn't I have a lawyer?" "You are not under arrest, and you haven't been charged with anything yet. This is just an interview. Nothing you say will be taken down. This is just between the three of us. I don't even know if any crime has been committed yet. It's been shown that your wife's death was an accident, so I don't know what we are dealing with at this point."

"Ok, what Cornel told you, is just what happened. The castle was evil. It killed my wife, just like it killed all those people in the past. I know, I saw it all." "You saw it all. You mean you saw the people in the past killed also?" "No! That was all in the records. I know what happened to Kristy, and to me." "But you did burn the castle down, did you not?" "Yes, like Cornel said, I had to stop it's rein of terror." "I see." Lucian called in an officer. "Take Mr. Hart out in the hall and stay with him. I'll call you when I want him to come back in the office." "Yes, sir, follow me Mr. Hart."

"Mr. Abbot, I don't think you need any help from this office. I think you should take him to see Dr. Dominik Candea, he is a psychiatrist, over at the Central Mental Hospital, at 29th and Olive. After listening to your story, and his response, I feel he has had a mental breakdown. Dr. Candea can do more for Mr. Hart, than we can. As for burning the castle down, that is up to the state to decide what they want to do. They are probably glad it's gone anyway." The DA called for the officer to bring Larry back in the office. "Mr. Hart, I see nothing here that is criminal. Therefore, there will be no charges made. I have told Mr. Abbot to take you over to see a doctor at the hospital. He may be able to help you out with your problem. Mr. Abbot, I will call ahead, and let the doctor know you are on your way." "Thank you for your help, Mr. Lupul."

Larry and Cornel entered the doctor's office. The receptionist said the doctor was expecting them, to go right in. "Mr. Abbot, Mr. Hart, please sit down. Lucian called and said I might be able to help you with a problem." "Yes, Larry here, has a dilemma, and if you listen to his story, maybe you would understand, and be able to help him." "Well, I'll give it a try. Larry, suppose you start from the beginning, and tell me what's been happening that upsets you." Larry started his story, again. Larry was getting tired of telling people what was going on, and nobody would believe him.

After Larry finished his story, the doctor studied Larry for a minute, "Larry, tell me about you and Kristy, before you settled in Medias to write this book." Larry told him about being a writer, and writing a couple of books about castles before this one. "So, this is the third castle you have written about. Did the other two castles' have a history just like this one?" "Oh, no. Naturally, they had their couple of skeletons in the closet, so to speak. Maybe a couple of scandals, but nothing like the Benes' Castle." "What did you know about castles, before you started writing about them?" "Nothing, really. I knew they had a reputation of being cold, eerie, and sometimes haunted." "So, you started writing about them, hoping they would be cold, eerie, and haunted." "Well, I never thought of that when I decided to write about them." "I see."

"But you did find out this castle was cold, eerie, and haunted." "Kristy and I both found that out as time went by." "You have no doubt." "No, sir." "The Benes' Castle is responsible for Kristy's death?" "Yes, I know it is. I saw it cause that chandelier to fall." "It couldn't have just been old and finally let loose?" "No way. It happened because we wanted to leave, and the castle wouldn't let us. Then the laughter. They wouldn't stop laughing." "Who was laughing?" "The people that were buried down in the vault room." "Ok, I think that's enough for now." "What do you mean for now? I have to get back to the castle, and get my book."

"I'm afraid that won't be possible right now." "What do you mean?" "Larry, I want you to stay with us for a while. I think we need to talk some more about this. We have a nice room you can stay in." "Aw no, you're not going to lock me up. You think I'm crazy, don't you? Well, I'm not. Everything I told you is the truth." "Larry, I didn't say you were crazy, but you need to rest for a few days. Try and sort out truth, from fiction. That's all I'm saying. We will take good care of you."

"Mr. Abbot, your responsibility is finished now. You can go back to Medias. We will take over responsibility of Larry, and do what we can for him." "Thanks Dr. Candea. Good luck, Larry. I hope you'll be better soon." "Cornel, don't leave me here! They'll lock me up, and no one will ever hear from me again. I'm not crazy!" "Relax, Larry, I'll tell you what I'll do, I'll check in with you every so often, to see how you are doing. Then you'll know you are not forgotten. The villagers are all pulling for you."

So, Kristy is dead, Larry is in a mental hospital, supposedly crazy. But is he? Two more victims of Benes' Castle? The castle is gone. The villagers are glad. But, is it over? If it wasn't the castle, who knows, if, or when, one of the villagers, or the next family, or person, that moves to the village, might go off the deep end? If, the castle was controlling it's residents, why? A question that will probably be ask, but never answered. The castle was only stone, and blocks, and mortar. The vault room, and the torture room, are still there, underneath the castle. If, the castle was the controlling entity, is it still there, waiting to carry on?

People can, and will speculate, and argue about the castle, and the events that took place there. I for one, know the secrets of the Benes' Castle. I know that the journals, and the history of the castle are real. I know, because I experienced them. I am, Larry Hart.

End

Epilogue

The remains of the castle lay for 20 years, until the year 2000. The state decided to clean up the rubble of the castle, and then put the land up for sale. A demolition company was hired to clean up the mess. All the equipment was assembled, and the job began, of hauling away what was left of the castle.

On the third day of cleaning up, the machine operator was trying to level up the ground, when he uncovered a large area of concrete. He stopped what he was doing, and called the foreman over. Evidently there was a room, or something, underneath the concrete. The foreman called back to the office to let them know what they found. The company called an archaeologist to see if he wanted to check the site out, before they continued grading.

Paul Darius arrived at the scene, to see what he could discover. He had no knowledge of the castle. "What kind of building was here before it was destroyed?" "The order said it used to be a castle. But I don't know anything about it. I'm just trying to clear it off." "We need to uncover as much of this concrete as we can, and hope to find an opening."

As they cleared off the concrete, they found some heavy panels of wood covering a stairway leading down below the concrete. They cleared it off; lit a lantern, then Paul and the foreman, started down the steps.

The lantern revealed the vault room. "Would you look at the number of vaults down here." They started checking the names and dates. "Everybody that ever lived here must be down here. Some of these dates go clear back to the early 1600's." They looked at several of the vaults, then the foreman noticed the door leading to torture room.

The door to the room was part way open. They entered, and looked around. There was a lot of dust, and debris, from when the castle collapsed. The lab portion was still there, and there was quite a bit of broken glass around. They spotted the dungeon, and several sets of chains on the wall. "Look at that jail cell, and those chains on the wall. It looks more like torture room." In walking back toward the door, they passed the brick walls. Some of the bricks had fallen out of the wall when the castle collapsed, but neither man noticed. The foreman was shaking his head, "I have a strange feeling. I don't like it down here." "I'll tell you, there is nothing here that interests me in any way. But the state may want to do something about that vault room. They may want to move the vaults. Other than that, the company can do whatever they want to do.

You can tear all this out, or just fill it in." "Ok, I'll check on that. Let's get out of here." "Good idea. But I'll tell you one thing." "What's that?" "I'll bet this place had one hell of a history."